DADDY'S SASSY SWEETHEART

LAYLAH ROBERTS

Laylah Roberts

Daddy's Sassy Sweetheart

© 2022, Laylah Roberts.

Laylah.roberts@gmail.com

laylahroberts.com

ALL RIGHTS RESERVED. This book contains material protected under International and Federal Copyright Laws and Treaties. Any unauthorized reprint or use of this material is prohibited. No part of this book may be reproduced or transmitted in any form or by any means, electronic or mechanical, including photocopying, recording, or by any information storage and retrieval system without express written permission from the author / publisher.

Cover Design by: Allycat's Creations.

Editing: Celeste Jones.

Photographer: Golden Czermak; Furious Fotog.

Cover Model: Kevin R Davis.

❦ Created with Vellum

LET'S KEEP IN TOUCH!

Don't miss a new release, sign up to my newsletter for sneak peeks, deleted scenes and giveaways: https://landing.mailerlite.com/webforms/landing/p7l6g0

You can also join my Facebook readers group here: https://www.facebook.com/groups/386830425069911/

BOOKS BY LAYLAH ROBERTS

Doms of Decadence

Just for You, Sir

Forever Yours, Sir

For the Love of Sir

Sinfully Yours, Sir

Make me, Sir

A Taste of Sir

To Save Sir

Sir's Redemption

Reveal Me, Sir

Montana Daddies

Daddy Bear

Daddy's Little Darling

Daddy's Naughty Darling Novella

Daddy's Sweet Girl

Daddy's Lost Love

A Montana Daddies Christmas

Daring Daddy

Warrior Daddy

Daddy's Angel

Heal Me, Daddy

Daddy in Cowboy Boots

A Little Christmas Cheer

Sheriff Daddy

Her Daddies' Saving Grace

A Little Winter Wonderland

Daddy's Sassy Sweetheart

MC Daddies

Motorcycle Daddy

Hero Daddy

Protector Daddy

Untamed Daddy

Her Daddy's Jewel

Fierce Daddy

Savage Daddy

Harem of Daddies

Ruled by her Daddies

Claimed by her Daddies

Stolen by her Daddies

Haven, Texas Series

Lila's Loves

Laken's Surrender

Saving Savannah

Molly's Man

Saxon's Soul

Mastered by Malone

How West was Won

Cole's Mistake

Jardin's Gamble

Romanced by the Malones

Twice the Malone

Mending a Malone

Men of Orion

Worlds Apart

Cavan Gang

Rectify

Redemption

Redemption Valley

Audra's Awakening

Old-Fashioned Series

An Old-Fashioned Man

Two Old-Fashioned Men

Her Old-Fashioned Husband

Her Old-Fashioned Boss

His Old-Fashioned Love

An Old-Fashioned Christmas

Bad Boys of Wildeside

Wilde

Sinclair

Luke

Standalones

Their Christmas Baby

A Cozy Little Christmas

Haley Chronicles

Ally and Jake

TRIGGER WARNING

Death of a partner, which happens in the past and off page.

1

Kiesha glided down the street.
The wind whipped at her cheeks, making her eyes water.

Shit.

She was late again.

Not that it was that big of a deal, but she couldn't sit through another Ed lecture.

The man sure knew how to make talking boring. She loved talking, but she didn't like listening to him go on and on about responsibility and punctuality.

So, she pushed herself faster. She was almost there. Almost there...

Slam!

The guy came out of nowhere. All right, he might have stepped out of the diner. But sheesh, didn't he know to look left and right first?

That was just common sense.

Especially at this time of the morning, when she was racing to work.

She threw her weight forward, slamming onto her knees as he turned toward her.

Ouchie.

That was going to bruise later.

Ah, well. What were a few more bruises?

"Are you all right? Are you hurt?" He ran his hands over her.

She sucked in a breath, trying to still her nervous tummy. "Stranger danger! Stranger danger!"

"What?" He withdrew his hands immediately. "I apologize. I was just checking to see if you were all right. I didn't mean to make you uncomfortable."

He had a slight accent that she couldn't place. Australian? And to be honest, he hadn't made her uncomfortable. At all.

"I'm all right, just a couple of scraped knees. I'm really good at falling. I was taught how to fall properly by a stuntman."

"You were?"

"Yes. Why? Don't you believe me?"

"Why wouldn't I believe you?" he asked.

She huffed out a breath. "Us roller skaters know that you should always try to fall forward so that our knee pads cushion the fall."

"But you're not wearing knee pads."

"Right, but if I had been, that would have been the perfect fall."

She would have worn her knee pads if she could find them. She wondered where they were . . .

"Miss? Miss? Are you sure you're all right?"

She looked up, studying him. Recognition tickled her brain.

Not a stranger.

"You're Mari's step-uncle, right?"

"Ah, something like that," he replied. "I'm Harrison. Or Harry. I think of Mari as my daughter."

"Oh yeah. That why you're here in Wishingbone? You're visiting Mari?"

"I am."

"Where are you from?" she asked as he reached out his hands to her.

"Houston."

Taking his hands, she was shocked by how strong he was as he lifted her to her feet. He kept hold of her to make sure she was steady.

His hands were warm, and she felt a zing of something rush through her as she took in his features. Hazel eyes studied her back. His dark hair and neatly trimmed beard were interspersed with gray. He was the type of guy who looked like he was only growing more attractive the older he got.

"Oh yeah, you're like some big-shot lawyer dude, right?"

"That is my exact job title." He grinned at her.

"Nailed it. I have an amazing memory. I really should go on a game show or something. I could probably win millions."

"No doubt. We should get your knees looked at," Harry told her, staring down at her legs. "Your tights are ripped. My car isn't far from here. I can take you to the doctor."

"Pfft. Over a couple of scrapes? Nah, I'm fine. I'll clean them up at work."

"You want to go to work with scraped knees?" He looked surprised.

"Wouldn't be the first time. Are you all right? You're older than me. Your bones are probably all brittle and stuff. Would you like me to take you to the doctor?" she asked with concern.

He blinked. "Just how old do you think I am?"

"Hey, no insult or anything. I mean, fifty is the new forty, right? And guys just get hotter as they get older. Well, most of them." She scowled as a red truck drove past, slowing down. "You keep moving, Jonny Jacks! Nothing to see here." She turned back to

Harry, taking a deep breath to calm herself. "Sorry, that was just my arch-nemesis."

He looked down at her for a long moment, then over to the red truck. "You have an arch-nemesis?"

"Doesn't everyone?"

"Um, no. I don't believe so."

"Huh." When she thought about it, she was the only person she knew with an arch-nemesis. "You could be right. Well, I have one and his name is Jonny Jacks. There's a man who is growing uglier with age. Let me tell you."

Harry ran his hand over his face. "Right. Can I take you to work, at least?"

"Oh shit! I've got to get to work! No time to stand around and chit chat or Ed will actually beat my butt this time. Bye! Say hi to Mari for me."

She sped off, heading toward the police station.

Shoot.

Now she was definitely going to have to sit through that scolding.

∼

Fifteen minutes later, she sat in Ed's office while he doctored her knees, thinking about how nice Harry's hands had felt against hers. He'd made her feel small and delicate with the way he'd just picked her up, and she definitely wasn't a lightweight.

"Kiesha? Are you listening to me?" Ed demanded.

"Of course, I'm listening to you. How could I not be listening to you? You're right there. And I hate to tell you, Ed, but you aren't exactly quiet."

"Really?" he asked dryly. "You hate to tell me that?"

Well, maybe she enjoyed telling him that. But she wasn't going to say that, was she?

"And I'm pretty sure that instead of listening to me, you were daydreaming."

"I know exactly what you said, and you owe me a bag of suckers for doubting me."

"Fine." He stood, and she glanced down at her knees. One knee had a large pad on it. The tape he'd used to secure it had images of monsters all over it. The other knee had just one Band-Aid with an alien on it.

Perfect.

"Repeat what I said," he commanded.

"You were telling me how I have to be more careful. That I can't go speeding down the sidewalk. It's not safe. For me or the citizens of Wishingbone. I need to wear more safety gear and go slower. And that I have to leave earlier so I don't have to speed and I get here on time. I have responsibilities and I need to take them seriously. How am I doing?"

Ed just eyed her. Then he crossed his arms over his large chest and leaned against his desk. "So, if you are listening to me, then why do you never actually *listen* to me?"

"Um, you realize what you just said made no sense, right?"

"It made perfect sense. If you understood me."

She scratched at her head. "After all these years, you'd think I'd understand Ed-speak."

"Here's something you can't misunderstand. No. More. Speeding. Any more skating-related incidents, and I'm confiscating them."

She jumped to her feet. Luckily, she'd put her shoes on. They were her favorite sneakers. One was blue and had the face of a one-eyed monster on the front. The other shoe was red and had a smiling, big-toothed monster on the top.

"You can't do that!"

"I can and I will."

"You're not the boss of me, Ed Granger!"

"That's exactly what I am."

"At work. I wasn't at work when I fell over."

"You were late to work. And my job is to keep the citizens of Wishingbone safe. You knocked a man over today, Kiesha. What if you'd really hurt him?"

She did feel kind of bad about that. Especially with him being so old and all. She sighed. "Okay, I get it. I could have hurt him and it would have been partially my fault."

"Partially? Kiesha, I just want you to be safe," Ed told her quietly. "You could fall and hurt yourself or dash out on the road and get run over. Please, can you do this for me?"

"Did it hurt you to say please? You likely strained something, huh? Is that why that little tic is going beside your eye? Does it have a name? I'd call it Ticcy."

"I call it Kiesha," he grumbled.

"That's stupid. That would get really confusing. When you call for me now, I'm going to think you're talking to the tic by your eye."

"Kiesha," he said in a low voice.

"See, now who are you talking to? Wouldn't it be better to call it Ticcy?"

"Fine, we'll call it Ticcy."

"Gosh, Ed, I'm not sure why you don't listen to me all the time. I'm always right." She turned to the door.

"I have a headache."

"Probably because of Ticcy," she called back. "You might want to check your blood pressure. Men your age shouldn't get all stressed out. Oh, and you owe me a bag of suckers."

She grinned at his grumbling. Grabbing her bag, she moved into the women's bathroom. She needed to change out of her ripped tights. Luckily, she always brought spares. Her spare ones were lime green, which went perfectly with her black pleated skirt and white T-shirt. Today's T-shirt was one of her favorites. It had a picture of a toucan dancing and said: *In A World Full Of Pigeons, Be A Toucan.*

Yes, she knew it was meant to be a flamingo. But she didn't like to do what everyone else did.

She checked that she didn't have helmet hair. Ed insisted she wear one. He was such a stickler for the rules. But at least her helmet was awesome. It had monster images all over it and googly eyes on the top.

Finally, she was ready for work. Gosh, Ed went on and on about being on time, then he delayed her for half an hour to lecture her.

He really had to get his priorities right.

∽

WHAT WAS HE DOING?

Harry knew he should just turn around and leave. That would be the smart thing. He shouldn't be here. It wasn't normal to buy a gift for the woman who mowed you down.

Trouble was, he'd spent all day thinking about her. And he'd been unable to settle until he'd done something about the fact that she was skating around without proper protection.

So here he was. Standing outside the police station holding a bag with knee pads, elbow pads, and a high-visibility vest.

As he walked up the stairs, his phone rang, and he drew it out of his pocket.

"Hello, Barbara."

"Harrison," Barbara replied. "How are you?"

"Good, thanks. Is there something you need?"

"I can't just call a friend?" she asked.

"I apologize. Of course you can." He guessed she was a friend. He had worked with her for years. They were both senior partners at a law firm in Houston.

"I wondered when you were coming home?"

"Well, I only just got here. I'm visiting my daughter."

"She lives in Colorado, right?"

"Montana," he replied evenly.

"Yes, yes. It must be so annoying for you to have to visit there. Can't she come visit you? I mean, there's nothing in Montana except ranches and cows, is there?"

"There's a bit more to it. And no, it's not annoying." This place was strange, filled with unusual people, and he'd been a bit taken aback the first time he'd come here. But for all their quirks, the people here were warm and welcoming.

"Yes, well. I look forward to seeing you when you return. When do you think that will be?"

"I've taken a few weeks off." He needed them. He was starting to burn out. At fifty-one, he never thought he'd feel so lost. So untethered. He had money, power, a successful career and yet at the same time, it felt like he had nothing.

"Goodbye."

He frowned down at his phone, then shook his head. Pushing Barbara from his mind, he headed up the stairs and into the main office of the police station. For a small town, it was a busy place. They seemed to have more than their fair share of criminal activity.

Of course, his ex-wife was one of the reasons for that. Her ties to the Devil's Sinners had brought a lot of problems to Wishingbone.

But she was in jail, where she belonged. And Marisol was free from that viper.

Looking around, he found Kiesha sitting at the main desk. She was typing on the computer and frowning.

"Kiesha?" he said, approaching her.

"How do you spell douchebagette?" she asked without looking up.

"Uh, is that actually a word?"

"Of course, it's a word. I just said it."

"That doesn't make something a word."

"Huh. That's a good point. Let's look it up. Help me spell it?"

"Um, I imagine it would be spelled d-o-u-c-h-e-b-a-g-e-t-t-e."

"Uh-huh. See, here it is! Douchebagette. Told you it was a word."

"Well, I suppose you learn something new every day," he said.

"I know I do. There. Sent. Take that, Mayor Jacks."

"Did you . . . did you just send something to the mayor about a douchebagette?"

"Nah, I called the mayor a douchebagette."

"You what?"

"Relax, I'm joking with you." She reached down and grabbed a sucker out of a drawer, popping it in her mouth before looking up at him. "Hey, it's you."

"Do you often have conversations without realizing who you're talking to?"

She shrugged. "More often than you'd think." She spoke around the sucker in her mouth.

"So, you weren't emailing the mayor? That was a joke?" Of course it was.

"Oh no, that part wasn't a joke. I sent the mayor an email telling him that his brother is a douchebagette."

"Right. That's so much better."

She grinned at him, removing the sucker. "Relax. I know the mayor. He'll laugh. You're strung a little tight, aren't you?"

"I didn't think I was."

"You don't seem like you smile much. You're kind of stressed out. Did you go gray early?" She ran her gaze over him.

"I don't . . . believe so?"

"Don't worry, you're totally rocking it."

"Ahh, thank you. I think?"

"You're welcome." She popped her sucker back into her mouth. "Oh, I'm sorry. You want a sucker?" Grabbing one, she handed it to him.

"No, thank you."

She shrugged and unwrapped it, sticking it into her mouth with the other one.

"Uh, do you realize you have two suckers in your mouth?"

She pulled them free. "Yep. Double the fun. I like having things in my mouth. Stops my hands from doing things they shouldn't. I don't know why it works like that, it just does."

Do not go there, Harry. You're better than that.

She started giggling. "You should see the look on your face."

Maybe he was wound a bit tight. Had he always been this way? Or was it just lately? He wasn't sure.

"How are your knees?" he asked, to distract himself.

"They're fine."

"That's good. I bought you something."

Her eyes lit up. "For me?"

"Yes." He held up the bag.

She stared at it as though she was a kid eyeing up gifts under the Christmas tree. She was practically vibrating with excitement. Although that could have been from a sugar rush. But she didn't reach for the bag.

He frowned as he noticed the way her hands had tightened on the arms of the chairs. She was going to hurt herself if she kept that up.

Which was completely unacceptable.

"Kiesha? You okay?" He moved around the desk and lightly touched one hand. She immediately released it.

"Oh, yeah. Sorry."

"If you don't like my gift, don't feel obliged to accept it. I was just worried about your poor knees and, well . . ."

He drew the knee pads out of the bag and her eyes widened,

her bottom lip dropping open. Before the suckers could fall from her mouth, he quickly grabbed the sticks.

"Wow. Those are so beautiful."

Beautiful wasn't quite the word he would use. But they were cute. He'd noticed that her helmet looked like a monster, and he'd managed to find some bright green knee pads from a bike shop a few towns over. They'd also sold monster decals, which he'd stuck on them.

"I couldn't find monster knee pads, but I thought you might like the decals. Of course, if I've overstepped and you don't like them..."

"Are you kidding? I love them. How could anyone not like monster knee pads?" She gaped up at him as though that was an impossibility she simply couldn't comprehend.

"Indeed. I also got elbow pads too." He placed the knee pads on the desk and pulled the elbow pads from the bag.

Kiesha reached out and drew a finger along the knee and elbow pads. "These are so gorgeous. But why would you buy them for me?"

She sounded so confused and awed that it shocked him. Had no one ever bought this girl anything?

"Do you want something in return? I can't get you out of parking tickets. Ed was really clear on that. Cleo was pretty upset about that, probably because Noah told her that if she got one more parking ticket, he was going to put her over his knee and take her keys. I think she's more upset about him taking her keys than the spanking."

She drew her long dark hair back, somehow securing it into a bun at the back of her head. Her brown eyes sparkled with laughter as she stared up at him. "Although Noah has these really big, meaty hands. So, I bet that spanking would hurt. Still, I reckon Cleo gets spanked lots, so she'd be used to it by now. No, I think she'd definitely be more upset over the threat to take her wheels."

"Do you always say what you're thinking?"

"Mostly. Ed says I have impulse control issues. Where did I put my suckers? Oh, there they are! Hey, if you want one I can give you a new one. I have lots. See?"

She drew open a drawer, which was filled with an obscene amount of candy.

"How do your teeth cope with all that sugar?" he asked, unable to help himself.

"Eh, they're tough. Plus, I just never go to the dentist. Problem solved."

"I think we have different ideas of what problem solved means. That isn't solving the problem."

"It works for me. So, like I was saying, if you have parking tickets I can't fix them for you. Sorry. I have no access to anything that might help with any court cases, either." She popped the suckers into her mouth, crunching down on them.

Ouch. His teeth felt sore just watching.

She didn't notice, though, as her gaze was fixated on the knee and elbow pads.

"Ah, no, I'm not wanting you to do me any special favors. I just. . . I was worried about you skating around without proper safety equipment, that's all." He pulled out the neon pink high-visibility vest. Her eyes lit up in delight.

"So, you just bought these for me because you were worried?"

"Yes. That's all. No ulterior motive. I promise."

"That's really kind." She stared up at him as though she'd never met someone who was kind before.

She was killing him.

"I don't know what to say," she told him.

"Thank you is all that's needed."

"Thank you," she said quietly.

"Just tell me you'll wear them, okay?"

"I will. I promise. You're sure you're all right? I didn't break your butt, did I?"

He had to grin. "No, I can assure you that I don't need a new bum."

She giggled. "Bum. You have a slight accent. Where are you from?"

"Well, I've lived in the states for most of my life, but I was born in New Zealand. My mother was from Texas. We moved back there after my dad died."

Jesus, man. You've gone from having no words to blathering on about shit that she doesn't want to hear.

What was wrong with him?

He was usually much more suave than this. He could feel his cheeks growing red as he realized how much he'd just blurted out.

"I'm really sorry about that," she told him. "My dad's dead too."

"I'm sorry."

"You shouldn't be. Turns out he was a jerk. So it was no great loss. But you might have liked your dad."

"I did." He really wanted to ask her about her father, but he was aware this wasn't the time or the place. And that she probably didn't want to talk about her father with a virtual stranger.

"Well, have a nice day," he told her before leaving. When he was outside, he stopped and shook his head with a groan.

Really? Have a nice day?

Was that really the best he had to say?

Heading to his car, he drove out to Sanctuary Ranch where Mari lived with her boyfriend, Linc.

After getting through the security gate, he drove slowly to their cabin, waving at Clint and Charlie, who were headed out of the barn toward the main house.

Getting out of the car, he grabbed the flowers he'd bought for Marisol. He hadn't even gotten to the stairs that led up to the front porch when the door opened and she raced out toward him.

He caught her with one arm.

"Pop! Pop! Guess what?"

Damn. He'd never tire of hearing her call him that.

"Marisol!" Linc scolded. "Don't run down the steps like that!"

"I'm fine."

"And you nearly knocked Harry over."

"Oh, sorry, Pop."

"That's okay, Banana." He gave her a tight hug after Linc stood up. "I can see you're excited about something."

"So excited! Look!" She held out her hand. "Linc proposed! And I said yes."

"Thank goodness," Linc added with a grin as he came up and shook Harry's hand. He wrapped an arm around Mari's waist. "If you'd said no, I'd have had to take drastic measures."

"As if I could ever say no," she replied, looking up at him dreamily.

He was so happy for them. If anyone deserved to be happy, it was Mari.

"I'm so happy you're here," Mari said with a huge smile as she wrapped her arm around his and leaned into him.

"I'm glad to be here, Banana." He kissed the top of her head. "And that is a beautiful ring."

"Linc chose it. I think it's perfect." And it was. Simple, but stunning.

"Here, I bought these for you." He held out the bright pink gerberas.

"You didn't have to do that! They're gorgeous." Mari took the flowers, dancing around with them. "I'm so excited."

Both men grinned at her.

"Congratulations, Linc," Harry said, whacking the other man on his back. "About time you made an honest woman out of my girl."

"Pop!" She rolled her eyes at him. Then she narrowed her gaze at them both. "Wait. I smell a rat." She pointed at Harry. "You knew, didn't you? That's why you brought me flowers."

"I would buy you flowers for no reason at all. But yes, I did know."

"I could hardly propose without asking your father first," Linc said.

Mari's eyes filled with tears.

"Teeny, that wasn't supposed to make you cry," Linc protested, gathering her close. He hugged her tight. "Hey, what's wrong?"

"Nothing. I'm just so damn happy."

Relief filled Linc's face, and he shrugged his shoulders at Harry, who rescued the flowers from Mari's tight grip.

"Why don't we go inside and celebrate?" he suggested. "I've actually got a bottle of champagne in my car." He moved to the back seat and drew it out. As they walked into the house, Marisol told him how Linc had gotten down on one knee to propose while they were roasting s'mores by a campfire. Harry sat at the kitchen counter and listened.

"I'm so happy for you, Banana. I've already set up a credit card and a bank account to pay for the wedding."

Silence filled the room.

"Harry, we can't ask you to pay for the wedding," Linc said.

Mari nodded.

"Of course I'm paying for the wedding. Am I not the father of the bride? That's my job."

"Yeah, but . . ." Linc trailed off, looking uncomfortable. "I'm not a young kid. I can afford to pay for it."

"Of course you can," Harry agreed. "But Mari is my daughter and it would be my privilege to do this for you. Please."

They glanced at each other, then Mari reached over, hugging Harry tight. "Thanks, Pop."

Tears entered his eyes, and he closed them. "Welcome, Banana."

"So, what did you get up to today?" Mari asked as they sat down to dinner.

"Ahh, not a lot, actually. It was kind of odd to do nothing at all." And it didn't sit well with him. He wasn't used to stopping. To taking it easy.

"I get it," Linc said. "Not sure I could do it."

Mari frowned. "Is everything all right with you? It's not like you to take time off work."

"Everything is fine," he told her with a warm smile. "Just thought it might be nice to take some time off work and relax."

"Do you know how to relax?" she asked.

"Apparently not. Or at least, not successfully. I thought I would sleep in, but I woke up at five, the way I usually do. Had breakfast at the diner. Then as I was coming out of the diner, I nearly got bowled over by a roller-skating monster."

"Wait, what?" Linc asked.

"Kiesha banged into you, huh?" Mari asked. "Was she running late for work?"

"Seemed to be. That's a common occurrence?"

"Ah, yep. She's a character," Mari said with a grin. "Lots of fun."

"But she needs to think more about safety," Linc said with a frown. "It's not that long ago that she was nearly run over."

"What?" Harry snapped, dropping his fork. "She was nearly run over?"

"Yeah, one of Juliet's boyfriends nearly hit her. She went straight out in front of him, apparently," Linc said. "Someone needs to give her a firm talking to about being more careful with her safety."

Mari sighed. "I do worry about her sometimes. She's such a kind, caring person. When Saber kidnapped me, I was so glad that she and Georgie were with me."

That's right. How had he forgotten that Kiesha had been kidnapped with Marisol?

"What about her boss? The sheriff? Can't he have a word with her?"

"Oh, I'm sure he's tried," Linc said. "Those two are close. Ed's like her brother. But I'm not sure that Kiesha really listens to anyone."

Seemed like someone needed to put their foot down with her. Or at least try to curb her wilder tendencies while continuing to allow her to be herself.

But putting herself in danger? Yeah, that had to stop.

"You all right?" Mari asked. "You weren't hurt, were you?"

He had to grin. "Despite my ancient age, I'm not going to break. I'm fine. I did buy her some more safety gear, though."

"Aw. That was so kind of you."

"She was almost shocked that someone would buy her something without wanting anything in return."

"That's sad," Marisol said.

The more he learned about Kiesha, the more he wanted to know.

"Are you sure you won't come stay here?" Mari asked as they finished eating. "There's plenty of room and I don't like you staying in a hotel. It's not very homey."

"Thank you. I appreciate the offer, but I like being in town. I'm used to the city, remember? And besides, you two lovebirds need your own space."

And he didn't need to hear them. Linc gave him a knowing look.

Harry just winked back at him. He remembered what it was like to be young and in love.

He wasn't that old.

2

Harry walked down the footpath. What the hell was he doing? He'd been here five nights, and he still wasn't feeling any more relaxed.

He squeezed the stress ball in his pocket as he headed into the park. A familiar dark-haired woman was sitting on one of the swings, pushing it back and forth as she read something on her phone.

"Kiesha?"

She gave a scream as she slid right off the back of the swing, landing on her butt with a groan.

Shit! He hadn't expected she'd be so startled.

"Kiesha, are you all right?" He ran to her, bending over her. She squinted up at him.

"Stranger danger! Stranger danger!" she yelled, pointing at him.

He shook his head. "Kiesha, it's me. Harry."

"Harry?" She sat up with a groan. "Sorry, the sun was in my eyes."

Bending down, he reached out a hand to help her up. The

sleeve of her long-sleeved T-shirt fell back, revealing faded bruises on her arm. He frowned, wondering how she'd gotten those.

"Are you all right? Do you hurt anywhere?" he asked, running his gaze over her.

Today she wore bright purple tights, a black and white pleated skirt and a purple T-shirt that had the words: *I Wear My Happiness On The Outside* written along the front.

"Am I hurt? I just fell off a swing. Of course I am."

"What hurts?" he asked.

"My butt."

"Do you want me to rub it?"

"Dude. You've got to buy a girl dinner first."

Mortification filled him. "Sorry. Yes, of course. I, uh, that came out wrong."

"Calm, Harry. I'm not going to sue you for pushing me off a swing."

"I didn't actually push you off the swing."

She shot him a look.

"But yes, thank you. I apologize for startling you."

She sighed. "It was probably a good thing. I was about to buy stuff I can't afford."

"How did you get those bruises on your arm?" He winced after saying that. He didn't normally just blurt things out.

She put her hand over her arm. "Oh those, they're a few weeks old. I fell over, I think."

Somehow, he wasn't sure that she was telling the truth. "What about your knees? Are they all right after the other day?"

"Yeah. They're all good." She patted herself down. "Darn it, I lost my sucker."

He looked around the ground, but couldn't see it anywhere.

She sighed. "Don't suppose you've got some candy in your pockets."

"Funnily enough, I don't carry around candy in my pockets."

"Yeah, probably a good idea. Especially when you're creeping up on people in the park. They might get the wrong idea."

"I wasn't creeping . . ." he trailed off with a grin. "You're trouble."

"I've got a T-shirt that says just that." She winked at him.

"Sorry, the only thing in my pockets are my balls."

"Your balls are in your pockets? Harry, I'm sorry."

"What? No!" He stared at her in horror.

She bent over, cracking up. "You should see your face."

He rolled his eyes. When she straightened, he drew out his stress balls. He kept one in each pocket. "My stress balls. See?"

"You keep stress balls in your pockets? You must have a lot of stress."

"I suppose so. It's one of the reasons I'm on holiday. Would you like one?" He offered her one.

She stared down at it with a frown. "Guess it won't hurt." She took it and started squishing it. "Oh, it's kind of like one of those squishy toys!"

"What?"

"Oh, Harry." She looked at him sadly. "Haven't you seen them before? That's just sad. They're really soft toys that you can squish. We need to get you one. More exciting than a stress ball."

"I'm sure. You have some?"

"I have one big one. But not any of the little ones. Maybe I need a little one to carry in my pocket."

An alarm sounded on her phone, and she quickly silenced it. "I've got to go! Thanks, Harry. For the stress ball, not for pushing me off the swing and bruising my butt."

"I didn't actually push . . ." he trailed off as she took off.

She was so unusual.

And he couldn't stop thinking about her.

∼

"Harry!"

He paused in his jog, looking over to find Kiesha roller skating toward him. He was pleased to note that she was wearing her safety gear. Her dark hair was tied into two braids and she had on a pair of bright blue yoga pants and an oversized pink sweater with an alien on the front of it.

"Kiesha, good morning."

"What you doing?" She eyed him suspiciously as she came to a stop.

"I'm jogging."

Her eyes widened. "Why? What's chasing you? Shit, I don't have my mace."

He shook his head with a grin. "Nothing is chasing me."

"Then why are you running?"

"For exercise."

"Harry, that's awful." She gave him a sympathetic look. "My condolences."

"What? Why?"

"On the loss of your good sense. The only reason to run is if something is chasing you. Ooh, I've got a T-shirt somewhere that says something like that. Don't you know it's Sunday morning? You should be sleeping in. Maybe watch some cartoons. Although you look like a documentary and news kind of guy."

Well, yes. He guessed he was.

"Shouldn't you be doing the same?" he asked.

"That would be nice. But I've got to go over to Mr. Clearly's to walk his dog, Oscar."

"That's really sweet of you."

"Well, Mr. Clearly is about a hundred and two, and Oscar needs the exercise. Want to come?"

"If you're certain I won't be in the way." For some reason, whenever he was around her, his stress levels started to drop. It was like she was a giant stress ball he wanted to squeeze.

Okay, what's wrong with you?

That was just terrible.

"Oscar will love you. He's a sweetheart. A giant cuddle bunny."

∼

WELL, she got one part of that right. Oscar was a giant. The biggest dog he'd seen in his life.

He was waiting on one side of a white picket fence that didn't even reach the top of his legs. But he didn't move until Kiesha went through the gate. Then he rushed at her so quickly that Harry didn't have time to move before Kiesha was flat on her back, with Oscar licking her face.

"Kiesha!" He reached for Oscar's collar. But the huge, fawn-colored dog with dark ears turned and growled at him.

"Oscar, hush! Be nice to Harry. He's come to take you for a walk."

Yeah, Oscar didn't look impressed.

"It's okay, Harry. He's just happy to see me."

"So you won't sue him for bruising your butt?"

"Of course not. He's a dog." She gave him a look like he was nuts. Maybe he was. He definitely didn't feel sane.

The door to the house opened, and a small, wizened man stepped out. "Oscar, off."

Immediately, Oscar climbed off Kiesha and sat down, looking every inch the obedient dog.

"Here you are, dear. I see you've brought a gentleman friend with you," the man said, handing over a harness and lead.

Kiesha quickly put the harness on Oscar. "Yeah, Mr. Clearly. This is Harry."

"Pleased to meet you. I'll see you all when you come back. Thanks, dear."

"No worries, Mr. C."

They moved out of the gate. "Isn't Oscar just the cutest?" Kiesha asked as the dog moved along obediently beside her. Harry moved up to a light jog.

"Very cute," he agreed. Oscar turned and snarled at him.

Yeah, he got it. He didn't like him.

"Mr. Clearly's kids all live a long way away, and they got him Oscar to keep him company. Oh, I love this house." She stopped and pointed to an older house that was set back from the street on park-like grounds. It was yellow with white trim and had a wrap-around porch with a turret. It looked a bit tired, but grand.

"No one lives there?" he asked.

"No, it's been for sale for a while now. It's just screaming for a family to move in and love it. You got any other kids, Harry?"

"Ahh, no. When I was younger, I was in an accident and lost the ability to have children."

She gasped, coming to a stop. He stilled, turning to her. Just as well, since she threw herself at him. He stumbled back, then righted himself as he wrapped his arms around her to keep her from sliding back on her bottom.

Oscar growled at them both.

Right. I get it. You don't like me touching her.

"Harry, I'm so sorry!"

"Oh. Yes, well, it was a long time ago." He patted her back as she clung to him. It had been ages since he'd really thought about it.

"Did you want kids, though?" She leaned back to look at him. "Oscar, honey, hush."

The dog sounded like he was about to unleash the demons of hell.

"You sure he's not part hellhound?" he asked jokingly.

Kiesha gave him a serious look. "He could be."

"Ahh. It was a joke."

"Never joke about hellhounds, Harry. Never."

He gaped at her. Then she grinned. "Got'cha. I know hellhounds aren't real. Now, aliens, they're real. I'm going to go find them one day."

"Are you still joking?" he asked.

"No."

Right.

"I always knew I couldn't have kids. And I guess I was a little sad as I got older about it. Especially once Mari left. But the truth is, my life wasn't conducive to kids."

"Do you have one of those word of the day calendars?" she asked.

That was completely off topic.

"Ahh. No?"

"Huh, so I guess you just like big, fancy words."

Big, fancy words?

"I'm really sorry you can't have kids, Harry." She gave him a soft look, without any pity.

"Thank you."

The rest of their time together, they kept their talk light. When he veered off to head back to the motel, he felt better than he had in a long time.

3

"Hi Harry! What you eating?"

Harry glanced up from his muesli and yogurt as Kiesha sat down next to him at the diner.

"Hello Kiesha." He took off his glasses.

"What is that stuff?" She wrinkled her nose as she stared down at his bowl.

"Um, muesli."

"Huh. Can't you just put that in a bowl at home? I didn't even know that they sold healthy food here. Have you tried the French toast? It's out of this world."

"It does look delicious, but I'm happy with the muesli." He studied her with a smile. "You're wearing your new safety gear."

"Yeah, it's so awesome. Thanks for buying it for me. It's one of the best gifts that I've ever been given."

"I'm glad," he replied. What kind of gifts had she received in the past that she thought these were so amazing?

"Are you having breakfast?" he asked.

"Hmm? Oh no. What are you doing? A crossword? Wow, I

didn't know people still did that on actual paper." She glanced over at his newspaper.

"Well, I am ancient," he said dryly.

"True." She grinned at him. "Do you even know how to use the internet?"

"What's that?"

Leaning back her head, she cackled with laughter then whacked him on the arm. "I like you."

Warmth unfurled inside him. "Good. I like you too."

"Are you starting work soon?" He glanced at his watch.

"I'm early for once," she told him. "Ed doesn't think I can do it, but I'm going to prove him wrong." Her tummy grumbled.

He frowned. "Haven't you had breakfast?"

"Nah, but I'll have something when I get to the office."

"And by something, do you mean the candy in your drawer?"

She grinned. "You bet."

"You know that's a terrible breakfast, right?"

Way to go, Harry. Lecture her like you're her father. That's going to help her view that you're old and decrepit.

Not that he cared. It wasn't like he was trying to impress her. Or was he?

Was he having some sort of mid-life crisis? It would make sense. Or maybe it wasn't a mid-life crisis and more of an epiphany.

He needed to get himself together.

"Of course I do." She leaned in and her scent teased him.

Sugar and cinnamon.

Sweet. Delicious.

"That's what makes it so good." She grinned at him then stood. "Just don't tell Ed, yeah? What he doesn't know can't hurt him and I don't need another lecture. I'm at my limit."

"Um, Kiesha," he said quietly.

"I swear that man likes the sound of his own voice too much.

Blah, blah, blah, Kiesha, don't do this. Kiesha, don't do that, blah—"

"Ah, Kiesha," he tried to interrupt her.

"Blah, blah. I don't really listen. I just nod and pretend to."

"That's good to know," Ed said.

Kiesha's eyes widened at Harry. "Oh shit, he's standing right behind me, isn't he?"

Harry's lips twitched as he fought hard to hold in the laughter trying to break free. He glanced up at Ed who stood behind Kiesha. The sheriff rolled his eyes in clear exasperation.

"Why didn't you warn me?" she asked him. "I thought we were friends."

"He tried," Ed replied. "You weren't listening. Apparently something you do quite often."

"Damn you ears! Why won't you fulfill your primary function?" She threw her arms up into the air. And Harry couldn't help it. Her dramatics were adorable and hilarious.

He let out a belt of laughter. He tried to hold back, not wanting her to think he was laughing at her. But to his surprise, she just smiled at him.

"You're cute when you laugh, Harry. You should do it more often." Then she spun on her skates to face Ed. "I'm on my way to work, boss man. See? I'm even early. You should be smiling, not frowning. Really, Ed, you're gonna get frown lines. Maybe you should be thinking about retiring before you age prematurely. I can see some more grays. And Ticcy is back."

Ticcy?

Was she referring to the tic by the sheriff's right eye? Dear Lord, she was trouble.

But rather than being irritated by her irreverence, he found her amazing. And cute. Kiesha was someone who didn't live life by anyone else's rules. That was rather refreshing.

"All of these grays are because of you," the sheriff informed her.

"Hey, that's not fair! I'm sure a few are from Georgie. She's a handful."

Ed just shook his head at her. Her stomach grumbled again and Harry frowned, not liking that for some reason.

"Did you skip breakfast?" Ed asked, sounding concerned.

"I had to in order to get to work on time." She glanced at her watch. It had a wide, black strap and surrounding the face was a monster's mouth, opened wide so you could read the time between its fangs.

"I've got to go! I'm gonna be late and my boss is a real hard-ass. Bye, Harry! Have fun with the crossword. You ever want to learn how to use the internet then come see me." She spun back at the door. "Hey, Harry, how are you at trivia?"

"Ah, I guess I'm all right."

"All right is good enough for me. How would you like to come to quiz night tonight? You can be an honorary member for our group."

"How come he gets to be a member, but I'm not allowed to join?" Ed asked, sounding piqued.

"Because Harry's fun. You're not. What do you say, Harry? Tonight at the Wishing Well. Eight p.m. Don't be late. Wear something pretty."

"Wear something pretty?" he asked.

"Yeah, it's girls only usually. But I'm making an exception for you. See you there. Bye!" She skated out the door, not even looking first.

Harry stared after her in shock. "I'm not sure whether to be flattered or alarmed."

"Alarmed," Ed advised, staring at him curiously. "They've never had a man on their team before. Why you?"

"I have no idea. She probably feels sorry for me, sitting on my own, doing a crossword."

"Guess I'll be seeing you tonight. In something pretty." Ed's lips twitched at that.

"Can you take her something to eat for breakfast?" Harry asked. Shoot. He hadn't meant to ask that. He made sure to keep the look on his face of mild interest. "I'm happy to pay."

"I was already going to order her something. But it's interesting you care."

He shrugged. "She seems like a sweet person."

"She is. She's also under my protection. Just thought I'd let you know." Ed continued to study him.

"Of course. I'm glad she has your protection."

Yeah, he managed to spit out the words without frowning. Because he didn't like her having anyone else's protection except for his.

Which was utterly ridiculous.

4

He wasn't going to turn up. She didn't know why she was here waiting for him. It was silly. She wasn't even certain why she'd invited him.

She could tell herself that she'd felt sorry for him, sitting alone and eating breakfast, doing his crossword.

But it would be silly to feel sorry for Harry. Because there was nothing sad or down and out about him.

All he'd have to do is look up and click his fingers and people would likely fall all over him. There was a confidence about him, he was the sort of guy you looked to in a crisis because you could just sense he'd know what to do.

And it wasn't about the gray hair, either.

Jonny Jacks had gray hair and no one would turn to him in a crisis.

Turning away, she let out a sigh. She should be used to being let down by now.

Stupid girl.

"Kiesha!"

A smile lit her face, but she quickly wiped it away.

Don't let him see how excited you are to see him.

Once her face was under control, she turned, her eyes widening.

"Hi," he said, strolling up to her.

In a pink shirt.

What the heck?

"Are you all right?" he asked.

"You're late," she told him.

Damn, how could he look so good in a pink shirt? That wasn't possible, was it?

"I apologize," he replied even though they both knew he wasn't late. There was still twenty minutes until the quiz started.

But she had to say something in order to keep herself from drooling over how hot he looked.

"It's okay. But don't make a habit of it."

"You mean I'm going to get invited back a second time? I gather from Ed that it's unusual for you to extend an invitation."

"Pfft, Ed's just sour because he's not allowed to join. But he's one of the DDBs."

"DDBs?"

Oh crap. She hadn't meant to say that. Now what to say . . . but then, maybe Harry already knew since most of the guys that lived on Sanctuary Ranch were Daddy Doms. Including Linc.

"Um, well, it doesn't matter."

"Inside joke?" he asked lightly.

She blew out a breath. "Sort of. DDB stands for the Daddy Dom Brigade." She watched him closely for his reaction.

"I see and because I'm not a Daddy, I'm allowed to join your team?"

Oh. So, he wasn't a Daddy? That was disappointing. Not that she was looking for a Daddy. She certainly hadn't been hoping that Harry was one. Nope. No way.

Well, maybe a teensy bit.

She might have wondered a few times if that's why he'd bought her that safety gear, and had been concerned over her teeth while she was eating candy, and had made sure Ed brought her some breakfast. It had been a healthy breakfast, but still she'd been grateful and surprised that he cared when she barely knew him.

He was a nice guy.

Too nice for you. You'd walk all over him.

"Um, well, yeah. You're wearing a pink shirt," she blurted out.

Good one, Kiesha.

When are you ever going to learn to think before you talk?

"Excuse me," he said in a cold voice. "I'll have you know that this is not a pink shirt."

Oh, shoot. Now she'd insulted him.

Idiot.

"This is a salmon shirt. There is a huge distinction. And you did tell me to dress pretty."

Relief flooded her. She had no idea why she cared so much about his feelings. "Yeah, but I didn't expect you to do it. Did you already own that shirt?"

"Of course."

Hmm, it looked suspiciously new to her. But she wasn't going to call him out on it. Because it was awfully sweet if he had gone out and bought it.

"Come on, let's go. I hope you have your brain up and revving. Did I tell you that we're the reigning champs?"

"Ah, no, you didn't."

"Yep. So, you better do us proud, Harry. Or you'll be out on your ass."

"Right. I better dust the cobwebs off my brain then, huh?"

She smiled at him. "Just joking. To be honest, Juliet answers most of the questions. The rest of us are just eye-candy."

He grinned. "So now I'm eye-candy."

"Why, Harry," she said in a shocked voice, placing her hand on her chest. "You're the biggest piece of eye candy of them all."

He let out a bark of laughter that had her bouncing up and down on her toes in delight. She loved when he laughed.

"Let's go inside," he suggested, holding out his arm. She slid her arm into his elbow. "I don't want you getting cold."

She'd never had someone offer their arm to her. Very proper and sweet.

She liked it.

Jonah would have just told her to get her ass inside. Which could be sexy, if said in the right tone of voice.

"I'm never cold," she told him. "I don't sit still long enough to get chilly."

"I have noticed you like to be on the move. No roller skates tonight?"

She pouted. "No, Noah banned me from wearing them in the Wishing Well."

"Really?"

"Uh-huh, mean, right?" She saw Noah over at the bar as they grew closer. "Hey, Noah, Harry thinks it was mean of you to ban me from wearing roller skates inside."

"Actually," Harry said firmly. "I don't believe that is what I said."

Whoa.

Where had that tone of voice come from? And the look on his face . . . he appeared almost stern.

Where was the mild-mannered guy from before?

This Harry wasn't sweet and chivalrous.

No, he was sexy as hell.

And she might be in trouble.

Harry ordered their drinks and Noah told them he'd bring them over.

"Our table is over there," Kiesha said, setting off.

She didn't have any trouble getting through the crowds of people. Did everyone in Wishingbone come to quiz night?

Several people gave him questioning looks as they called out to her. Tonight, she was wearing a pair of bright yellow tights that had white ghosts on them. Over them, she wore a long, black floaty top. Her hair was back in a high knot and a yellow ribbon was tied around it.

When he was around her, he felt lighter, happier. More alive and relaxed than he had in a long time.

An older man stopped in front of Kiesha, dropping to his knees.

"Kiesha, me darlin', when are ye gonna make an honest man of me?"

Harry walked up beside her as she sighed. She sent him a wink and he relaxed slightly. But he still kept an eye on the man on his knees.

"Is that supposed to be an Irish accent?" he asked. "Or Scottish?"

"Scottish? Scottish?" The man got to his feet. "That there is a true insult. I demand retribution. I call ye out, sir!"

"Oh, dear Lord." Kiesha smacked her hand against her forehead. He reached out to gently pull her hand down.

"No hitting yourself," he told her as she gave him a surprised look.

"You're a strange man, Harrison, uh, what is your last name?" she asked.

"Taylor. I'm the strange one considering this guy just proposed to you and is calling me out? Whatever that means?"

"Oh, it means he wants to duel you for insulting him," she explained seriously.

He waited a few beats, expecting her to grin or tell him she was joking. But she just stared at him seriously. So did everyone else around him.

"A duel? You do realize this isn't the eighteenth century?"

"Ye insulted my accent," the man told him.

"Come on, Irish Mick," Noah said, coming over to them. "He didn't know. He's new here. Why don't I pour you a Guinness on the house and we'll call it even?"

"Ack, well, I suppose he is new. And a city slicker. Can't be trustin' 'em. Kiesha, me darlin'. I'll expect an answer to me proposal."

"I'll let you know Thursday next year," Kiesha replied.

"Good enough, darlin'. Good enough." He waved a hand over his shoulder as Noah led him away.

"What just happened?" Harry asked.

"Noah saved your ass," Kiesha told him. "Don't worry, I wouldn't have let Irish Mick actually shoot you. He's got a soft spot for me."

"You don't mean he was serious about that duel stuff?"

"Oh, he's very serious. He's a good shot too. But Ed's banned him from using actual bullets. Now, it's paintball guns. They still leave bruises. And you've got delicate skin."

"I do not," he replied. *Delicate skin?*

"Hmm, it looks delicate." She ran her gaze over him then walked off again.

Jesus help him.

She stopped at a table where several women sat. He really was the honorary bloke tonight.

Ed was standing behind Georgina, who he'd met during a previous visit to Wishingbone. He leaned in to whisper something in her ear that had her shifting around on her seat.

What was he saying to her? Something sexy? A scolding?

Since when did he become so interested in what happened in other people's relationships?

He needed a hobby. Golf? Bowling?

Keeping Kiesha's butt out of trouble?

Now, that would definitely be a full-time job.

"Kiesha!" A small woman dressed in cowboy boots and sparkly shorts and top smiled up at her. "There you are. Usually, you're the first one here. I was worried you were sick or something."

Kiesha snorted. "Even if I was on my deathbed, I'd throw myself out of it and crawl here on my hands and knees just to kick Loki's ass one last time!"

She said that last part loudly and a few tables over, a huge guy stood up. "You're not beating us tonight, Kiesha!"

"Watch me, big boy. You and your little friends are going down! You're going to lose so badly that you'll be crying for mercy. And I'll show you none!"

Ed straightened then nodded to Harry. "Harry, you remember, Georgina?" Georgina stood and reached out a hand to Harry as Kiesha and the other man traded insults. Harry wasn't sure whether he should get involved or not.

"Hi, Harry. Don't worry about the trash talk. That's just the way Kiesha and Loki warm up."

"Loki?" He eyed the other man curiously.

"Yeah, Loki's Warriors are always trying to beat our team at quiz night."

"But they always lose," Kiesha added, turning to Harry.

"Because you have Juliet," Loki called out, pointing to the quiet woman sitting between Georgina and the girl in the sparkly outfit. She wore a black top with a sparkly pink crown on the front. Her long chestnut-colored hair was pulled back into two braids. "Juju, when are you going to leave the dark side and come over to the good side? We'll treat you right."

A well-built guy, whose gaze had been running over the crowd, turned to frown at Loki who simply smiled back at him. "You can come too, Brick. More the merrier over here with Loki's Warriors."

The men sitting with him started to chant, "Loki's Warriors. Loki's Warriors."

"Starting to wonder what you've gotten yourself into?" Ed asked, wrapping his hand around the back of Georgina's neck.

"Ah, perhaps a little bit. But it definitely beats sitting alone in a hotel room, eating a microwave meal."

Everyone stared at him.

Ahh. Awkward.

"Dude, that's just sad," Kiesha told him.

It really was.

"Everyone, this is my friend, Harry. Harry, this is Isa."

The tiny woman in the sparkly dress waved at him.

"And Cleo."

Cleo was tall and curvy. He remembered Kiesha saying that she was involved with the bar's owner, Noah. Something about speeding tickets and spankings. Cleo frowned at him suspiciously, then turned to Kiesha. "Really?"

"He's wearing pink," Kiesha said, as though that explained something.

"True." Cleo nodded. "He's on probation."

"Fair call," Kiesha replied.

"Do I want to know what they're talking about?" he asked Ed quietly.

"Probably not," Ed replied. "My advice, keep your head down and only talk when you're spoken to. Then you might survive the night."

"Ed!" Georgina protested, smacking her hand against his chest. "We're not that bad, Harry. Honest. This is all just for fun."

"It totally is not!" Kiesha replied. "We play to win and for bragging rights. And the bar tab."

"The lot of you have such a large bar tab that you could go

months without winning and still be flush," Noah commented, walking up with their drinks.

"Last, but not least, this is Juliet," Kiesha said, softening her voice.

Juliet gave him a hesitant wave as the well-built guy Loki had called Brick stepped up behind her. It was obvious that she was with him. And that he was protective of her. He eyed Harry for a long moment. Harry just gave him a calm look back.

He was used to how protective the men were of women in these parts. And he didn't take offense as Brick sized him up.

Finally, he gave Harry a nod, then stepped back. Juliet turned and smiled up at him. His face softened as he glanced down at her and he ran a finger over her cheek.

Harry felt a curious longing inside him. His life had been filled with work and little else. It wasn't until he was reunited with Marisol that he'd realized how lonely he was. Was it too late to find someone? To have what Brick and Juliet obviously did?

"Was Irish Mick giving you problems?" Ed asked, glancing over to the bar where the fake Irishman was sipping a Guinness.

"No, he wanted to duel with me over an insult about his terrible accent, but Noah distracted him. I owe you," he called out to Noah who grinned.

"Don't worry, you're not the first person I've saved from the paintball gun."

Ed sighed. "I'll have another chat with him."

"Don't worry. I'm not concerned."

"Yes, but one day he'll challenge someone who does care. And then I'll have a real mess to clean up." He frowned as he glanced over at Cleo. "Cleo, Jace said he pulled you over for speeding. Again. You need to slow down or I'm taking your license."

If looks could kill then Ed would be writhing on the floor in a huge amount of pain.

"What the hell, Ed?" Cleo snapped. "That's private."

"Private? I don't think so." Ed crossed his arms over his chest as Georgina gave him an exasperated look.

Noah turned to Cleo, raising his eyebrows. "You were pulled over for speeding? Again?"

"I was barely over the limit."

"You were doing fifty in a forty zone," Ed said.

"Well, aren't you Mr. Helpful and Informative tonight," Cleo drawled at Ed.

Noah turned her chair around so she was facing him. He placed one hand on the table and the other on the back of her chair. "What did I say would happen if you got another speeding ticket?"

Cleo turned her glare on him. "You are not taking my keys!"

"Oh, I am. And just wait until later tonight." He leaned in and whispered something that had Cleo going bright red.

"Happy with yourself?" Georgina glared up at Ed. "Did you have to do that?

"Better that Noah heat her ass than she gets into an accident and hurts herself or someone else," Ed countered.

Georgina sighed, but nodded.

"Excuse me a moment, I need to talk to Mick while he's still sober enough to listen." Ed moved through the crowd, which parted easily for him. Maybe because he was the sheriff. Or because he'd lived here a long time.

"Have a seat," Georgina told him.

"Sorry, I'm late," another man called out as he walked through the crowd to them. "Hey, Twink."

To Harry's surprise, the newcomer leaned down and kissed Juliet's cheek.

"Juliet has two men," Georgina told him, watching him closely. Probably wondering if he was going to react negatively.

"Right. I've heard there are a few relationships like that around here." He didn't quite understand how the men worked together to share a woman, but from the look on Juliet's face she was happy.

"Right, who's ready for this? Harry, you got your brain cells firing? Dusted off those cobwebs? You'll be good at the history questions, right?" Kiesha said as she took a seat next to him.

"Because I lived through it," Harry guessed dryly.

"Exactly."

"Kiesha!" Isa scolded. "You can't say that."

"I didn't." Kiesha placed her hand on her chest. "He did."

Harry nodded good-naturedly.

"Harry isn't old. He's probably the same age as Ed," Georgina told her. "Ed's fifty this year."

"We're close in age. I'll be fifty-two in a few months."

"Damn, you look good for nearly fifty-two," Cleo commented. He noticed that Noah had disappeared.

The new arrival was saying something quietly as he crouched by Juliet. She nodded, but didn't answer back. Had he heard her speak yet?

"Juliet doesn't generally talk to anyone she hasn't known for a long time," Georgina told him. "So, don't be insulted if she doesn't speak to you."

"I won't be."

"We have to give Ed a big surprise party for his birthday," Georgina said.

"I've already bought his gift," Kiesha told her.

Georgina grimaced. "Do I want to know?"

"You should, since it's gonna benefit you too. I got him some little blue pills and a packet of adult diapers."

Harry spat out the mouthful of drink he'd just taken as everyone gaped at Kiesha.

Then Georgina broke out into giggles and the rest of the girls followed.

"Oh man, I can't wait to see his face when you give him those,"

Cleo stated.

"Kiesha, you can't give him that," Georgina scolded.

"Why not? I thought it was a good gift. I thought about getting you a vibrator for the days when he couldn't get it up, but I figure those blue pills will help." Kiesha shot him a look. "When did you say your birthday was, Harry?"

Oh no, she didn't. He leaned in to speak quietly to her. "I don't need any blue pills, Little Monster. And you can bet that if you have a vibrator, it will only be used as a starter, not during the main course."

Kiesha stared at him wide-eyed.

Oh fuck. What had he just done?

He'd pushed that too far. She'd been teasing him and he'd gone and flirted with her.

Idiot.

Then she grinned. "Well, Harry, aren't you full of surprises?"

He hadn't thought so until tonight. He'd always thought he was rather boring and mundane.

He couldn't remember the last time he'd gone to a social function that wasn't work-related. Well, other than having dinner with Marisol and Linc.

"Wait, this guy is playing?" The guy who'd been talking quietly to Juliet stood up and pointed to him. "How come he's allowed in and I'm not?"

"Because you're super unreliable, Xavier," Kiesha replied. "You're always running off because of 'emergencies'." She did air quotes with her fingers as she said emergencies.

"I'm a doctor. Those are actual emergencies."

Kiesha waved away his reasoning. "Excuses are not welcome. Now, toddle off to the DDB wall."

Xavier just shook his head but kissed the top of Juliet's head. "Knock it out of the park, Twink."

"She always does," Kiesha said proudly.

5

For the next thirty minutes, Juliet proceeded to answer pretty much every question. He knew several of them, but his input wasn't needed.

Not that he was bored. How could he be with Kiesha around? She was gentle with Juliet, a smart-ass to Cleo and Isa. With Georgina, she was a combination of both. All between yelling insults to Loki and talking to whoever stopped by the table. She was a whirlwind, and he wondered how she found the energy.

"We have tallied the results and the winner is Beersal Suspects!" the quiz master, Red, yelled out.

Kiesha jumped to her feet and did a victory dance. Loki let out a cry, like he'd been mortally wounded as he fell to his knees. Suddenly, Kiesha climbed onto the chair and bounced up and down.

It wobbled precariously and Harry quickly stood up, grabbing her around the waist to lift her down. She glanced at him in confusion.

"All victory dancing has to happen on the ground," he told her. "I don't want you getting any more scrapes and bruises."

"Well, that's no fun. What about the table?"

"No dancing on the tables," Noah called out as he walked up to them. He drew Cleo close, wrapping an arm around her. "Congrats. Your bar tab has been added to."

Juliet's two men walked forward to collect her.

"Come on, Duchess. Your brain must be exhausted after that work-out," Brick said to her. "Kiesha, you want a ride home with us?"

"Nah, I'll sort something out," Kiesha replied.

Brick looked to Ed, who'd come back from his talk with Irish Mick sometime after the quiz started. "Don't worry, I have her."

"Hey! Nobody needs to have me. I can get myself home."

"Right, like the time you told everyone that someone else was taking you home, then you walked home in the dark," Brick said with a scolding look.

"That was one time. One time."

"I'll take her home," Harry stated.

Brick stared at him assessingly. Juliet tugged on his sleeve and he bent down as she whispered in his ear. Then he nodded. She wrapped her hand up in his top.

"All right," Brick replied. "If that's okay with Kiesha."

"I don't know why you're so concerned about how I get home," Kiesha stated. "If you care so much then how come you tried to run me over that time?"

"I didn't try to run you over," Brick growled back. "If I'd been trying to hit you, I would have."

"What?" Harry asked.

"Don't worry, he didn't hit her," Georgina stated.

Right. Because that made things better.

"Harry can take me home," Kiesha stated. "We don't have to go right now, do we? Is it your bedtime yet? Because I want to do some dancing."

"I have a few more hours before I need to get my old body into bed," he replied dryly. "Of course, you can dance. I don't dance, though."

Brick, Xavier, and Juliet all left along with Ed and Georgina.

"Isa, dance with me!" Kiesha called out.

"I'll be back in a minute," Isa told her. "Got to pee. Tiny bladder." As she moved away, Harry noticed a big guy with dark hair watching her. He frowned, wondering if she knew him.

"Remy's watching Isa again," Cleo noted.

"He never seems to do anything but watch her," Kiesha said with a frown. "Do you think we should do something?"

"Would you like me to ask some questions about him?" Harry asked, startling them both.

"Oh, actually Linc will know him since they work together on Sanctuary Ranch," Kiesha said. "Could you ask him? Maybe just get a gauge of whether he's a good guy? Although, to be honest, I have a good creep-o-meter and he's not setting it off. I think he might just like her."

"I'll check anyway."

"Aww, thanks, Harry." Kiesha patted his shoulder. "You're a good dude."

"Thank you. That's what I strive to be."

"Even if you do talk funny sometimes." She waved at Isa as she worked her way back toward them. "Sure, you don't want to dance? I don't want you to be lonely."

"I'll keep an eye on the drinks."

"Eh, don't worry, no one here will spike them. Noah would string them up by their balls."

He frowned at her complacency. It seemed to him that she needed to take more care with her safety.

Or she needed someone to do that for her.

Not your business. You barely know the girl.

"Still, it always pays to be cautious."

"Are you always cautious, Harry?" she asked, tilting her head to one side.

"Yes, I suppose I am."

"What about when you were younger? Didn't you live it up? Get wild? Wasn't everyone smoking weed and having orgies back then?"

"Just when do you think I was born?" he asked.

"I dunno? The forties?"

"The forties? You little brat." He reached for her, but she danced back, laughing.

"I was born in nineteen-seventy for your information," he told her haughtily. "And sure, I had some fun. In my early twenties. But then I buckled down and worked hard and . . ."

Have done little else since but work.

Shit, he was boring.

"Maybe it's time to party again. Have some fun! Life is short, right? So why not live!" She twirled in the air then stopped to gesture at him, crooking her fingers. "Come dance with us, Harry."

"Kiesha! Come on!" Isa called out.

Harry shook his head. "No way. I'm staying here."

"Fine, but if you change your mind . . ." She turned and danced her way over to where Isa was surrounded by some big, burly guys.

He scowled, not liking the way those guys surrounded them, grinding in behind her and Isa.

Not your business. She's free to do what she likes.

"You know Kiesha."

He glanced up in surprise to find the big cowboy they'd been talking about earlier had sidled up to him.

"Uh, yes, sort of. Hello, I'm Harry. You're Remy, right?"

The other man narrowed his gaze. "Right."

"I'm Marisol's father." Standing, he held out his hand.

The other man just looked at it like it was a snake that might bite him.

"Marisol?"

"Uh, yes. Mari? She lives at Sanctuary Ranch with Linc. You know Linc?"

"I know Linc," he replied in a cool voice. He glanced over at the girls then back to Harry. "Just letting you know that Isa is mine."

Harry dropped his hand, staring back at the other man. So, there wasn't going to be any niceties, huh?

"Is that so?" he asked. "Does Isa know?"

"Not yet. She will." He spoke with a confidence that impressed him. But still . . .

"Her friends have noticed you watching her. You're not stalking her, are you?"

Remy turned his gaze to Harry. "If I was, I'd be a fool to tell you, right? And my mama didn't raise a fool. Just wanted to be clear in case you were thinking that Isa was going to be yours. She's not."

"Listen, I admire your confidence. But Isa will only be yours if she wants to be."

Remy's gaze narrowed.

"I'm not interested in her," Harry explained calmly. "But I am big on consent."

"She'll consent. I've never forced a woman, and I wouldn't force the woman I intend to spend my life with. Just want to make my intentions clear."

"Got it. For your peace of mind, I'm not interested in Isa."

"You're interested in Kiesha, she's a spitfire," Remy told him.

Harry couldn't tell whether he thought that being a spitfire was a good thing or not. "I'm not looking for a relationship."

"None of my business. Just so long as you stay clear of my woman."

Harry watched as the big man moved away, his eyes narrowed

thoughtfully. Was this entire town filled with eccentric personalities?

"Harry! Come on, come dance." Kiesha drank down her drink, then grabbed his hand.

"Kiesha, seriously. I have two left feet." But he let her tug him out onto the dance floor. Because wasn't she right? Life was short. And it seemed he'd missed a lot of it by working all the time.

So, he moved with Kiesha, trying to find the beat. He shuffled from side to side, throwing his arms around. Both women stopped and stared at him.

"What?"

"Nothing," Kiesha replied. She bit her lower lip.

Isa was doing the same.

He stilled, putting his hands on his hips as he frowned at them both. "Are you trying not to laugh at me because I'm such a bad dancer?"

"No. Not at all," Isa reassured him.

"Absolutely, yes," Kiesha countered. Blunt as ever. But that was surprisingly refreshing. It seemed that lately all he'd done was surround himself with people who told him whatever they thought he wanted to hear.

"Come stand here and we'll move around you. Just see if you can wiggle in time to the beat." Kiesha tried to direct him but he knew it was hopeless, he'd never been able to dance.

After about thirty minutes of sweating his ass off while doing very little, the girls decided they'd had enough. They headed back to their table for a few more drinks before they left.

As they walked Isa to her car, he swore he saw Remy standing off in the shadows, although he couldn't be certain. The other man had been dressed all in black, so he kind of blended into the shadows.

Harry kept a close eye on Kiesha as he walked her over to his car. She'd had a couple of pink flamingos and apparently she was a lightweight.

He was just glad he was the one taking her home and not one of those assholes on the dance floor who'd tried to dance far too close to her for his peace of mind.

"You really have no rhythm, do you?" She took hold of his hand and he spun her in and out.

She laughed, sounding so carefree. Then she stumbled and he had to tug her into his chest to keep her upright.

He stared down at her, both of them breathing heavily.

"I might not have rhythm for dancing, but I'm not lacking for rhythm in other places..."

"What do you mean?"

"Let's just say I have plenty of rhythm between the sheets."

Oh. Dear. Lord.

Did he seriously just say that? He couldn't have, right?

"Is that right?" she replied huskily.

He cupped the side of her face with his hand, leaning in to kiss her. The blast of a horn made them both jump and turn. Headlights flooded them, making him squint.

Someone's timing was shit.

"You asshole!"

For a moment, he thought she was talking to him. But then she stepped toward the car, her fist waving in the air. "Jonny Jacks! You have a nerve!"

The car backed up.

"Your arch-nemesis?" he asked. How much of a problem was this guy?

"Yes. Jerk. Now where were we?"

Well, he'd been about to kiss her...

"Oh yeah! Rhythm in the sheets! Harry, you're a hoot."

Right. So that moment was over. He should probably be

relieved she found it funny. Although he was slightly insulted that she thought it was hilarious that he could be good in bed.

Get it together, Harry.

For some reason, he kept making an idiot of himself in front of her.

"This is mine," he told her as they reached his rental car.

"Oh, nice. This doesn't really seem to suit you, though."

"It doesn't?" It was sensible. Economical and safe. Seemed like him.

When did he get so boring and predictable?

"I dunno, you just seem like you should be driving a red car."

"Because they go faster?" he teased, opening her door.

"Exactly!"

"Do you drive?"

"No, I'm not allowed to. I have trouble focusing. Ed says I'm a menace. But then, apparently, I'm also a menace on roller skates. I mean, I wish the guy wasn't so wishy-washy."

"Indeed."

She waggled a finger at him. "I know what that means, that means you agree with him."

"Not at all, sweetheart. Now, let's get you home. Okay?"

"All right."

She climbed up into the passenger seat and he shut the door, walking around to get in the driver's side.

He immediately noticed that she hadn't done up her seatbelt. Instead, she was rummaging in his glove box.

"What are you looking for?"

"Candy. Everyone knows that you keep candy in your glove box."

"Uh, I'm afraid I don't eat candy."

"Dude." She looked over at him. "I'm not sure we can be friends anymore. You don't eat candy? How are you still alive?"

"Not all of us have sugar running through their veins," he replied dryly.

"I don't get it. It's just not healthy."

"I think you'll find the opposite is true."

She shook her head. "You poor delusional man. Don't buy into the propaganda, Harry. It's veggies that will kill you."

He wasn't sure he wanted to know her reasoning for that statement.

Reaching over, he closed the glove box. "Do you want to put your seatbelt on?"

"Not really." She turned around on the seat, glancing into the back seat.

Harry stared at her wriggling ass, feeling his cock harden.

Totally inappropriate, asshole.

Feeling like a complete creeper, he cleared his throat. "Kiesha? I can't drive until you're sitting down with your seatbelt on."

There. That sounded reasonable and polite.

"Your car is shockingly clean."

"Well, it's a rental." Not that his own cars weren't as clean and tidy as this one.

"It's unnatural. Even with a rental, shouldn't you have empty food packets and stuff lying on the floor? I mean, what do you do with your garbage?"

"I don't really eat in the car."

She turned, plonking her butt back in the seat. He started the car, worried she was going to get cold if the heater wasn't going.

"But what about on a road trip? On a road trip, you'd have to eat in your car."

He grimaced at the thought. "I suppose so. Although, I don't really go on many road trips."

"I love road trips. Loud music. Junk food. New places to see." She sighed, looking out the window. "It's been a while since I went on a road trip."

"Perhaps we could go on one together sometime."

What are you doing?

He seriously needed to find his filter. He'd always been careful with his words, but now he was just blurting shit out all over the place.

Please don't let her remember any of this.

"Forget—"

"That would be so fun! Where would we go? Disneyland?"

Okay, so she didn't think he was a complete weirdo. "It might be a bit of a long trip to go to Disneyland."

She pouted and he felt the ridiculous urge to take that statement back. To tell her that he would drive her anywhere she wanted to go as long as she was happy.

"I love Disneyland."

"You went as a child?" he asked.

"No, I've never been. But I know I'd love it. Who couldn't? It's the happiest place on earth, right?"

"Right."

"I'll get there one day. Actually, I had a job offer there once."

"You did?"

"Yeah, they wanted me to be one of the seven dwarfs. Obviously, that wasn't going to work."

He cleared his throat, trying not to let her see how amused he was. "No, obviously."

She eyed him. "You don't believe me?"

"I, uh..."

"You shouldn't, Harry," she said sadly. "You shouldn't believe a word out of my mouth." Her shoulders were slumped as she turned to look out the window.

What the hell had just happened?

"Kiesha. Hey, look at me."

Nothing.

"Kiesha?"

Still nothing.

Ah, fuck it.

"Kiesha," he said in a deeper voice. One that he infused with steel. "Look at me."

She turned, giving him a surprised look. "Damn, Harry, here I thought you were all mild-mannered and stuff but you keep surprising me. You do alpha male really well."

"Thank you. I think. Listen to me."

"I'm all ears." She cupped her hands behind her ears.

Don't smile.

She was so adorable, though.

"Right. I'm not sure why you think that I shouldn't listen to you, but how about we make a pact to always tell each other the truth?"

She bit her lip. "That's the part I'm not good at, though. Telling the truth."

"So, everything has been a lie? You're not my friend? You don't think I should know the answer to all the ancient history questions in the quiz because I lived through it? You don't think I'm funny?"

"Nah, all those things were true. But there are other things . . . things I can't talk about. Or don't want to talk about."

"If there is something you don't want to talk about, then just tell me that. I know, how about if you tell me a story that isn't quite true, then you can give me a signal?"

"A signal?"

"Hmm, like every time you create a story, tap your nose with your finger."

"I like that." She gave him a big smile. "You're so smart, Harry. And kind. How come you don't have a girl?"

"I think that somewhere along the line I ended up married to my work."

She shook her head. "Don't you know that your work can't give you a hug? Can't make you laugh when you're sad or celebrate when you have a win?"

"It's taken me a while to realize that. I appear to be a slow learner."

"Silly Harry." Reaching over, she patted his thigh and he tried to ignore the way that her touch heated his insides. "Hey, we better get home. It's probably past your bedtime and all."

"My old bones do need quite a lot of sleep," he said dryly.

She bit her lip. "You know I'm just joking, right? About your age. I don't . . . sometimes I take the joke too far and I don't want to hurt your feelings."

"My feelings are pretty tough," he told her. "And the truth is, I could use a bit of fun. I've taken life very seriously for far too long."

"That's funny, because most people would say I don't take life seriously enough. But there's so much bad stuff that could happen and I just . . . I want to be happy when I can be, you know?"

"Yes. I think I understand."

She ran her hand over her face. "Wow, this got pretty in-depth and serious, huh? Home, James!" She pointed ahead of her.

"You need to put your seatbelt on first," he told her.

"I'll be all right. My place isn't far away."

"And the entire way, you'll be wearing your seatbelt," he said firmly. Finally, deciding not to wait any longer, he reached over and grabbed the belt, securing it over her. His arm brushed over her breasts and she let out a startled gasp.

He quickly belted her in. "I apologize. I didn't mean to, uh . . ."

Harry, get it together, man.

"It's okay," she told him, her voice slightly breathless. "Most action I've had in ages."

He groaned. "I was just doing up your belt."

"So, you're saying you didn't want to touch my boobs?" She

glanced down at her chest. "Sorry, boobs. That really was an accident. He's not interested in touching you."

"What? No, I would be happy to touch . . . I mean, it just . . ."

She burst into laughter. "Relax, Harry. I'm just having you on."

He let out a breath. "Have you always been this much of a brat?"

"Pretty much."

"Right, brat. Tell me where you live."

6

Kiesha directed Harry to her tiny apartment. She wished she could think of an excuse to spend more time with him.

You should give the guy a break, you're a lot to handle.

Like she hadn't heard that a lot. Well, not from her friends. She really did have the best friends. The people of Wishingbone understood her. She fit in here. But out there . . . in the big bad world?

That's where people could be mean.

Not that Harry was capable of being mean. Well, she guessed maybe he could be, but he'd been nothing but nice to her.

However, she couldn't take advantage of his niceness. He was sweet and polite and even though he seemed to have a dark edge, she had doubts that he could handle her long term.

Which was a shame, because when she was around him, she felt calmer. More centered.

But that didn't mean they couldn't continue to be friends. Maybe she could help him relax a bit more.

"Harry, you know what?"

"What?"

"I think you need me to help you live a little."

"Do you just? You don't think I know how to do that?"

"What's the last fun thing you did?" she asked, directing him to pull up outside her building.

"I just went to quiz night with a bunch of semi-crazy people. Does Loki always talk about himself in the third person?"

"Yep. Before tonight then? What's the last fun thing you did before you came here to visit?"

"I went on that walk with you and Oscar. Oh, and I went out to dinner with some associates. That was nice."

"Dude. That's not living. Right, it's decided. I'm going to teach you how to live."

"Should I feel worried?"

"Probably. I don't have the greatest safety record. And you do have those elderly brittle bones."

"I'm not that old, brat."

He turned off his car.

"This is where you live?" He glanced up at the gray building.

It didn't look like much, but it was cheap and in a good location.

"Yep, I know it's ugly but it does the job."

"I'll walk you up. Wait there."

Wow. He was such a gentleman.

"You're gonna spoil me, Harry," she told him as he opened her door and held out his hand. She undid her seatbelt. Annoying thing. She always felt like it was strangling her.

"Hardly," he replied. "Besides, I'm sure you could use some spoiling."

Aww. Sweet.

"I always thought I was made for a life of being spoiled." She winked at him to let him know she was joking.

The two vodka and raspberries she'd had were making her light-headed and happy.

Humming, she skipped along the footpath. Uh-oh. That was a bad idea. Her stomach rolled queasily.

"Kiesha? Hey, come back here."

Ooh. Harry had his stern voice out. She liked that voice. It did giddy things to her tummy.

Or maybe that was the skipping after drinking tonight. Yep, could be that.

"I was just doing some skipping. You should try it."

"If I can't dance, then I definitely can't skip."

"Everyone can skip, Harry."

"Not me. And I don't want you skipping away from me when it's dark out. Understand?"

There he went again. If he kept this up, her panties were going to get embarrassingly wet.

"Yes, Daddy!"

Um. Whoops. Where had that come from?

She saluted him, trying to make up for her embarrassing slip-up. He'd just think she was joking, right? Not like she thought he was a Daddy. Although . . . he did show some characteristics. But she was probably just seeing things. Or maybe it was wishful thinking.

Instead of giving her a look like she was insane or telling her how wrong she was, he just gave her a nod.

"That's better."

"Let's go!" Turning away, she hurried toward the door. Reaching out, he lightly grabbed hold of her arm. Right over the bruises that were still a bit sore.

She flinched, hoping he didn't notice.

"Did I hurt you? Did I grab you where you're bruised?"

He remembered?

"Oh no, I'm fine. You saw them the other day. They're nearly healed."

"I want to have a better look. Actually, it's too dark out here. Let's go inside."

"Inside? Into my place, you mean?"

Very few people came to her place. She usually met with her friends at the diner or the Wishing Well or their houses.

Not hers.

"Yes."

"My arm is fine. It's just a few bruises and they've mostly faded. You saw them the other day."

"Not closely, I want to see them again," he said firmly.

Whoa. She hadn't realized he could be this stubborn.

She sighed. "My apartment is a mess."

"Don't care."

"I have my panties and bras everywhere."

"I have nothing against panties and bras."

"And tampons. It's a complete, uh, tampon fest . . ." she trailed off.

Yeah, she'd just entered the realm of the ridiculous.

"What did we just say about making stuff up?" he asked in a stiff voice. "If you don't want me in your apartment, then all you need to do is say so."

"It's not that." She groaned. She didn't want him thinking it was about him. "It's not you, it's me."

"What? Are we breaking up?"

"I have . . . urgh you know what? I'm just going to show you. Come on, let's go." She grabbed hold of his hand and tugged him toward the main door. It had a key card entry.

"At least the security is good."

"Ed made the landlord put this in. Said he'd make his life supremely difficult if he didn't. He doesn't often throw his power around, it's not his thing. I mean, if I was the sheriff I'd probably be exploiting the heck out of my power. Probably a good thing that I'm not the sheriff."

"Likely."

"Anyway, like I said, Ed did use his powers for evil that time and we got a more secure building." Sort of.

"The security lights are out, though."

"Ah, yeah, I know. I've told the building manager, but he hasn't fixed them yet. We never see our landlord, but his nephew is the building manager and he's a dick. He doesn't like to do anything you ask him. I did think about threatening to have Reuben sue him. But then I'd have to follow through if he called my bluff and I really don't want to have to ask Reuben for anything. I mean, I'd get Juliet to do it, obviously. For her, he'd raze the world to the ground and take over as the lord and dictator. He's already got the dictator part down." She knew she was rambling but she was nervous.

Harry was coming into her apartment.

"Who is Reuben?"

"Oh, he's Juliet's brother. Sorry, I forget that everyone doesn't know him. But you've likely met him."

"I have?"

"Uh-huh, he's the bogeyman that your mama warned you about as a kid."

He barked out a laugh. "That bad, huh?"

"No. Worse."

It was clear from his grin that he thought she was joking.

She wasn't.

They had started to climb the stairs and she was feeling breathless. More from his close proximity than anything else. He didn't show the slightest sign of being out of breath as they got to the third floor. Dude was in shape.

She wondered what kind of body he was rocking under his pink shirt.

Bad, bad eyes. Behave yourself. Stop eating up Harry.

Reaching her door, she tried to unlock the door with her keys, only to drop them. She bent down at the same time Harry did, smacking her head into his.

"Ow. Ow. Ow."

"Oh, baby. I'm sorry. Are you all right?"

Did he just call her baby?

"Kiesha? Are you all right? Let me see." He reached for her.

Nah, she must have imagined that. Stupid imagination. Why would he call her baby?

"I'm fine. My brain just got a ding. Won't hurt it. There's not a lot in there to begin with."

"No," he told her firmly.

"What?"

"No saying things like that about yourself."

"It was just a joke." She stared at him, confused about why he was being so stern.

"It's not funny if you're saying negative things about yourself," he informed her.

Right. Okay.

She stared up at him in amazement.

"Here, let me get your keys, all right? When we get inside, we'll put some ice on your head."

"What about your head?" she asked.

"I have a hard head. Or so I've been told."

"Hey now, no putting yourself down." She waggled a finger at him.

He grabbed her keys and easily unlocked the door. Then he tried to open it.

"Did it not unlock correctly?"

"Oh no, it did. You've just got to put a bit of muscle into it."

"Pardon?"

"Like this." She pushed him gently aside then turned and rammed her shoulder against the door. Once. Twice.

Finally, it budged. "See?"

He was giving her a strange look. As though she'd grown a second head or something. Great. She didn't have something between her teeth, did she? Someone would have told her by now, surely.

"That's how you open your door?" he asked.

"Yeah."

"And you've told the building manager about this?"

"Yeah." For all the good it did her.

"When?"

"What?" she asked, giving him a puzzled look.

"When did you tell him?"

She scratched her head. "I don't know." She held out her fingers, counting backward. "Maybe three?"

"Three days ago. He should have been onto it by now."

"Uh no, three months ago."

His mouth went flat as he glared down at her. What did she do wrong?

"And he refused to fix it?"

"Like I said, he's a dick. And I didn't want to bother Ed about this since he'd already interfered over the front door."

"Sounds like you should have bothered him."

"If I go to Ed for too much help, his head gets really big. And then he'll insist I move in with him and Georgie and I need my privacy. And I really, really don't need to listen to the two of them getting it on." She shuddered. "That's a hard limit."

Harry grunted and pushed open the door, stepping inside. She reached up and turned on the lights, holding her breath as she waited for his reaction.

"I'm disappointed."

What? Why? He was?

She glanced around.

"Where are all the bras and panties?" he teased then he grimaced. "I can't believe I just said that. It was inappropriate."

"Relax, Harry. I'm your friend, not your client. Saying inappropriate things is A-Okay between friends. Or it is when you're friends with me. So I might have lied about the bras and panties. And the tampons." She walked around and picked up some clothes off the floor. She didn't mean to be messy.

It just happened. Sometimes she thought she had gremlins who came in to mess up her house when she wasn't here.

Yeah, that was it. It was totally gremlins.

When she had an armful of clothes and other items, she looked around for somewhere to dump them.

"You don't have to tidy up because of me. Do you have an ice pack, though?" he asked.

"Oh yeah." She pushed open the door to her bedroom and walked in to dump everything on the chair in the corner. "Just let me . . ." she trailed off as she noticed him standing in the doorway.

Crap.

She looked around the room, taking in what he could see. The monster decals on the walls. Friendly looking cartoon monsters, not the scary kind. Although she had one of those stickers on the bottom of her closet door that looked like eyes peering out of the darkness. It glowed in the dark. Most Littles would likely be scared.

But not Kiesha. To her, monsters weren't scary. They were unique and interesting and misunderstood.

A bit like her, she guessed.

Fairy lights were strung around the walls and she had a large bed with a monster bedspread. Which might have been visible if it wasn't for the piles and piles of soft toys she had loaded up on the bed.

There were all sorts of soft monster toys, as well as aliens.

They took up pretty much the entire bed except for right in the middle which is where she slept.

Surrounded by them.

"Cute room. You really like monsters."

It wasn't a question but she nodded. "Uh, yep. So welcome to my den of monsters and the occasional alien. You creeped out?"

"Why would I be creeped out?" he asked.

"Maybe that was the wrong word. I just . . . most people would find this weird."

"Most people would find the dead bodies in my basement weird." He winced. "I cannot believe I said that. What is wrong with me? I never say stuff like this."

He sounded so bewildered it made her smile.

"Don't worry. I'm not weirded out by dead bodies."

"You aren't?"

"No, that's a lie. I totally am. That's disgusting. Really. Don't they smell?"

"I think we better stop talking about it. I'm starting to feel queasy. Ice pack?" he asked again.

"Sorry." She walked out and into the tiny kitchen. Opening the freezer, she drew out an ice pack. With a one-eyed alien on it.

"This is the only one I've got." She grimaced.

"This is fine. Come. Sit down." He gestured to the sofa. She wandered over and sat. He gently placed the ice pack on her head where she'd banged it into his. "Hold this."

"Are you sure your head is all right?"

"I'm fine," he said soothingly as he crouched in front of her. "Do you have a headache? Do you want some painkillers?"

"Oh, no." She shook her head then winced. "Um, maybe."

"Bathroom?"

"Yeah, through the bedroom." She sat and waited then she realized where she'd sent him.

Oh shit!

I hope I put the vibrator away after washing it last night.

She let her hand drop away from the ice pack, turning to look through her bedroom. As though she could see through walls to where the vibrator lay.

Please. Please. Please.

It was pale green and curved with monster footprints over it and the end that rested against her clit was a small paw. It was epic. But not something you wanted your new friend to see.

It wasn't that she was shy or anything. But Harry might be. Some people were weird about vibrators.

When he walked back into the living room, she couldn't tell whether he'd seen it or not. Damn him, he had too good a poker face.

Moving to the kitchen, he grabbed a bottle of water from her fridge then walked over to sit on the coffee table in front of her. He handed her two pain killers. She took them, chasing them with gulps of water. He picked up the ice pack and put it back on her head.

"It's not going to help if you don't keep it on your head," he scolded. "Saw you've got something interesting in your bathroom."

All of her froze except for her heart which raced. "What? What do you mean, something interesting?"

Oh, hell. Oh, hell.

"Your toilet lid."

"I can explain, see—"

Wait. Her toilet lid?

"The monster on your toilet lid with its mouth open is unusual. Don't think I've ever seen that before."

"Right. Yes. My toilet lid. I love monsters."

"What did you think I was talking about?" he said.

"Nothing at all."

He eyed her for a moment then held out his hand. "Show me the bruises."

"I really don't think that's necessary."

"I do. Show me."

"I'm not sure I like this bossy side of you."

"Tough. We're friends now. Friends look after one another. Now, show me your arm."

Muttering to herself about stubborn men, she held out her right arm. He drew the sleeve of her top up gently, revealing the fading bruises.

"These are nearly healed."

"Told you they were." She put her sleeve back into place.

"How about your knees from the other day? Have they healed?"

"They're fine. Ed fixed me up. He's good for some things."

"The two of you are close?" he said as he laid her arm back down after looking it over.

"Yeah, we're like brother and sister. Sort of. I mean, he's a lot older than me. And really bossy. But he's been there for me always. I know he'll always back me up. No matter what. Our mothers are best friends. They actually moved down to Florida together. It's too cold for them up here. They're having a great time. They even went on a cruise a while back. Ed's mom had him early in life, while mama took a while to conceive me. And now Ed thinks he's my big brother and he gets to boss me around."

"It sounds like he's a good big brother."

She yawned.

"I'm going to let you go to sleep. You have work tomorrow. But I want to give you my number if that's acceptable?"

"Course it's acceptable, silly." She glanced around for where she'd dropped her handbag. Ahh, there it was. She was shocked she'd managed to hang onto it last night. Leaning over, she grabbed her phone.

She entered his number into her contacts then sent him a text.

"You bet. I've got to help you have some more fun."

"I'm looking forward to it. Come lock the door behind me, please."

"I'll get it before I go to bed."

"You'll get it now." His voice was calm, but she found herself standing to do his bidding.

Wow. He was good.

"Night, Harry."

"Night, Kiesha. I had fun tonight. Thanks for inviting me."

He closed the door behind him, having to tug at it.

She leaned against the door, smiling like a loon. Why did she feel so light and floaty? She hadn't felt like this since . . . since Jonah was alive. That wiped her smile off her face.

"Kiesha?"

She let out a squeak. "What? Did you forget something?"

Shit, he'd just given her a heart attack. She placed her hand on her chest.

"No, you did. Lock the door."

"Oh God. Have you been standing there the entire time?" What if she'd been sighing and saying his name like some lovesick fool?

Which she absolutely was not.

"Yes. Now lock your door."

"Yes, boss!"

Whew. At least she didn't call him daddy again. That would have been embarrassing. After locking the door, she headed into her bedroom to grab her favorite onesie. Then she moved into the bathroom and came to a sudden stop.

Because sitting there for the whole world to see, well, just Harry but that was enough, was her monster vibrator.

Holy. Hell.

Well, it was official. She could never, ever see him again.

7

Kiesha was in a grump.
It didn't happen very often. All right, it happened more often than she liked to admit. But she tried not to get grouchy. She blamed it on the vodka. And the late night.

And the monster vibrator next to her bathroom sink.

Yep. That had really made her frown this morning.

She opened the door to her apartment after work on Friday, nearly falling over as she shoved her shoulder against it and it just opened. What the heck?

Had Dennis finally fixed the door? Shouldn't he tell her he was going to do that? He couldn't just come into her apartment any time he liked!

Then she frowned as she saw an envelope on the floor. Picking it up, she gulped, feeling ill as she slid out the piece of paper inside it.

That asshole!

Really? He was going to evict her because she wanted him to do his fucking job? Well, she was going to give him a piece of her mind!

Turning, she walked out and locked the door behind her. Then she stomped along the hallway.

Dennis was going down.

She was going to kick his ass.

Well, maybe she couldn't do that. But she was going to . . . to give him a stern talking-to.

This is what happened when someone thought they were powerful and they were just a weaselly little asshole. With a pencil dick.

She didn't exactly know if he had a pencil dick, but she thought it was likely. She only had two hours to shower and get ready before heading off to her next job and she really didn't want to deal with this dipshit.

But he didn't get to serve her with an eviction notice without at least telling her face-to-face what the hell was going on.

She reached his door which was on the upper floor. Yep, he had the entire upper floor to himself. That was the perk of your uncle owning the building, she guessed.

She knocked on his door.

"It's not office hours," he called out.

"You don't have office hours, dipshit! You're the building manager."

"Is there a leaky pipe?"

"No!"

"Is there a fire? Electrical fault? Is the water out? Heating?"

"No, you bastard."

"I'm sorry, I'm going to have to tell you to leave. It's not acceptable behavior to call me names."

That rotten little asshat. Pulling back her leg, she kicked his door. She'd taken her roller skates off at the bottom of the stairs and put on her shoes. She'd learned the hard way that skates and stairs did not mix.

See? She could learn.

"I'm not leaving until you talk to me, you slimy little worm. Get out here and stop hiding behind your door."

"If you continue to harass me, I'm going to be forced to call the cops."

"Do it! In fact, I'll call Ed right now, shall I?"

"What? No! Fine. You asked for this. Just remember that."

The locks turned and then he was standing there.

Just dressed in a pair of boxers and some slippers.

"Ew. Ew. Are you serious right now? Put some damn clothes on!"

He held a bowl of ice cream in one hand. She watched in disgust as he ate a spoonful then licked his lips, leaving them glistening. They were thin and weaselly. Just like the rest of him. Well, except for the poochy stomach that stood out over his boxers.

But she was trying not to look too closely at him.

Also, she wasn't sure that she would ever be able to eat ice cream again.

"You knock on my door outside of my office hours, hurling abuse and demanding special treatment, then you complain about how I dress in my own home."

"This isn't your home. You get to live here and in return you're supposed to take care of this damn building."

"And that's what I do."

He burped and she started choking as the putrid scent reached her. That was it. She had to bleach her eyes and her tongue. Was that possible? Maybe she could be hypnotized to forget that this ever happened.

"Right, that's why it took you three months to fix my door? That's really taking care of the building."

"Pfft. It wasn't exactly a major problem was it? Some people have real issues, Kiesha."

"And you don't bother to fix those issues, either! And what the hell is this?" She held up the eviction notice.

"Your apartment has been deemed unfit for habitation."

"What? What the hell are you talking about?"

"You've got pests that need to be exterminated."

"I . . . what are you talking about? I don't have any pests."

"Fleas."

"I do not have fleas in my apartment."

"I'm afraid you do. In a routine inspection while fixing the door to your apartment, I found fleas. The whole place needs to be flea bombed or whatever it is they do. I'll be sure to send the bill on to you."

"This isn't happening. You cannot do this. I'm going to have to tell Ed about this."

She hated having to use Ed in order to get her way, but Dennis was being even more of a dick than usual.

"I'm sure he'll be interested to hear how you've been harassing me," Dennis replied, licking the spoon with his reptilian-like tongue. Seriously. How long was that thing? It was unnatural.

"Ogling my half-naked body, treating me like a piece of meat, abusing me."

"You are such a liar."

"Yeah?" He leaned in. "So are you."

Okay. That one stung. Mostly because it was true.

"Have you ever heard of a freaking breath mint?" she snarled, waving her hand in front of her nose. "Your breath smells like garbage."

He drew back, scowling at her. "Everyone knows how pathetic you are, Kiesha. They tiptoe around you, letting you do whatever you want. Grow up. And get out of here. You have five days. Which is very generous considering how mite-infested your apartment is."

"You said it was fleas."

He shrugged. "Whatever. I don't care what it is as long as you aren't here anymore."

She clenched her hands into fists. "You're a jerk, Dennis. And you're not getting away with this."

"Ohh, I'm shaking in my boots. Actually, I'm not wearing any. And I'm not scared."

"You will be if I call Reuben and bring him into this," she threatened.

She was desperate.

She knew that she couldn't afford a one-bedroom apartment anywhere else.

Dennis paled. Ah-ha. She had him. But then he seemed to rally as he glared at her. "You and I both know you aren't going to do that. Besides, why would Reuben care about you? You're nothing to him but his sister's friend."

Damn it. He'd totally called her bluff.

"Besides, you already brought in one lawyer, what do you need with another?"

She frowned. "What the heck are you talking about?" Had he been smoking something?

"That lawyer you brought in to threaten me. He came around this morning, said if I didn't fix your door within the next twenty-four hours that he was going to sue me. Well, now you've got what you want. Your door is fixed."

"How is getting evicted what I want?" she demanded. "You can't evict me just because I asked you to do your job."

"I wouldn't do that. That wouldn't be legal. I'm evicting you because of the rodent issues."

"You said it was fleas!"

"Whatever. We've also had complaints about you playing your music too loud."

"I never do that."

"Take that up with your neighbors. And maybe next time don't get a lawyer involved."

"I didn't get a lawyer involved this time!" She waved a hand in front of her face. Damn, he smelled bad. "Did you eat week old leftovers again?"

"No! That was one time. And you won't let me forget it."

"Because you stank. I've never smelled anything so rank in my life."

His entire face started to grow purplish-red. "Get out of here!"

"Not until you take back this eviction notice!"

"Why don't you go stay with your lawyer friend, since he's so worried about your safety."

"What lawyer friend? You are delusional."

"I'm not. What was his name . . . it was a last name as a first name. Jenkins. Simpson."

"Simpson? What kind of person is called Simpson?"

"I dunno," he sneered. "A friend of yours. That's it! Harrison."

She stared at him for a moment. Shit.

Seems she did have a lawyer friend. She just hadn't imagined that he would do this. She groaned. What had he been thinking? Would he really do this without telling her?

Shit. Shit. Shit.

"Harry came to see you today and asked you to fix my door?"

"He didn't ask anything. He got all demanding. And you know I don't like being dictated to." He puffed out his chest, like he thought he was all that.

"He wasn't dictating to you, asshole. He was asking you to do your job!"

"Well, that's not the way he was acting." He sneered at her. "He was all up in my face with his fancy words and shit. Thought he was better than me, just like you always do. Well, neither of you are. I'm the one in charge around here." He patted his chest like some ape.

"You're an idiot. And I'm going to fight this eviction notice."

"Bring it on. You and that fancy lawyer can't fight against facts. And your apartment is riddled with bats."

"Bats!" She threw her hands up in the air. "Lord help me, if the thought of touching you didn't gross me out I swear to God, I'd strangle you."

"Careful, you don't want me to have to call the sheriff and tell him you're threatening me."

He spooned some more ice cream, slurping it up.

"You are so disgusting! And would you please put that away!" She pointed at his crotch with a grimace.

"What?" he asked.

"Your twinkie has been winking at me this whole time."

"So what?" he asked. "Like what you see?" He leered at her.

"Nope. Pretty sure I just threw up a little in my mouth. But I also know that if I told Ed you were flashing me, you'd find your ass in jail quicker than you could get dressed. How well do you think Mr. Twinkie would do in jail, Dennis?"

He snarled. "Fucking bitch. We both know you're not going to Ed. I have a good reason for evicting you. It's legal and Ed has no standing here. In fact, involving him could hurt him."

"What the hell does that mean?"

"Coming up for re-election, isn't he? I'm sure he would struggle to get re-elected if someone with a lot of money behind them went up against him. My uncle would be very happy to bankroll Ed's opposition if he started creating problems for him."

"You fucking creepy, tiny-dicked bastard!"

"Go away. You have five days. Five!"

He slammed the door in her face. Fuck. He was such an asshole.

An alarm went off on her watch, reminding her that she had to get ready for her next job.

Running down to her apartment, she quickly got changed, and grabbed her backpack with her uniform. Then she headed out.

She'd have to deal with Dennis the asshole later.

And Harry. Shoot. What was she going to say to him? What

could she say? He'd only been trying to help her. It wasn't his fault that Dennis was an asshole of epic proportions.

She reached the bus station and sat to catch her breath for a moment. She'd go to work. Go home and check her apartment for cameras.

And then she guessed she'd have to find somewhere else to live.

8

Was it silly that he was disappointed that she hadn't been in contact with him?

He'd waited all of yesterday for her to text him.

Perhaps you should have called her.

Damn it. That's exactly what he should have done.

Idiot. How did he get so out of touch with how to behave around a woman?

Yesterday morning, he'd paid a visit to Kiesha's building manager. He was an unpleasant man but he'd assured Harry he would fix her door.

It was Saturday evening and he was back in his tiny motel room, with nothing to do. He needed to get out.

Picking up his phone, he sent off a text to Kiesha.

HARRY: *Hello. How are you?*

. . .

Shit. Was that too formal? Maybe. He needed something else to say. Something more relaxed.

Harry: *How was your head after the other night?*

He groaned. This was ridiculous.

They were friends. He needed to remember that. For some stupid reason, he kept getting this rush every time he thought of her.

But she wasn't his. She was too young for him. And they were opposites. Where he was staid, calm, and well, boring, she was fun and impulsive.

Nope, they'd never work.

So, he needed to pull himself together. He was a grown man.

After learning that Marisol was a Little, he'd decided to do some research. The idea of being a Daddy Dom had stirred something inside him. It had felt right. Especially the nurturing, caring side. He'd even taken some classes at a BDSM club back in Houston. But he hadn't had time to take things any further.

Sighing, he glanced down at his phone. It shouldn't matter that she hadn't texted back.

What he needed was a hobby.

Or to go back to work.

Yeah, that wasn't happening for another week at least. But he could go back to the city. Maybe he'd feel less lost. Surely, he could find something to do there.

Or you could stay here and hang out with a Little who likes monsters and stuffed toys and roller skating . . .

And now you're back to thinking about her.

This was ridiculous. He was going round and round in circles.

Picking up his keys, he headed out the door. Perhaps he'd go to the Wishing Well for a beer. Or drive around aimlessly.

Maybe you should just drive past her place.

What? And just hope that he saw her?

Now he was a stalker?

Pulling up at the Wishing Well, he knew he wouldn't go inside. There was nothing sadder than the idea of drinking on his own.

He could go see Mari, but she needed time alone with Linc. And he didn't want to interrupt anything they had going on.

Call her.

No. He wasn't going to do that. If she wanted to see him, she'd answer his texts.

Call her.

Fuck it. One drive by. It wasn't going to hurt, right?

When he found himself walking up to her apartment half an hour later, he told himself it was only because he wanted to make sure her building manager had fixed her door.

That was something a friend would do, right?

Not a weird-ass stalker. Which is what he was pretty sure he was becoming.

He knocked on her door.

Nothing.

What if she was ill? What if she couldn't get to the phone? He checked his messages. Nothing.

Well, he couldn't just leave without trying to call her. He'd feel terrible if he left and she was ill or hurt.

Or maybe she's not home.

That was a possibility. Because not everyone sat at home on their own at ten on a Saturday night.

But he still called her. Because he was an idiot.

It went to voicemail.

"Hi, this is Kiesha. If I'm not answering, it could be that I don't like you. Or I'm busy. If you leave a message and I don't call you back then you'll know which one it is. Bye!"

He had to grin.

"Kiesha, it's Harry. I'd appreciate a call back when you can. Hopefully. If we're still friends and you like me. I'm going to hang up now before I sound even more pathetic."

He ended the call.

"Wow, that was really smooth."

Harry glanced over to find the building manager he'd talked to on Friday morning, standing there, sneering at him. He had skin-tight jeans on with a singlet and open shirt over it. Harry supposed that look could be good. On someone else.

"Excuse me?" Harry asked.

"You got a crush on her?" Dennis asked, looking him up and down with a grin.

"A crush? Do I look like I'm fourteen?" Harry asked coldly. "I just want to check that she's all right. Did you fix her door?"

"Course I did. If she'd let me know earlier, I'd have fixed it straight away."

"She did let you know."

Dennis shook his head. "In case you haven't worked it out, Kiesha is a bit . . ." He made circles with his finger in the air by the side of his head.

"Are you insinuating that Kiesha is crazy?"

She was. But in the best way possible.

"Yeah, that's exactly what I'm trying to *insinuate*," Dennis spat out. "Course, she might have told me while we were fucking like rabbits. I don't listen well when I'm having my dick sucked."

Was he trying to say that he and Kiesha . . . yep, now he was definitely feeling ill.

And this dick had to be lying.

"You're trying to say that you and Kiesha are in a relationship?"

"No, not a relationship. But that girl is fucking needy, if you know what I mean. And when she gets needy, she comes and finds me."

Harry had no idea of what happened next. But one moment, he was standing by Kiesha's door and the next he had Dennis pinned to the wall, his face close to the asshole who was staring at him with wide eyes.

"I know you're talking out your ass because there is no way that a wonderful, amazing girl like Kiesha would ever let you touch her, you disgusting little worm."

Anger surged inside him even as part of him realized he was acting slightly irrationally. Kiesha wasn't his. And if she had been with Dennis the dick, he had no right to be angry.

But still, he couldn't stand the thought of this guy touching her.

"Fuck you!" Dennis slammed his hands against Harry's chest.

He stepped back, telling himself it wasn't okay to hit someone just because they were a worm.

"You're just as crazy as she is!"

Huh. Maybe he was. He smiled. "Stay away from her. Oh, and I better not hear that you weren't doing your job properly or I will ruin you. Understand me?"

"Y-yes."

"Now go away."

"Fine." Dennis slid away. "But if you're looking for her you're out of luck. She spends every weekend out partying until the small hours of the morning." He sneered, looking Harry up and down. "Give it up, grandpa. Chasing her around is just sad. You're old enough to be her father."

It wasn't anything that Harry didn't know. But for some reason this asshole's words struck him.

Harry breathed out a sigh as the little dick left. He wasn't wrong. He was way too old for her. And he didn't know her that well. After checking his phone one last time, he decided to find his dignity and leave.

Pathetic wasn't a good look.

~

"Fuck!"

"Hard night, sugar?" One of the other waitresses glanced over at Kiesha with sympathy. Kiesha leaned against the wall. She was exhausted. It wasn't working two jobs, one of which went until the wee hours of the morning. It wasn't even traveling an hour on three different buses to get here.

She was exhausted due to life. She was going to be thirty soon. And nothing had ended up the way she'd thought it would. By this time, she thought she'd have an amazing job, a gorgeous husband, and maybe a couple of rugrats. Although that part, she wasn't entirely sure about.

Not that she didn't love kids. She just wasn't certain she wanted any of her own. Besides, wouldn't she have to grow up before she had kids?

And she was pretty sure she never wanted to grow up. It seemed so boring. Thoughts of Harry filled her mind. Now, there was a guy who had it together.

And there was nothing boring about him. In fact, he was damn sexy.

Too bad he wouldn't look twice at her.

She sighed.

"Love life issues?" Margo asked, leaning against the wall with her. The other woman tugged at the top of her T-shirt, trying to cover her generous cleavage. They all hated the uniform. People seemed to think that just because they wore shorts that barely covered their ass and a top that was close to being completely indecent that it was fair game to touch them.

Look, but don't touch.

She'd told Geri that she should get that printed on the back of their T-shirts or maybe on a huge sign at the bar.

But their boss was all for getting as much money from patrons as she could. And if that meant letting them touch her employees, well, she wasn't going to change a thing.

Geri cared about her bottom dollar. Nothing else. Certainly not her employees' rights.

If only she didn't pay so damn well, then Kiesha would have told her to shove her job so many times. But she had debts that had to be paid. And she couldn't get behind on them.

A shudder ran through her at the thought.

Nope. That wasn't an option.

"Nah, not really. Just sick of those assholes out there thinking that they get to treat me like a piece of meat."

"I get what you're saying," Margo replied with a sigh. "I've had four guys slap my ass in the last hour alone and one of them got his fingers way too close to my asshole for comfort."

"Ew."

"I wish Geri was a decent person. It's not right she lets them treat us like this."

"Yeah, but unfortunately for us, Geri knows that we're desperate enough not to say anything. Not when we need the money."

"I know," Margo agreed. "And this is the only job I can get where I can make as much working two nights as I would working a full week anywhere else. And it means I can be home with my daughter during the week."

"Yep, she's got us over a barrel. Bitch." Kiesha looked around to make sure that Geri wasn't hiding around a corner. She wouldn't put it past her.

"So, not man trouble? I could have sworn that was the look on your face."

"What look is that?"

"You know . . . half-constipated, half-pleasure."

Kiesha burst into laughter. Then she groaned as she realized she had to get back out there. "Okay, maybe there is a guy. He's just a friend, though."

"Is that all you want him to be?"

"I don't know."

Margo gave her a knowing look.

"He's very different from me. And older. And I think I wouldn't be right for him. I'm a lot."

Margo shook her head. "If he doesn't appreciate that you're a sweetheart then he doesn't deserve you."

"That's so nice. But I'm not a sweetheart, I'm a total badass."

Margo grinned. "Sure, if you say so."

"And I've already determined that I'm not going to see him again, anyway."

"Why? Was he a jerk?"

"No, he saw my vibrator."

"Um. What?"

"He walked me into my apartment. He's really protective and chivalrous. He opens doors and makes sure I have my seatbelt on."

"Oh my God! Really? I thought those sorts of guys were only in books." When Margo was on a break, she usually had her nose in some book. Kiesha spent her breaks drooling over the half-naked men on the front of those covers and trying to stuff as much sugar into her mouth as she could manage.

Priorities.

"Anyway, obviously I wasn't expecting that. I'd also had a couple of vodkas, which isn't like me."

Margo nodded.

"He went into the bathroom and there was my vibrator, sitting right by the sink."

"Oh my God! It's like something out of a rom-com. What did he say? Do?"

"Nothing. That's the worst part. I'm not even sure if he saw it. But how could he miss it? It was right there. Now I'm in that awkward spot of having no idea whether he knows or not."

"Damn, girl. You live a way more interesting life than I do."

"Not usually!" Kiesha sighed. "I'd better go back out there. Are the girls straight?" She cupped her breasts.

"Does it matter?" Margo asked dryly. "No one here is going to care. They're boobs and these assholes are Neanderthals."

"Yeah, you're right."

Kiesha spent the next few hours dodging wandering hands, delivering drinks, and glaring at assholes who leered back at her. Yeah, she could likely make a lot more money if she was nice.

But who wanted to be nice to assholes?

And speaking of assholes. She still had to find a new place to live.

She'd have to deal with it tomorrow. The one day she had off where she could sleep in, watch cartoons, play hide and seek with her monsters and now, apparently, pack up her stuff so she could relocate to God-knew-where.

The only thing she knew was that she was not moving in with Ed. That would require an exorcism or a lobotomy. He'd boss her around even more than he did now. And then she'd likely have to smother him in his sleep which would upset Georgie.

Kiesha didn't want to do that. Maybe she could move into Juliet's pool house. That would probably be the best option. But then she'd have to explain to Juliet about Dennis the dick.

And then if Juliet got upset, she might tell Reuben...

Well, it would serve Dennis right if Reuben went all crazy on his ass. But then he'd likely come to visit to make sure Juliet was all right.

And no one wanted that.

Shit.

Isa didn't have any room. And Cleo . . . well, Noah basically lived with her now. And she really didn't need to hear her and Noah going at it.

"Hey, let me go!"

Frowning, she turned to glance over at where some sweaty, greasy asshole had hold of Margo's wrist. His big meaty hand engulfed her tiny one as he drew her slowly over to him.

His friends all laughed and hooted at his antics. "Come here, sweetie, you know you want it. No need to pretend. I've seen the way you look at me. Your titties swinging in my face."

Fucking asshole.

Kiesha started shoving through the bodies around her, glancing over toward where the bouncer was supposed to be.

Only, he'd fucked off like usual. Probably into Geri's office to fuck her over her desk. Or maybe Geri put on a strap-on and took Reggie's ass. Yep, that was more likely.

Kiesha didn't give a shit what people did in the privacy of their own homes or offices. But when it impacted her or her friends' safety, she did.

"Let her go, asshole!"

"Look, it's another little bitch to play with," Grabby Hands said. "Come here, slut, I've got another leg you can sit on."

"Let me go!" Margo kicked the asshole in the shin and he roared, dragging her over his lap to smack her ass. Kiesha stood in shock for a moment as everyone around them cheered the meathead on.

Help her, Kiesha!

"Let her the fuck go!" she yelled. She had no idea what she was going to do. Her Taser was in her handbag and this dickhead was twice her size. But what she wasn't going to do was let him abuse Margo.

She went to grab for Margo, then realized she still had her

drink tray in her hands. It was wooden and heavy. She'd often bemoaned carrying it around all night. But right now, as she drew it back and smashed the asshole across the face with it, she was damn grateful.

He let out a screech of pain that sounded exactly like a pig's squeal. His nose started to spurt with blood and he reached up with both hands to stop the spray. Margo immediately jumped off his lap and Kiesha grabbed her, pulling her back behind her.

"You fucking bitch!" he screamed, turning to her. "You broke my nose."

"You were touching my friend!" Kiesha yelled back. "Without my permission."

"I'll fucking kill you." He moved toward her. Oh fuck. Realizing she was still carrying the tray, she raised it above her head. But he had caught onto her by now and he grabbed the tray with one hand and reached for her with the other.

Kiesha yelped as he grabbed her by the arm.

Fuck! If he applied much more pressure, he was going to break her wrist. She could feel the bones rubbing against each other. Gritting her teeth against the pain, she used it to try and clear her head. Georgie's self-defense lessons flitted through her mind.

"Nose!" she yelled, punching out at his face.

Make a proper fist. Don't break your thumb.

But fuck, his face was like concrete and her knuckles immediately screamed out in pain.

He roared.

Instead of hitting his throat next, she aimed for his stomach.

Then she brought her knee up.

"Nuts!"

Okay, she'd hoped that one would be more effective than the guts one, which hadn't done anything. But he didn't move. Then he let out a strange wheezing noise and dropped to his knees.

Fuck! Thank God. Turning, she grabbed Margo by the arm,

prepared to shove her way out of there. All they needed was for meathead's friends to decide they wanted some revenge. She could barely fight off one guy, she couldn't manage any more.

But as they turned a huge guy appeared in front of them, grabbing her and Margo by their upper arms and dragging them away.

Fucking awesome.

9

"Ow. Fucking hell, Reggie," she complained, twisting her arm out of his hold as they walked into the back of Chubby's Bar.

Yep, that was the name of the classy bar. Its name wasn't quite as bad as Suck 'n Blow, which was a bar owned by Markovich on the outskirts of Wishingbone, but it was close. The ironic thing was that Suck 'n Blow was a far nicer place. And she was betting the employees were treated a lot better.

The only reason she hadn't tried to get a job there was that she ran the risk of running into Ed. Or someone else she knew.

And she didn't want to explain to anyone why she needed a second job.

"Watch it, you're hurting us," she snapped at Reggie.

"Get in the office and wait for the boss."

Fuck.

Had Geri seen what happened? Another boss might've booted those guys out, would likely care about their employees' safety.

Geri was not that boss.

"Oh God, Kiesha," Margo said as they walked into Geri's office.

It was surprisingly clean and bright, considering the rest of the bar was run-down and dark. Then again, the darkness worked in Geri's favor. People could hide what the hell they were up to in a dark corner and they didn't see that the place hadn't been cleaned properly since nineteen-eighty-five.

She shuddered. There was a reason why she never ate her free meal and always brought a sandwich.

Okay, she never brought a sandwich. She brought a few suckers and a candy bar.

But she'd never touch the food they served here. How the sanitation department had never closed them down, she didn't know.

Actually, wait, she did know. Geri gave regular blow jobs to the guy that came around to inspect the place. Kiesha actually walked in on that once.

Her eyes were never the same. She really needed that eye bleach. Badly.

It still wasn't as bad as seeing Dennis's dick.

"Kiesha? Are you all right? What are you thinking?" Margo asked as she paced up and down the room, chewing on her fingernail.

"Oh, I was just thinking about Dennis's twinkie."

"What?" Margo gaped at her.

Get it together, girl.

"What? Sorry, I had some weird brain fart or something. Oh my God, are you okay? Did that asshole hurt you?"

Margo shook her head, but she was trembling. "I'm all right."

"No, you're not! Fucking bastard. What right did he have to grab you like that? I hope I broke his fucking dick."

"Kiesha, focus." Margo grabbed her wrist. Unfortunately, she managed to grab her right where that bastard did. She flinched and drew her arm away.

"Oh God! I'm sorry! Did I hurt you?"

"No, I'm fine. That meathead just grabbed me hard. I'm more

worried about you. Are you sure you're not hurt? I could take you to the emergency room."

"I don't need the emergency room. Kiesha, do you think we're going to lose our jobs?"

Margo was pale, her eyes wide as trembles rocked her body.

"No, of course we're not. Geri's a bitch, but she won't fire you because some guy threw you over his knee and started spanking you. I've always thought of spankings as sexy but that was just wrong on so many levels. Where's the consent, asshole? Consent is sexy. Force is the, uh, opposite . . ." she trailed off as she realized that Margo was staring at her like she had two heads.

She got that look quite often. She couldn't figure out why.

The door opened before she could ask Margo what was wrong and Geri stormed in. She glared at them both. "What the fuck was that? Who behaves that way?"

Geri was gorgeous. Long, blonde hair and a body that didn't quit. She was wearing a low-cut red dress. Her outfit was completely out of place in this bar, but somehow, she made it work.

"I know!" Kiesha said, nodding. "That asshole grabbed Margo and when she told him to let her go, he dragged her over his lap and spanked her. And like I was saying, spanking with consent is hot. Or like, if you've agreed to a relationship where spanking is given as punishment. That's all good. Spanking from some sweaty, meathead with a Godzilla complex isn't cool, am I right?"

Geri narrowed her gaze at Kiesha. "I wasn't talking about the paying customer's behavior! I was talking about the two of you!"

"What? Why?" Kiesha asked.

"What is my motto?" Geri asked in a low voice.

Uh-oh. Kiesha was starting to get an idea of where this was going and it wasn't good.

Not good at all.

"The customer always gets what they want," Margo whispered. She was so pale that even her lips had lost all of their color.

"But that doesn't mean that they get to manhandle us!" Kiesha protested. "Margo was terrified. I mean, we put up with a lot. I can't tell you how many times my ass has been slapped or pinched tonight. Sitting down is going to be a bitch tomorrow, but come on, Geri! That was way beyond that. And it's unacceptable."

"What's unacceptable is you bashing a customer over the head with your drink tray, breaking his nose then kicking him in the balls!" Geri stated. "You'll be lucky if he doesn't sue."

Kiesha scoffed. "Whatever. He was in the wrong."

"Both of you get your gear and get out. You're not getting any pay for tonight, either."

"What? You can't do that!" Kiesha argued as Margo let out a pained noise. "Come on, Geri! That's ridiculous even for you."

"Now you're calling me ridiculous?" Geri snarled. It wasn't a pretty look. "Get out!"

"You can't fire us. You need us," Kiesha insisted.

"I have loads of girls just waiting for a spot to work here."

"Then you at least need to pay us for the night."

"Do I? Who is going to make me? The two of you?" Geri let out an evil cackle that would have done Cruella De Ville proud.

"Please, Geri," Margo whispered. "I need this job."

"You should have thought of that before you behaved how you did."

"But it was Kiesha who hit him and broke his nose!" Margo protested.

"Wow. Way to throw me under the bus." Kiesha stared at Margo, trying to mask her hurt. She'd thought they were friends, but it seemed she was delusional.

"You were both there," Geri said dismissively. "Reggie will go with you to make sure you don't steal anything."

Margo turned and left with a small sob.

"This is going to come back to bite you in the ass, Geri," Kiesha warned. "Bad enough you treat me like this, but Margo is the victim in this."

"Ooh, I'm so scared I'm shaking in my Louboutins. Go. And don't bother ever coming back. I don't do second chances."

Fuming, knowing that she couldn't do anything right now, Kiesha stormed toward the door. Turning back, she glared at Geri and put two fingers up to her temples.

"What the hell are you doing? Are you having some sort of weird seizure or something?"

"No, I'm just hexing you. Have a nice life G-bag."

Geri's eyes widened and she started storming toward Kiesha.

Time to go.

Turning, she raced to the employee room where Margo was already clearing out her locker. Reggie stood leaning against the wall, his gaze on Margo's ass.

Creep.

"So, now you're doing your job, huh?" Kiesha asked, storming up to him. "Where were you twenty minutes ago when that bastard was manhandling Margo!"

Reggie gave her an uninterested look and just continued to chew his gum.

"Asshole!"

"Kiesha, just stop!" Margo cried.

Oh crap. What kind of friend was she being? Not a good one. Turning, she gave Margo a reassuring smile.

"Sorry, Margo. Don't worry, everything will be all right. Geri can't do this to us. We can fight it. Get your job back—"

"Stop, Kiesha!" Margo yelled, holding her hands out in front of her. "You never know when to fucking stop, do you?"

Kiesha jolted as though slapped, she stared at her friend in shock. "What do you mean?"

"You just keep going and going and going. Always making

things worse. Always getting mixed up in things that have nothing to do with you."

"Are you talking about what happened tonight?" Kiesha asked. She felt like someone was ripping through her stomach, grabbing her insides and tearing them out of her.

"I didn't ask for your fucking help, Kiesha!" Margo snapped, tears running down her cheeks. "And now, because of you, I've lost my job. How am I going to feed my child? Put a roof over her head?"

"I . . . I'm sorry. I thought—"

"No, you didn't! That's it, you didn't think. You're impulsive and just plain ridiculous and you've ruined my life."

Kiesha sucked in a breath and tried to tell herself that she didn't mean it. She was just scared.

"Just stop trying to do what you think is best, because all you ever do is make everything worse," Margo said quietly. Grabbing her stuff, she stormed out of the room while Kiesha just stood there, gaping after her.

What the fuck?

Reggie let out a huff of laughter. "Guessing that didn't go the way you thought it would. She really let you have it."

"Nobody asked you, Reggie," Kiesha replied, grabbing her own stuff and heading for the door. She tried to ignore Reggie following her. At the door, she paused and looked across the dark parking lot.

Shoot. She didn't want to walk to the bus stop on her own. Margo always gave her a ride to the depot.

Groaning, she sat on the step and tried to figure out what to do.

"Hey, you can't stay around here," Reggie said, prodding her with his foot.

"Stop it, asshole!" she snapped, turning to glare at him over her shoulder. "What the hell? You're going to kick me when I'm down? Wow, you're a great guy, Reggie. Really awesome."

He sighed. "You want me to call you a taxi or something?"

"I can't afford a taxi, just lost my job. I'll call for an Uber."

It would still cost more than she could afford. But what could she do? She couldn't call and ask someone to get up at two in the morning and drive an hour to collect her.

Bringing up the app, she requested a ride. Ten minutes. Freaking awesome.

"Just don't tell Geri I let you wait here."

"Your secret is safe with me."

She saw that she had a couple of messages. Opening them, a smile crossed her face as she saw that they'd come from Harry.

When she read them, she chuckled. He was so awkward at text messaging. Was he not used to texting someone?

She debated whether to answer him, but decided she didn't want to risk waking him. He needed his sleep. Telling herself she'd answer tomorrow, stood as a car drove up.

Taking Ubers made her nervous. She hated getting in a stranger's car. Especially at night.

It's just like a taxi. Stop being a wimp.

Still, as she climbed in the car, she kept her hand over the Taser in her handbag. Sometimes, she remembered to be careful with her safety.

10

Shit!

She was running late for work. Racing down the stairs in her apartment building, a sense of sadness filled her as she realized that she'd have to leave soon.

How was she going to find a place to live by Wednesday? This was a nightmare. After getting home in the early hours yesterday morning, she'd slept in late then walked Oscar before spending the entire day searching for somewhere to live that she could afford. She had two options. Rent a room from old Mrs. Yardley or move into her grandpa's place.

Mrs. Yardley was lovely, but she always smelled like old cheese and Kiesha knew there was no way she could live in a house that smelled like old cheese.

Which left Grandpa's place. Which no one had lived in since he'd died, because her mom refused to do anything with it.

On the plus side, it was free. On the negative side, it was a shack in the middle of nowhere with no power or running water.

Awesome.

Maybe she could live with the smell of cheese.

You could ask for help.

But asking for help made her feel icky. Like she was accepting charity. She didn't want to burden her friends like that.

And apparently, she wasn't as good a friend as she thought. Well, Margo didn't seem to think so. She'd stuck her nose in where it wasn't wanted and made things worse.

Ouch. That had really hurt her feelings.

It wasn't until later on in the afternoon that she'd remembered to text Harry back.

And she still hadn't heard from him. Which worried her. Did he think she'd been ignoring him? What if she'd hurt his feelings?

What if he'd decided she was rude and didn't want anything to do with her anymore? She took in a deep breath and let it out slowly as she put on her roller skates at the bottom of the stairs.

It would be all right.

She started skating frantically toward work. She moved onto the road since the sidewalk was busy. A truck drove past and she grabbed onto the back of it without thinking, crouching down so the driver didn't see her in the rear-view mirror.

Yep, it was dangerous as hell, but it was also fun. And the truck went far faster than she could skate.

She turned her head to the side, just in time to see a familiar truck drive past in the opposite direction.

Fuck!

Did that asshole drive around searching for her? She swore that he did. The truck slowed for a stop sign and she raced away down the street. By the time she got to work, she was hot and puffing. She was still tired from not getting much sleep over the weekend.

And she was in a mood.

Which is why she'd dressed in what she called her badass shit-kicker clothes. Bright pink tights. A black, pleated skirt with a T-shirt that said: *Monsters Do It Better.*

She'd split her hair into five sections and then braided each section. In each braid, she'd woven a different colored ribbon and used monster hair ties at the ends.

Reaching the police station, she climbed up the few steps on the front of her skates. Yep, sometimes she managed to end up on her ass. But today was not one of those days!

Winning!

Skating into the main area, she headed to her desk. A quick glimpse at the clock told her that she was only ten minutes late.

Perfect. That was totally within her grace period.

Sure, Ed didn't believe in such a thing as a grace period but he was way too rigid in the way he saw things.

"Kiesha!" he bellowed from his office.

Shit. And she hadn't gotten her skates off yet.

"I'm working!" she yelled back. She waved at Jace, one of the deputies, as he headed back to the break room. She quickly turned on her computer and pretended to be typing as Ed stormed out of his office.

Uh-oh.

Ticcy had a friend. That was not a good sign. Not good at all.

She smiled bright and decided she best just bluff her way out of whatever had put him in a mood.

"Morning, boss man. You want a coffee?"

His eyes widened. "A coffee? You're offering to make me a coffee?"

"Yeah, why wouldn't I? What's the matter? Don't you trust me? I'm not going to put arsenic or anything in it."

"No, but I don't trust that you won't slip in a laxative or salt," he muttered.

She stood, putting her hand over her chest with a gasp of outrage. "Boss man, I would never do that."

"You have before."

"I have? Huh, well, obviously you were being an ass and deserved it. Now, coffee?"

"You've told me a number of times that if I want coffee, I have to get off my ass and make it myself. So, what gives?"

Damn. She was acting too far out of character.

"You're right. I was going to put some laxative in your coffee," she lied.

"What? Why?"

"Because you were gonna yell at me."

"What? How do you know that?"

"Ticcy and Ticcy junior are exhibit a. The way you bellowed my name is exhibit b. You stomping out here is exhibit c."

"So, you just bring laxatives in your bag every day in case I'm about to yell at you?" he asked, looking smug.

"Sure do." She rummaged around in her bag and drew out the small bottle of laxatives. "See?"

His mouth dropped open. "I cannot believe this."

"Wanna try it? See if it's the real deal? Is that why you look so, um, grouchy? Are you constipated?"

"Stop. Enough. Get into my office. I need to lecture you in private."

"I'll bring this just in case, shall I?" She glided toward his office, laxatives in hand, ignoring the way he breathed down her neck as he followed behind her.

"Sit."

"I really think I should make you a coffee. Put you in a better mood."

"You're never making me coffee again."

She sighed. "Fine. But I think you're being awfully rude."

"Kiesha," he grumbled.

"Yes, boss man?" She sat demurely, hands folded in her lap and giving him a smile.

"I just got a disturbing phone call."

"Ooh, is it a good crime scene? Because I also brought my detective kit with me."

He blinked and his face seemed to soften. "Is that the one that I got you for your tenth birthday?"

"Uh-huh."

"You kept it all this time?" he asked softly.

"Of course, I did. You gave it to me."

"That's awfully sentimental of you, Kiki," he replied, using her childhood nickname.

"Shut up. I am not. You know I don't do mushy."

"I know."

"So, do I need my detective kit? I always thought I'd make a great detective. Is it a gruesome murder? Oh no, it's not someone I know, right? I don't think I could deal with that."

"There's no murder scene."

"Oh, whew. That's a relief."

"Yes, it is. Also, if there was one there's no way in hell you'd be going."

"Hey, you can't ground your best detective."

"You're not my best detective," he pointed out. "You're not even a detective."

Semantics.

"And besides, the call was about you."

"Well, I know I haven't been brutally murdered."

"No, but you nearly ended up as roadkill," Ed snapped. All that softness bled from his face, replaced by fury. "What the hell were you thinking? Holding onto the back of a truck? Do you not know how dangerous that was? Damn it, Kiesha. I ought to take you over my knee."

She held up a finger at him. "I'm an employee. That's harassment."

"I wasn't talking to you as your boss, I was talking to you as your big brother. But if you want me to come at this as your boss, then I can point out that shit is dangerous and you could be charged and fined."

"With what?"

"Reckless endangerment."

She scoffed. He was totally making that shit up. Then something occurred to her.

"Wait? A phone call? From who?" She scowled. "As if I didn't know who . . . Jonny Jacks. That weaselly, tattling asshole! I'm gonna get him."

"Kiesha!"

"Don't worry, I'll make it look like an accident or something. Huh, actually, I probably shouldn't say that to you. Being the sheriff and all."

"You shouldn't say it at all. Jonny is only looking out for you and you know it. If he was the one to call me that is," he finished awkwardly.

"We both know it was him. Only a sneaky snake would call someone's boss and rat on them." She narrowed her gaze. "Vengeance will be mine."

"Kiesha," Ed said on a sigh, leaning forward to rest his elbows on his desk. "Jonny didn't do anything wrong. He simply reported someone being reckless with their safety. What if you'd accidentally let go and gone under that truck? How do you think the person driving it would have felt if you'd gotten hurt or worse? Did you think of them?"

Fuck. He had a point.

She glanced away. She hadn't thought of anyone but herself. Again. Wow. How had she not realized how selfish she was? Is this how she'd always been? Did she just go through life, not giving a shit about anyone else and doing whatever she wanted?

Seemed that she did.

"I'm sorry."

Ed stopped mid-rant and gaped at her. "Um, what?"

"I said I'm sorry," she told him in a hoarse voice.

Don't cry. He'll never let you forget it.

And besides, that would be freaking embarrassing.

"You're sorry?"

"Yes."

"Oh, dear Lord, what did you do?" He gave her a horrified look.

"What do you mean? Jonny Jacks called and told you what I did."

"No, but what are you apologizing for? You never apologize. Or rarely anyway. Which means you did something. What is it? Is there a laxative in something else around here?"

"No, Ed, you doofus. I'm sorry for what I did this morning. For grabbing hold of that truck. You're right, it was dangerous and foolish. So yeah, I'm sorry. I won't do it again. Is that everything?"

"I . . . I . . . no. I just . . . that's it? You're not going to argue with me?"

"Nope."

"But you always argue with me." Ed scratched at his chin. "I'm not sure what to do now. I had a whole lecture prepared. It was a full twenty minutes' worth. Then I was going to lecture you again before you left for the day. Now . . . now, I'm lost."

She snorted. "I'm sure Georgie will do something that you can lecture her about."

"Nah, when Georgie does something wrong she gets a spanking."

"Yeah, well, we're not doing that. I need coffee. Sure, you don't want one?" she asked, shaking the laxative bottle to try and make him feel better. She needed to give the guy something to complain and worry about clearly, or he just became all lost and pathetic.

It was sad, really, how much he relied on her to keep him sane.

"No coffee!" he barked. "And that laxative needs to stay at home, understand?"

There, his color was much better now that he had something to scold her about.

"Aye-aye, boss man!" she saluted him then rolled her way out of his office.

"And put your shoes on."

"So bossy," she muttered, but she sat and put her shoes on. Then she got on with her job. She actually loved her job. But it could be stressful and exhausting. By lunchtime, she'd gone through four suckers and had a low-level headache.

She should go get something to eat, she hadn't had time to pack anything this morning. But she didn't want to spend the money when she was going to need it to relocate.

Leaning back, she closed her eyes.

11

What was he doing?

Harry stood on the footpath, staring up at the police station.

But he couldn't leave without seeing her again. Just for a few minutes. A quick goodbye.

Friends did that, right?

Urgh, why was he finding this so hard? He should have replied to her messages yesterday. But he'd been unsure what to say.

Where have you been?

Why were you out half the night?

Why would your building manager claim that the two of you were fucking?

Yeah, none of those things were actually any of his business. And he'd worked something out last night as he'd found himself grinding his teeth with a mix of possessiveness and irritation.

And he'd finally realized he was jealous.

Jealous that she was out having fun without him. That she might have had a relationship with that dipshit building manager, although he still thought the asshole was making shit up.

And after realizing that, he'd felt like a complete asshole.

What right did he have to be jealous? Absolutely none.

So now he was here, hoping she'd let him take her out for lunch to make up for his behavior. Even though she didn't know he'd been having these thoughts.

When he walked into the police station, he frowned as he saw her. She was slumped in her chair, her eyes closed and her pink-painted lips were slightly open.

There were bags under her eyes that he hated. She looked tired and delicate. Why hadn't he noticed how exhausted she was?

Probably because her personality was so huge when she was awake.

But right now, all he saw was someone who needed some coddling and to be bundled into bed for a long nap.

Easy, man.

You're not her Daddy. Hell, you're not even a boyfriend.

Friend. That's all.

"Kiesha?" he called out quietly.

She was wearing a black T-shirt with the words, *Monsters Do It Better,* written on the front in pink cursive.

He shook his head. He was surprised that Ed let her wear that. Her hair was tied into five braids all over her head in a crazy arrangement. He peered closer at the ends. Were those monsters on her hair ties?

Damn, she was adorable.

Rein it in.

"Kiesha?"

Should he let her sleep? But she couldn't sleep here. Maybe he could convince her to let him take her home and put her to bed.

"Kiesha?" he said again. "Kiesha?" He reached out to touch her shoulder. Did she always sleep so deeply?

"What? I was just resting my eyes!" she yelled out, sitting up.

She slid right off the end of the chair and fell onto her ass with a thud. He winced. Ouch. That had to hurt.

"Kiesha? Are you all right?" He rushed around the desk to check on her.

She groaned. "Ouchie, my butt-butt hurts."

Okay, that was cute. He forced himself not to smile. He didn't want her to think he was laughing at her.

Bending, he held out his hands. "Here, let me help you."

She slid her hands into his and he had to bite back a groan at the feel of her warm, smooth hands.

Really? Should you get turned on by holding a girl's hand? What are you? A horny teenager?

Sometimes he felt that way around her.

He easily pulled her up.

"Whoa, careful, Harry. You don't want to put your back out."

"I'm not so old and decrepit that I can't lift you."

He expected her to make some smart-ass comment back, instead she winced, looking upset.

What the hell?

"Little Monster, what's wrong?" he asked gently.

"I . . . what happened?" she asked, clearly not wanting to answer him.

"I was coming in to ask if you'd like to have lunch at the diner with me. I saw you were sleeping and tried to gently wake you up." He pulled a face. "Seems I failed. I'm sorry that I gave you a fright. How's your bottom?"

"Sore." She rubbed at it without a hint of self-consciousness. Made him think about what she'd do after a spanking and . . . nope, not doing that.

"Do you need me to take a look?"

He waited for her to say something cheeky back. He'd given her the perfect opening. But she simply stared at him blankly.

What was going on with her?

"Ah, no, pretty sure it's not broken."

"Okay, sweetheart," he said in a quiet voice. "That's good."

Why did she seem so fragile? Where was his bigger than life girl? With her thirst for adventure and fun?

"You look exhausted, Little Monster. Why don't I take you home and you can go to bed?"

There were no quips about him trying to get her into bed. No teasing grins as she gave him hell. "No, I've still got a few hours left of work."

"I'm sure Ed won't mind."

She shook her head again.

"Can you really do your job properly if you're exhausted?"

Again, she looked upset.

What. The. Heck.

He had no idea what was going on with her, but he felt a pressing need to find out.

"You don't think I can do my job properly?"

"No, sweetheart." He held his hands out. "That's not what I meant. I just . . . hell, I should stop talking. I keep getting myself into trouble. You know, I'm usually considered quite good at conversation."

Her lips twitched. An almost smile. He was counting that as a win.

"You just seemed tired, that's all. I wanted to make sure that you're taking care of yourself."

She seemed to rally at that statement, giving him a stern look. "I wasn't sleeping," she claimed. "Just resting my eyes."

"Do you always drool when you're resting your eyes?"

She gave a huge gasp. "I was not drooling, Harrison middle-name-unknown Taylor. Ladies do not drool."

"Hmm, are there any of those around?" he teased, glancing around then peering beneath her desk. "Under here? Nope."

"Stop it!" she said with a giggle that eased his tension.

Finally, she was acting more like herself.

"I'm the lady."

"Nooo." He shook his head. "You can't be."

"I am."

Aww, she was adorable as she pouted. If she stomped her foot then he swore he was going to throw her over his shoulder and carry her away to his cave where he'd keep her forever.

Shit. You need some pills or something, man.

"Are you sure?"

"Yep. I have all the right parts. You want to check?"

He choked on his laughter. "Um, urgh, uh, what?"

She laughed, throwing her head back and grasping hold of his arm to keep herself steady.

Damn, she was beautiful when she laughed. She was gorgeous all the time, of course. But when she laughed it was like she drew everyone to her. There was something so freeing about the sound. As though she gave her everything into that laugh.

"Relax, Mr. Uptight Lawyer, I wasn't about to strip off and let you see me naked. At least not before you get me this lunch you were talking of."

He ran his hand over his face. How did she always seem to be three steps ahead of him?

"So, you have time for lunch?"

"Sure, just let me tell Ed I'm going now so he can cover the desk. It's quiet in here today."

Instead of walking into the office, she threw her head back. "Yo, Ed!"

"Yeah?" he bellowed back while Harry stared at her.

"I'm going to lunch at the diner with Harry!"

"Got it! Bring me back the special! And leave the laxatives here."

"One special with extra laxative, you got it!" She gave Harry a cheeky grin, winking at him.

She was such trouble.

"Kiesha," Ed rumbled.

"Let's go," she said to Harry, grabbing his hand and racing toward the door.

He didn't get what was going on exactly, but he tugged on her hand, slowing her down. "Walk, sweetheart."

"But he might get me."

"I won't let him get you," Harry reassured her.

"Are you going to protect me from the boss man, Harry?"

"I will. I'll protect you from everything, if you need me to."

Urgh.

What was with the deep declaration, idiot?

"Because that's what friends do, right?" he added weakly.

"Right," she said as they walked out the main door. "That's what friends do. Only, I don't think I'm a very good friend, Harry."

"What makes you say that?" he asked.

"Maybe I stick my nose in where it's not wanted and I make too many jokes and don't take life seriously."

He turned her to him, his hands on her shoulders. "I don't know what's happened, but you listen to me, sweetheart. You are amazing exactly as you are. I've met your friends and they love and adore you. They wouldn't feel that way if you weren't wonderful. Understand?"

She gave him a small smile. "Thanks, Harry."

"Now, you have a little . . ." Without thinking, he licked his thumb then wiped it over the corner of her mouth.

"What was it?"

"Some dried drool."

She narrowed her gaze at him. "I don't drool. You just wanted to touch my chin, admit it."

"You caught me. I have a chin fetish. It's a sickness."

"I knew it." She grinned then transferred her hand to the crook of his elbow. "Let's go eat. I'm starving."

As if to back up her claim, her stomach started grumbling. Loudly.

"Dear Lord, is there a monster in your tummy?"

She giggled. "Uh-huh."

"Did you eat breakfast?"

"Umm. I think so? I was in a rush this morning." They reached the diner and he opened the door for her. Walking in, she took a seat at a booth while he held the door open for the older women behind them.

One of them gave him an appreciative look. "Thanks, hot stuff."

"Uh, you're welcome." He walked over as a waitress approached Kiesha.

"You can't sit at a booth, Kiesha. You have to sit at the counter."

"I'm going to sit here, thanks so much, Leslie."

"And I said you can't. If you're on your own, you have to sit at the counter. Don't make me get the manager."

Kiesha just snorted. "Go ahead."

"Actually, she's not on her own," Harry said from behind the bitchy waitress. "And we'd like a new waitress. If your manager has a problem with that, they are welcome to speak to me. I'd gladly have a chat with them about your customer service skills."

The woman, who appeared in her early-thirties, turned to him. Her mouth dropped open then closed. He just waited for a moment for her to gather her thoughts.

"Fine." She stomped away.

"Well, she's charming," Harry commented as he sat across the booth from Keisha. He really wanted to sit next to her. As much to protect her from the outside world as to feel her up against his body.

Okay, maybe the main reason was to feel her pressed against him.

Friends.

Just friends.
Lord, you are in trouble.

"Urgh, I went to school with her. She's always disliked me. I don't know why exactly. But yeah, she takes great delight in lording anything over me that she can. And then you came in like a white knight, saving me." She smiled at him.

"As long as I don't have to ride a steed," he stated with a grimace. "Me and horse riding do not mix."

"Is that because you've got no rhythm?" she said with mock-sympathy.

"What? No! What has rhythm got to do with horse riding?"

"Well, you've got to be able to move in time, right? You know . . . wiggle your hips up and down. You can't do that. Your hips are totally out of time with your feet. It's really a wonder you manage to walk without falling over."

Before he could answer, another waitress came to their booth. She was younger and Kiesha started asking her all sorts of questions about her children. Kiesha started giggling as the woman told her a story about her twin boys and Harry watched as everyone turned to smile at her.

Well, most people. That other waitress scowled.

Not a fan of his girl then.

She's your friend, not your girl.

Damn, he needed to get that tattooed on his hand.

"Harry? Harry!"

"What?" He turned to look at them blankly.

"I think he's losing his hearing," Kiesha mock-whispered to the waitress. "Happens when you're two hundred and thirty-three."

"Excuse me," he said coldly. "I'm only two hundred and thirty-two."

"My apologies," Kiesha said solemnly.

The waitress giggled. "What would you like, sir?"

"You've ordered?" he asked Kiesha.

"Yep. My usual. Burger and fries. Extra pickles."

Right. He ordered the healthiest thing he could find on the menu. A chicken salad.

"It will be here soon," the waitress promised.

"Do me a favor and make sure Leslie doesn't spit in it," Kiesha said.

"If she does, I'll make sure she regrets it," Harry said in a dark voice.

He was suddenly aware of both women gaping at him. The waitress with trepidation and Kiesha with glee.

"Whoa. Got a dark side, doesn't he?" the waitress said.

"Yep. I love it." Kiesha smiled at him as he tried to rein his dark side in. Seemed he didn't like any sort of threat toward his Little Monster.

Yep, definitely in trouble here.

12

Kiesha ate her lunch with gusto. The burger was cooked to perfection and the fries were greasy and hot. She glanced over at her companion and his bowl of leaves. Yuck.

"Is your burger all right?" he asked her.

"Uhummm," she replied.

He grinned. "I'm guessing that's a yes. Here, you've got a bit of ketchup on your chin." He grabbed a napkin and cleaned her up.

She swallowed her mouthful, trying to tell her body that she wasn't turned on.

It had to be mortification making her entire body zing. That was definitely it.

"Careful, your chin obsession is getting more obvious," she warned, trying to sound carefree when her body wanted to get up and do a victory dance.

"Yes, I shouldn't let it out in public. People will think I'm debased."

"Well, you can't stop what people think, but yeah, probably a good idea. You want a fry?"

"I shouldn't."

"Why not? Harry, I know I tease you about being old and I'll stop if you want . . ." She grew pensive, thinking about Margo's words. Was she a terrible friend? Was she annoying?

Did she make everything worse?

"Kiesha? Sweetheart, what's wrong?" Harry asked, staring at her in concern.

"Oh sorry. I'm just tired. I zoned out. What was I talking about?"

"Did you stay out too late Saturday night?" There was a strange note in his voice that she couldn't figure out.

Wait . . .

How did he know she was out on Saturday? Was he watching her? Stalking her?

Okay, this was taking an interesting twist.

Unless he'd just guessed that because she hadn't answered his texts. That was more likely. Still, she could have been doing anything. Volunteering, visiting friends, toilet papering Jonny Jacks' house.

Damn, she wished she had time for that. And the money for the toilet paper.

"What was it you were saying to me before?" he prompted

What?

What had she been saying?

"Oh yeah, I was saying that even though I tease you about being old, you're actually freaking gorgeous. You're manly. Distinguished. Yeah, that's a good word for you, distinguished. Wait, are you blushing?"

"I don't know what you're talking about."

"You so are." And it was damn cute. She didn't think he was the type to blush. Then again, he wasn't arrogant, puffed up, and full of himself. He was humble and kind. And just when you thought you had him pegged, bang! He'd hit you with his more dominant side.

Was it any wonder why she found him kind of irresistible?

They were opposites, and she never thought that would be something she'd want. Someone calm and serious.

And yet...

"I was saying that you should have some fries. Because your body is smoking hot and a few fries aren't going to change that. You're not on one of those diets, are you?"

"Ah, not exactly. But I've had it pointed out that I need to take care of my health. Fries are a treat."

"Nah, Godiva chocolates are a treat. Burgers and fries? They're a staple."

"Little girl, you need watching over." He froze. "I apologize. That was inappropriate. I hope I didn't make you uncomfortable."

Wow. He was wound up tight. Did he think she was gonna throw a fit? He hadn't spent enough time around her and Ed if he thought him calling her little girl and pulling her up on her eating habits was going to upset her. "Takes a lot to make me uncomfortable."

"Yes, well, friends don't really talk that way to each other."

"Are you a Daddy, Harry?" she asked bluntly.

She watched with amusement as his eyes bulged. Then his mouth opened and closed.

"Careful, you'll get flies in there." She dipped a fry in ketchup then mayonnaise, because everyone knew that was the best combination and held it out to him. "Here."

He stared down at her offer. "Um, what?"

"Try it. It's delish. Promise. I didn't poison it."

"I didn't think you would have." He leaned in and took a bite. He hummed. "That is surprisingly delicious."

"I know, right. But do you know what's even better?"

"What?"

"Pickles in your mayonnaise. All chopped up then you dip stuff in it."

"What sort of stuff?"

"Dude, whatever you like." Then she realized how suggestive that sounded. Harry licked his lips.

Damn, was everything he did sexy?

"So, are you? It's okay if you don't want to tell me," she hastily added. It wasn't like she didn't have stuff that she didn't tell people. "Sorry, that was really rude of me to ask that."

"No, that's all right. I understand why you asked. Truth is, I didn't know much about Littles and Tops until Mari told me she was a Little. Then I did some research and the idea of being a Daddy just resonated with me. I took some classes at a local BDSM club, but I never had the time to do anything more. I don't know that I would make a great Daddy."

She tilted her head to the side. "I think you would."

"I've worked sixty to seventy hours a week for pretty much all my life. Perhaps if I'd paid more attention to Rosalind, things wouldn't have derailed the way they did."

"Okay, so I don't know what happened and I guess there are always two sides to every story, but that Rosalind was bad news. And you can't blame yourself for her actions or the way she was. That wasn't on you. It was all on her. Understand?"

"I suppose you're right."

"Pfft. I'm always right. Maybe we should get you a T-shirt saying that Kiesha is always right."

"Hmm, I'll get right on that," he told her.

"Seriously, though. You can't blame yourself for what happened. Sure, you might have worked too much. But it sounds like she was a psycho bitch."

"Yes, but I left Marisol with that, uh, psycho woman."

Her lips twitched as he avoided using the word bitch.

"I often think I should have put up with her. Ignored the cheating and the lies for Mari's sake."

"My dad left my mom when I was small," she blurted out. "My mom never said anything bad about him. He'd send me presents for birthdays and Christmas, only it turns out he wasn't the one sending them."

"What?"

"My mom did it. She created this big lie about him being a good guy and he wasn't. He was selfish. And he didn't bother to even try to get in contact with me once he left us."

"Kiesha, I'm so sorry. Why would your mom do that?"

"When I asked her, she told me it was because she'd never had the greatest relationship with my grandpa. My grandpa wasn't an easy man to get along with. She wanted me to see my dad as good. But in the end her deception just hurt me more."

"I'm so sorry."

"Yeah, I love my mom but it took me a long time to forgive her for the subterfuge. Hey, look at me using big words. I'm going to start to sound like you."

"I'm sorry that happened, it sounds like she was trying to do what was best for you."

Reaching across, she grabbed his hand, squeezing it. "You're a good man, Harry. You deserve to be happy."

"Thank you," he said quietly. "You're a very good listener."

"Did you think I wouldn't be? Is it because I talk so much? I can do both, you know. Sometimes even at the same time."

"That is very impressive."

"Yes, well, I am impressive." She grinned at him.

"Yes, you are." There was something soft on his face that she couldn't quite figure out. "I spoke to your building manager about your door."

"Thank you, but you really didn't have to do that, you know."

"I did," he replied firmly. "It was a safety hazard. It's unacceptable that you had to shove your door open every time you wanted to get into your apartment or leave."

"It was good if I forgot to lock the door, though. I knew no one would likely think to shove their way through."

"How often do you forget to lock the door?" he asked.

"Ahh." The look on his face told her that the answer better be never.

Damn, she hated to disappoint him.

"Well, see, sometimes I'm in a rush and I just forget to lock it behind me. No big deal."

Oops, there was that stern look that she kind of freaking loved. "Kiesha, that is a big deal. And you will not do that again."

"I won't?"

"No. No matter how late you're running, you won't forget to lock your door. Do you understand me?"

She found herself nodding emphatically. She didn't think anyone would deny Harry when he used that voice. She certainly didn't want to, and she was quite fond of defying people.

Well, Ed. She was quite fond of defying Ed. But he needed it to keep his ego in check.

"I'm going to need you to reply verbally."

A shiver ran through her at his words. Damn, Harry was good. "I won't forget to lock my door."

"Good girl."

Yikes. That sent a flush of heat through her. Harry didn't seem nervous or out of his element at the moment.

Nope he was very much in his element.

Just as well he didn't know what she'd done today, though. If he thought leaving her door unlocked was dangerous, he'd likely have a heart attack if he found out that she'd been hanging onto the tailgate of a truck on the way to work this morning.

Yep, best he didn't find out about that.

"Your building manager is . . ." he trailed off, obviously trying to search for the word he needed.

"A dick? Just plain wrong? A slimy worm? Something like that?"

"Incompetent. Has he done anything inappropriate?"

"What? No. Well, he answered his door in just his boxers. That was pretty gross. But yeah, he's incompetent all right."

"In just his boxers? That's disgusting."

"I know. I puked in my mouth a little."

"I went to your apartment to see you Saturday evening, and ran into him. He told me that you were out. And he implied that you and he . . . uh . . . had a relationship," he told her.

"No, we don't. Ew. You mean sex?" she cried.

Again, everyone stopped talking and stared at them.

"I can't believe that weasel. As if I'd touch his cheese-encrusted dick with a ten-foot pole."

"And now I've officially lost my appetite," he drawled.

"Right. Uh, sorry. But that's so disgusting. You didn't believe him, did you?"

"No, I didn't. But it's unacceptable the way he was talking about you and I might have, uh, threatened him a little bit."

"You did?" she asked.

"I didn't like the way he was making up lies about you. If he does anything inappropriate, I want you to tell me. I'll take care of him for you."

"Aww, thanks, Harry." Should she tell him about the eviction notice? It didn't seem fair to ask him to fight her battles. That wasn't what a good friend did, right? It wouldn't be right to burden him with her issues. But he had offered to help.

Before she could decide whether to tell him, his phone rang. With a frown, he glanced down at it. "I apologize, Kiesha. This is work. Just give me one moment."

"Go for it."

Kiesha watched him through the front window of the diner. Damn, he was a fine-looking man.

The man would absolutely kill in a pair of tight jeans.

"Ew, it's disgusting the way you're panting after him. He's old enough to be your father. Then again, you've always had daddy issues, haven't you, Kiesha?"

Kiesha sighed. "Go away, Leslie. I've got little interest in dealing with rodents today."

"What?"

"Rodents. I'm calling you a rodent. You do know what a rodent is, right? Shoo. Scram. Get." She flicked her hands at the other woman.

"You're such a bitch, Kiesha," Leslie snarled at her. "You're not the perfect princess everyone seems to think you are. So superior, looking down on everyone but you're no better than anyone else."

"I don't think I'm better than anyone else," Kiesha told her. Honestly, where did this woman get her delusions from? "Just you."

Leslie's face went all blotchy. It really wasn't a good look. "At least my parents didn't abandon me. Your father couldn't stand being around you, seems now your mother feels the same way. How does it feel to run everyone out of your life, huh?"

It wasn't true. She was just being a bitch, like usual.

But Kiesha found herself without a reply and Leslie smirked at her, knowing she'd made a hit.

Bitch.

Turning, she walked off and Kiesha grabbed her handbag to search for some cash. She couldn't afford to pay for lunch, but she also didn't want to stay here any longer.

Did she have daddy issues?

But she wasn't looking at Harry and seeing her father? No, she looked at Harry and saw someone that she wanted to jump. That she wanted to laugh with. Go on adventures with. Have him scold her for the hundred and one foolish things she did every day.

She looked at Harry and saw forever.

Which was the absolute stupidest thing she could do. He didn't even live here for goodness sake. He'd go back to his fancy job in Houston and she'd . . . do what?

Soon she wouldn't even have a place to live. Where was she going to go?

There was only one option. One that wasn't appealing at all. But at least it would be free.

Unless you ask for help.

Harry stepped back into the diner and she tried to give him a smile that was friendly but not 'I want to fuck you' creepy.

He stilled by the table and frowned down at her. "What's wrong? Is your tummy sore? Do you have indigestion from your lunch?"

"What? No! Why would you think that?"

Sheesh. That wasn't exactly a question you asked someone you were attracted to, right?

"You looked a bit off."

"I was trying to smile."

"That wasn't your smile. Your smile is gorgeous. That looked like you were in pain. You didn't hurt yourself again, did you?"

She sighed. This was ridiculous. "No, I didn't hurt myself."

"You need to be more careful with your safety. You used your safety gear this morning?"

"Yes."

"Good girl." He reached into his pocket to grab his wallet, pulling out some cash. Then he picked up the money she'd put down and gave it back to her. "No."

She stared down at the money, then up at him. "No?"

"No. When we're out together, you don't pay. Now, put that back in your purse."

She huffed out a breath, shaking her head. "You shouldn't be paying for me."

"I asked you out, I pay."

Hmm. Well, that did seem like a fair rule.

"All right." She took the money and put it away. He gave her a satisfied look. Before he held his hand out to her. She slipped her hand into his and he helped her out of the booth.

"How are your bruises?"

"Uh, which ones?"

"The ones on your arm and knees." He glanced down at her legs as though he could see through her pants.

"Oh, they're fine. I heal quick. I once had a doctor tell me that I heal at an almost superhuman speed." She rubbed her nose as she said that. And Harry nodded without comment.

You're such a dork.

Why do you keep saying these things?

She wasn't sure that it was better that she could give him a signal to tell him she was making stuff up.

"I'm sorry to cut lunch early," he told her.

She caught Leslie scowling at them as they walked past and made certain to flip her the bird behind her back as they left the diner.

"That's okay. I should probably get back to work. Ed can't do anything without me. It's pretty pathetic, really. Grown man like that being unable to function without me at the helm."

"Yes, I can see that Ed is highly reliant on you."

Huh, she couldn't tell if he was being sarcastic or not.

"Didn't hear any good gossip while I was there, though. That's disappointing. You ever play poker?" she blurted out.

"Uh. I've been known to dabble."

Dabble? Who even used that word?

"Once a month a few of us like to meet up to play. It's coming up soon if you want to come."

"Thank you," he told her as they reached the police station steps. "Unfortunately, I won't be here. I've got to go home."

Wait. What?

"Now?"

"Yes." He frowned. "That was work calling. I need to get back rather urgently."

"Is everything all right?"

"Yes, just a case that needs me."

"Oh well, then. I guess this is goodbye. But, I mean, you'll be back soon. To see Mari," she added hastily.

"Yes, to see Mari. And you. We're friends, after all, right?"

"Course we are." She smiled at him. No way could she tell him about Dennis now. "We're friends."

"You have my number if you need anything."

She wasn't sure what she'd have to call him about, but she nodded anyway.

"And you'll call me if you need anything," she told him.

"I will."

This was the most awkward conversation she'd had in her life.

She had to leave. Before she did something stupid like blurting out that she didn't want him to go.

"Well, bye, Harry." She held out a hand.

He stared down at her hand for a moment until she started to feel antsy. Didn't he want to shake her hand? Reaching out, he grasped hold of it.

"Goodbye, Kiesha. Remember, call me if you need me." His gaze was intense on her and she felt a familiar itchiness under her skin. That feeling that told her she had to leave now or she was going to do something stupid.

Like cry.

Or beg.

Or throw a tantrum.

Yeah, that wouldn't be cool.

"Bye." Slipping her hand from his, she rushed up the steps and into the police station.

Back to her normal.

Without Harry.

Which is how her life was going to be. Because he didn't belong here. And she didn't belong with him.

Best she remembered that.

13

Harry had made a mistake.

He'd come back to work, thinking he'd be happier.

Since returning, he'd fallen into old habits. Working all hours. Eating whatever was on hand. Ignoring everything else in his life.

And for what?

For a client who was self-absorbed and egotistical? Would they care if he keeled over one day from stress? Nope, they'd step over his body to find a new lawyer.

When the hell had he started thinking that work had to be his life? Maybe because he didn't think there were other options.

Now, he realized there were. There was Marisol, who was planning her wedding without his input. And likely skimping in areas that she shouldn't in order to save him money.

There was Wishingbone, a town filled with crazy, strange residents. People who he would have never seen himself as liking, let alone missing. And now...

Now, he wanted nothing more than to be back there.

But mostly, there was Kiesha. What was she dressed in today?

Was she still wearing the safety gear he'd given her? Was she living off sugar?

Most of his thoughts centered around her. She was hard to forget. Not that he wanted to.

He wanted to be with her. Because when he was, he felt alive.

Why was he even here?

Fuck it.

"Harry, good, you're still here."

He glanced up, barely managing not to grimace as Barbara stepped into his office. When had her voice started to grate on his nerves?

"What am I saying?" she said with a titter. "You're always here." She walked in, carrying a bag. "I ordered us some dinner."

She sat across from him, drawing out two containers filled with beef noodle salad.

"I'm so glad you're back. We couldn't function without you."

"I know that's not true," he said dryly, picking at the salad which he had no appetite for. He wondered if Kiesha had touched anything green all week.

If she was his . . .

But they were just friends. She'd sent him plenty of text messages, filled with bad jokes. Apparently, they'd whipped ass at quiz night, even without him there to answer the history questions.

"What's funny?" Barbara asked.

"Oh, sorry. I was thinking of something else."

Barbara gave him a miffed look. "I'm sorry I'm not interesting enough to keep your attention."

"That's not the case, Barbara," he told her gently. "I apologize for my inattention."

She seemed satisfied. "I'm glad you're back, Harrison. We need you around here."

"Actually, I don't think you do."

"What?"

He leaned back in his chair and looked at her, then around the office. "I'm not needed here and I'm not sure why I was called back from leave to return."

"Because you're needed here. The client—"

"We both know the client didn't care who took on this case as long as it was a partner. So why did you call me?"

"I thought you were needed," she said stiffly. "I apologize for interrupting your holiday."

"Apology accepted," he replied. "But I do intend to take the next flight back to Montana as soon as I've finished handing this all off to Andrew."

"What? You can't do that." She gave him an alarmed look.

"I can. I've spoken to Andrew and he's more than happy to take it on. The client is fine with it. And I need to return to my daughter. She needs help with her wedding."

Barbara sniffed. "I'm sure she can manage to plan a wedding on her own. Without your help."

"Perhaps it's not her that needs me then, but the other way around."

"But . . . but . . ."

"Thanks for dinner. I'm going to try and get some more work done. Good night."

She frowned. "Of course. Good evening."

He shook his head. He probably could have handled that in a nicer way. But right now, all he wanted was to get this done so he could get back to Wishingbone.

His phone dinged an hour or so later and he reached for it, smiling when he saw who it was.

KIESHA: *What's red and bad for your teeth?*

Harry: *I don't know. A raspberry sucker?*

Kiesha: *Pfft. No. A brick!*

Dear Lord. Her jokes were awful.

Harry: *That was terrible.*

Kiesha: *Hahahaha. Terribly good! I think I could have been a comedian. I might convince Noah to have an open-mic night. What you doing?*

Harry: *Working.*

Kiesha: *Dude. You're always working. Don't you ever do anything for fun?*

Harry: *I talk to you.*

Kiesha: *Well, I am the funnest person I know.*

Harry: *I don't believe funnest is a word.*

Kiesha: *It should be. It's an awesome word. I once got offered a job making up words. I'd have been fanterrful at it.*

Harry: *Do you mean fantastic?*

Kiesha: *Nope, I mean fanterrful. It's a mash of fantastic, terrific, and wonderful.*

Harry: *You're right, you would have been fanterrful at it.*

Kiesha: *See? It's taking off. I'm a trend-setter.*

Harry: *You are. Are you all right? Have you been wearing your safety gear? Have you had any more issues with Dennis?*

Kiesha: *Harry, you worry too much.*

Harry frowned. That wasn't actually an answer. Did that mean she was having trouble with Dennis? That she wasn't wearing her safety gear? Had she had any more accidents?

Damn it.

He didn't like this. At all.

He tapped his fingers on the desk. He was well aware that he didn't have any right to demand she give him an honest answer. Maybe he should call Ed.

But no, he wouldn't go behind her back.

The sooner he got back there, the better...

Friends could protect each other, right?

HARRY: *Maybe what you need is someone worrying over you more.*
Kiesha: *I'm fine, Harry. Better let you go back to work. Night!*

FUCK.

Now, he'd driven her off.

And it made him wonder even more just what the hell she was hiding from him.

∼

KIESHA TURNED HER PHONE OFF, trying to save some of her battery life. Urgh, why hadn't she remembered to charge it at work?

So stupid.

A shiver worked its way through her and she dragged the blankets tighter around her.

This sucked.

This sucked big time.

She'd only been here three nights and she was already considering caving. The battery powered lamp on the table next to her flickered and she bit her lip, hoping like hell the damn thing wasn't going to go out.

She wasn't sure that even she was brave enough to stay in this shack in the dark.

Nope. That might be enough to have her calling Ed to rescue her.

Thankfully, the lamp stopped flickering and she breathed out a sigh of relief. But she needed to get some back-up batteries.

What was she doing?

This was insane.

And someone would soon realize that she'd been kicked out of her apartment. Wishingbone wasn't big enough for her to keep that a secret.

Then Ed would find out where she was living . . . and there would be hell to pay.

Truth was, she hadn't expected this place to be as bad as it was.

Which was stupid. Of course, it was going to be bad. No one had lived here in years.

This place didn't exactly hold good memories for her.

But it was a roof over her head.

Was it really, though? Because the roof was rickety and old, like the rest of the place. Was this really worth her pride? Right now, she could be sleeping in Juliet's pool house.

But she didn't want to be a burden. A terrible friend. Margo's words still had the power to hurt her.

"You're such an idiot, Kiesha."

Another shiver ran through her.

Rolling over, she tried to ignore the wind howling through the trees as she dug down under the covers.

Sleep wasn't going to come easy tonight.

∾

Kiesha glanced around the crowded bar. The Wishing Well was always like this during the weekends. Luckily, Noah always kept their table for them.

For the last few days, she'd been living in her grandpa's old shack. But she couldn't keep staying there. She swore the roof had more holes than it did iron, and sometimes in the middle of the night it had started to rain. She'd ended up wet and cold.

Now, she felt more tired than ever and ready to just give in. Which is why she was here. She was going to come clean and ask Noah if she could crash at his place. She'd offer to pay rent, of course. He had an apartment upstairs, but he spent all his time at Cleo's. And if she could just stay on the couch then she would be warm and dry.

It wasn't a permanent solution. But it could stop her from freezing to death. Or getting sick.

"Kiesha."

She glanced up with a tired smile as Noah sat across from her. "Hey, Noah."

"Red said you wanted to talk to me?" Red worked as a bartender some weekends.

Noah glanced over at some of Loki's friends as they roared with laughter.

"Yeah. I did. I—"

Another roar interrupted her. Noah glanced over again. "Fuck, that's about to turn into a brawl. Head over to the bar. Understand?"

Kiesha nodded. Wasn't like she wasn't used to a brawl. That was old news. She practically swayed on her seat, her eyes growing heavy-lidded.

Shoot. Now was not the time to sleep.

A wave of dizziness washed through her. She guessed she probably should have eaten something more substantial for dinner than a handful of candy. But she was stressing. She always ate candy when she was stressing.

All right, she ate candy all the time. But she consumed more when she was worried about something.

Add to her sleepless night last night and it was no wonder she was feeling slightly out of it. Plus, it was warm and cozy in here. Even if it did smell like beer and sweaty bodies.

She felt safe here.

Despite the brawl breaking out just to her right.

You're meant to be heading to the bar.

And she would in a minute. She caught a glimpse of Noah in the middle of a pile of guys, trying to break things up between one of Loki's friends and some guys she didn't recognize.

Right. Probably time to find the energy to move.

The chair next to her was pulled back and she glanced over to greet the person, only to freeze in fear and shock.

"What are you doing here?" she asked quietly, glancing around frantically to make sure no one was looking. Luckily, the fight was pulling everyone's attention.

"You're late with your payment, Kiesha," the large man sitting next to her said.

"You shouldn't be here. Someone will see you."

"So? That's your problem, not mine. Guess the sheriff wouldn't take kindly to you associating with me, huh? Not a good look when you work for him."

Ed wouldn't give a shit about that. What he would care about was how she knew someone like Bodhi. And then he'd throw a fit when he learned the truth. It could give him a heart attack. Lord knew, his heart had to be weak, trying to pump blood around that huge body of his.

She couldn't be responsible for killing him.

"What do you want?"

"Like I said, you're late with your payment."

"Seriously? Vance can't even give me a bit of leeway? I'm never late."

Bodhi sighed. "Babe, you're constantly late. You're the only person that he wouldn't have cut their fingers and toes off already as interest payments."

Nausea bubbled in her stomach as that image filled her mind. She knew that Vance was dangerous but part of her had always believed he wouldn't hurt her.

How did she get herself into these situations?

"Well, those are stupid interest payments aren't it? Fingers and toes aren't going to be any use to him and they're awfully useful to the people they belong to. They need them to work jobs to pay his God-awful interest rates."

"You borrowed the money from him," Bodhi said.

"I didn't exactly borrow it. And I never asked for Vance's help." She turned to glare at Bodhi.

Losing Jonah had been bad enough. But to have the men he'd thought would take care of her turn on her . . . yeah, that made everything so much worse. Sometimes she couldn't even breathe when she thought of the betrayal.

Which is why she tried not to think about it too much. Because then she'd never get out of bed.

"Jonah would be fucking horrified if he knew the way you all treated me after he died. He thought you'd look after me, Bodhi!"

She was aware that she needed to keep a smile on her face, the tension out of her shoulders, but as she turned to look at Bodhi, she allowed her anger and fear to fill her face.

"You think I haven't tried, Kiesha?" Bodhi said with frustration. "Who do you think has topped up your payments every time you've been short? Me, Axe, and Coop. We've talked him down every time he threatened to come get you. You should have rejected him in private."

"Yeah, I get that now."

"Then you also get why he has to save face and make you pay this debt."

She heaved in one breath then another.

"We're doing the best we can to protect you, Kiesha. But when we turn up to collect a payment and you're not there, things get difficult."

Deep, slow breaths.

"I had a problem with the building manager, I had to move out of my apartment."

"You want me to pay him a visit?"

"No. I don't want any more favors. From any of you. I just want you to leave me alone."

"Fine. I paid this month's installment to buy you some time."

"What do you want in return?"

Bodhi sighed. "Nothing, Kiesha. I don't want fucking anything. I know Jonah would fucking kick my ass for everything that's happened and I'd deserve it. I'll meet him in the afterlife. Just don't hide from Vance. Because if you do and he comes after you, I can't protect you."

She snorted. She didn't feel all that protected now.

"Believe it or not, I'm doing the best I can."

She held back her reply that his best was shit because he had paid this month's installment which gave her some breathing room.

"I'm not going anywhere."

"Nobody wants this, Kiesha. This could have all been prevented."

"What? If I'd given him what he wanted? You know, for a moment there I was thinking you were a somewhat decent guy. The deal he offered me wasn't right and you know it, Bodhi."

She smiled at a couple of locals as they walked past, giving her curious looks.

"Doesn't matter what's right and wrong, Kiesha, you should know that. What matters is what Vance wants."

"I'll have your money in a month's time."

"I'll text you the meeting place just before the time." He disappeared into the shadows.

She glanced over to see the brawl was getting closer. Shit! Something flew by her head and she ducked down under the table. She slung the strap of her handbag over her head so she didn't have to worry about carrying it. She might have to move quick.

"Kiesha!" Noah roared from somewhere. She peeked out to see if she could see him. A chair crashed against the table she was under.

This was insane.

There were brawls and then there were brawls. She heard sirens in the distance.

Shoot. Ed would blow his stack when he heard she was in the middle of everything.

"Kiesha!" Noah yelled again.

"I'm coming!" Obviously, he needed her help if he was calling for her. And she couldn't leave him out there on his own. He could get hurt without her backing him up.

Something smashed.

"Kiesha! Go!" Noah screamed at her.

She finally spotted him. He was trying to make his way toward her.

"I'm coming, Noah!"

"Get out! Right fucking now."

Well, how did he expect her to just leave him? What if he got hurt? She'd never forgive herself. No, better she make her way to him and cover his back. She crawled out from under the table, preparing herself to jump up and shove her way through the crowd, when someone grabbed her ankle.

And started slowly hauling her back...

14

Turning onto her back with a scream, Kiesha kicked out at whoever had a hold of her.

"Stranger danger! Stranger danger! I have a Taser and I'm not afraid to use it!"

Images of Bodhi coming back to grab her and take her to Vance raced through her head.

She smashed her foot against a firm shoulder and the person holding her let go, then grabbed her by the waist.

"Kiesha! It's me. It's Harry."

"H-Harry?"

He had her back under the table by now. Unable to stop herself, she launched into his arms. They fell back on the floor with her on top of him. And everything around them faded. There was just her and Harry.

Her heart raced. Only this time, it wasn't in fear. It was with arousal. She could feel his hard body beneath her, and she had to resist rubbing against him like a contented cat in the sun.

"Oh, thank God because my Taser isn't charged."

A loud bellow of anger made her jump and Harry scowled.

Sitting, he set her to the side.

"Harry, what are you doing here? How did you get here? Don't you have to work?"

"Questions later, Little Monster. Right now, we need to get you out of here."

They did? Oh yeah, the brawl. Shit!

"Noah! I need to go help Noah! You stay here, Harry. Where it's safe. I'll make sure no one hurts you." Turning, she tried to crawl back out from under the table.

"Kiesha. No!" Harry grabbed hold of her again. She tried to ignore how his touch zinged through her blood. "Come back here."

"I have to go help Noah, Harry. Don't worry, if you stay here you should be safe."

"I don't care about my safety. I care about yours. Come on. We're leaving."

"I can't leave Noah. He needs me."

"He needs you to be safe so he can concentrate on this mess."

The sirens sounded really close now and she felt the floor tremble as people raced for the door, yelling at each other.

"What?"

"You're not going out there. It's not safe. Come on." He tugged her free from the other side of the table.

"But Harry—"

"No buts." Harry turned and gave her a stern look. "Any more arguments and I'm throwing you over my shoulder and carrying you out of here. Then I'll turn you over my knee. Got me?"

She gaped at him. "You couldn't carry me."

Really, Kiesha? That's all you've got to say? The man just threatened to spank you.

Yeah, but that kind of made her curious. What would it be like if Harry went all Dom on her ass?

Hot. Really hot.

"You want to try me?"

Oh yeah. She wanted to try him, all right. The thought of her riding him like a cowgirl entered her mind. Hmm. Harry would look damn fine in a cowboy hat and nothing else.

"Why do you think it's cowboy and not cowman?"

"What?" he asked, glancing back at her.

"Like you're definitely not a boy, but you could be a cowman."

"Kiesha, focus. I'm going to hold your hand and get you out of here but I need you to do as I say, all right?"

"Will you spank me if I don't?"

"I shouldn't have made that threat. I apologize."

"Jeez, don't apologize, Harry. That was hot."

He gave her a shocked look then glanced over as a body flew past them. Shit, this was the biggest brawl she'd ever witnessed.

She really hoped Noah was all right.

"Hot? Really?"

"Yeah, that stern thing you have going on really works for you."

"Good to know. Do not let go of my hand. Or your ass is going to be toast. Got me?"

"My hearing is just fine, so yes."

He stood and drew her up next to him. Holy shit. This place was a disaster. She cried out as a glass flew past not that far from her head. Harry wrapped his arm around her head, drawing her in close to him as there were yells from the front of the bar.

"Police! Stand down! I repeat, stand down!"

Shit.

Harry kept himself half-wrapped around her as he led her through the crowds. She spotted a couple of frightened faces peering out from a table over to her left. Shoot. It was Leslie and her sister, Luna. Both women weren't very nice, but she couldn't just leave them.

"Harry! Over there!" She pointed at the two women. Harry spared them a glance. "We should get them."

Harry pulled her down, shielding her as more glass went flying. "We can't!"

"We can't leave them. They could get hurt."

"Fuck!" he swore.

Whoa. Had she even heard Harry swear before? It sounded so wrong coming from him. But then again, these were trying circumstances.

"I'll go get them. Stay right here." He hit her with another firm look. "I mean it."

"I know, otherwise you'll spank me. Harry, you've got to stop. Now is not the time to be turning me on."

He gave her a shocked look, then shook his head. Did his cheeks go slightly pink?

Nah, must have been her imagination.

She crouched down under another table, watching as Harry worked his way toward the women. A big guy fell into him, nearly sending him flying. She winced as she saw it was one of Loki's friends, Zane.

Ouch, he didn't look like he was in a good way. Harry moved past him, focused on getting to the two women. Zane sat up, looking dazed, his hand pressed to his forehead.

Shit.

He didn't look like he even knew where he was. Someone nearly trampled all over him trying to get toward the side exit.

Yeah, she wasn't just leaving him there.

Getting up, she rushed over, keeping her head down.

"Kiesha, get back," Harry yelled, moving toward her with the two women next to him.

"Sorry, Harry! You can spank me later."

"Ew, do you have to subject us to your disgusting sex life," Leslie complained.

"Feel free not to come with us if we're offending you," Harry snapped at her. "Otherwise shut up."

Leslie gaped at him, then blanched in fear as someone screamed.

"Shut up, Les," her sister told her.

Kiesha always thought she was the smarter one of the two.

"We have to help Zane!" Kiesha told Harry.

"No, we don't!" Leslie cried. "We need to get out of here."

"I'll come back for him," Harry told her, letting go of Leslie to reach for her.

Leslie screeched and grabbed hold of him. "Don't! Leave her! She's not worth it."

Damn, she was a bitch.

Harry gave her a withering look which had her actually stepping back in fear. Leslie moved around by Luna and they clung to each other.

"I've got him." Kiesha leaned down and tried to help Zane up. But the guy was enormous. Harry helped her, grabbing his other side and heaving his arm over his shoulders.

"You two, stay behind us."

"We're all gonna die," Luna cried, tears running down her cheeks.

They slowly made their way toward the exit.

They managed to make it without too much drama. Harry nearly copped a fist to the face and she'd almost dropped Zane twice when objects flew toward her head.

"Come on, Zane the Pain," she muttered to herself. "Jesus, dude, you need a diet or something."

There was a searing pain in her arm where something had hit her, it was at the same time that Harry was pushing some asshole away from them, so she didn't think he'd noticed. She'd take a look at it when they got outside.

Right now, she was just focused on putting one foot in front of the other.

"Kiesha!" She glanced over as they made it outside, seeing Jace rushing toward them.

Thank God. She nearly collapsed under Zane's weight. Now that adrenaline was no longer flooding her, she was aware of how badly she was shaking. Of how heavy Zane was.

Jace quickly grabbed hold of Zane. Without his weight as an anchor, she felt herself swaying. The world tilted around her as she collapsed onto the ground, heaving for breath.

"Kiesha!" Jace cried.

"I'm all right," she said as Harry rushed over, falling on his knees next to her.

"Kiesha. Little Monster, what's wrong?" Harry asked urgently.

The night was lit up from all the emergency vehicles, so she could easily see the concern on his face. She tried to reach up to pat his face, but her arms didn't want to work.

"Don't look so concerned. I'm okay. Just exhausted."

"Medic!" Jace yelled.

Ryan came racing over, kneeling beside her. "What happened? What's wrong?"

"I'm fine," she told him. "Help Zane. I'm just tired. He's hurt."

"You just collapsed!" Harry protested from her other side. "I want her seen to immediately."

"Rye! Some help!" Jace called out.

"Are you bleeding? Hurt?" Ryan asked, taking her pulse.

"Nope. Like I said. Go!"

"Stay with her," Ryan told Harry. "I'll be back in a moment. What the fuck were these idiots all thinking?"

She didn't think they were meant to hear that last part.

"I can't believe he just left you," Harry said, glaring at Ryan.

"He knows there are more important people to take care of."

"More important people? What bullshit is that? There is no one more important than you are."

"Aww. Harry, you always say the nicest stuff."

She pushed with her hands to sit up.

"What are you doing? You shouldn't be moving."

"Ahh, it's cold down here and I'm fine."

"If that paramedic isn't going to do his job, then I'll find someone who will. And I'll sue his ass."

"Sue his ass? Is that a technical lawyer term?" she teased.

"Yep."

"You can't do that. Rye's just doing his job."

"Not very well," he muttered. "Which is unacceptable when it comes to you."

Harry rubbed her back. She leaned against him tiredly, her face pressed to his chest. "Can we leave?"

"Not until you get seen by a professional. And I mean someone who knows their job."

"Kiesha, Ed is on his way," Jace called back.

"Ah, fuck. That's all I need," she grumbled. "I'm fine. Just wanna sleep."

"Which worries me," Harry told her. "Fuck, you're trembling. Are you cold? Let's get you somewhere warmer."

"You said fuck again. That's twice. I never heard you swear so much."

"Extenuating circumstances."

"I like when you talk all fancy," she told him.

"That's fancy?" he asked.

"The long words in your accent sound fancy. Say something else." She stared up at him with a silly grin on her face. Yep, she was aware she was acting odd. Another tremble rocked through her.

Harry frowned down at her. "Are you sure you're all right?"

"I am one hundred thousand percent sure that I am okay. Harry, did you know that your nose is really cute?"

"Thank you. But you are still getting checked out."

"I'm just cold. And tired. And my arm hurts."

"What? Why? What happened to your arm?"

"It got hit by something."

"You got hit? Where? How the fuck did that happen?" He gently took hold of her right arm, feeling it.

"It's the other one."

He carefully moved his hand over her left arm. "Fuck, you're bleeding."

"I am? Huh, wonder how that happened. You know, my boob hurts too."

"What?" He moved his gaze to her chest.

She grinned at him. "Harry, my eyes are up here."

"Kiesha, now is not the time for joking around."

Seemed like the perfect time to her. He was so worried and he didn't need to be.

"You must have been hit with something sharp. Fuck, how did I miss that? Damn it, I should never have let you talk me into stopping to help other people. I should have just gotten you out of there."

"It was the right thing to do."

"Screw the right thing. I should have just taken care of you." He cupped the side of her face. "And now you're hurt. That's on me."

"Harry, what happens to me isn't your responsibility."

"And if I want it to be?"

Whoa. Where had that come from? Sure, she thought he was hot and gorgeous and smart. But she hadn't thought he'd care this much about her.

"Let's go get you checked out," he said gruffly when she didn't reply.

Was that disappointment on his face?

"Harry?" she asked, grabbing his arm as he went to stand.

"Yeah?"

"Being responsible for me would turn the rest of your hair gray."

"You wouldn't like me with a full head of gray?" he asked.

"I think you'd just get sexier. Which seems impossible right now, because you're already pretty damn sexy."

The tension that had built in his shoulders dissipated and he grinned at her.

"You're good for a man's self-esteem."

"Poor Harry, was it suffering before? Had it gotten all shriveled and tiny?"

"Are we still talking about my self-esteem?"

"I don't know. I thought men's self-esteem was tied up with their—"

He put his hand over her mouth. "I'm going to stop you there before you say something that you can't take back."

Why would she want to take it back? But she nodded and he let go of her mouth. Once he was standing, he reached down and helped her up, holding onto her for a moment before he swung her into his arms.

"Harry! You can't carry me."

"Funny, because that's what I'm doing."

"You'll hurt your back, though."

He frowned down at her. "Are you making negative comments about your weight or my strength?"

Uh-oh.

"Ahh, which one will get me in the least amount of trouble?" she asked, giving him a hopeful grin.

"Brat," he grumbled. "You better not have been making comments about being too heavy. You're already owed a spanking."

"What? Why?"

"I told you to stay where you were and you moved. Right into the middle of danger."

"But I had to help Zane."

"No, you had to stay where you were and keep safe. I would have helped Zane."

"You were busy with the witches of Wishingbone."

He simply shook his head as they reached one of the ambulances.

Ryan walked up to them. "Kiesha? Tell me what hurts."

"She's hurt her arm. And she's light-headed. I want her taken to the hospital," Harry said in a low voice.

Whoa. Even when he was bossing her around, he'd never sounded this commanding.

Ryan raised his eyebrows then nodded. "Let me assess her first and we'll see."

"She'll be going to the hospital," Harry countered. "I want her seen by the best. I'll fly someone in if I have to."

"Harry, dude, you don't need to stress. It's just a cut or something. I don't need the hospital or some specialist flown in. I don't even like normal doctors, don't want some guy who thinks he's even more special coming around and poking and prodding me."

"You nearly fainted. That's not normal."

"Hey, ouch, Ryan Mathison!"

"What are you doing to her?" Harry stepped up, getting between her and Ryan.

Okay.

So, obviously she'd made a mistake. Because she had seriously underestimated Harry's alpha maleness. On the scale, she'd put him at around a three. Most of the guys she knew in Wishingbone, especially those in the DDB squad were at a nine.

She'd never expected Harry to react so protectively to her being harmed. He was bordering on the ridiculous. And fast making his way up the scale.

"You're reaching a seven there, dude."

"What? I'm a seven? Only a seven?" He gave her a disgruntled look.

"What do you mean, only a seven? You were a three before!"

"What!" He looked horrified.

"Uh, I think you two might be talking about two different things here," Ryan said. "Kiesha, you want to tell him what you're talking about?"

"My alpha male scale, of course. Some might call it the OPI scale."

"OPI?" Harry asked.

"Over-protective idiot scale."

"Wait, so you're saying that I was a three on your overprotective idiot scale and now I'm a seven?" He glared at her. "I'm an overprotective idiot, am I?"

"Well, you are standing between me and my patient," Ryan pointed out.

Harry turned to glower at him. But he did step back and away from her. "Do not hurt her again."

Ryan sighed. "I was just trying to look at the wound. For what it's worth, it doesn't look like it needs stitches, just cleaning up and a bandage."

"Ooh, have you got any monster Band-aids?" Kiesha asked.

Ryan smiled. "I've got unicorns and diggers."

"Pfft. That's boring."

"Kiesha! Where are you?" Ed boomed.

"Aww shit." Kiesha ducked behind Harry. "Who the hell told him I was here?"

"I'm betting any of a dozen people," Ryan replied dryly. "Did you really think you could keep your presence a secret?"

"I was hoping to."

"What's wrong?" Harry asked, turning to look down at her. "Are you scared of Ed? Were you not supposed to be here?"

"I can go anywhere I like. I'm in charge of me."

"For the moment," Harry muttered.

She gave him a surprised look, then turned to glare at Rye as he grinned. "What are you smiling at?"

"Just thinking that it's time someone took you in hand."

"Hey! You can't say things like that. Take me in hand. Pfft. No one is taking me in hand. I'll bite that hand."

Harry leaned into her, brushing his lips against her ear. "Every time you bite, baby girl, I spank. Just remember that."

Holy. Crap.

Yep. Her insides just exploded.

The more she got to know him . . . the more she wanted to know.

"Kiesha!"

"Oh crap. He's reaching Defcon One. Prepare yourself for the explosion."

Ryan just shook his head at her. "She's over here, Ed!"

"Ouch, shit! What did you just put on me? Battery acid?"

"What?" Harry barked. "What did you do to her?"

Crap. She'd forgotten that she needed to stay chill for Harry's sake.

"Just cleaning it," Ryan said dryly. "She's going to be fine."

"Fine? I don't think I'd call this fine. This is definitely three suckers' level of owie. Where are your suckers?"

"No suckers," Harry said.

She gaped at him, her mouth dropping open. "No suckers? What is this bullshit? Are you trying to kill me?"

Unfortunately, she said that last part right as Ed caught up to them.

"What?" he boomed. "Who is trying to kill you? I'm going to kill those assholes that started this."

"Ed, she's fine," Ryan told him. "Nobody is trying to kill her."

"That's totally not true," she countered. "Harry is trying to get between me and my suckers. I need them. I can't survive without them. Therefore, he's trying to kill me."

She glared at Harry, who appeared completely unrepentant. He crossed his arms over his chest.

Just what the heck was going on with him? When he'd left, he'd been the easy-going, affable, cautious Harry who was her friend. And now, he'd come back, alpha, bossy, domineering Harry.

And sure, it might be hot as hell. Until he attempted to get between her and the candy she needed as much as she required air to breathe.

Not happening, dude.

Not. Happening.

Ed let out a huff. "Sounds like he's more likely to be a dead man." Ed shot Harry a look she couldn't decipher. "What happened? Rye, is she all right?"

"She's fine. She just got hit by a piece of glass or something sharp. I've now bandaged her arm up, and she's free to go."

"She was dizzy before," Harry said. "I want her checked over more thoroughly. I'll take her to the hospital myself."

"What?" Ed barked. "What's wrong with her, Rye?"

"Her blood pressure was a bit low. When was the last time you ate, Kiesha?"

Crap.

All three men were staring at her intently.

"Uh, I had dinner."

"Yeah?" Harry asked, staring at her intently. "What was it?"

Drat. She'd been hoping he wouldn't ask that.

"Handful of M&Ms and some orange juice. But the juice has Vitamin C so that's something, right? I mean, I'm not going to get scurvy."

She patted herself on the back for remembering that.

But if she was expecting congratulations from the three men

glaring at her, she was unfortunately going to be waiting a long time.

"Sheriff!"

"I need to go deal with all of this," Ed said grimly. "Rye, make sure you check her over thoroughly. If she gives you any problems, let me know. I'll get Georgie to meet you at the hospital, KiKi. She can take you home to our place."

"Uh, no. I'm not going to the hospital or home to your place."

"Yes, you are. Because you were just in the middle of a brawl, you were hurt, and you're dizzy. You need someone to watch over you and I'm it."

"You are not it."

"I am it," Ed countered.

"Sheriff!" Noah walked over, looking worse for wear. There was a gash on his forehead and one eye was swollen shut.

"Noah!" Kiesha gasped. "Are you all right?"

"I'm fine. Are you okay?"

"She'll be fine," Rye said, drawing a scowl from Harry.

"Why didn't you head to the bar immediately like I told you to," Noah said, sounding exasperated.

"I was going to," she muttered.

"Noah! Sheriff!" someone called out.

"I have to call Cleo before she hears this from someone else. Ed, you have her?"

"I'll sort her out."

"Actually, I'll be taking care of her," Harry interjected before she could argue.

Ed narrowed his gaze. "You?"

"Yes. Me."

"I'll be fine, Ed," she told him. "Leave Georgie at home. She doesn't want to come out at night."

Ed let out a deep breath. "Fine. Just let me briefly take your statement."

She quickly told him what she'd seen, which wasn't much.

"All right, text me once you're home. And I'll be calling you in the morning. Rye, keep me informed about her health."

Just as she was about to murder the bossy bastard, he leaned in and brushed her forehead with a light kiss. "I'm glad you're all right, Kiki. I was scared out of my mind when someone told me you were here. Just keep out of trouble, all right? Leave me with some hair that's not gray."

"I'll try," she muttered. Now she felt bad for thinking he was a bossy bastard.

Then he drew back and shook his finger in front of her face. "Behave. Listen to Rye and Harry. They'll tell me if you don't."

And yep, the bossy jerk was back. That was short-lived.

15

"I really didn't need to come to the emergency room, Harry," Kiesha grumbled as he walked her out to his car.

He had his arm wrapped around her waist. All he could think about was the way she'd just keeled over. She could have been seriously hurt.

Because you didn't keep a close enough eye on her.

He knew about her propensity to be impulsive and not think about her own safety. And he'd still left her while they were in the middle of a brawl.

What had he been thinking?

He needed to do better than this. If he wanted to be her man, then protecting her came before everything else.

And he did want to be hers. He wanted her to look to him for everything. He intended to ensure that she was well taken care of. No matter what he had to do to make sure that happened.

He was not off to a good start.

"You fainted."

He debated picking her up but decided he wanted to see how well she could walk. While she was leaning on him, she didn't seem dizzy again. The doctor had reassured him that it was likely due to low blood sugar and the surge of adrenaline. Not to mention, she was probably a bit in shock and exhausted.

None of those things were a good combination.

"I didn't faint. I felt faint. There is a huge difference."

"Not to me."

"Rye said I was fine. I didn't need to come to the hospital. I don't like hospitals, they're filled with sick people."

Harry snorted. "I wasn't trusting that idiot's opinion. I still don't know if I should trust that doctor."

"Harry! Xavier is a really good doctor."

"Didn't seem that way to me. I need to do some research into his qualifications. And he made you wait far too long before he saw you. Unacceptable."

"Shh," she said, looking around frantically. "You can't insult Xavier. Or go around making threats."

She had his jacket around her. It fell past her ass and she looked adorable. Like a little girl dressing in her daddy's clothing.

Which is exactly what he wanted to be to her.

"I wasn't making threats." Well, not overt ones. And what was she so worried about? "Are you scared of him? Has he said something to you?" He stopped as they reached his car, turning her toward him.

"What? No! Xavier wouldn't do that. I've known him for years. But he belongs to Juliet."

"Yes. I know. Why? Has she threatened you?" Juliet seemed like the most unthreatening person he'd ever met in his life, but appearances could be deceptive.

"What? No, of course not. Juliet couldn't harm a fly. But if you upset her, then Reuben will come for you. There won't be anywhere you can hide. So you see the problem?"

"Not really. If I look into Xavier's qualifications then . . ."

"Juliet might get upset."

"And if Juliet gets upset..."

"Reuben will get upset."

"And Reuben getting upset is bad."

"Very, very bad. Remember, he's the bogeyman."

He didn't like the idea of her being afraid of this Reuben.

"There is nothing he won't do for Juliet and I do mean nothing. Bad things happen to people who upset her."

"What is he? Like a mafia boss?"

"No. Worse. He's a lawyer."

He blinked down at her. She didn't realize what she'd just said, right?

"Ah, Kiesha?"

"Yes."

"I'm a lawyer."

"Yeah, yeah." She waved a hand in the air dismissively. "But you're all Harry. And he's Reuben." The last part was said in a soft whisper.

"And what does being 'all Harry' mean?"

"You have a moral code. You're gentlemanly and quiet and polite and stuff. You don't go around destroying people for upsetting Juliet. I mean, I'm totally on Reuben's side for doing that shit. But I don't want his attention on you."

"So you think I'm soft and sweet and that I can't take care of you? That I couldn't protect you against this Reuben?"

Right now, he was starting to get pissed off.

"Uh, well, Harry, that's not it. I, uh... it's just, he's ruthless."

"Kiesha, I might seem like I always play by the rules. But when it comes to the people I care about I can be every bit as ruthless."

The look on her face told him she wasn't convinced, but he would show her.

"I will protect you. No matter what."

Her mouth opened, then closed. "Harry, that's really sweet—"

"It's not sweet, damn it, girl," he grumbled at her. "It's meant to be sexy."

"S-sexy?"

"Yes. Sexy. You don't see me as sexy? You look at me and you only see an old man in a suit who can't look after you?"

"Harry, are you all right?"

"Kiesha, I'm better than I have been in a long, long time. Tell me you know I'll look after you."

"It's not me I'm worried about, though," she whispered. "Juliet wouldn't allow Reuben to hurt me. It's you I'm trying to protect."

"That's sweet of you to worry." He grasped her waist and turned her so she was between him and the car. He knew he should get her in the car, that it was cold out here. But there were just a few things he needed to make clear. He cupped the side of her face with his hand, heard her breath hitch.

"But you do not need to worry. You leave that to me. That's my job."

"Your job? As a lawyer?"

"Nope. My job as your protector."

She shook her head. "Harry, it's not your job to look after me."

"Perhaps not yet, but it will be."

Ease up, man.

But he didn't want to.

"I'm taking you home now. And I'm staying the night to look after you. And I won't hear any arguments."

"Have you always been this bossy?"

"You bring it out in me."

"Oh, so it's my fault? Rude."

"You're complaining?" He placed his hands on the roof of the car behind her, leaning into her. "Do you not like my bossy side? Do you not like me fussing over you? Wanting to make sure you're safe and well? Tell me you don't like it, Kiesha and I'll stop."

"No, you won't," she whispered.

"No," he replied quietly. "I won't." He stared down at her, studying her. "I'm going to kiss you now, Kiesha."

"W-what? Why?"

"Because I want to. And I think you want me to. But if you don't, you need to tell me now. If you don't find me attractive or sexy. If you don't want me touching you or taking care of you, this is the time to say so. Because once my mouth touches yours, it belongs to me."

"What? You can't own my mouth!"

"I can, Kiesha. I intend to own all of you."

"What is happening right now?" she muttered, staring up at him, wide-eyed.

"Tell me, Kiesha. If you say no, I won't be angry. I'll only be upset with you if you lie to me. Do you want me? Do you want to belong to me?"

"I barely know you."

"So get to know me. Date me. Let me take you out. Give me time. But just tell me now if you're not interested, if you don't find me attractive, and I'll back off."

"Harry, I'd have to be blind, deaf, and dumb not to find you absolutely fucking gorgeous."

"Even though I'm ancient? And apparently come across as weak?"

"You don't come across as weak."

He raised an eyebrow.

"I didn't mean it that way. You're not weak. It's just you've never met Reuben."

"What's his last name? Maybe I've heard of him."

"Um, Jones. He has a different last name from Juliet to protect her."

"Shit, Reuben Jones? Boston lawyer?"

"Yes. You know him?"

"I've heard of him. Wow, hard to believe Juliet is his sister.

Look, it doesn't matter who he is. I can be just as ruthless when I need to be. You don't need to protect me. Tell me."

She stared up at him, her breathing coming in sharp, fast gasps. He worried she was going to pass out for a moment. His timing could definitely be better. But then she straightened her shoulders.

"Harry, I think you're the sexiest man I've ever seen. And I want to get to know you better. And that's the truth."

"Good girl," he murmured. "And now I'm going to kiss you."

"About time."

Leaning in, he kissed her. The kiss started gently. He was testing her. As a soft hum came from her mouth before she parted her lips and allowed him entrance, he knew he was right.

She wanted him just as much as he desired her.

What she likely didn't realize was just how serious his feelings were for her. Because this wasn't a fling. This wasn't something small or simple.

Nope, his feelings were big. And they were becoming more and more difficult to contain.

And while his rational side tried to warn him that he'd only known her a short time, those caveman instincts he hadn't realized he possessed were rearing their head. They were pushing at him to claim and protect.

Seemed her being in danger had pushed away all thought of going slow or not scaring her off and tipped him over into the more irrational, must-protect-at-all-costs mode.

Not that that was necessarily a bad thing in his mind. He would do whatever he had to in order to keep her safe.

Tonight, he thought he'd fucked up. He should have put her before everyone else. She'd worried him when she'd grown all dizzy and he'd realized she was injured. And perhaps he'd gotten a bit overprotective. But it was going to take a while for him to get over that.

He slid his hand around the back of her head as he kissed her like he wanted to own her, devour her.

Like she was fucking his.

Because that's what she was going to be.

"Wow, Harry," she said breathlessly as he drew back. "You really know how to kiss. Guess that comes with experience, huh?"

"There's some advantage to kissing an old man."

"Who called you old?" she demanded hotly.

"You did. Many times."

"Ah, yeah. But as long as no one else did. It's okay for me to call you old, but I'll bleed anyone else who does."

"So bloodthirsty," he murmured. "Strangely, that turns me on."

"Yeah?" she asked, biting her lip. "That mean you'll kiss me again?"

"You want more kisses?"

"Uh-huh. Lay one on me."

He moved his mouth down to hers, then slid it to the side at the last moment to kiss her cheek.

"Hey! That wasn't a proper kiss."

"I know," he replied. "Because you're going to have to earn the next kiss."

"What? What kind of bullshit is that?"

"It's not bullshit," he countered. "It's my way of getting you to behave."

"Never! I'll never behave! It's against my code of conduct."

"You have a code of conduct?"

"Doesn't everyone? Like things you will and won't do. Beliefs, rules, moral codes. A code of conduct."

"Yes, I suppose so. And yours says you can't behave?"

"I don't like rules. They're confining."

"That's too bad," he told her, cupping her face between his hands. "I really did enjoy that kiss."

She stared up at him in shock. "You can't be serious."

"About enjoying that kiss. I'm very serious."

"No, about not giving me any more."

"Well, if you're not going to follow the rules then I have no choice, do I? You have to earn your rewards."

"That's just . . . that's so mean!" she wailed.

He had to hide his smile. Lord, she was anything but boring. She was so full of life that he knew he was going to always be on his toes, trying to keep up with her.

But he wouldn't be lonely. And he wouldn't turn to work because he had nothing better in his life.

She made him feel alive, but more than that, she made him want to live.

Then he felt her tremble. Shit. He should be shot for keeping her outside like this when she'd just been in a brawl and injured. Moving away from her, he opened the passenger door.

"In you get."

She climbed in and he bent down to pull the seat belt over her.

"I was going to do that."

"Doesn't matter," he replied. "It's my job now."

She stared at him, completely dumbfounded. He drew back and walked around to the driver's seat. He needed to start carrying a blanket in his car. And perhaps some sort of booster seat. Was she safe in the front seat? Or was she better in the back? These were all things he needed to do research on.

But for now, his main priorities were making sure she was warm, safe and fed.

"Are you all right? Or have I shocked you into silence?"

"I'm never without something to say. There's something wrong with me." She grabbed his hand and put it on her forehead. "Have I got a fever? Am I delirious?"

"You're not dreaming, baby," he told her. "This is your reality now. You're going to have to get used to someone else being the boss."

"The boss?"

"Yep."

"And that's you? You're now declaring yourself the boss of me?"

"You agreed to date me. Told me I was sexy. You kissed me."

"Yes, but I'm not sure I agreed to let you be the boss of me."

"I told you I'm going to protect you."

"Ed protects me. Doesn't mean he gets to be the boss of me."

"Yes, but unlike Ed, I don't see you as a little sister. I see you as mine."

16

Kiesha's mind was whirling as she rested back in the seat. Harry turned the heated seats on when he saw her trembling. He was muttering something about keeping blankets in all his cars. Which was kind of weird, but she didn't have time to worry about why he was obsessed with blankets.

And just how many cars did he have?

She was too busy trying to get her mind to catch up on what had just occurred.

Harry had kissed her.

Harry wanted to date her.

Harry was claiming her.

Now that she could think more clearly without his kisses and sweet words affecting her, doubts started creeping in. What was going on? Why would Harry want her? She was nothing special. Well, she was. But she was the kind of special that was hard work. She knew that.

Why would he want to date her? Maybe because he didn't know her well enough... and when he did he'd leave.

Suddenly, she was aware that they'd come to a stop.

Right outside her old apartment building.

Shit.

Now she had another problem. She hadn't had a chance to talk to Noah about his apartment. And the last thing she wanted was to go back to her grandpa's place. Even though all her stuff was there.

It wasn't like she had much choice, though.

And then there was Harry. How to explain to him what had happened?

"Hey, are you all right?" Undoing his belt then hers, he turned and reached over to cup her chin. Turning her face to his, he studied her. The light the streetlamp provided barely lit up the interior of the car. Yet, he still seemed to sense something was going on with her.

Probably because you're not talking. That's not exactly normal for you.

"When you find out I'm too much hard work, you're going to leave me."

Fuck.

That wasn't what she'd meant to say. She should have said something about the weather, the heated seats, the brawl at the bar. Anything except about how he was going to leave her.

Now, she'd put that idea into his head.

Was she an idiot?

His hand tightened slightly on her chin. "Is that something you do often?"

Was what something she did often?

"Come here," he murmured. Moving his hand from her chin, he opened out his arms. She looked over at where he was sitting, doubting she could fit between him and the steering wheel.

"Come here, Kiesha." This time, his voice was filled with steel and she found herself moving before she thought about it. He slid his seat back slightly as she climbed over the middle console and into his lap.

"This is a bit weird. Pretty sure I'm too big to be sitting on your lap, Harry. Am I squishing you?"

"If you say anything disparaging about being too heavy for me, I will turn this cuddle into a spanking," he warned.

Her mouth dropped open. "That's not very nice. Here I was, worried about your poor legs and you're threatening to warm my bottom."

"Got a feeling that's going to be a common occurrence."

"What is?" she asked suspiciously.

He lightly patted the side of her thigh. "Me warming your ass."

"I don't see why it would be. I'm a good girl."

"You're impulsive, show little concern for your own safety, and you don't take very good care of yourself."

"Hey! None of that is true."

"Really? Because when I told you to stay safely under the table, you instead ran out into the middle of a brawl."

"It wasn't the middle of the brawl. That was somewhere over to the right of us. I had to help Zane."

"No," he said warningly. "You had to keep yourself safe. I would have helped him."

"But who is keeping you safe?"

"Me."

"All right, well, but none of that means that I can't take care of my own health," she stated.

"What did you eat for dinner, Little Monster?"

Oh, shove it.

Why didn't she just keep her mouth shut?

Idiot.

"There were extenuating circumstances."

"And what were those?" he asked, his hand going up and down her back.

"I was stressed."

He frowned. "About what?"

"Lots of stuff. Everything." She glanced away.

"Uh-uh, don't do that." Gently, he touched her chin, turning her back to face him. "We both know that wasn't a proper answer. Do you always try to push people away because you think that they'll eventually hurt you?"

"That's not what I do!"

Did she?

Maybe.

Well, shit.

"I have lots of friends. I don't push them away."

"I'm not talking about your friends. I'm talking about a relationship. Do you look for the worst? Do you always make assumptions about what someone else will think and do? Or is it just with me?"

She licked her lips. "I haven't been in a relationship for a long time."

"Good."

"Good?"

"Yes, good. Because neither have I. It means that we can work this all out together. But what it doesn't mean is immediately deciding that the worst will happen. It doesn't mean pushing me away before I can prove to you that I'm in this for the long haul."

"Harry, you can't know that. You barely know me."

"I know that when I left here, it felt wrong. I know that every moment I was away from you, it felt wrong. And I know that when I saw you hiding under that table in the middle of a brawl, I wanted to murder everyone putting you in the slightest bit of danger. That when I saw you leave the relatively safe place I put you, that I was tempted to leave everyone else behind, grab you and carry you out of there. That when you . . . when you nearly fainted right in front of me I almost had a heart attack from fear."

"Be careful, we have to look after that heart of yours."

"We do. Which is why I need you to be safe. Always. I know I'm going too fast, but I warned you when you let me kiss you. Bit by bit, all of you is going to be mine. You just need to be a little brave, to have some faith, to just trust in me and I'll do the rest."

Tears filled her eyes, blurring her vision. She so wanted to believe in him, but this all felt so bizarre.

"Fuck, baby. Don't cry. Please, don't cry." He leaned his forehead against hers. "I don't want to upset or scare you. I just want you to not push me away. Work with me. Have some faith in me and I'll show you that I'm not going anywhere."

"Even if I'm hard work?"

"Do you know how I feel when I'm with you?"

"Well, I'm guessing you feel murderous by how many people you seem to want to take out," she replied.

He grinned and drew back to tuck her hair behind her ears. "It does seem that way, doesn't it? You bring out the alpha caveman in me. Usually I just annihilate people with my words, in the courtroom, but tonight I felt physical. And I felt alive. For the first time in a long, long time, I have something to live for. Meeting with Mari again gave me a new focus, something to aim for, a reason not to work so much and live a little more. But meeting you, Kiesha? It showed me just how much of life I've missed out on and how little inclination I have to miss out on anymore. I don't want to spend the rest of my life alone and bored. Working and not living."

"It doesn't sound like much fun."

"It's not." He ran a finger down her nose and over her lips. "When I'm with you, I feel alive. I have a reason to get up in the morning. Being with you, it's not ever going to be boring, maybe not always easy, but I'm always going to feel alive. That's what you do for me."

"You sure it's not some midlife crisis?"

"I think I'm old enough to know what I want. And what I want is you. I can take it as slowly as you need me to. What I won't allow, though, is for you to push me away without even trying. So long as you see a chance, I'm going to run with that. And I'm not letting you go, not until the day you tell me you don't want me. Fuck, even then I'll have a problem."

"Have you always been this possessive?"

"You know, I don't know. I don't think I've ever had someone that I wanted to be this possessive of. You're special, Kiesha. And the kind of special that's worth fighting for."

"Just remember that when I do something to embarrass you in front of your fancy lawyer friends," she muttered.

He tilted her face back, his finger under her chin. "I don't have fancy lawyer friends. I have work colleagues. But they aren't my friends and I don't care what they think. Of you or me. All I care about is how you feel. And if they upset you then you never have to see them. Actually, you won't be seeing them anyway, since I'm quitting."

"You . . . you what?"

"I quit."

"You quit?" she squeaked.

"Handed in my notice yesterday evening."

"Harry! You can't do that!"

"Why not?"

"B-because that's your job. You love it, right?"

"I used to. But somewhere along the line, it became my crutch not my career. I don't want my job to be who I am. And that's what happened."

"But you can change that. Maybe work a little less. Take up a hobby, tennis, golf, you know something boring with a ball."

"Something boring with a ball?"

"Yeah, maybe not football. I don't think that would be very wise."

"I always wanted to be an All Black you know."

"What the hell is an All Black?"

"New Zealand rugby team. You've never heard of them?"

"I don't really like anything where I have to play with balls."

"That's a shame," he said dryly.

Oh, crap.

"Walked right into that one, huh?"

He grinned at her. "Yep. And I'm not going through a midlife crisis. I don't need to take up golf. What I want is to quit my job, move here and be with you."

She rubbed at her chest as it tightened in panic. "So, no pressure, right?"

"I didn't say that to scare or worry you."

"No, but you've quit your job, you're uprooting your life and moving here because you think we could be something. I think I'm entitled to a bit of panic over that, Harry! We've barely kissed. You don't know me that well, not really. I'm a terrible bed hog, I take up the whole thing and I like to wrap myself up in the covers like a burrito.

"You'll likely end up on the floor and cold. I'm not even human until I have a sucker in the morning. I'm grouchy and moody. I cry at every sad thing on TV and most of them aren't even that sad. Cartoons, advertisements, movies, TV shows. It's really pathetic. And my jokes are just awful. Really bad. I don't like sports, I'm not interested in politics. I'm not sophisticated or worldly or good at anything! And I don't even know what I want to be when I grow up because I don't ever want to grow up! Harry, there's no way you want to be with me. You can do so much better."

"Right, Little Monster. Let's get one thing clear. There is no one that is better than you, got me? And if this car wasn't so damn small and you hadn't nearly fainted just a few hours ago, you'd be over my knee. In fact, I'm going to postpone that spanking for when you get your other spanking that you're owed."

"What? How did I end up being owed two spankings?"

"You moved when I told you to stay put and you were talking badly about yourself. Two rules. You'll listen to me when it comes to health and safety and you won't speak badly of yourself."

"I told you I don't believe in rules."

"That's too bad then. Because your bottom is going to pay the price. I don't ever want to hear you say I could do better than you. Because that's so blatantly untrue."

"Pretty sure it's not."

He moved his mouth to her ear then tugged on the lobe lightly with his teeth. "Keep going, Little Monster. You're not going to be sitting for a week by the time we get done."

Oh, just kill her now.

Heat flooded her, along with a hint of nervousness. Just how serious was he about this spanking stuff? Because sure the idea was sexy . . . but what about the reality?

She wasn't sure her butt could take too much of a pounding. Then again, how hard could the spankings be? Harry was probably just talking about a few slaps on her butt. And it was a well-padded butt. Plus, she liked the idea of a light spanking. That sounded sexy.

Yeah, she wouldn't worry too much about that.

He turned her face to his and kissed her. Slow and sweet. Then the kiss turned hotter. Deeper. She squirmed on his lap, her heart racing.

Fuck. There wasn't enough room in here for her to turn around and face him. To touch him properly.

"Time to claim another part of you," he murmured as he drew back.

Oh, fuck yes.

Please.

"But before I do, I want to make a few things clear. If you need to be a burrito, I'll wrap you up with me. It will stop you being a bed hog too. If you're grouchy, I'll just have to work hard to put you in a better mood. And I don't care that you don't know what you want to be, that you don't want to grow up. Truth is, what makes you you, is what I like about you. And I don't ever want you to change."

"Really?" she whispered, feeling those tears from earlier leaking down her cheeks.

He wiped them away then kissed his way down one cheek, then up the other. "Really. Bit by bit, I'm stealing you, Kiesha. You're going to be mine."

And damn if being his wasn't all that she wanted to be right then.

"You talk a good talk, Harry."

"I'll show you I can walk the walk, too."

"I do love a good rhyme," she said on a sigh.

"Come on, enough serious talk. You're exhausted. You should be sleeping right now, not sitting in a car in the cold."

Reaching over, he turned off the car which wasn't cold in the slightest. And that's when she remembered her other problem.

"Uh, Harry?"

"Just let me open the door then you can get out first," he told her, reaching for the car door. "We'll get you into bed soon."

"No, it's not that. It's just . . . Harry, you can't stay with me tonight."

17

Harry froze.

Okay, so she was going to take more convincing than he'd initially thought.

That was okay. He had all the time in the world now. Sure, he'd have to go back to Houston and wrap up some business and his apartment and belongings. But once that was done, he would be here for good.

He'd expected some pushback. And he hadn't meant to blurt everything out tonight. His timing needed a lot of work.

"You don't want me to stay tonight?" he asked. "I'll sleep on the couch. There's no pressure for anything else. I just want to make sure you're all right."

He really didn't want to leave her alone tonight. He wasn't sure that he could. And he was pretty certain her building manager would be all over his ass if he slept outside her apartment door.

"No, it's not that. Oh shit. I don't live here anymore."

"You don't?" He gave her a surprised look. That happened quickly.

"No."

"Well, you move quick. But at least you won't have to put up with that building manager anymore. Where do you live now?" He shifted her over to her seat, relieved that she wasn't trying to tell him he couldn't stay. Just that they weren't staying here.

"At my grandpa's place. He died about three years ago. My mom inherited the property, but she doesn't want anything to do with it. She moved away to Florida and it's just sat there."

He frowned. "Leaving you to look after it? Why didn't you live there?"

"It's kind of out of town and I don't drive. Plus, it doesn't hold the best memories, I guess. After my dad left us, mom couldn't afford the rent on our place and had to move back in with my grandpa. He mostly ignored me, but he wasn't very nice to her."

"I'm sorry, sweetheart."

She gave him a small smile.

"Why don't you direct me to where it is? We can head out there."

"Actually, do you think you could just take me to the motel? I can't deal with being there tonight."

Harry studied her for a long moment. He wanted to press her on her reasons. Why would she want to stay at the motel instead? Was it more than just bad memories? How was she getting to work if it was that far out of town?

But as much as he wanted answers, he didn't think now was the time. He'd pushed her too much tonight. She was exhausted and he was cursing himself for not immediately taking her home and tucking her up into bed.

Reaching over her, he put on her seat belt. She huffed a breath at him.

"Safety first."

"Yes, sir." She saluted him.

Daddy would be better. But he needed to stop, pull back, give her a little space to breathe.

By the time they reached the motel, she was half asleep. He glanced at the clock. Fuck. It was nearly two in the morning.

"Wait there."

"What?" she asked tiredly.

"I'll come around and get you."

"I can do it."

"You can. You won't. Wait there."

"So bossy. And spanky. You're bosspanky."

"Yep, I'm bosspanky. So stay there."

He moved quickly, not wanting to give her enough time to defy him. At some stage, he was going to have to make good on those threats to spank her.

Not that that was any hardship. But he didn't want to do it while she was tired and had just hurt her arm.

He opened her door and she tried to get out. But the seat belt threw her back.

"What's happening? The car's got hold of me! Run for your life, Harry! Save yourself!"

He couldn't help but chuckle.

Definitely not boring.

"It's just your seat belt," he told her calmly, reaching over to unbuckle her. "The car isn't out to get you."

"What? A seat belt? I knew I hated those things."

"That's too bad, since you'll be wearing one every time you're in a moving vehicle."

"I'm not good with vehicles. I think I failed my driver's test like ten times, all the times I've tried to drive haven't ended well."

He frowned as he reached his motel room and sort of propped her up against the wall with his body as he unlocked the door.

"You don't have a license?"

"Nope. All those driving suggestions . . . yeah, I can't follow them."

"They're not suggestions, Little Monster. And you are definitely not getting behind the wheel of a vehicle again without a license. And my express supervision."

"Eh, no great loss. I mean, it is going to be a bit of a nuisance once it's snowing now that I'm not on a bus route. Yep, that's going to suck. Guess I'll need some good snow boots to get to work. Maybe I can ski. That's no good when it's raining, though. Actually, an electric scooter could work. How much do you suppose those are and do you think I could rig an umbrella up to cover me?"

"You are not getting around on skis or an electric scooter," he told her as he ushered her inside. "Also, while we're at it, no going to bars on your own." He led her into the small bedroom and carefully helped her sit on the bed. She lay back, spreading out like a starfish.

"I wasn't on my own. I knew lots of people there."

"But none of them were charged with being responsible for you. Noah was doing his best, but he had a lot on his hands and he couldn't take care of you."

"Harry, you're talking like a Daddy Dom."

"I am a Daddy Dom." Saying the words felt a bit nerve-wracking but also freeing. Like this was something he'd been all his life but only realized it recently.

She sat up as he started drawing off her boots. They were a bright purple. The black shoe laces had these little monster figurines on the end that looked like they were biting down on the end of the laces, trying to eat them. "You're not *my* Daddy, though."

"You don't want me to be?"

"I ... I ..."

He tensed, waiting for her rejection. To tell him they needed to slow down. That they hadn't even dated yet.

"I think that would be amazing. But I can't even wrap my head around it."

"Then don't think about it right now. It's time for sleep. I'm going to find you something to wear." He moved to the drawers, opening one.

"You unpack your clothes?"

"Ah, yes, you don't?"

"No. Who does that? I never unpack when I'm staying in a hotel. I just live out of my suitcase. It's easier, in case you have to leave quickly."

"Why would I have to leave quickly?"

"I dunno, you might not pay your bill."

"I'm not going to skip out on the bill," he told her dryly. "Here you are." He handed her one of his T-shirts. "Go use the bathroom and put this on."

"I don't need the bathroom. I'm just gonna sleep like this."

He shook his head at her. "Would you like me to get you undressed and into my shirt then put you on the toilet?"

Her eyes opened wide and she shot up. Then she groaned, holding her head.

Fuck!

"What is it? What's wrong? Kiesha?"

"I'm fine. Just sat up too quickly."

"Come on, I'm going to help you." He drew his jacket off her then reached for the bottom of her sweater. It was neon green with a huge yellow blob on the front.

"No, I got it." She slapped at his hands, then moaned.

"What's wrong?"

"Just my stupid arm. Whatever drugs Xavier gave me are wearing off. I knew he didn't give me the good stuff. Sneaky bastard probably had them hidden out the back. That's what doctors do, you know. They keep all the good stuff for themselves."

"He better not have," Harry said with a scowl. "Do you want me to take you back? Demand some better pain medication?"

She stared up at him and to his surprise, she smiled. "Aww, Harry. You're so sweet. But nah, I'll be all good."

"I've got some acetaminophen. You can take that. Although I wish you had something in your stomach. I think I've got a protein bar around here. Let me help you get this off. You don't want to hurt your arm."

She grumbled, but let him draw off her sweater.

"Why is there a blob on your sweater anyway?" he asked, hoping to distract her as he drew off her T-shirt underneath.

"It's a monster blob."

"Right. That makes perfect sense."

She giggled, making him smile. Along the front of her pink T-shirt were the words: *That's a terrible idea. I'm in.*

He shook his head as he took her T-shirt off. He tried desperately not to notice the way her red bra cupped her gorgeous breasts, all that smooth skin on display. He wanted to lick every inch of her.

She's injured. Go slow.

Fuck. He felt like a horny teenager. His dick was hard, pressing against his pants and he quickly whipped his T-shirt over her head.

"I've got to get my bra off. Can't sleep in it."

"I'll get it," he reassured her. "Thought you would want something covering you while I took it off."

"Eh, they're just boobs. Lots of us have them, right?"

"Right. For the record, I don't."

Why the hell did he say that?

She giggled again. "That's good to know, Harry."

He shook his head. "I think I need some sleep. I'm losing my ability to talk properly." Reaching around behind her, he slid his hands under the T-shirt to undo her bra.

"Whoa, you're good at that, Harry."

"Well, yes." He could feel himself blushing slightly as he

helped her slide the straps off then get her arms into the sleeves. "I went to an all-boys boarding school and one of the boys stole his mother's bra so we could practice..."

She started giggling. "Seriously?"

"Yes. We all got quite good at it. Unfortunately, that never actually helped us get to the stage where a girl was willing to let us undo her bra." He winked at her. "Being at an all-boys school was not conducive to learning how to speak to girls. The first boy-girl dance I ever went to, the boys stood on one side of the hall, the girls on the other and we all just stared at each other."

"Oh no. An all-boys school, huh?"

"Yes, it wasn't my choice." He helped her stand, then crouched down and reached under the bottom of his T-shirt to undo her jeans. Instead of finding a zipper, he encountered just smooth material. "My mother found it hard to cope with raising a teenager on her own. So, she sent me away."

"Oh, Harry. I'm sorry."

He shrugged. "I didn't say that to make you feel sorry for me. I still had a good life. My grandparents came and got me every holiday. My mother did what she could, but she was lost without my father, I think. Now, where the heck is your zipper?"

"Huh? What? Oh, these aren't jeans. They're jeggings."

"Jeggings?"

"You've never heard of jeggings?" she asked as he drew her pants down. "They're a cross between leggings and jeans."

"Uh, no."

"Harry, where have you been living? Jeggings are amazing. All the comfort of leggings and the style of jeans. Mind you, I don't know if they make them for men."

"I'm missing out," he told her with mock-seriousness.

"You are. Ooh, maybe I'll make my millions inventing men's jeggings."

"Put your hands on my shoulders. One foot up. Good girl. Now the other one. You're doing so well."

"I'm just standing here, Harry."

"Yes, but you're listening to me. That's nearly a miracle."

She made a scoffing noise. After he had her leggings off, he stood and guided her to the bathroom. "Pee. There's a new toothbrush in the cupboard under the sink. Call out if you need me, I'm going to leave the door cracked open slightly so I can hear you."

~

He was going to leave the door cracked open slightly so he could hear her? Yeah, she so didn't think so. There was no way she was starting off a relationship letting her man hear her pee.

Her man. Yikes. That would take some getting used to.

She closed the door and locked it.

"Kiesha," he growled through the door. "Unlock and open the door."

"Can't hear you."

"You can hear me just fine. Unlock and open the door. Right. Now."

She wanted to obey him. She really did. But she just couldn't.

"I will in a minute, I'm peeing." Then so she wasn't lying to him, she sat on the toilet to pee.

Panties off first, Kiesha.

Good Lord. She was tired. Her brain was so foggy she'd nearly peed with her panties on.

Idiot.

Standing, she slid them off then peed. Okay, maybe she had to go and hadn't realized it.

After, she washed her hands and face. Then she found the brand-new toothbrush.

Seriously, who traveled with a spare toothbrush? That was kind of anal. And also, kind of Harry.

But it suited her since her teeth were feeling gross and she hadn't relished going to bed with stinky breath. So, she quickly brushed her teeth then stared down at the mess she'd made of the sink with the toothpaste. Really? How did she always manage to make a mess? Was there something here she could use to clean it up?

"Kiesha, open the door."

Uh-oh. Now he was getting mad.

"I will in a second, I'm just cleaning up the mess."

"What mess? Why is there a mess?"

"Uh, well, it might look like there was a toothpaste massacre in here," she told him with a grimace.

"Kiesha, open the door."

Moving to the door, she unlocked it. He reached out, wrapping his arm around her waist and drawing her into him. "So you brushed your teeth?"

"Yep."

"You peed?"

"Yep."

"Then get your ass into bed." Turning her to the bed, he smacked his hand against her bottom.

"Hey, ouch!" She rubbed her bottom and glared over her shoulder at him. "That wasn't very nice."

"Neither was locking the door when I told you to keep it open."

She waggled a finger at him. "I am not letting you hear me pee, Harrison Taylor!"

"Why does it matter if I hear you pee?"

"Just does. Takes away the romance."

He smiled at her, crossing his arms over his chest. "You want romance?"

"I dunno. I guess. Don't most women?"

"Maybe. I'm not sure. To Rosalind, romance was me giving her jewelry."

"I don't need jewelry. That's not what romance is to me."

"What's romance to you, Little Monster?" He walked over and drew back the covers.

"I dunno. I guess picnics and walks and talking and sharing stuff." She could feel herself growing hot. This was embarrassing. "Saying nice things to each other. Sitting and watching a show together. All of that."

"Flowers?"

"I like flowers," she told him, climbing into the bed. "But I like monsters more."

"I'll remember that." He tucked her in. "I'm just going to clean up whatever mess there is and then brush my teeth."

"All right, but the mess wasn't my fault. Toothpaste can be tricky, ask anyone. Actually, don't ask anyone. Just ask me. I'll tell you." Her eyes were growing heavy. Then something occurred to her. "Wait! Why aren't I on the couch?"

"What do you mean, why aren't you on the couch? Why would you be on the couch?"

"I can't take your bed."

"Oh. Well, I thought we might sleep together. But I can take the couch."

No, that wasn't what she wanted. Could she sleep with him, though?

"No, I don't want you to take the couch," she told him. "We can sleep together."

"You sure, sweetheart? I don't want to make you uncomfortable."

"You could never make me uncomfortable. Now, make sure you leave the door open so I can hear you pee! Or in case you get into difficulty. Although I draw the line at some things. Remember, romance."

"I'm not leaving the door open, brat. Go to sleep." Leaning over her, he bent down to kiss her on the forehead.

"Uh-huh, sure, I'll get right on that," she mumbled. Like she was going to be able to fall asleep knowing that he was going to be climbing into bed with her.

Would he sleep naked? Nah, likely not. He probably had button-up, striped pajamas.

Damn, now she wanted to see him in button-up, striped pajamas.

Unfortunately, she was asleep well before he left the bathroom.

18

Kiesha woke up, stretching.

Damn. That was a good night's sleep. Normally, she woke up two hundred times. And half the time, she ended up falling out of bed. That wasn't fun.

As she moved her arm, she groaned as pain shot down it.

"Easy, Little Monster."

Okay. Wait. What?

Where was she and what the hell had she done last night?

"Kiesha? Are you all right? Are you in pain? Want some painkillers?"

Was that... Harry?

Why was Harry... had the two of them... oh no, wait.

"I didn't fuck Harry," she whispered.

"Ah, no, you didn't," an amused voice answered.

"And I just spoke out loud," she added.

"Is this how you normally wake up?" he asked.

She cracked an eye open. "What do you mean?"

"All sleepy and cute. Muttering to yourself."

"It can take a while for my brain to function. Candy. I need candy."

"No candy first thing in the morning."

"I need it to function."

"No, you don't."

She gave a huge gasp of horror. How dare he?

"Harry, are you trying to change me?"

"I'm just trying to save your teeth."

Grumbling to herself, she opened her other eye, looking around. Unfortunately, Harry was dressed.

That was a huge disappointment.

"Hey, where are your pin-striped jammies?"

"What?"

"The jammies. I wanted to see you in them. I bet they were navy blue with a white stripe. Classy and sophisticated, like you. Maybe if I had pin-striped pajamas, I'd be classy and sophisticated too."

"I'm sorry to burst whatever fantasy you have going on, but I don't have pin-striped pajamas."

"That's another disappointment."

He grinned. "And you don't need to be classy and sophisticated. I like you just the way you are."

"So, you're saying you don't think I'm classy and sophisticated?" she asked with mock-outrage.

"What . . . no . . . I . . .. that's not what . . ."

Aww, he was cute when he was floundering.

"It's okay, Harry. I was just teasing." She pushed herself up with her good arm so she was sitting. Harry immediately moved over to support her, grabbing some pillows to put behind her back.

That was sweet, if unnecessary.

"You were teasing me?" he asked, sitting on the bed facing her.

"Yep. I know I'm not classy or sophisticated."

He gave her a stern look. "That sounds like you're saying negative things about yourself."

"Only if I wanted to be those things. Since I'm not worried, I can't be putting myself down, right?"

"I have a feeling you're going to try and run rings around me."

She thought she already was, but she wisely kept that thought to herself.

"Brat. Don't think I don't see that smug look on your face." He reached out and tickled under her good arm.

"Eek! No tickling! No tickling! I'll pee!"

"Oh, very ticklish, are we?" he said in a mock-evil voice. "Good to know." He tapped his fingers together, raising one eyebrow to give her a devilish look.

She giggled at his silliness, studying him. Damn, he looked fine in the morning. He looked gorgeous all the time, of course. But morning might be his time to shine.

He was wearing a white button-up shirt and black pants. She guessed this might be dressed-down for Harry.

Unless it wasn't. Unless he was planning on working.

Oh shit! What day was it?

Then she realized how light it was inside the room. "Oh fuck! What's the time? I'm gonna be late for work! Ed is going to kill me!"

"Kiesha!" He reached for her, holding her around her hips as she attempted to dive out of bed.

"Harry, I gotta go!"

"Kiesha!"

"Ed will be having a fit! Where's my phone?"

"Kiesha, it's Sunday!"

"What?"

"It's Sunday."

She leaned back against the pillows, breathing heavily. "Oh my God. Don't scare me like that."

"How did I scare you?"

"By making me think it was Monday."

"How did I make you think that?" he asked.

"You're dressed in Monday clothes, of course."

"I am?"

"Harry, those aren't Sunday clothes. Sunday clothes are T-shirts and jeans or tights or something more relaxed." She eyed him for a moment. "Do you own anything like that?"

"I'm not sure if I packed them or not. I think I might have some jeans."

"Do we need to go shopping?"

"Ahh, perhaps."

"That's good. I love shopping. I once had a job as a personal shopper for this really rich dude."

"You did?"

She rubbed her nose. No, she did not.

Understanding filled his face as she out and out lied to him. Why was she like this? She wasn't sure she liked rubbing her nose to let him know when she was telling porkers. That meant he'd know how many stories she made up.

Just to make her life seem better than it was.

Not that things were bad now . . . but it had taken some shitty years to get here.

To where she was lying in a motel bed with a seriously cute, understanding, smart guy.

"I'd be grateful to have your help while shopping," he said in a gentle voice. He placed his finger under her chin, tilting her face up so she was looking at him. There was nothing but understanding in his face and it floored her how kind he was. "It's been a long time since I shopped for myself."

Jealousy flooded her. "Someone else did it?"

"Yes, a guy named Jacques. I think his name was really Jack and the French accent was fake, but he rocked it."

"He sounds like fun."

Harry smiled. "I suppose he was."

"You're a really good guy, Harry," she told him. Because he was. There weren't many people who'd not only put up with her bullshit but still wanted to hang around her.

"I have a lot of people who would say differently."

"Then they're all idiots."

He huffed out a laugh. "I guess so. I'm going to go and get us breakfast and bring it back here. I want you to stay in bed while I'm gone and rest, all right?"

Reaching up, he brushed his fingers through her hair.

Eek! Her hair! She had to look like a mess. She tried to smooth it down, but yep, it had to be sticking up everywhere.

Damn it. Normally she tried to braid it before bed. But last night, she'd been so tired that she'd fallen asleep without even thinking about that.

And she hadn't even felt Harry come to bed.

"My hair is a disaster!"

He grinned. "It does seem to have a life of its own. It's cute."

"It's not cute. I should have taken the time to braid it." She tried to use her injured arm to tame it down, wincing as it pulled at her sore skin.

"Easy," he warned. "Don't move that arm much."

"It's fine. I didn't even need stitches. It's annoying more than anything."

"I still don't want you moving it around too much. If you do, I'll put it in a sling," he warned.

Her mouth dropped open. "I don't need a sling!"

"And you won't have to wear one if you don't use your arm." He gave her a knowing look.

"Xavier said I didn't need one."

"Xavier isn't your man, I am."

She gave him a shy look. "You are, huh? I didn't dream that part?"

"Well, if you did then so did I." He ran a knuckle down her cheek then tapped her on the nose. "And I don't want that to be a dream."

"You really do want to date me? That wasn't the adrenaline talking? Because adrenaline can do weird things. I once went out and bought a pair of plain black shoes after a scare. Can you believe it?"

"The horror."

She smacked him lightly on the arm at his teasing. Then she winced as she pulled at her cut again.

"What did I tell you?" he grumbled. "Hurt yourself again and there are going to be consequences, Little Monster."

"But I might like them."

"You want a sling? For me to feed you? Dress you?"

Damn, he was just making that option more and more appealing.

"Bathe you." He studied her closely. "Then again, I think you quite like the idea of me doing those things for you."

She licked her lips. "And you?"

"I like the sound of that too. More than you probably know."

"Harry, did you really quit your job?"

"Yeah, baby. I did."

"But . . . won't you miss it? Won't you regret leaving? What if things don't work out here? What if—"

He slid his hand across her mouth. "First, deep breath. In. Out." He removed his hand, and she took a couple of calming breaths.

"Would it help if I told you that I didn't quit because I wanted to pursue a relationship with you?"

"It would."

"Then I didn't quit because I wanted to be with you."

"Good." She eyed him. "Are you telling me the truth?"

"Partially." His eyes twinkled. "The full truth is that I haven't been interested in my work for a while. It's a chore. It was my life. I need something more. You weren't the entire reason."

"Huh, well, that's rude."

"What?" He gave her a shocked look.

"I'm joking again, Harry."

"I'm beginning to see how Ed got that tic by his eye."

"Isn't Ticcy cute?"

"I'm not sure I'd call him cute," Harry said slowly. "So, we're still good? You still want to date me?"

"I'd like that."

"Good. Because I want to claim another part of you."

Excitement moved through her. She knew what this meant. Leaning forward, he laid the sweetest kiss on her forehead.

Damn.

Her heart melted. She cleared her throat as he moved back. "You know, my boobs are feeling very unclaimed."

He grinned. "Your breasts seem to be very needy."

"They are. Greedy bitches."

A chuckle escaped him, right as her tummy started grumbling. Why was her body so needy?

"Right, enough talk of that. We can discuss our first date during breakfast. But I need to feed you. Do you have any requests?"

"Where are you going? I'll come with you. It will just take me a minute to shower."

Too bad she didn't have any clean clothes with her. Maybe she could sneak something from Harry's wardrobe. She really needed to get him some colorful shirts.

Maybe he really had gone out and bought that pink shirt just for quiz night.

He really was the sweetest.

"No, I want you to rest today. You still look exhausted. You can get up later, after another nap."

Her mouth dropped open. "A nap? I don't need a nap."

"The bags under your eyes say differently."

"Harry!" She slapped her hand over her eyes.

"What are you doing?"

"Covering up my eyes, since they obviously look terrible."

"They don't look terrible," he countered, tugging gently at her hand. "Remove your hand. Good girl."

She bit her lip and he pulled it free from her teeth. "Hey, be nice to my lips, I claimed them, remember? And you look as beautiful as always. But after last night, you're bound to be tired. You said you hadn't been sleeping well, so I want you to rest. That's all."

"But I slept amazing last night! I didn't even wake up once. Well, not that I can remember. I didn't wake you with any dreams, did I?"

"No."

"Did I move around a lot?"

"A little.

"Did I kick you?" she asked.

"Once or twice."

"Sorry, did I steal all the blankets and wrap myself up like a burrito?"

"You tried, but I figured out a way to keep you still."

"You did? How?"

"I just wrapped myself around you."

Her eyes widened. "Really?"

"I was a bit worried that you'd wake up and be frightened. But you just sighed and went still. Then we slept like that the rest of the night."

"I don't usually like being touched while I'm sleeping. Huh. I can't believe I slept so well."

"I'm happy to offer my services every night," he told her with a wink.

"I dunno. Can I afford your fees?"

"Hmm, they are steep. Endless kisses."

"Ouch. That is expensive. I hope you don't offer these services to just anyone?"

"Nope. These rates are special just for you."

"Good to know." She nodded solemnly. "I'll take your offer under consideration."

"I offer a lifetime warranty too."

"That's a long time," she whispered.

He cupped her face. "Longer for some of us than others. That's something to take into consideration."

For some reason, tears entered her eyes. "That's rather morbid. Should you be trying to talk me out of your services?"

"No. It's rather foolish of me. But I don't want you to have buyer's remorse."

She closed her eyes and turned into his hand, snuggling against it, breathing in his scent. His hand was so warm, comforting, strong.

"I can't have buyer's remorse when you're so damn perfect."

He gave a laugh. "I think you'll find I'm far from perfect, Little Monster."

"Perfect for me."

"Well, if you like someone who is stubborn, protective, and possessive then I'm probably your man."

She grinned. "Well, maybe not completely perfect."

He threw his head back and laughed. She squirmed in delight at making him laugh like that. She got the feeling that wasn't something he did often.

Then her tummy grumbled again, making him frown.

"Right, breakfast." He stood and grabbed his keys and wallet off the nightstand. "Any requests?"

"French toast. And soda."

"You can't have soda with breakfast."

"Sure, I can. It helps break everything up."

He eyed her. "No soda. Try again."

"Fine, I can see that stubborn part of you is rearing its head."

"I did warn you."

"Chocolate milk then."

"Chocolate milk it is." He placed his hands on the mattress on either side of her, then leaned in to kiss her lightly. "I'll be back soon. I expect to find you in the bed, resting. Understand?"

"I can't spend all day in bed. I have things to do. I'll be bored."

"Not all day. But I want you to get more rest. I'll let you turn the television on if you're bored."

"Gee, thanks," she said sarcastically as he handed her the remotes.

"You're welcome. Text me if you need anything more."

Oh shit! Her phone. She hadn't checked it lately and if Ed was trying to get hold of her . . . he could be flipping his lid.

She dove off the bed after he walked out the door, and searched for her handbag. There it was.

Shoot. And she had to pee. Grabbing her phone out, she rushed into the bathroom.

A wave of dizziness washed over her.

All right, don't move too fast.

Harry might be right about her needing more sleep. And something to eat that wasn't sugar.

But she'd never tell him that. As she peed, she looked at her messages. She winced as she saw she had texts from everyone. Deciding the best way to handle things was a group text she sent one out.

. . .

Kiesha: *I'm fine everyone. Got a small cut on my arm. Nothing to get worried about.*

Almost immediately, her phone was flooded with more texts. Tears entered her eyes at the way her friends all expressed their concern for her.

She loved these guys. They were her family; her closest friends and she was so glad she'd come home to them rather than staying in the city. She hadn't belonged there. And even if in some ways her life would have been easier with Vance, it wouldn't have been a happy life.

She wouldn't have her family.

Juliet: *Are you sure you're all right? Xavier said Harry brought you into the hospital and that you just had a cut on your arm, but I've been so worried.*

Kiesha: *I'm fine! Xavier is right. Just a cut. Promise.*

Isa: *Are you sure? Do you need me to come over?*

Kiesha: *I'm good, babe. But if you have time to walk Oscar that would help.*

Isa: *Consider it done.*

Cleo: *Noah said that you were in the thick of it but that Harry came to your rescue? Is that why he took you to the hospital? Why did you need the hospital if it's just a cut?*

Juliet: *Do you want to come stay with me? You can stay in the pool house and I'll take care of you.*

Georgie: *Where are you?*

Wait. Hmm. That didn't seem like the way Georgie would text. If that rat-bastard Ed had stolen her phone...

. . .

KIESHA: *Hey, Georgie, how is Ed's anal bleeding?*
Juliet: . . .
Isa: . . .
Cleo: . . .

HER PHONE STARTED RINGING in her hand. Georgie's name was on the screen.

"Hello, Ed," she answered the call, putting it on speaker.

"How did you know it was me?"

"Well, first of all you didn't even ask how I was, if I was all right, all you said was where are you."

He grumbled something to himself. "I don't have time for social niceties."

"But you have time to steal Georgie's phone and read her messages?"

"You weren't answering your phone or my messages! I had to do something. Where are you? I went by your place and there was no answer."

She sighed. She wondered if Dennis the dick hadn't rented it out yet.

"I'm with Harry."

"With Harry," he repeated. "With Harry where exactly?"

"Oh, we're running naked down the middle of Main Street. What? Is that not okay?"

"Kiesha, I'm fucking serious here."

A stab of guilt filled her. She knew she was a trial to Ed. But she figured it was every little sister's prerogative to rile up their brother. Right?

"Sorry, Teddy-Eddy," she told him. She rubbed at her temples as she stared into the bathroom mirror at herself.

Damn it, she did have dark bags under her eyes. And her hair looked like she'd had a shock. It was a wonder Harry could stand to look at her this morning, let alone kiss her.

And ew, she hadn't even brushed her teeth.

"Don't call me that," he grumbled. "That's a terrible nickname."

"But you're like a giant teddy bear. All gruff on the outside and marshmallow on the inside."

"I am not a teddy bear, nor am I marshmallow. And if you don't tell me where the hell you are right now, I'm gonna track you down and . . . and . . ."

"What?"

"Lecture you until you cry."

She rolled her eyes at the threat. As if she'd cry from one of his lectures.

Please.

She was made of tougher stuff. And it wasn't as if she wasn't well used to his scoldings.

But she heard a loud gasp coming from the background.

"Ed! What did you just say? Who are you talking to? And on my phone!"

"Now, Georgie," Ed said in a placating, soft voice. "This isn't what it seems."

"And how does it seem? Because it seems to me that you just threatened to make someone cry. And you're on my phone so I'm guessing it's someone I know."

"It's just Kiesha."

Just Kiesha? Wow, how rude.

"Kiesha! Why are you talking to Kiesha? Wait, is she all right? Is something wrong? Does she need my help?"

"See, that's the way you talk to a friend, Ed," she told him. "Not just a grumpy text demanding to know where I am."

"I'll remember that for next time," Ed replied dryly. "She's giving me lip, so it seems she's just fine."

"I want my phone back. You shouldn't be on it. We're going to have words about this."

"Give him hell, Georgie!" Kiesha said. She shifted the phone to speaker so she could set it down and brush her teeth. She listened to Ed and Georgie talking as she brushed her teeth then washed her face.

Finally, they remembered she was on the line.

"Kiesha?" Georgie asked.

"Yeah my saintly sister?"

"Why is she saintly?" Ed asked.

"Because she puts up with you, of course."

Wait, didn't she have a spare hair tie in her handbag? Picking up her phone, she moved into the bedroom and grabbed her handbag, searching through it.

Why weren't hair ties easier to find? She ended up tipping the handbag over the bed then searching through it. Mints, a few suckers. Yum, she really needed one of those. Opening a red one, she popped it into her mouth as she kept searching. The remains of three broken pens, some smiley face stickers for when people earned them. Because did anything make you feel as good as earning a smiley face sticker? Bedazzled Taser that she'd bought after being kidnapped that time with Georgie and Mari. She really needed to find the charger for that. Her wallet, a mirror, neon pink lipstick. Ooh, that one was her favorite shade. She took out the sucker and put some on. And a hair tie! Uh-huh.

She moved back into the bathroom.

"Kiesha! Kiesha? Are you listening?" Ed boomed from the phone's speaker.

Oh right. She'd actually forgotten that she was on the phone with Ed and Georgie.

"Of course, I'm listening," she bluffed. "What else would I be doing?" She tied her hair up in a messy bun. There, at least it was off her face. And her lipstick was on-point. She stuck the sucker back in her mouth.

Shower time.

"Well, are you going to answer me?" Ed snapped.

"Not if you're going to talk to me like that," she replied. "Sheesh. What twisted your boxers into a bunch this morning?"

A strange sound came from her phone.

"Are you okay? Is it your anal bleeding?"

"Kiesha, I do not have anal bleeding. And you're going to tell everyone that, too."

"You want me to go around telling people you don't have anal bleeding . . . kind of weird, but okay."

"No, I just," he sighed.

Oh crap. Too far. She closed her eyes. "I'm sorry, Ed."

"What?" he asked, shocked.

"Sorry. I just . . . teasing you is normal and feels safe and I'm still a bit out of sorts after last night."

And she wasn't just talking about the brawl.

"So, I'm sorry. The others all know I was joking. I promise, no more mention of anal bleeding, okay?"

The last thing she wanted was to push Ed away. Out of everyone, he was really her family. Her brother in all the ways that counted.

"I really do love you, you know."

"Where are you?" There was an urgent note in his voice, rather than the bossy, exasperated tone from before.

"Why? What's wrong?"

"Ed, what is it?" Georgie asked in the background. Obviously, Ed hadn't put her on speaker.

"What's wrong? You just told me you were sorry, and that you loved me. I want to know where you are right now. I'm coming to you. There's obviously something wrong."

She rolled her eyes at his craziness. Then moving to the shower, she turned it on. "There's nothing wrong. I'm fine. I can't tell you that I love you without you freaking out?"

"No, you can't!"

"Jeez, you're crazy, Teddy-Eddy. I've got to go. I need a shower. I'm fine."

"Then why won't you tell me where you are?"

Great. He'd picked up that she was trying not to answer him. She'd hoped that she'd gotten away with it.

"I'm at the motel."

"What? Why?"

"Because that's where Harry's staying."

There was a beat of silence. "You're really staying with Harry?"

"She's what?" Georgie asked. "Oh my God! Get off my phone so I can text the others. Kiesha, you stayed with Harry? He's so hot."

"He's what?" Ed snapped.

"Not hotter than you, obviously," Georgie soothed.

That girl was going to find herself with a hot ass if she wasn't careful.

Ed said something quietly that she couldn't make out.

"All right, I'm gonna go now!" Georgie said. "Kiesha, call me later. I'm here if you need anything."

"Thanks, Georgie! Bye!"

"You really stayed the night with Harry, Kiesha?" Ed asked.

"You got a problem with that?"

"I don't know," Ed grumbled. "I mean, Harry seems like a good guy..."

"But?" she prompted, knowing there was going to be one.

"I don't think anyone is good enough for you."

"Ed, no mushy stuff."

"How long have you two had something going on?"

"I dunno, eight hours or something."

"Eight hours?"

She sighed. "Yes, look, I've gotta go before all the hot water is gone."

"I want to talk to you about last night. Are you all right this morning? Are you feeling okay?"

"I'm fine. Just a small cut on my arm. Haven't you already talked to Xavier?"

"Yes, but I just wanted to check in."

"You were worried about me?"

"When don't I worry about you?" he asked, sounding tired. Poor Ed. He'd had a big night and he was old.

"You don't need to worry about me. I'm a big girl, I can take care of myself." She crossed her fingers behind her back as she said that, even though he couldn't see her.

"I'll still worry about you when you're eighty and using a walking stick."

"Dude, you're hopeful of a long life if you still think you'll be alive then."

"Brat. Are you sure there's nothing I need to know?

"Nope. Nothing. Got to get in the shower, bye."

Sheesh, talk about suspicious. Just what did he think was going on?

Whatever he thought it was, he was probably nowhere near the truth.

After stripping off, she climbed into the shower with a sigh, letting the hot water work into her tense muscles.

19

Harry whistled as he walked into the motel suite. When was the last time he'd whistled? Had it really been that long since he was happy?

When he entered the bedroom, his stomach dropped.

She'd left?

He didn't think she would just leave like this.

Then the sound of running water registered.

She was in the shower?

Relief made his legs weaken even as he frowned. He'd distinctly told her to rest.

Yep, it was going to be interesting getting her to listen to him.

After setting out breakfast on the small table in the living area, he heard the water shut off. Then someone moving around in the bedroom. He knocked on the door and winced as she shrieked.

"Sorry, Little Monster, didn't mean to scare you. Was just letting you know I'm here. I have breakfast."

"I'm getting dressed."

He frowned. "I don't want you using your arm."

"I'm being careful."

He shook his head in exasperation.

Standing by the table, he crossed his arms over his chest and waited for her to walk out. When she did, he had a hard time controlling his body from reacting.

Damn it. He wasn't a teenager anymore. He shouldn't get hard-ons at just the sight of his woman wearing his shirt.

But his dick was hard and throbbing, pressing painfully against his pants. He cleared his throat, taking in her legs. The shirt ended mid-thigh and she'd rolled up the sleeves.

To hell with lingerie.

Kiesha in a dress shirt was all he needed to reach boiling point.

Although he wouldn't mind seeing her in lingerie either. Maybe red or emerald. Lacy cups for her breasts, then something that billowed out.

Okay. Stop.

"Are you all right, Harry? Are you upset that I stole one of your shirts? I'll wash it. I won't even put it in the dryer."

"I don't care what you do with it, as long as you promise to wear it like this for me again."

She looked startled then she gave him a wicked smile. "You like?"

"Baby, I more than like," he murmured back huskily. "If I liked that sight anymore, I might just embarrass myself." He adjusted himself while giving her a rueful look.

She turned shy. Her gaze lowered.

That intrigued him. He wasn't sure he'd ever seen her shy. Moving forward, he reached out slowly and cupped her chin, tilting her face back.

Was she not used to this? To someone finding her so damn irresistible?

"Hello there, beautiful girl."

She bit her lip and he rescued it from between her teeth. "Harry, I'm not beautiful."

"Hush," he told her firmly. "You are beautiful. And what did I say about chewing on that lip?"

"That it's yours. And I wasn't to hurt it since you claimed it."

"That's right." He ran his thumb over her lower lip. "I don't want you to hurt yourself." Bending, he kissed her. She reached up and wrapped her arms around his neck as he deepened the kiss, tasting her, playing with her.

"You taste like sugar," he murmured as he drew back.

"Oh, ah, yeah, I might have found a sucker in my handbag."

"Is that so?" He gave her a stern look. "We need to make a rule, no sugar before breakfast."

"I told you that I don't like rules."

"You need them, though." He reached around and patted her ass. "And you'll soon learn to follow them, unless you're fond of sitting on a sore ass."

She rolled her eyes at him, some of her sass returning. "Rules, schmules."

"Naughty girl, hot bottom."

"Hey, that doesn't rhyme."

"Some of us just aren't as good at rhyming as you."

She sighed. "That's true. Don't worry, Harry. One day you'll be as good as me."

"I can only aspire to be."

"Is breakfast ready?"

"Yes. Sit. Eat. We'll talk after about your inability to follow an order."

"What?" she asked as he led her over to the table and pulled out her chair. "Harry, you don't have to be so fancy. I'm just me. Plain, simple, boring old Kiesha."

"There is definitely nothing plain, boring, or simple about you. And if you're old then I'm ancient. And I like doing things for you. Like pulling out your chair, opening doors, buying you breakfast. So, get used to it, please."

"I'm guessing you think adding please will make me more agreeable to being bossed around," she said, sitting down.

"Doesn't it?"

"Nope. Well, perhaps a bit."

Kiesha sat and let Harry push her in. Why was she so nervous around him? Her tummy was filled with butterflies. She hadn't felt like this around a man since Jonah, and even with him her nerves hadn't been this bad.

Chill, dude.

Placing his hands on her shoulders, he leaned down and kissed the spot where her neck and shoulder met. "Just claiming another part of you."

A shiver of arousal raced through her and she pressed her thighs together.

Dear. Lord.

He was so potent. He moved away from her to sit in his own seat and she just sat there, barely able to breathe.

"Kiesha? You all right?"

"Uh-huh."

"Can you use your words?"

"Nuh-uh."

He cupped the side of her face with his hand, turning her toward him. "Try for me, please."

There was a firmness to his voice that cut through her arousal.

Yikes. How embarrassing.

Get it together, Kiesha!

"Sorry, what?"

"You're back with me? You seemed to zone out."

"Sorry, I, uh, yeah. You have that effect on me."

He gave her a pleased look, which made her feel better for just blurting that out like that.

Sheesh, girl.
You've got problems.

One simple touch and she was ready to go up in flames.

"Just answer one question for me, please," he said in a very polite voice as he dished out some food onto a plate for her. He'd already laid out the plates and cutlery.

"Actually, would you like me to heat this for you?"

"That was your question?"

"What? Uh, no. It wasn't. But would you?"

"Nah, I don't like eating my food too hot. Sensitive mouth."

"I'll remember that." And he looked so serious as he said it that she knew he would. She had the feeling that she was going to enjoy being Harry's. Even if it didn't last, while she was with him she could tell that she'd be his focus. That he'd pay attention to her.

"Kiesha? Are you all right? Is something not to your liking?"

"Well, I'm not sure what this is." She poked at something on her plate.

"Um, it's cantaloupe."

"Is it supposed to be that color?"

His eyes widened slightly. "You've never had cantaloupe?"

She had to grin. "Course I have. Got you."

He just shook his head at her. "You sure did, my baby."

She ducked her head, pretending to cut up her French toast, wanting to hide the pleased look on her face.

My baby.

She loved being called that. Almost as much as being called Little Monster.

It made her feel special, cared for. Noticed.

"Do you not like me calling you my baby?" Harry asked suddenly.

"What? No, I like it." She glanced up at him. "I like it a lot."

"Good." Reaching over, he gently took hold of her knife and

fork and started cutting up her French toast. Did he want to try some? But then why was he cutting it into small pieces?

It looked amazing and her mouth was watering as she waited for him to give her back her cutlery. He'd put some other stuff on her plate, more fruit and a small cup of yogurt, but she wasn't interested in that.

Then he forked up a piece and held it up to her mouth. "Open."

"I don't need you to feed me."

"Just indulge me, Little Monster."

"But your food will get cold."

"I'll eat it in a minute. I like feeding you. I like the idea of taking care of all of your needs."

"Hmm, some more than others, I'm hoping," she grumbled.

He grinned at her. "Is someone getting frustrated?"

"Someone is. Someone's boobs are greedy, remember?"

"They'll just have to wait. Open."

She opened her mouth obediently and he popped the French toast into her mouth. She groaned with delight. "So good."

"Good girl. Eat the rest. I want that plate cleared."

Her eyebrows rose. "All of this? I don't think I can do it all."

"Do what you can then. Be a good girl for Daddy."

He eyed her as he said that. She sucked in a sharp breath, pleasure filling her at those words.

She picked up another bit of French toast and shoved it in her mouth before she started begging him to take her to bed.

What was wrong with her? She hadn't been this turned on in . . . in forever.

Harry put his food into a bowl. Muesli and yogurt. Yuck. He also had a coffee. Her chocolate milk was in a cup with a straw. She reached for it with her injured arm, frowning slightly at the pain.

"Hey, if you need something just ask." He grabbed the cup and held the straw to her mouth. She stared at him as she sucked. His eyes heated as he stared down at her lips.

And yeah . . . she wondered what it would be like to take something else into her mouth. She loved giving blow jobs and it had been so damn long. She squirmed in her seat.

Easy. Chill.

Was everything sexual right now? What was wrong with her? She had sex on the brain for sure.

He set the drink down then started eating.

"What was your question?" she asked after a minute.

"I think I better wait to ask until after you've eaten." He gave her plate of food a pointed look.

"That bad?"

"What? No, not bad at all. Just distracting." He ran his gaze over her. "See, I was just wondering if you have anything on under that shirt."

"Oh." She squirmed and he reached over to place his hand on her leg, right under the edge of the shirt. His fingers moved lightly up and down her inner thigh. "N-no."

"No? No, you don't have anything on under this shirt?"

"No."

"No panties, no bra?" His fingers moved further up her inner thigh.

"No."

"That's just become my favorite shirt."

"That's a shame because I'm pretty sure it's just become my shirt."

"Oh, you're stealing my clothes now?" he asked.

She nodded her head. "That a problem?"

"Nope, baby girl. Part your legs."

"Oh, Lord. Harry."

"Do as you were told," he said firmly. "Part your legs or I'll stop. And I don't think you want me to stop, do you?"

She shook her head. Nope. She didn't want him to stop.

"Words, please."

It was crazy how he could sound so polite yet be so in charge and dominant at the same time.

"I don't want you to stop." She slid her legs slightly apart.

"Good girl. I like to be in control in the bedroom, that a problem?"

"N-no. Although I think you like it all the time."

"You could be right."

"I'm not always very obedient."

"Oh, I know that. All that means is that you'll spend time sitting on a hot ass. Do you have an issue with that?"

"Spankings?"

He nodded.

"No."

"Good. I know you like to push boundaries. But you also like to please, don't you, Little Monster? You like to make other people happy."

"Well, I don't think I make all that many people happy."

"Don't you? I think you'd be surprised."

She gasped out as he moved his fingers further up her thigh.

Oh, Lord.

Was he going to touch her pussy?

And here she thought he'd move slowly. That was the vibe he'd been giving off anyway.

"You're not eating, Little Monster."

"I can't concentrate on eating right now." All she could focus on was the feel of his fingers on her upper thighs, so close to her pussy.

Dear. Lord.

"You're going to, though," he told her firmly, his fingers stopping. "Because I'm not moving until you eat."

She groaned. That was so not cool.

But when she glared at him, he stared calmly back at her. Then he spooned up some more muesli, his hand still on her thigh.

Grr. Fine.

She picked up her fork and ate a piece of French toast. "I'm eating. I'm eating."

"So eager. Do you want me to touch you?"

"Oh yes. Please."

"I like when you tell me what you like, what you want. I always want to hear what you're thinking."

"I don't usually have a problem letting people know what I'm thinking."

"Is that so?" he murmured. "So, what do you want?"

"For you to touch me. Please, please, touch me."

"Where?" he asked. "And remember to keep eating please."

She forked up some more of the French toast.

Damn, it really was delicious.

Reaching over, he grabbed her drink with his free hand and held it up to her mouth. "Drink."

She gulped some chocolate milk down.

"That's my good girl. Now, this is what I want you to do. I want you to wrap your feet around the legs of the chair and spread your legs nice and wide, can you do that for me?"

"Yes." She moved her feet into position, her legs spread apart as far as she could get them to go.

"Now, I'm going to feed you and if you're a good girl and eat what I give you, then you get a reward. If you're naughty, then there's no reward for you. Ready?"

"Yes." Maybe. Not really. Lord, she really wasn't certain. Could she ever be ready?

"I want you to close your eyes."

He was killing her. What was even happening?

"Am I going too fast? I can slow down. This was meant to be just breakfast." He shook his head, looking rueful. "It's just the sight of you in my shirt made my blood heat. Fuck, I'm definitely going too fast."

He drew back and she reached out to latch onto his wrist. "No! No, no, no, no, no."

He raised his eyebrows, looking amused. "Is that a no from you?"

"It's definitely a no from me. Please don't stop. You can't leave me like this."

"Poor baby, are you in pain?" he asked with mock-sympathy.

"Uh-huh, so much pain."

"Do you need me to help you?"

"Yes."

"Are you going to ask nicely?"

"Yep. I can ask nicely. Please, please, Harry, will you touch me? Play with me? I need you. So badly."

"All right." He placed his hand back on her thigh, under her shirt then reached out with his other hand to pick up her fork. "Eyes closed."

She closed her eyes immediately. Her insides were humming with excitement. She was already so wet it was kind of embarrassing and she hoped she wasn't leaving a wet patch on the chair.

Yikes.

"Open your mouth."

She opened her mouth, then her nose wrinkled in distaste as something wet and cool was placed on her tongue.

"Eat it and Daddy will give you your reward."

She chewed with a grimace. "Ew, Daddy. What was that?"

"Cantaloupe. You don't like it?"

"It's healthy," was all she said.

"Something being healthy isn't a good enough reason to dislike it."

"Seems like a good enough reason to me," she countered.

"Well, you ate it and that means you get a reward."

Her breath came in faster pants as he moved his fingers up her thigh, closer and closer to her pussy.

"Damn, I think I can smell you."

She stiffened. That couldn't possibly be a good thing, right?

"Shh, stop worrying. You smell delicious. You're going to taste delicious. There isn't a single thing about you that I don't desire, Kiesha."

"Just wait. I'm sure you'll find one."

He smacked his hand down lightly on her thigh. "Would you rather turn your reward into a punishment?"

"Nuh-uh, nope, no way. I earned my reward." She opened her eyes and glared at him.

"You did. But then you were naughty. Talking badly about yourself. Opening your eyes when you were told not to." He removed his hand. "That means I have to stop."

"Nooo," she cried. "Can't you just spank me or something instead?"

"Nope. We have to start again. Close your eyes."

Darn. This sucked.

But she quickly closed her eyes and opened her mouth, sticking her tongue out. She heard him chuckle, then something else was placed in her mouth. This time she knew what it was straight away.

Yogurt.

"Urgh, that's unsweetened. That's just criminal. Yogurt needs sugar to taste good."

"Some sweet yogurts are as bad as ice cream."

"Yum, ice cream. Now that's a decent breakfast food."

"We need to improve your diet."

"Why? I really don't think it can be improved. It's at optimum sugar performance."

"It's at optimum performance for giving you cavities and shortening your life. Now, you were a good girl, so we can start again."

His hand rested just above her knee then moved slowly up. But it didn't reach her pussy before he stopped and she whimpered in frustration.

"Higher, please," she begged.

"Not yet, we had to go back to the beginning, remember? Now, you're going to have to be a good girl and take what I give you. Open your mouth."

"Dear Lord, I know you're talking about giving me food but I so wish it was something else."

"And what were you hoping for? Chocolate milk?"

"No, dick," she said bluntly. "I really want your dick."

There was a strangled noise and a burst of laughter. "Just when I think I know what you're going to say or do you surprise me."

Damn, she wished she could open her eyes and look at him. "Is that a good thing or a bad thing?"

"Hey," he said quietly, cupping her face. "Open your eyes."

She opened her eyes slowly, staring into his face. A face filled with acceptance, understanding, and affection. The tension in her melted away.

"You seem to think that you're going to push me away, and that's okay. Because my job is to prove to you that I'm not going anywhere. I'm here for good, Kiesha."

"I've heard that before." Shoot. She hadn't meant to say that. She bit her lip and he reached up to free it, giving her a stern look.

"I'll keep that lip busy if you keep biting it."

"Please. I'd like that. You can keep them busy anytime."

He grinned at her. "So eager for my kisses?"

"Is it that obvious?"

"Just slightly," he deadpanned. "And maybe I can't promise that I won't leave you. I could walk out the door and get run over tomorrow. But I won't willingly leave you, Kiesha. There's something I've only recently understood."

"What's that?"

"That I only get one life. I've wasted so much of it and I don't intend to waste any more. I intend to live every second of it the way I want to, in a way that makes me happy. And being with you makes me happy."

Damn. He was good.

She stared up at him, studying him.

"You keep surprising me, keep me wondering, and you bring me joy."

"Like a Christmas tree?" she asked.

"It's been a long time since I had a Christmas tree."

"Is that a euphemism for something or do you really mean it's a long time since you had a Christmas tree?"

"Both, actually. I think the last time I bothered with a Christmas tree was when Marisol lived with me."

She gasped, horrified. "Harry, that's terrible. No Christmas tree? That's practically criminal."

"You're quite right, I deserve to be punished. But perhaps this will be the year I have one."

She shook her head with pity. "Poor Daddy, I'll show you everything you've been missing."

Happiness filled his face and she ducked her head shyly as she realized what she'd called him.

"You think you could see me as your Daddy?"

Be brave, Kiesha.

She looked back up into his gorgeous face, so full of hope and while she knew that the safe thing would be to push him away . . . she couldn't do it. She didn't want to.

Because he was right. Tomorrow could be gone, but they had today.

"I could see you as my everything, Harry. And it's honestly

terrifying. It's scary because you don't really know me. Not all of me. And what if you don't like me when you do?"

His kind gaze didn't change. He didn't grow mad as she told him her fears. Didn't insist that everything was going to be fine.

"Then that's my goal. To get to know you better. For you to know me. And for me to show you that I want all of you."

"Okay," she whispered.

He brushed the strands of hair back off her forehead. "All you have to do is know that you're mine and I'm yours."

"You really are the sweetest, Harry."

"For you, I'm sweet." He leaned back. "Do you want to keep playing or are you ready to go back to bed for a nap?"

"What? No! No, nap!"

"Then you best be a good girl and close your eyes and open your mouth."

20

She immediately complied and he rested his hand on her thigh, moving his fingers in light circles.

Trickles of arousal swam through her blood as something crisp and tart landed on her tongue. Apple. Seemed he was determined to get some healthy stuff into her.

Apples were all right. She swallowed and waited for his fingers to move up her thighs. He circled higher and higher until his fingertips just brushed over her lips.

"That's my good girl. Open your mouth again. I have a drink of water for you."

Urgh. Water. But she drank it without complaint.

"That's it. Open."

A piece of orange. She practically inhaled the bit of fruit, knowing he had to touch her pussy now.

And he didn't disappoint, his finger ran along her slick slit, just pressing between her lips, barely brushing past her clit.

"Harry!"

"You're so wet, my baby. You need to come, don't you?"

"Y-yes."

"Hmm, should I let you, though? You weren't a very good girl, were you?"

"Yes, I was!" She ate all the fruit, what was he talking about?

"Really? Are you sure about that? Because I distinctly remember telling you to stay in bed, but I came back here to find you in the shower."

Drat. He had her there. Damn him.

"I needed to pee and then I thought I'd have a shower and brush my teeth. I didn't want stinky breath. That's never cool."

"I expected you to wait for me to return. Next time, I'll be very careful in the way I word orders. Luckily, you've been a good girl and eaten your fruit and breakfast and for that I did promise a reward."

She breathed out a sigh of relief.

"But you need to eat a little more," he decided.

She groaned, but obediently opened her mouth. This time she got a strawberry. Yum. Now, strawberries were something she could eat all the time.

"More?" she said hopefully.

"You like strawberries?"

"Uh-huh. They're delicious."

"All right. Open."

Another strawberry landed on her tongue and she ate it happily, moaning as Harry pressed a finger deeper into her lower lips, running it up and down her slit then circling her clit.

"Harry!"

"I bet you taste even better than that strawberry," he murmured. "Open your mouth."

She parted her lips and his finger moved from her pussy. Then he pressed it into her mouth. "Suck."

She hummed. The taste wasn't that interesting to her, but the whole gesture made her hot.

"Good girl, clean me up. Now, I'm going to turn the chair around."

She gasped as he spun her chair.

"Move your bottom to the edge of the chair."

"Are you going to claim something else?" she asked him, excited about the thought of his mouth on her pussy.

"Give me your right hand."

She held out her hand, frowning slightly and wishing she could see him. Maybe she could crack her eyes open just slightly.

But he might catch her and the last thing she wanted was for him to stop.

He pushed her hand carefully down to her pussy.

"If you don't like anything we do just say 'red' and it stops immediately, all right?"

Did she trust him to stop?

She wouldn't be here if she didn't.

"All right," she agreed.

"I want you to push your fingers deep inside yourself," he told her. "Coat yourself in your juices then hold them up so I can see them."

Oh crap.

Yep, she'd never imagined doing this. She could feel herself heating up with a mix of embarrassment and need. But she moved her fingers to her opening, pushing two up inside her. She groaned as she drew them slowly out, holding them up.

"Good girl. Well done, you're doing so well. I'm so very pleased with you right now."

Well, fuck.

Was he trying to make her come just from his words alone? Because he was doing a damn good job.

"Open your eyes and look at me," he commanded.

She watched, her breath trapped in her lungs as he grasped

hold of her hand and drew it toward his mouth. Then he took her fingers into his mouth and sucked.

A whimper escaped her as she felt her body buzz.

So hot. His beard tickled at her hand, making her wonder what it would feel like on the sensitive skin of her inner thighs.

"Baby, you taste better than delicious," he murmured to her. Then he kissed each of her fingers. "Mine."

Yes. His.

That was what she wanted. For all of her to be his.

With his eyes staring into hers, he ran his hands lightly up her thighs to her pussy, cupping it.

"Please," she whispered.

"Do you need to come, my baby?"

"Yes, yes, please."

"How badly?"

"So damn badly. It's been so long."

"So long? Since you've come? Didn't you use that vibrator I saw in your bathroom?"

"Oh my God!" she cried. "You did see it!"

"Hard to miss it when it was lying right there."

"That's it, I'm going to die from embarrassment." She covered her face with her hands and he chuckled.

"No need for that, Little Monster. I thought it was cute. You're also going to use it one day while I watch."

She pulled two fingers apart and peered out at him with her right eye. "Really?"

"Really. I can't wait. You'll look so hot when you come." Reaching up, he tugged her hands away from her face. "Now, keep your arms down. I'm going to play. And I still have to give you your reward."

He started undoing the buttons of her shirt.

"Harry," she said hesitantly as he parted the shirt, staring down at her.

"Hush, baby," he told her gently. "I'm having some play time. And I'm not stopping unless you say your safeword. What is it?"

"Oh, uh, I'll just go with red."

"Good. If I hear any nonsense out of your mouth that is derogatory about your beautiful body, I'm going to turn you over my knee and not let you come."

"You wouldn't!"

"Baby, I don't make threats I don't mean."

Fuck. There was no way she wanted him to stop. So, she sat still and uncomplaining as he studied her. His big hand cupped her breast. His hand was warm and firm and she whimpered as he twisted her nipple lightly.

"Beautiful. You are so damn gorgeous. I could stare at you all day. Maybe I'll do that soon. Have you spend the entire day naked, bare to my gaze, available for my touch whenever I desire you."

Holy crap.

Yes, let's do that. Right now! No, wait. I'm not quite ready for that. Am I?

Her body was. Her mind wanted a minute to catch up.

"But not now," he said soothingly, almost as though he could read her mind. It was a bit scary the way he did that. She'd always thought she had a good poker face.

He ran his thumb over her stiff nipple and she gasped, trying to push her chest out. She grabbed hold of his wrist with her hand as he went to move away.

"Uh-uh, hands down," he warned. "I won't tell you again."

Shoot. She dropped her hand, keeping both at her sides, watching as he moved his hand to her other nipple, playing with it before cupping her breast.

She wished he'd lower his mouth and claim her. He ran his hand down her stomach. She tried to suck it in. This wasn't a good angle. But he must have felt her move, because he lightly slapped the side of her thigh.

"Stop."

"What?" she asked.

"Stop sucking your stomach in. You don't need to be anything other than what you are. Don't you know how hot I think you are?"

Reaching down, he adjusted himself with a rueful grin.

"I could help with that, you know." She waggled her eyebrows in what she thought was a sexy move. It likely wasn't. Especially since rather than falling all over her offer, he just grinned.

"Soon," he promised.

She groaned. Why soon? Why wait? Why couldn't she just get down on her knees, open his pants and take him into her mouth like she wanted?

Waiting was so hard sometimes.

"I love how much you want to touch me," he told her with a hint of awe in his voice.

Jeez, surely he knew how hot he was.

Unless he didn't? Huh, she hadn't thought of that. Maybe she could show Harry how delicious he was.

"No sucking your tummy in or trying to hide from me. You need reassurance, you're feeling down or bad about yourself, you come find me and I'll tell you the truth. That you're a gorgeous, beautiful goddess."

Yikes.

How had she lived this long without someone talking like this to her?

She had no idea.

But everyone needed a Harry. Only, they'd have to find their own one. Because this one belonged to her.

Suddenly, he moved onto his knees between her legs.

"You have no idea how I want to take you into that bedroom and fuck you."

"Do it. Just do it. Life is short, right?"

"Soon."

"Harry!" she groaned. "Waiting sucks."

"I know," he reassured her. "Hush now, though. I'm playing." He moved a hand up to her mouth. "Open."

Two fingers entered her mouth, probably to keep her from complaining anymore. Smart.

His other hand moved between her legs, and he ran one finger along her slick lips.

"So wet. So hot," he told her, pressing two fingers deep inside her while his other fingers slid into her mouth. In and out, they moved at the same time, making her groan. She ran her tongue around the digits in her mouth, sucking on them until she heard him groan.

And then his thumb touched her clit. Her breath caught in the back of her throat. Waves of need crashed through her. More. She needed more.

"Oh baby, you need this so badly. I can tell. Hush, it's all right. You're okay. I'm right here. I won't let you go."

She hadn't realized that she was whimpering. Her body shook. She sucked on his fingers like they were her anchor, something to cling to in the storm.

"Come, my baby. I can feel how much you need to. Come around my fingers. Let go."

She had no idea that an orgasm could be this good. It beat anything she'd given herself in the last few years. Likely anything Jonah had given her as well. She screamed, pulsing around the fingers in her pussy, her body shaking.

He slid his fingers from her mouth and she let out a protesting cry. But he moved closer, replacing his fingers with his mouth. She fell into the kiss gratefully as he slid his fingers from her pussy.

Drawing back from her, he stared down at her with satisfaction then pressed his fingers that were damp with her dew to her lips. She opened her mouth.

"Clean me up. That's my good baby." He let out a deep shuddering breath as she moved her tongue around his fingers, then sucked them strongly.

"Fuck, yes."

Sliding his fingers from her mouth, he gathered her against him. She rested her face between his shoulder and neck, feeling the energy draining out of her. But unlike last night, this was a good sort of tired. The kind where your mind was blank, your body sated.

"Thank you. Thank you for giving that to me. For trusting me with your pleasure." He wrapped his hand around the back of her neck then drew back to kiss along her cheek to her ear then down her neck. "My precious girl. Come on, time for a nap."

She made a protesting noise, even though she didn't really mean it. Because she really felt like a nap. But she didn't want him thinking that this was going to be a regular occurrence. She had a lot more interesting things to do than nap.

Lifting her up into his arms, he carried her into the bedroom and laid her in the bed. Then he climbed in with her, wrapping her up in his arms.

She sighed happily. If all naps were like this, then she'd consider taking one more often.

"After your nap we'll head to your place," he told her.

Ah, drat. She knew that the bubble had to burst at some time.

This wasn't going to be fun.

21

This definitely wasn't fun.

Harry turned to look at her. They were sitting in his car outside her grandpa's old cabin. He'd driven them slowly up the rutted path to get to the cabin. It couldn't even be called a driveway. She'd tried several times to convince him to let her come on her own.

But he'd just given her a look like she was crazy.

And so, here they were. She was burning hot with embarrassment and worry over his reaction. He stared at her in disbelief.

"This is where you've been living?"

"Yep, pretty surroundings, right?"

"The property is beautiful. But that building is not habitable."

"Oh, it's not so bad once you're in it. Why don't you wait here and I'll just go and get changed?" He wanted to take her out for an early dinner.

Their first date.

Was it weird that he'd fingered her to orgasm, and that she'd slept in the same bed as him before they'd even gone on a date?

Maybe a bit.

"Stay right where you are," he commanded.

Well, drat.

"You don't leave the car without me opening the door for you," he told her.

"What? Really?"

"Yes, really." His face was serious, voice firm.

That seemed like an old sort of rule.

"What 'if we've fallen into a lake and we need to get out quickly?"

He eyed her for a moment then shook his head. "Fine, in an emergency situation, then you can get out yourself. Under all other circumstances, you're to wait for me, understood?"

"Huh, what about—"

"Little Monster, stop trying to procrastinate. You know the rule now. I expect you to follow it."

"Or what?" she challenged.

"Or you'll be in trouble," he replied. "And depending on what rule you broke will determine your punishment. For instance, getting out of the car without my help, that would result in you getting some lines or a couple of pops on the ass. Something more serious and you wouldn't be sitting comfortably. You understand?"

"Loud and clear."

"Is there anything that is a hard no?"

She licked her lips. "Wasn't exactly expecting to have this conversation right now."

"If you're not ready, we can postpone this conversation and come back to it later."

"I . . . I've just never had a relationship like this, so I'm not exactly sure what I want or don't want. I was with my boyfriend, Jonah, for years. But he wasn't a Dom. We were friends and it developed into something more. We moved away from Wishingbone, thinking we could make a better life for ourselves. That didn't work out so well, especially after he got sick."

"Oh, baby."

"It was cancer and it was bad. He fought for six months but it was too far gone by the time we found it. Jonah treated me like a queen. He was a really good man. And when he died, I didn't want to keep going. A friend of Jonah's moved me in with him to watch over me. But I was stifled there. Cared for, given everything I wanted but not able to breathe. I told him I had to leave and I called Ed. He drove up and got me."

"Baby, I'm so sorry."

"Me too. Jonah deserved a long and happy life." She sighed. "I'm not sure exactly what my limits are, but I do know that I wouldn't like to be ignored or humiliated. Don't stop talking to me or walk away from me. If I do something wrong, tell me."

"Communication is always important. We'll work out your other limits together. And the rules. Just be honest with me if you're feeling upset or uncertain of something. Okay?"

"All right, I'll try."

How did her life get so messy? Would being with her put him in danger? It shouldn't. Vance didn't care about her beyond using her.

She took a deep breath, then let it out slowly.

Reaching over, Harry squeezed her hand with his. He'd insisted she take some painkillers before they left, so her arm was feeling pretty good. But she was starting to develop a low-grade headache.

"You're going to insist on coming inside with me, aren't you?"

"Yes, I am. I don't even want you stepping foot in that place. Are you certain it's safe?"

No, she wasn't certain of that at all.

She bit her lip.

With a sigh, he reached up and freed her lower lip. "Kiesha, just tell me what's going on. Why are you living here? It's not safe. And I'm not just talking about the fact that this building looks like a stiff wind would topple it. You're in the middle of nowhere. You don't drive. What if something happened? What if you hurt yourself? How are you getting to work each day? Do taxis come out here?"

"Ah, no, they don't."

"A friend has been picking you up?"

She squirmed on the seat. "Noooo."

He closed his eyes, looking like he was in pain. "Dear Lord, I'm not going to like your answer, am I?"

"Likely not." She gave him a bright smile. "You look like you need some candy. I've got some in my handbag." She rustled around and found some suckers. "Grape or strawberry?"

He shook his head and took them both.

"Hey! One of them is for me."

"You get a sucker after you give me straight answers, Little Monster."

Oh man. There was his Dom voice.

"I've been roller skating to work. I obviously walk down the driveway since you can't skate on it. Then I skate the rest of the way."

"The rest of the way? How long does that take you?"

"A while," she muttered. "I've only done it for two days. I moved in here Wednesday night." She'd had to move her stuff over several days to get it here. She'd borrowed a trolley that Mr. Clearly had in his garage and had covered her stuff with a tarp. She'd even come up with a story about cleaning up her grandpa's place in case anyone saw her.

To her surprise, they hadn't.

"And that makes it better?"

"I dunno. Maybe?"

"Does Ed know this?"

"No, not yet. I mean, it's probably only a matter of time until someone tells him. Likely that tattle-telling rat, Jonny Jacks." She pumped her fist through the air at the thought of that jerk. "He's always tattling on me."

"Okay, let's go back to why you moved out here. Why aren't you in your apartment?"

"Rats."

"What?"

"Well, one rat anyway. Dennis the dick evicted me."

It felt like all the air was sucked out of the car as he stiffened. "He evicted you?"

"Yes, the asshole claimed that there was a flea infestation. Then he said it was mites or rodents, I can't remember. It was all bullshit, of course. He also said that there had been complaints about my music being too loud. He probably made that up or threatened my neighbors to get them to complain. Although Mrs. Long across the hall has never liked me. I'm pretty sure she has a voodoo doll of me. Every so often something pricks me and I'm certain it's her. Hey, maybe I should get a voodoo doll of Dennis. But then I'd have to touch something that looked like Dennis. And that's just ew."

"That fucking bastard," Harry said, looking enraged. "I can't believe he evicted you."

"I'm just surprised he didn't do it earlier. He's still mad because I wouldn't suck his twinkie."

"What?"

"You know, give him a blow job. I was late on my rent once and he offered . . . you know what? Never mind," she said hastily as his face started to grow purple.

"That. Asshole. Is. Dead."

"Damn, Harry. You're sexy when you're angry."

He turned those raging eyes to her. "Why didn't you tell me immediately?"

She held her hands up. "Now why would I do that?"

"Because I could help you, Kiesha."

"I'm fine. I don't need help."

"You're living in the middle of nowhere without a car, in a shack that looks like it's about to fall down! And I'm guessing no one else knows, since no one would allow you to live here."

"Nobody allows me to do anything. I do what I like."

"Not anymore, my baby."

22

Well, that was just rude.

She turned to glare at Harry. But he met her gaze with his own firm one.

"I mean it," he told her.

"I can take care of myself, Harry. I'm a big girl. Just because I like monsters and suckers and roller skating doesn't mean I'm not an adult who takes responsibility for herself."

"That doesn't mean you have to do everything for yourself. Like deal with asshole building managers. Do you think he did this because I made him fix your door?"

She tried to hide her wince but he must have caught it because his face grew red.

"Oh, he's going to pay for this."

"Dennis is a dick, but there's not anything we can do about it."

He eyed her with interest. "And why would you say that? For that matter, why did you let him get away with that shit? Why not tell someone? Ed, for instance."

Drat. What to tell him?

"And you best tell me the truth, or you're going to find yourself bent over the closest tree stump, getting your bare butt walloped."

"That's not very nice."

"Why didn't you tell anyone?"

She sighed. "Because he said that if I did he'd make life difficult for Ed. He's coming up for re-election and as much as I like to tease him otherwise, he's a really good sheriff and I don't want to do anything to jeopardize his campaign."

"How could Dennis do anything to hurt Ed's job?"

"He said stuff about his uncle getting involved. I know he's some rich dude who lives in New York."

"Hmm, might need to do some research into that." He was silent for a moment, staring out at her grandpa's place with narrowed eyes. "Leave this to me, I'll take care of Dennis. And there won't be any blowback on you or Ed."

She frowned. Should she ask him for information? Likely. But she was worried about Dennis pulling this with other tenants. Someone needed to make sure that didn't happen.

"All right."

"Yeah? No questions asked?" He gave her a surprised look.

"As long as nothing comes back on Ed or you."

"Oh, there's no way someone like Dennis can touch me. And I'll keep everyone you care about safe. Don't worry, Dennis is going to pay."

"Good," she said with satisfaction.

"So, after Dennis evicted you, you came to live here." He gave her grandpa's place a skeptical look.

She sighed. "I didn't think things through very well."

"Really? Surprising."

"Hey! Sarcasm is not welcome."

"I'm sorry, Little Monster," he said, running his hand over his face. "You're right, that was uncalled for."

She stared at him in shock.

"What? What's wrong?"

"Oh, nothing. I'm just not used to such a quick apology. Normally, I tell Ed he's being a dick, he tells me I'm a brat, we bicker then one of us gives up. Usually him. I'm more stubborn."

"I'm not Ed."

"No," she said quietly. "And thank goodness for that. Last thing I want is to lust after my brother."

"You're lusting after me, huh?"

"You hadn't worked that out already?" she asked with a grin. "And here I thought I hadn't been subtle."

"I don't think subtle is a word I'd use to describe you."

She shook her head with a laugh. "No, likely not. Anyway, I kind of felt like I didn't have any choice but to come here." She winced as he shot her a look of disbelief. "All right, I had options. But I don't like asking for help or feeling like a burden. When we had to move in with my grandpa, he always made my mother feel so bad. It just . . . I guess it affected me more than I thought."

"I'm so sorry, baby. But you have to know that your friends aren't like that."

"I know. Just a habit that's hard to break. It felt like a failure to admit that Dennis evicted me and that I didn't have anywhere to live. But after I spent the other night constantly emptying buckets and bowls and cups because the roof on this dump leaks like a sieve, I decided that I needed another option. So, I was at the Wishing Well last night to ask Noah if I could crash in his apartment for a few nights. He's basically moved in with Cleo now and it just sits empty above the bar."

"This place leaks?" he asked. "And you stayed here?"

"Ah, well, yeah."

"Bloody hell. And an apartment above a bar doesn't sound safe."

"It's safer than a house with a door that an eight-year-old could kick in."

"What?" he barked. "Right, I think it's time we went into this place."

~

As soon as Harry entered the tiny cabin, he knew that he wasn't going to allow her to stay here a moment longer.

Actually, that wasn't true. He'd known before he even walked into the place. The front porch was rotted and she'd had to direct him where to step so he didn't fall through. That had him tightening his jaw in anger at Dennis, at her friends for not knowing what she was doing, at Kiesha for not asking for help.

But mostly at himself.

Because while he was at home, in his nice warm apartment with plenty of security, complaining over the hours he was working and his sheer boredom in his job, she'd been here. . . living in a place where he could see through the damn walls. He could literally see through her walls to the outdoors.

There were bowls and cracked mugs around the living and dining area. Most of them were full of water from the rain they'd had during the night.

The place smelled damp and there were cobwebs in every corner and dust coated the windows and furniture.

An old, worn sofa lay against one wall and had a monster duvet lying on it. As well as a pillow at one end.

She'd been sleeping on the damn sofa? In a cold, mold-ridden cabin in the middle of freaking nowhere.

"Uh, Harry, are you all right?" she asked worriedly.

No. No, he really wasn't all right. In fact, he thought his blood pressure had just shot through the roof. But he let out a deep breath.

"I'm all right."

"Because you kind of look like you want to murder something then run over it, then set it on fire."

Yep, that's pretty much how he felt.

"Is there no bedroom?" he asked.

"Uh, what?"

He waved to the sofa. "You were sleeping out here, right? Is there no bedroom?"

"Oh yeah, there's two actually. This place is bigger than it looks from the outside. One was my grandpa's and the other was where my mom and I slept."

Fuck.

He knew it was likely better back then. Surely, there hadn't been holes in the walls and cracks in the roof. But it still didn't make him feel much better.

"So why were you sleeping on the sofa?"

"Oh, because the fire is out here. There was still some wood in the shed outside, lucky, huh?"

"Lucky?"

"Well, yeah. It was lucky because without the fire it would be damn cold in here."

"There's no heater?" He glanced around but he couldn't see one. Fuck, he hated to think about how cold it had been in here at night. Even with the fire going, it wouldn't be easy to heat the place when there were holes in the fucking walls.

"I don't think so, even if there was one there's no electricity to run it."

"There's no electricity?"

She eyed him warily, probably wondering at why his voice had grown so high-pitched and he was repeating everything she said. "Uh, no. No one has lived here since my grandpa died. My mom refused to do anything with the place. She hated living here and didn't want any part of it. I pay the property taxes on it and that's it. I don't have the money to fix it up."

He had to close his eyes and count slowly to ten.

One. Two. Three.

Nope, he couldn't do it. The rage was still there.

Four. Five. Six.

"Harry, are you all right?"

"I'm counting."

"Ah, yeah, people do that around me a lot," she told him. "I'll give you a minute, shall I?"

She went to step away but he gently reached out and took hold of her wrist.

"Please stay right here."

"There you go saying please again, but I don't think you're asking."

"I'm not. I don't want you walking around here, I don't trust the floor not to give in or the roof or just . . . I can't let you out of my sight right now. All right?"

To his shock, instead of balking at his words, she turned and rubbed her free hand up and down his arm.

"Careful of your arm," he warned.

"My arm is fine, fuss-pot," she told him gently. "You, on the other hand, look like you need a stiff drink and a lie down. Or maybe a blow job. I can help with that." She winked at him and he knew she was trying to lighten the situation.

But this was . . . this was beyond a joke.

"I can't stand thinking about you living here, not even for a few nights."

"I'm all right, Harry. But yeah, this wasn't my smartest idea. That's why I went to see Noah."

"I don't like the idea of you there, either. I want you to go wait in the car. I'm going to pack up your stuff and then you're coming back to the motel with me."

Then tomorrow, he was going to start searching for a house to buy.

"The motel? You want me to stay with you?" she asked, sounding surprised.

"I'll pay for you to stay in a different room if it makes you feel more comfortable, but I really want you with me. After last night, then learning about Dennis, now this . . . I'm trying very hard to keep myself calm and sane and reasonable. But knowing you were in danger, that you were out here on your own . . . it's very hard for me to remain calm."

She stood there, gaping at him.

"There isn't much that riles me up, that tests my temper and control, but someone I care about being in danger, that's going to do this to me every time."

"It's all right. I'm okay. I'm like a cat, I have nine lives."

"I don't want you to need nine lives. And you're not a cat. You just have one life. I want to make sure you live a long, happy one."

"You keep talking so sweet to me, Harry, and I won't ever let you go."

"That's the plan, Little Monster." He drew her close to him, wrapping his arms around her and just holding her until he felt himself calm.

She was safe.

She hadn't been harmed.

And he'd do whatever was necessary to protect her.

23

Half an hour later, all of her stuff was packed into the trunk of Harry's rental.

It helped that she didn't have much and hadn't really bothered to unpack.

"That everything?" Harry asked. He was looking slightly rumpled. His white shirt had dirt down the front, his hair was mussed and he had more dirt on his cheek. Reaching up, she wiped it off.

His eyes danced as he stared down at her. She leaned up on her tiptoes to kiss him. "Thank you."

"For what, Little Monster?"

"For caring."

He placed his hands on her hips. "Always. You hear me? And you never have to thank me for that. Now, is there anything else you need?"

"No, that's it. I've got my stuffies, my duvet, my roller skates and clothes, Taser and phone charger, so I'm good. All the furniture belongs here. I travel pretty light."

"Come on then, let's go before it starts getting cold and dark. I want to get you settled before we head for dinner."

He helped her into the car and fastened her seat belt for her. She yawned then covered it up, trying to smother it quickly.

"You're tired."

"I'm fine."

"We've missed lunch."

"We had a huge brunch, though. An amazing brunch. I've never had a better one."

He grinned over at her. "Is that so?"

"Uh-huh. Wouldn't mind another brunch like that one."

"I'll have to see what I can do. What about instead of going out for dinner, we get take-out and stay in tonight? Watch a movie, snuggle, and go to bed early. What do you think?"

"I think that sounds like the perfect way to spend the night."

∼

Later on that evening, she groaned as she sat on the couch.

"You okay?" Harry asked.

"Ate too much. Gonna explode. Need some sweatpants before I burst through a button."

"Aren't those jeggings?" he asked as he sat next to her. "They don't have a button."

"Yeah, you're right. I should have said before I split a seam. I can't keep eating like this, I won't fit into my clothes soon."

"You barely ate anything. But I'm sorry you don't feel great. Here, let me see if I can help." He was sitting on the chaise end of the sofa, and he spread his legs, patting the seat in front of him.

She eyed him for a moment. "You're going to help huh?"

"I'll try."

"I'm not feeling all that sexy at the moment."

He grinned. "Come here."

She moved between his legs and he wrapped his arms around her, squeezing lightly.

"Ahh, you're gonna squeeze the food out of me? Bit gross, but okay," she said jokingly.

"Hush," he told her. Then he raised the hem of her top and rubbed his hand over her belly in slow, soothing sweeps of his hand.

Ohhh, that was rather nice. She relaxed back against his chest.

"That better?"

"Yeah," she told him, her eyes closing slightly.

"Tired?"

"Little bit."

"Maybe we should skip the movie and head to bed."

She tensed slightly. To bed, huh?

"Not for that, Little Monster," he chided, kissing his way up her neck to the back of her ear. "For sleep."

"Well, that's disappointing."

He chuckled.

"As appealing as going to sleep at eight at night sounds, I want to watch a movie and snuggle. You did promise."

"All right, what would you like to watch?"

"Monsters movie!"

He chuckled. "How did I know that would be your choice? Let's see if I can find it. I don't know what movies they have."

Getting up, he grabbed the remote, managing to find the movie.

"I think we need popcorn. And ice cream. You can't watch movies without popcorn and ice cream."

"What happened to your sore tummy?" he asked her.

She waved a hand through the air. "It was sore because I ate too much food-food. Ice cream and popcorn are entirely different."

"Is that so? I'm afraid I don't have either of those."

She sighed. "All right, I'll suffer through without."

"I know it's a grave disappointment. I'll try to make it up to you."

"Oh yeah? And how do you intend to do that?" she asked as he sat next to her.

Reaching down he grabbed her feet and brought them up onto his lap. "How about a foot rub?"

"Well, now we're talking."

Harry rubbed her feet as she giggled her way through the movie. When it was over, she sighed in pleasure. "Let's watch another movie!"

"It's bedtime."

"Not tired."

"I am," he countered.

"Poor Harry. I'll keep the noise down." She sat up and moved over to grab the remote.

Smack!

His hand landed on her ass, making her jump slightly. "Harry!"

"If you put it in front of me, then I need to smack it."

"I don't think so." She waggled a finger at him. "Bad Daddy."

She eyed him a moment, seeing the satisfaction fill his face. It felt so right, calling him that.

"Not bad Daddy. But there is a naughty little girl in front of me."

"I am not."

He raised his eyebrows. "Really? Didn't I just tell you that it was bedtime? Not time for another movie."

"But it's not even ten! I don't go to bed until midnight most nights."

"And you're exhausted," he pointed out gently. "You need more sleep, Little Monster. A routine."

"Nuh-uh, I don't need a routine. That sounds way too boring."

"You can still have fun and get enough sleep and proper food."

She eyed him suspiciously. "Not sure I believe you."

"How about you give me a chance to show you? Please."

"There you go again, saying please like you're asking and all reasonable and stuff."

"You don't think I'm reasonable?"

"I think you hide your more dominant side behind all those 'pleases' and 'thank yous'."

"They're called manners, Little Monster." Reaching out, he drew her onto his lap so she was straddling his thighs, facing him. He cupped her face between his hands. "Rules and discipline don't have to be boring. You can still be you, I'd never take that away from you. I just want to make sure you're safe and healthy. Because I intend for the two of us to be together a long, long time."

Her breath caught in her throat at his words.

"I know I can't promise forever, baby. But while I'm here I will take care of you with every part of me."

"Damn it, Harry," she muttered, leaning her forehead against his. "I was going to be all indignant and fight back, then you go being all sweet. Wind. Sails. All gone."

He huffed out a laugh as he grabbed her ass, squeezing it. "I'm sure you'll have other things you can argue with me about."

"Yeah, no doubt."

He cupped her face, drawing it back so he could kiss her. His tongue ran along the slit of her lips. She pressed herself against his cock, feeling how hard he was. A whimper of need escaped her as she ran her hand down his chest, toward his cock. Running her hand up and down the shaft, she loved the groan that escaped him.

"I could take care of this for you."

"We're supposed to be going to bed." He ran his hands up her thighs. "You're so gorgeous. It's difficult to think of anything other than stripping you off and claiming every inch of you."

"Yes, let's do that."

"You need sleep."

"I'm not going to sleep like this. I'm too wound up. And so are you. Please."

She leaned back and gave him a pouting look. He shook his head at her, running his finger along her lower lip. "No pouting. Doesn't work on me."

"You have pouting immunity?"

"Yes."

"Good to know. What about puppy eyes." She made her eyes wide and batted them a few times.

"Nope. Doesn't work on me."

"Begging? I could beg. Just slide on down to my knees then put my hands like this." She slid off his lap to kneel on the floor between his legs, with her hands in a begging pose. "How about this?"

"No."

"What about if I were to lean in and do this?" She placed kisses along his cock. Too bad there were layers of clothing between her and his dick.

Then she was certain he wouldn't be able to resist.

"I would tell you good try. But I'm not letting you top from the bottom."

What? She wasn't doing that. Was she?

Urgh. Maybe she was.

Well, that just sucked. Jonah totally would have stripped off his jeans by now. Then again, all she'd have to do was tell him she wanted to suck his cock and he'd get naked.

Harry was a different kettle of fish and she wasn't sure it was a good thing. She liked getting her own way far too much.

"No more pouting," he warned as he held out a hand to her, drawing her up off the floor. "You'll get to have my cock in your mouth soon. Once you've been a good girl."

"But what if that never happens?" she cried.

"What? You being a good girl?" he asked as he got to his feet.

"Yes! I'm not sure it's in my DNA."

"Little Monster, you're a good girl. You're always a good girl. I shouldn't have worded it that way. What I meant is that you'll get my cock as a reward for good behavior, not for trying to push me into it." He cupped her face. "I adore you. But you are not in charge here."

Well. Crap.

That seemed like a really bad deal.

Leaning in, he kissed the tip of her nose then her chin. "My nose. My chin. I'm going to claim all of you until you're completely mine."

Her breath caught in her chest as he lightly brushed her lips with his. How was this going to calm her down? She couldn't sleep when she was all worked up like this.

It definitely sucked.

"Now, I'm guessing you don't want another shower since you had one earlier?"

Maybe if she had a shower she could take care of things herself . . . her monster vibrator was waterproof after all. And ultra-quiet.

"Okay, that's your scheming face."

She had a scheming face? And he knew what that face looked like? This was not good. Not good at all.

"Am I going to get away with anything with you?"

"No."

She let out a loud, dramatic sigh.

"Because you're going to tell me whenever you do something that I wouldn't approve of, aren't you, Little Monster?"

"I dunno. That seems like a sure way to end up with a hot bottom."

"Oh, it is. But it could be the difference between one spanking and several. Or my hand and my belt."

But she might just like his belt. He wasn't wearing it right now which was really too bad.

"Are you fantasizing about my belt?"

"Of course, I am. You can't talk about your belt then not expect me to think about it. I've never been spanked with a belt. Jonah would sometimes slap my ass, but I've never been, uh, well . . ."

"Disciplined when you were naughty?"

Damn. Did he have to word it that way?

Killing her.

"Don't know what you mean. I'm never naughty."

He moved his lips across her cheek to her ear. "No lying. That's very naughty." He slid his arm around her waist and laid several hard smacks on her ass.

She squealed then arched against him. Okay, those slaps were hard!

"Shit! Daddy!"

"No swearing," he warned.

Really? What kind of a rule was that?

"Who knew you'd have a concrete hand?" She rubbed at her bottom.

"That was just a small warning," he told her.

Yikes.

He eyed her for a moment. What was he thinking about? She tensed, worried.

"You need to change any of your limits?"

Oh, he was worried about her?

She shook her head. "No, Daddy. But I think we might need to discuss this whole no swearing thing."

"It will be tough, but you can do it."

She sighed. "All right, Daddy. I'll try."

"You're to tell me if anything I do or say upsets you."

She shot her hand up in the air.

"Yes?" he asked, clear amusement in his face.

"Giving me a bedtime upsets me."

"Noted and dismissed."

"What? You can't just dismiss that."

"I can. I have. If you need something, you're to tell me. I want to be the first person you call. Especially if you're in danger or something has upset you. Understand?"

She bit at her lip.

"Kiesha?" he asked, freeing her lip gently.

"I understand. I'll try. I'm not good at asking for help."

"I get that it's hard. I want you to try. And I'll be very upset with you if you were in danger and you didn't call me. Or your health was at risk, understand?"

"Yes."

"You're to keep yourself safe and healthy. And if you can't do that, then I will step in."

"That doesn't sound good."

"It could be. It all depends on what you need. Sometimes you might need more rules, you might need me to take more of the reins and I am here for that. Other times you might need me to stand back. Not going to lie, that will be harder. But everything comes down to what you need, Kiesha."

"But what about you?"

"Oh, don't worry. I'm getting exactly what I need. You."

"You say the most delicious things. I could eat you all up. Too bad, you won't let me." She pouted.

"Poor baby. It's hard to be Kiesha."

"It really is! I'm glad you understand that." She winked at him.

"Right, enough procrastination, Little Monster. It's time for bed."

"It's really not."

"Bedtime is ten during the week. Later on the weekends."

"Ten! Ten is so early."

"I can make it earlier," he warned.

"Well, da . . . ugh, I mean darn it. Fine. But I want it noted that I protested this grotesque form of injustice."

"I'll note that down. I might need a notebook, because I fear there will be more protests."

"Good plan. And cause you're old and will forget." She jumped away with a squeal as he gave her another slap on the ass.

"Just remember I can still move fast. And I have a hand like concrete."

"Noted, Daddy! Noted!"

She dashed into the bedroom and looked around for her bags. They'd left some of her stuff in the trunk of his car, but she'd brought in all her stuffies and clothes. She'd felt bad about leaving her stuffies alone last night.

Bad stuffy mama.

But where had all of them gone?

"Daddy! Quick! Daddy!" she cried out worriedly. Huh, that word was coming very easily now.

"What is it? What's wrong?" He rushed into the room, glancing around. Grabbing her around the waist, he drew her behind him. As though he thought something might attack her.

That was really sweet, if totally unnecessary.

"Someone stole my stuff! All my clothes are gone!"

"Oh, you nearly gave me a heart attack. I thought something was really wrong." He put his hand on his chest and she felt a moment of worry.

"Are you all right? I'm sorry." She placed a hand on his chest. "Maybe you should sit down."

He shook his head. "I didn't mean that literally."

"Well, don't scare me like that!" She smacked her hand on his arm. "Don't you think that was overly dramatic?"

"Yes," he said dryly. "I believe that in this relationship I am definitely the dramatic one."

"Well," she sighed. "I didn't want to say anything . . . but wait!

There is something wrong! All my clothes are gone!"

"Baby, I put them away."

"Some asshole has come in here and stolen everything!"

"First of all, no swearing."

"These are extenuating circumstances. I think there should be a clause that says swear words are allowed in trying times."

"Your stuff isn't gone. I put it away."

"What?"

"I put all your clothes away." He opened the wardrobe and there were her favorite dresses, skirts and pants hanging up. Then he drew open some drawers to show her sweaters, T-shirts, pajamas, bras, and panties.

"You put away my panties?" She gaped at him.

"Yes."

"You folded them?"

"I did. Is that wrong?"

"Uh, no. I just didn't know that people folded panties."

"I did it while you were in the shower earlier. You didn't notice that your bags were all missing when you walked through here?" He drew out a pair of pale blue pajamas that had a smiling monster face on the front of the top and then bright pink blobs on the long pants.

"Ah, no, I'm not always very observant. I can't believe you put them all away."

He eyed her. "Too presumptuous? I want you to stay here with me, but if that makes you uncomfortable . . ."

"No," she said quickly. "No, it doesn't make me uncomfortable. Kind of the opposite. I like knowing you want me here, that you expect me to stay."

"Good. Because if I do something that upsets you . . ."

"Then I'm to tell you. I know. I remember." She tapped her forehead. "Thanks, Harry." She wrapped her arms around his waist and squeezed him.

"You're welcome, baby." He kissed the top of her head. "Your stuffies are still packed up as I didn't know whether you'd want me to touch them."

"That's so thoughtful. Although I need to get them out, they'll be suffocating."

"I'll get the suitcase in soon. Let's get you ready for bed first. Are you all right with me undressing you?"

"Yes," she said in a soft voice. "I'm okay with that, Daddy."

"Good, because I want to do this every night for you."

"Yeah?"

"I like taking care of you, Kiesha. And what's more, I think you need it." He reached for her sweater, drawing it up then her T-shirt.

Leaning in, he kissed along one shoulder, then down across the base of her neck to her other shoulder. "Neck like a queen, the bearing of a princess and the butt of a brat."

"Hey!" she protested, but couldn't help the giggle that escaped. "What does the butt of a brat look like?"

"Why, I'm glad you asked, Little Monster. Red, it looks red."

He drew off her bra, admiration and heat in his gaze. Biting her lower lip, she felt her nipples tighten. Would he take one into his mouth?

Please, let him take one into his mouth.

But he just picked up the pajama top and helped her get into it.

Darn it.

Not fair.

"But my butt isn't red, Daddy," she pointed out.

"Not currently." He reached around to pat her bottom lightly. "But soon."

She rolled her eyes at him. "You're so sure I'm going to earn a spanking. I might not ever get a spanking."

That actually sounded like a good plan.

"You're right," he told her. "I'm making some terrible assumptions. You might never get a red bottom—"

"Thank you."

"Except for the fact you're already owed several spankings, aren't you?"

She was? Oh yeah, for disobeying him in the bar. And for saying naughty things about herself.

"But I wasn't actually yours then . . . I mean, ah, we weren't, we didn't have a relationship, you never. . . feel free to stop me at any time!"

"Why? I was enjoying you getting all flustered."

She grumbled while staring up at him.

"You're very cute." He kissed her lightly. "You are mine and I am yours. You can get a T-shirt stating that. Actually, that's a good idea. Or a bracelet."

"Why not tattoo your number on me so if I get lost people know who to call," she said dryly.

"Good plan. Wasn't sure where you stood on tattoos."

"You can't do that!"

He winked at her, then crouched down to pull off her tights. She held onto his shoulders to steady herself.

"You want new panties on?"

"What?" she squeaked.

"Are they wet?" he asked slyly.

"I can do that!"

"Baby, I've had my fingers on you and in you, I've tasted you. And you're balking over me changing your panties?"

"Yes, well, if you're not going there for pleasure, then is there any need to go there at all?" she asked in a hushed voice.

Seriously! He couldn't really want to change her damn panties, right?

A loud bark of laughter escaped him. "Oh, baby. You have a lot to learn. Lie on the bed."

"Daddyyy," she moaned.

"Lie back." This time there was no mistaking the stern note in his voice. She moved onto the bed, placing her arm over her eyes. She definitely needed to change her panties. Sleeping in wet panties was not high on her checklist.

Ick.

But for him to do it . . . yeah, that wasn't something she was expecting.

"Good girl."

A shiver of pleasure ran through her.

"You're being such a good girl for Daddy, aren't you? Hmm? I know this isn't easy, but what you'll soon realize is that there is absolutely nothing that I wouldn't do for you."

She was beginning to see that he did.

He slid her panties down her legs and she lay there, resisting the urge to cover herself up. Did he like what he saw? Did he think her too big? Too small?

"Hush, baby."

"Oh shit, did I say all of that out loud?"

"No," he soothed. "But I could tell you were thinking hard. You need to stop worrying so much. I'm going to tell you as often as you need to hear it how gorgeous you are."

"I might start listening one day."

"Poor baby, these panties are soaked. You definitely needed some clean ones."

Something that was partway between a squeak and a squeal escaped her. Well, that was embarrassing. She hadn't been aware she could even make a noise like that.

"I think I need a shower." Then she could take care of her throbbing clit. And clean herself up.

"You wouldn't be thinking of trying to take care of things yourself, would you?"

"Um, I don't know. What would happen if I was?" She leaned

up on her elbows to stare down at where he knelt between her legs.

"Bringing yourself to orgasm without permission isn't allowed, so that would definitely warrant a punishment. Have you ever been edged?"

Her eyes went wide and she shook her head. "No, and that sounds like a terrible idea."

"Oh, I think it would be a fitting punishment for a naughty girl who couldn't keep her fingers off her pussy. I'd handcuff your hands and secure them to the bed. I'd spread these legs and feast on your pussy until you were begging to come. Then I'd draw back. Then I might finger fuck that gorgeous ass of yours while I fucked your pussy with my tongue. And when you were screaming with need, I'd pull back."

Okay, note to self. Never come without permission.

Also, note to self. That finger fucking thing sounded hot.

"You've gone all quiet and thoughtful. That's never a good sign."

"I love anal play."

And whoops.

"Also, I say things without thinking them through first."

"I would never have guessed."

She could tell he was trying not to laugh. "You're lucky you're cute."

He leaned over her, and drawing up her top, laid kisses over her stomach. "Another part of you claimed. I'm glad you blurt things out. Keeps me from having to wonder what you've got scheming in your smart brain. And baby?"

"Yeah?" she groaned.

"Anal play is very high on my list too. In fact, because you've been such a good girl and you're in such need . . ."

"Yes?"

Please tell her he was going to let her come? Please?

24

He laid more kisses over her tummy. "Well . . . I shouldn't let you come. Not when you were just punished."

"I'll be a good girl. I know how to do that. Please. I'll sleep better."

He grinned. "Good. I want you to move up the bed and grab your vibrator from the nightstand."

"Just kill me now," she said dramatically, placing her hands over her eyes. "You unpacked my vibrator?"

"I sure did. Now, do you want to come or would you like to go to bed like this?"

"I want to come. I want to come," she said hastily. "I just can't believe you unpacked my vibrator. That stuff is personal."

"Not anymore."

Shivers.

She sat then turned to crawl up the bed only to realize she was naked from the waist down. Pausing, she looked back over her shoulder at him. "You're going to stare at my ass as I move, aren't you?"

"Be a crime not to."

Moving as quickly as she could, while trying not to flash him too much, Kiesha made her way up the bed. Opening the drawer of the nightstand, she drew out her vibrator. She'd wrapped it up in one of her tops.

"Nearly whacked myself in the face with it when I was pulling your clothes out," he told her.

She groaned again, but made her way back down to him. "Um, what am I doing with this?"

He raised an eyebrow. "What do you mean? What have you been doing with it up until now?"

"Wait . . . do you want me to . . . oh pumpkin pie!"

"Pumpkin pie?" he asked, looking confused.

"Well, I can't swear so I've got to say something."

"Yes, but pumpkin pie?"

"Don't make me put the cream on top!" she said, pointing at him sternly.

"We wouldn't want that. I don't think." Moving around the bed, he grabbed a couple of pillows, placing them beside her. "Lay back, put your head on these pillows. Then spread your legs, bend your knees and put your feet flat on the mattress. I want you to show me how you use your vibrator."

"Harry," she moaned. "I don't know if I can do this."

"Why not?" He sat next to her, then reached over to cup her chin turning her face toward him. "What's worrying you?"

"Ahh, everything! I mean unless you're planning on leaving me alone to do this?"

"No, I'm not leaving. I told you no more orgasms without permission."

"You could give me permission then leave."

"I'm not leaving, baby. I want to see you come. I want to hear those delicious noises you make. I want to watch you use your vibrator. Can you do that?" He moved his hand down to her pussy, cupping it. "Because your orgasms already belong to me." He swirled the tip of his finger around her clit, making her gasp and shift around where she was sitting. Then he slid his finger lower. "Part your legs."

She pushed them apart.

"Lie back."

She arranged the pillows behind her head as she lay back.

They were doing this. She was going to do this.

A whimper escaped as he slid a finger deep inside her.

"Just close your eyes, baby. That's it. Good girl. I'm going to give you another finger now. That's it. Good. You're doing so well. See, it's not that hard, is it? Giving Daddy all of your pleasure. I want you to put your feet flat on the bed, but keep those legs nice and spread."

Oh, hell. Oh, hell.

She thought about saying no. For all of two seconds. Because at this point stopping wasn't an option.

"That's it. I want you to pull your top up over your breasts. Good girl." He slid his finger from her pussy as she raised her top. His fingers were wet against her skin as he ran them up to her right nipple and brushed them over the tight bud.

Then his fingers went back to pumping in and out of her pussy before moving up to her left nipple.

Please claim them. Please claim them.

She was dying to feel his mouth around her nipples, pulling on them, sucking strongly.

"I think I'm going to have to clean them, aren't I? Or you'll have to have another shower. Take hold of the vibrator and put it inside you. Good girl."

Hell. Her breath was shallow, her heart racing fast as she picked up the vibrator and ran the thicker part of it through her slit.

Grabbing hold of her hand, he drew it up to her mouth. "Take it into your mouth. I want you to make it nice and wet. That's it.

Pretend it's Daddy's cock. Good girl. Keep it in your mouth until I say otherwise. Hmm, you look so hot with something in your mouth. Might have to keep your mouth filled more often. Maybe a pacifier."

She frowned up at him and slid the vibrator out of her mouth. "Are you trying to say that I talk too much?"

"No," he said. "I'm not. And you weren't given permission to remove that from your mouth."

Oh, pumpkin pie with whipped cream on top.

"I'm sorry," she said, worried he wouldn't let her come now.

He rubbed his chin, staring down at her hungrily. "I shouldn't let you come."

"Please, Daddy."

"Tell you what, I'll give you a choice."

There was a devilish look in his eyes that she did not like.

"What is it?"

"I'll clean you up, get you dressed in your jammies, put you to bed and cuddle you, but no coming. That's choice number one."

Please let choice number two be better than number one. Please.

"Choice number two is ten spanks."

Well, hell.

"But I get to come?" she asked desperately.

"Yes. But I'll warm your ass first."

"Okay, option two."

Satisfaction filled his face. It was obvious which option he'd been hoping she would take.

"Reach down and pull your legs back against your chest."

"What? Why?" she asked.

"Because I'm going to spank your bottom."

In the diaper position? Could he have chosen a more embarrassing position? This wasn't cool.

"Can't you spank me while I'm on my tummy? Or over your lap? That's a classic for a reason, you know."

"You made your choice, baby. I'll give you one opportunity to change your mind. And that's it."

"I'm not changing my mind," she moaned, reaching down to grab her legs. She drew them back to her chest. She couldn't believe this. She was now totally on display. And he didn't stay sitting beside her, where he couldn't get a good view. Oh no, he stood up at the end of the bed and ran his hand down her thigh over one butt cheek, then the other.

"Daddy! Please!"

"Please what? Please punish you? Why would I do that?"

"Because I was naughty?"

"Yes, naughty girl. Hmm, you know what I've never been a fan of?"

"What?"

"Mirrored wardrobe doors. Until now. I want you to scoot around until your bottom is facing the mirrored door then get back into position."

Killing her. He was killing her.

She couldn't believe he expected her to lie with her bottom on display like this, with a mirror showing him everything no matter where he decided to position himself for her spanking.

But when she stared up at him pleadingly, he just gave her a firm look back. So, he wasn't going to bend?

Just. Awesome.

She scooted around, and then lay back with her hands behind her knees holding her legs up. Then she closed her eyes.

"Good girl. Don't close your eyes."

She opened her eyes, staring up at him in shock. He moved so he had one leg bent and, on the mattress, next to her hip, the other still rested on the floor. Then he smacked his hand down on her ass before turning his head to look in the mirror as he rubbed the sore spot.

"Perfect."

Not perfect. Really not perfect.

Another smack to her other cheek. More staring into the mirror. And here she'd been foolish enough to hope the spanking might be over quickly. He did remember she had a bedtime now, right?

"Let's speed this up," he said almost as though he'd heard her thoughts.

She was starting to wonder if he might have secret mind reader abilities.

Another two smacks landed. Then two more. And she was starting to regret her wish to have this over with quickly.

"Ow. Ow. Owie!" she cried out as he paused to study her bottom.

"Last four. Do you need to say your safeword?"

Did she?

"Nooo," she groaned.

"Good girl for being honest."

Slap! Slap! Slap! Slap!

All four smacks were hard and fast. By the time he finished, her bottom was hot, throbbing and she was starting to regret her choice.

"Baby, you look so beautiful. Look at you lying there with your pussy and ass on display for me. Is your bottom sore now?"

"Yes!" she cried, thinking she might get some sympathy. And that maybe next time he'd take things easier on her. Because, let's face it there was always going to be a next time.

But he simply nodded. "Good."

Good? Was he serious right now? That wasn't good. It was terrible!

"You can release your legs."

She put her legs down gratefully and he lay beside her, drawing her into his chest and rubbing her back until her breathing grew more even and her tears dried. Reaching for a tissue from the nightstand, he even cleaned her up.

"All right?" he asked.

"My butt hurts, but otherwise I'm all right."

"That's my good girl. You want to keep going?"

"Yes!" Was he insane? Of course she did.

He grinned down at her. "I thought that might be your answer. Bend your knees, feet flat on the mattress and put your vibrator back in your mouth."

"Stop frowning at me, little girl or I'm going to think I didn't spank you hard enough."

What? Eek!

"You did, Daddy!" she cried. "You totally spanked me hard enough. Any harder and I'd never be able to sit again."

"I think you'd sit just fine, Little Monster. Now, here is your vibrator. I'd take it before I change my mind and decide you don't get to come either."

Sheesh and here she thought he would go easy on her.

Showed her what she knew.

He pressed the vibrator to her mouth and she parted her lips. He slid it in and out of her mouth and she found herself starting to relax, pleasure flooded her.

Oral fixation? Yep. She guessed she definitely had one of those.

"That's my good girl," he murmured, his gaze intent on hers. "Take hold of the vibrator and get it nice and wet for me. I just need to check you're ready for it."

Oh, she was totally ready for it. But she wasn't going to argue if he wanted to touch her some more.

So long as he wasn't planning to spank her.

No more spanking!

She might get a tattoo of that on her butt. Yeah, only it might have the opposite effect that she was after.

Then she gasped as he knelt on the floor. He parted her pussy lips. "Look at this pretty pussy. It's so wet. Did someone like her spanking? Did she enjoy having Daddy put her in the diaper position so he could spank her naughty ass? Did she like that she was on display in the mirror?"

No! She hadn't liked any of that stuff? Right?

Oh, Lord. Her body certainly seemed to think differently. She arched up and he flicked his finger over her clit. She was glad that she had the vibrator in her mouth now, gave her a good reason for not answering him.

Although she was shocked that he wasn't demanding a reply.

Then again, her body probably spoke for her. He slid his fingers deep inside her.

"So wet. So warm. I can't wait to claim this part of you, baby."

Then do it! Do it now!

She slid the vibrator in and out of her mouth, her heart racing as he moved again, kneeling next to her on the bed. He ran his fingers, which were damp with her arousal, over her nipples.

Please. Please.

"Take the vibrator out, then slowly push it into your pussy," he commanded.

She slid it from her mouth and lowered it, staring up at him as she did. His gaze was intent on hers until she pressed the thicker end against her passage. Then he turned to stare at her in the mirror. She let out a small whimper as she pushed it inside her.

"Good girl. Look at it fucking you. That's so hot. We might have to make this at least a weekly thing. I'm going to get you a range of vibrators and you can fuck yourself with every one until we find your favorites."

Oh, hell. Oh, hell.

When it was situated, he reached down to take hold of her

hand. Then he pushed her pussy lips back, studying the vibrator where it pierced her.

Wow. He was far more commanding and involved than she'd expected when it came to sex.

And dirtier. Definitely dirtier.

"Pull it out then thrust it back in," he ordered. "God, yes. You don't know how hot that is, baby."

She was feeling it. Her body was flushed. She wanted more. Needed it.

"Turn it on, but do not come until you have permission," he warned. Then he cupped one breast in his hand and lowered his mouth to flick his tongue over the tight nub.

Holy. Heck. Yes! Finally!

"Mine," he told her.

Yes, all his.

She let out a low moan, almost coming straight away. It was so much sensation to deal with. Too much. She couldn't hold back.

"Do not come," he warned. "You come and tomorrow I will edge you from the moment we walk through that door after you finish work until you go to sleep."

Hell. Hell. Hell.

Didn't he know how hard it was to hold back?

"Please, Daddy!"

"No. You're to hold on."

"You're so mean!" she cried out as he moved to her other nipple, flicking his tongue over it lightly. It wasn't enough. She needed more.

"I know. I'm so mean. But you're going to learn to do as you're told. Because if you don't, there are consequences and you don't want them, do you?"

The small end of the vibrator buzzed against her sensitive clit to the point where it was nearly too much. She couldn't take much more. Suddenly, he sucked on her nipple. A scream ripped out of her.

"Shh, hush. You need to be quieter. We don't want anyone next door calling the cops, do we?"

Dear. Lord. No, they didn't want that. She could just imagine one of the guys she worked with turning up at the door wanting to know what the hell was going on.

She'd never live it down. She'd never be able to work there again, that was for sure. Although if they were going to call, she'd figure they'd have done it by now. She hadn't exactly been quiet during her spanking.

Reaching up, he grabbed her a pillow. "Use this to muffle any screams."

She took the pillow gratefully, holding it over her face as her other hand kept the vibrator in the right position.

"Just don't suffocate yourself," he warned, before his mouth returned to her nipple.

His facial hair brushed against the bottom of her breast, his mouth was smooth and warm in contrast. The vibrator buzzed inside her. She needed to come so badly. She was right on the cusp of falling over that edge.

Then he brushed her hand away from the vibrator, taking over. She held the pillow with both hands, letting out low cries.

"Please, please, please."

"What was that?" he asked.

She slid the pillow away, staring up and him pleadingly. "Please let me come, Daddy."

Oh Lord, if there was someone in the unit next door, then they'd likely heard more than they ever wanted to. She cringed thinking about it.

At least they hadn't banged on the wall or anything.

"I'm not sure you're quite there yet."

"I am! I am! Please, I can't . . . I can't hold on."

"All right, baby. Come for Daddy. Come now!" He injected his voice with steel and it was like her body knew she had to obey him. Because she arched up, her entire body trembling as she came with a strangled scream.

Her orgasm was intense. She pulsed around the vibrator, her breath coming in sharp pants as she came. He slowly lessened the vibrations then slid it from her pussy.

Panting, she stared up at him through blurry eyes.

"Good?" he asked.

Good? Nuh-uh, you couldn't describe that as good. She shook her head, still trying to catch her breath.

"Not good?"

"Better than good," she managed to get out. "Mind. Blown. Can't. Talk."

A smile kicked up the edges of his mouth. "Just wait until I claim that part of you. I'm going to eat you out until you come screaming my name."

"We might need to move venues before we do that. I don't think the walls are thick enough to handle my screams."

A thoughtful look filled his face. "Yes. Staying here is all right for short bursts. But we need a long-term solution."

Happiness flooded her at the idea of him living here in Wishingbone. She just hoped he didn't get bored or regret the decision further down the track when he missed the city.

She pushed those thoughts from her mind. He was old enough to know what he wanted.

Of course, she still didn't know where she was going to live. She needed to take another look around. Maybe the smelly cheese house was her best bet.

A yawn escaped her.

He glanced at the clock. "So much for your bedtime. We better get you into the shower then straight to sleep, young lady. Do you like to sleep with a soft toy?"

A soft toy?

Was he serious?

"Wellll, usually I sleep with all of them."

"All of them?"

She got why he looked so shocked. Her soft toys took up one whole suitcase. And yep, she usually slept with all of them. But then, she didn't usually have a man in her bed.

"Uhh, yep."

"Do you have a favorite?"

"Daddy!" She gave him a horror-filled look. "That would be like trying to choose a favorite child or limb. Sorry, left leg, right leg is my favorite. Off you go!"

"My apologies," he replied gravely. "I'm not sure what I was thinking asking you to choose. But perhaps you could swap them around? Maybe sleep with a different one each night."

Hmm.

"I don't want the rest to get lonely, though." It was a huge dilemma.

"Do you think they will understand that without a bigger bed they can't all fit? Perhaps some of them could sleep on the floor."

"To be honest, Daddy. I'm pretty certain they think that you should sleep on the floor. But I guess I'll get out the triplets to begin with. They're the neediest."

He drew the suitcase out from the top of the wardrobe. Then he set it on the bed and opened it. Soft toys sprung out from inside.

"My poor babies. You hate being in the suitcase, don't you?" she said, patting each of her toys. "They can't breathe in there, Daddy."

"Yes, I can see that. What if we set them out on the sofa? Will that make them feel better?"

She sighed. "I suppose."

They quickly put all of the soft toys out on the sofa, lining them up. Harry even found a spare blanket to put over them so they wouldn't get cold.

"What if someone breaks in and steals them?"

"I'll hear if anyone tries to break in," he reassured her as she grabbed the triplets.

"I take it these are the triplets?" he asked.

"What gave it away?" she teased as she held the identical monster stuffies. They were all purple and fluffy with one eye and open mouths filled with teeth. Totally ugly. But that was part of their appeal.

"There's a slight resemblance between them," he replied dryly. "What are their names?"

She held one up at a time. "Oogly. Doogly. Moogly."

"Of course," he said with a nod. "Good names."

"Thanks, Daddy." They walked into the bedroom after she said good night to her other stuffies. She was still a bit worried about them and made sure Harry checked that the door was locked again.

"Who do you want to sleep with tonight?" Harry asked as they entered the bedroom. "Oogly? Doogly? Or Moogly?"

"All of them?"

"I'm sorry, Little Monster. Just one."

"But it's so hard to choose. I'll hurt the others' feelings. They're triplets. They're meant to stick together."

"What if we make a bed on the floor for the other two?"

"Not happening."

With a sigh, she nodded. Then she decided the only fair way to choose was with the tried and tested method of closing her eyes and pointing at one.

"Moogly, it is," Harry said.

"Daddy! How did you know it was Moogly?" she asked, suitably impressed.

He tapped the side of his nose with his finger. "A Daddy always knows."

Harry made a bed out of a few cushions and his jacket for Oogly and Doogly.

Five minutes later, she was nearly swaying as she stood in front of the bathroom sink trying to get toothpaste on the darn toothbrush. Why did they make the hole of the toothpaste so big? It just seemed to go everywhere. She needed one of those pump ones. Did they still make those?

"Here, baby." Harry moved up behind. He was dressed in a pair of black pajama pants and a white T-shirt.

Hmm. Not what she'd expected.

"I'll take you shopping this weekend," he promised, taking the toothpaste and toothbrush from her. He expertly put some paste on the bristles without it going everywhere.

Damn. How did he do that?

He slid in behind her so they were both facing the mirror. She stared in the mirror at him. His kind eyes that could twinkle with humor or harden with sternness. That sexy beard. He was handsome and put-together and smart.

"Keep looking at me like that and we won't ever get to sleep."

"Promises, promises," she replied huskily.

He reached around her, holding the brush to her mouth. She went to grab it but he shook his head. "Let Daddy help you. Or you'll make a mess."

Well, she couldn't argue with that. Still it felt a little odd to let him brush her teeth. She found herself leaning into him as he cleaned them for her.

When he was finished, he wiped her mouth then kissed the tip of her nose. "Have you used the toilet?"

"Yes," she groaned.

"Good. Come on, then. You should have been asleep ages ago."

With a yawn, and her hand wrapped up in his, she followed

him to the bed where he tucked her in then went over to the other side and climbed in.

He spooned her from behind her and she sighed happily. It had been so long since she'd slept with someone. Last night didn't really count because she couldn't remember it.

But there was nothing like having your man wrap himself around you protectively. Even if she was likely to start kicking him as soon as she fell asleep and he'd probably end up on the floor.

Poor guy.

Just as she was drifting off, she remembered what he'd said earlier.

"Daddy?"

"Yes, Little Monster?"

"What are we going shopping for?"

"Pin-striped pajamas, of course."

Oh, goody.

25

Kiesha sat up with a gasp.

She looked around her. Where the heck was she? What was going on? What day was it?

Fuck! Was she late for work?

She threw the covers back and jumped out of bed, stumbling to one side and smashing up against the nightstand.

"Ow! Owie!"

"Kiesha? What's wrong?" Harry rushed into the bedroom and over to her.

Tears had filled her eyes and she sat on the bed, rubbing at her leg. "Banged my shin on the nightstand."

"Oh, baby," he crooned, coming to crouch in front of her. "Let me see."

"I have to hold it or it will hurt worse." Everyone knew that, right?

"Let Daddy see," he said with a firmer voice. "I need to make sure you're not really hurt."

"I am really hurt," she countered. "It's bad."

"Hmm. Do you need a Band-aid?"

"I don't know, have you got any monster ones?"

"I don't. Which is remiss of me. I'll have to fix that today." Reaching over, he grabbed a tissue from the nightstand and patted her cheeks, wiping away the tears. "Let Daddy see, baby girl."

Slowly, she removed her hand. There was nothing there. It didn't mean that it didn't hurt, but still, she did feel a bit put out.

"It really does hurt."

"I'm sure it does," he soothed. "Would you like some of Daddy's special kisses?"

"Special kisses, huh? Kisses that only I get?"

"Of course."

"Okay then."

Running his hand along her leg, he laid some soft kisses on the sore part of her leg.

"Wow, Daddy. Those really are special kisses."

He smiled at her. Then he leaned in and kissed her lips. "Told you."

"More?" She wrapped her arms around the back of his neck. "I think I might have hurt my lips too."

"You did? Well, we can't have them hurting." He gave her another few kisses.

Then awareness filled her. She was late! And she hadn't brushed her teeth yet.

"Oh God!" She drew back, putting her hand over her mouth. "Ihaventbrushedmyteethandimlate."

He gave her a puzzled look. "What was that?"

She moved her hand. "I haven't brushed my teeth! I just kissed you with morning breath! And I'm running late." She attempted to wriggle past without inflicting him with any more of her terribly stinky breath.

He placed his hands on her thighs.

"I want you to stop and take a breath," he ordered in a low voice.

"But, Harry, I—"

"Stop. Breathe. In. Out."

She stilled, knowing he wasn't going to budge. In. Out.

"Again."

"In. Out."

"It's not good to wake up so stressed. Is this the way you wake up every morning?"

"Uh, well, I suppose. Usually, I keep some suckers by my nightstand. And I pop one in my mouth to give me a sugar boost. That would likely help with the stinky breath too."

"No candy first thing in the morning. That's not a healthy breakfast. And you're not late."

"I'm not? But I'm always late."

"I was just coming in to wake you up. You have plenty of time to get dressed. We'll have breakfast at the diner and then I'll take you to work."

"I have time for breakfast?"

"Yes."

"You're taking me to work? But what about my roller skates?"

"You don't need them, I'm driving you. I'll pick you up as well. I don't like the look of the weather. It's meant to rain later."

As he spoke, he drew her up and led her into the bathroom.

"It is?"

"Yep. Use the toilet, don't brush your teeth as I'll help you with that. What would you like to wear today?"

"Ahh, it's Monday. I always start the week off extra bright. So, my neon pink or yellow tights with a skirt and a T-shirt."

"You got it."

An hour later, Harry was walking with her into work. They'd already eaten breakfast at the diner. He'd made her get a side of fruit salad with her stack of pancakes. And when she hadn't bothered to eat it, he'd placed his hand on her thigh and asked her if she needed help.

Damn if her body hadn't instantly gone on alert. She'd managed to eat a few bits on her own.

As they walked in, Ed was coming out of his office. He came to a sudden stop looking from her to the clock on the wall.

"Do we need to change the batteries on the clock? It has to be going slow."

She put her hands on her hips. "It's not going slow. I'm early."

"You can't be early. You're never early. Are you feeling all right?" Ed came forward and reached out to put his hand over her forehead. "You don't feel hot."

"I'm not ill. It's all due to Harry that I'm here early."

"Harry." Ed gave him a polite nod before staring down at her. "How is it due to Harry that you're early?"

"Because he got me up early. And he took me for breakfast. He's trying to change me already, Ed! It's terrible." She winked at Harry.

He shook his head at her.

"You stayed with him last night as well?" Ed asked in a low voice.

"Oh no. You don't get to do that overprotective shit with me. You don't own me, Ed Granger. I'll sleep with whoever I like."

One of Ed's deputies had just walked into the room. He turned and walked away. Probably wise.

"I'm looking out for you. Your mother put me in charge of your care."

"Really?" Harry drawled. "Then how come you allowed her to stay in that shack with holes in the ceiling and walls and no electricity in the middle of nowhere?"

She groaned. "Damn it, Harry. You weren't supposed to tell him. Now he's going to be insufferable."

"What? What's he talking about, Kiesha?" Ed demanded.

She sighed. "Before I tell you, promise you won't lecture me for half an hour like you did the other day."

"You put yourself in danger. You were holding onto the back of a truck while on your roller skates."

"What?" Harry demanded.

"I was running late," she said to Ed, ignoring Harry. "It got me here quicker. Isn't that what you want?"

"No, what I want is for you to be safe. Now what the hell was Harry talking about?" They were moving closer to each other as they argued.

"I was kicked out of my apartment and so I went back to stay at Grandpa's place."

"What the hell? Why wouldn't you tell me that? Damn it, Kiesha."

Suddenly, she was drawn back against a firm chest, an arm wrapped around her waist.

She glanced up at Harry who was glaring at Ed.

Uh-oh.

"Do not swear at her," Harry warned in a low voice. "And do not take that tone of voice with her."

Ed eyed him for a long moment. "I'm practically her brother."

"I get that. But it doesn't mean you get to swear at her. Or speak to her like that."

Kiesha patted Harry's arm in what she hoped was a soothing gesture. "Harry, it's all good. This is what we do. We bicker like siblings. But Ed has my back. He always has. He's just worried about me."

"But you're right," Ed said suddenly. "I shouldn't be swearing at her. She just worries me. All. The. Time."

Guilt filled her. "You don't need to worry about me. I can take care of myself."

"Clearly not, since you've been living in your grandfather's shack." He glanced around, noticing how public they were. "Come into my office. Please," he added after glancing at Harry.

Harry moved her, pressing her tight to his side as they walked into his office. Ed shut the door behind him. "Have a seat, you want a coffee?"

"I can make it," she offered, eager to get out of this conversation. Having your bossy pseudo-brother and your new boyfriend/Daddy Dom in the same room discussing your behavior wasn't high on her to-do list.

"I don't think so," Harry said, drawing her over to Ed's desk.

Hmm. She wondered what it would be like to have Harry on the other side of the desk, calling her in for her naughty behavior. He might direct her to bend over the desk, then draw up her skirt and pull her panties down and . . . then Ed came into her line of vision.

Yikes, that was one way to cool her fantasies off.

"Have a seat," Ed said, taking his own across the desk.

Harry sat then drew her onto his lap, wrapping an arm tightly around her.

Whoa. She hadn't expected such a show of ownership from Harry.

Damned if it didn't make her hot as hell, though. She'd kind of thought he'd be more chill than this. But knowing that he was so possessive of her . . . yeah, she found that way too sexy for her own good.

Probably shouldn't let him know that. He'd go caveman on her ass all the time and she'd have to carry a five pack of panties in her handbag.

Ed leaned his forearms on the desk, taking in the way Harry was holding onto her.

"What the two of you get up to is none of my business."

Okay, that was unexpected. "What's the catch?"

"Pardon?" Ed asked.

Yeah, he could look all innocent but she knew him.

"There's a but. There has to be. You're being too reasonable."

"But I'd like to know Harry's intentions."

"Oh, good Lord." She threw her arms up in the air. "We don't live-in eighteenth-century England, Ed! You can't ask his intentions."

"I'm looking out for you. I want to make sure you don't get hurt." He gave her a calm look.

"We're getting to know each other and seeing where this goes. That's what's going on."

"Yeah? And what happens when Harry leaves?"

She tensed but Harry squeezed her waist with his arm. "Easy, baby. I've got this. I care greatly about Kiesha. I think she's amazing, beautiful, funny, and kind. And I want to get to know her better. I'm also planning on moving here."

Ed gave him a shocked look. "You're moving here? To Wishingbone?"

"Yes."

Ed shot her a worried look.

She sighed. "He's been thinking about it for a while. He's not moving here just because of me."

"Well, all right then."

"Jeez, don't be so effusive in your encouragement and well wishes," she told him sarcastically. "It's getting embarrassing."

Ed sighed. "I'm sorry. You're right. It just took me by surprise. You're right, Kiesha is all those things. And you're lucky to have her."

Aw, see sometimes Ed could be so sweet.

"She's also impulsive, reckless and needs constant watching. You up for that?"

And then he went and said something completely dickish and ruined it all.

"Hey!" she protested. "I am not impulsive or reckless and I definitely don't need close watching."

Both men stared at her and she squirmed on Harry's lap.

"She doesn't take good enough care of herself," Ed said darkly. "And what she fails to see is how lost we'd all be without her."

Oh crap.

Mushy stuff.

This was something she definitely didn't expect from Ed. They didn't usually do this sort of thing with each other.

"No, you wouldn't," she muttered. "You'd go on with your lives. Have lots of babies with Georgie. How is that going, anyway? Because I've got some little blue pills that could be very helpful if you're having trouble in that department."

Ed sighed. "And she tries to deflect whenever you attempt to talk about anything she deems mushy."

"Hey!"

"Yes?" Ed asked. "You want to dispute that?"

"No, not really." She glanced up at Harry. "How about you? Do you need . . ."

"I think we both know I don't need help in that department." Harry gave her a stern look.

"Well, can't say as I know for sure," she muttered quietly.

Ed groaned. "I really don't need to know about this stuff."

"You brought it up."

"No, I didn't. I was warning Harry about your lack of self-preservation and little regard for your own health and safety. I just want to make sure he's up to the job of taking care of you. No offense, Harry."

"None taken," Harry replied. "And yes, I believe I am. What Kiesha needs is someone steady, reliable, who can be firm when needed. I'll have plenty of time on my hands to look after her."

"Can we not talk about me like I'm a Labrador," she grumbled.

Harry winced. "Yes, you're quite right. I apologize."

"Good." She smiled up at him and he kissed the tip of her nose. Then his face grew stern again.

"But I would like to hear more about you holding onto a tailgate while roller skating."

Uh-oh.

26

Harry could feel Kiesha growing tense in his lap.

"We don't really need to talk about that. It's in the past."

"This seems to be a behavior that happens often, Kiesha. Putting yourself at risk."

"What else has she been doing?" Ed asked.

Kiesha squirmed.

"That's between Kiesha and I." Harry held his hand up as Ed went to protest. "I know the two of you are as close as siblings and I'm not trying to push you apart or take over. But some things are between us."

"Fair enough," Ed said with a sigh. "Although I'm always going to be protective of her, no matter who she's with." Ed shot him a warning look. Harry knew that if he ever hurt the gorgeous woman in his arms that he'd never be welcomed back into this town.

And he liked that she had a protector. But what Ed would come to realize is that no one would protect her as completely and thoroughly as Harry.

"Can you two please stop talking about me like I'm not even here," she said with obvious exasperation.

"I'm sorry, baby. We should stop doing that." He kissed the top of her head and she melted against him.

"That's okay," she told him, smiling up at him.

Ed watched them with raised eyebrows. "Huh, interesting."

"What is?" Kiesha asked.

"Ah, nothing. Why were you kicked out of your apartment? Did you forget to pay the rent?"

"No, I didn't forget to pay the rent. Dennis was just being a dick."

"I think it might have been in revenge for me getting him to do his job," Harry said darkly.

"What? Why?"

"Kiesha had a stuck door and even though she'd told him three months ago, he still hadn't fixed it."

"What? That asshole. Why didn't you tell me you were having problems with him?" Ed demanded.

"Because I don't need you to fight my problems for me. I had it under control."

"Only I went and told him to do his job and then suddenly, Kiesha gets an eviction notice."

"Bastard. What reason did he give?" Ed asked.

"Lots of reasons," she said dryly. "He couldn't seem to settle on just one."

Ed stood. "Oh, he'll come up with just one. I'll go talk with him now."

"No, wait, you can't!" she said, climbing off Harry's lap. Harry let her go, knowing she needed to tell Ed this part herself.

"Why not? He had no right to evict you, Kiesha. I can't believe you didn't come to me as soon as you got the notice."

"Because he threatened your job."

Ed stilled then turned to look down at her in disbelief. "He what?"

"He threatened to make things difficult for you to get re-elected as sheriff. That's why I didn't tell you."

Harry waited for Ed's reaction. He was pretty sure what it was going to be, but he could be wrong.

"That fucking tiny-dicked asshole!"

Okay, he wasn't wrong.

"Language," he warned Ed.

Ed flicked his furious gaze to him.

"Watch your language around Kiesha."

Kiesha waved a hand in the air. "I work with criminals, Harry. I hear that language all the time."

"You don't work with criminals, baby," Harry countered. "There shouldn't be criminals anywhere near you."

Ed winced. "Sometimes there are. And sometimes she does hear shit like that. But you're right, she shouldn't hear it from me."

Okay, he didn't like the sound of that. "She better be safe," he warned the other man. Or there was going to be a problem. A big one. He couldn't allow her to go to work each day if she was in danger.

"Of course, she's safe," Ed countered, sounding offended.

But Harry wasn't apologizing. "Her safety is my utmost concern."

"Urgh, the two of you are doing it again! Unless my invisibility powers have kicked in, I am right here."

"Sorry, baby. No invisibility powers."

She sighed. "That's really too bad. They're coming one day. I know it. I feel it."

"She's safe," Ed insisted. "I wouldn't allow her to be otherwise. Although obviously, she doesn't know that she should come to me with any threat." He glared down at Kiesha as he said that.

"Kiesha was trying to protect you," Kiesha said. "Kiesha can keep herself safe. Kiesha might just start talking about herself in the third person since the two of you like to ignore her."

"You should know that Dennis can't touch me," Ed replied. "He's a little man who thinks he has some power when he has none."

"I know exactly what kind of a dickhead Dennis is," she said. "I know that his overinflated sense of self-importance is in compensation for his undersized twinkie. Gag."

"He needs to be taught that he cannot treat you the way he has," Harry stated.

"I second that. Don't worry, Harry. I'll help you hide the body," Ed announced. "Let's go now."

"Whoa. What's happening right now?" Kiesha flung herself in front of the closed office door. "Stop it. I cannot be the voice of reason in this room! It's unnatural. No dead bodies allowed."

Dennis deserved to be strung up by his tiny twinkie.

Urgh, he had to stop calling it that.

Kiesha held out her hands. "You two need to stop and think. You're a sheriff." She pointed to Ed. "And you're a lawyer." She moved her finger to Harry. "You can't go around beating guys up."

"Of course, we can," Harry said. "The trick is not to get caught."

Kiesha shot him an exasperated look. "But you will, because Dennis will squeal as soon as he can. Ed, don't make me call Georgie."

Ed raised his eyebrows and crossed his arms over his chest. "You can't threaten me with Georgie."

"Just did."

"You don't think she'd agree with me teaching Dennis a lesson?"

"She'd tell you to be sneakier about it."

The longer they stood there talking, the more Harry realized getting physical with the little weasel probably wasn't the way to go. No matter how tempting it was.

"I have some ideas about how to destroy his life," Harry told Ed.

"Really? That sounds interesting."

"Probably best I don't give you any details."

"Good idea," Ed agreed.

"Okay, the two of you are being weird," Kiesha stated. "Have you stopped acting like idiots?"

"I don't know if we were acting like idiots, what do you say, Harry?"

"Not at all, Ed."

THEY BOTH TURNED to look at her.

No. Nope.

"Uh, no!" Kiesha pointed at them both. "This is not happening. You can't start getting along. That's not cool. Nope, first you make me be the voice of reason and now you're friends. Not. Cool."

"You'd rather we fought?" Ed asked.

"No, I'd just rather you never spoke to each other. I have a feeling that would be far better for me."

"Not happening. We need to talk in order to know what's going on with you," Harry told her. "Come here." He crooked a finger at her and she walked over to him. He drew her onto his lap and kissed her.

Ed cleared his throat and she blushed as she remembered that they had an audience.

Whoops.

She turned to face him. "So, is that all? I've really got to get to work. My boss is a real jerk if I'm late."

"Your boss says you're to stay here and tell him why you thought that asshole could affect my re-election."

"He said that his uncle had a lot of power and money and he could make things very difficult for you."

Ed sighed. "Kiki, you believed him? Dennis' uncle couldn't give a rat's ass what happens here. He only bought that building and gave Dennis a job to keep him away from him."

"Oh."

"Yes, oh."

"Well, I didn't know. I mean, it makes sense if I think about it. Why would anyone want Dennis the dick around? Nobody would. But I figured this guy was family so he might be blind to his dickishness. And I didn't want you to have problems because of me."

"Even if he could make trouble for me, I wouldn't care. You are far more important to me than my job."

"Urgh, no mushy stuff, Ed. It makes it harder for me to put laxatives in your coffee."

Harry shot her a look. "You put laxatives in his coffee?"

"Well, not all the time. Just when he annoys me. And sometimes I do other things to get back at him."

"All right, so why go stay in your grandpa's cabin? That thing is derelict. I don't know why your mom doesn't sell the land or something."

She didn't either. "I know. But I didn't have any choice."

Red started to fill Ed's cheeks. "No choice?"

Whoops.

"Any long-term choices," she said hastily. "I mean, obviously I could have stayed with you. But you guys need your privacy. I really don't need to be scarred for life hearing Georgie ride you like a cowgirl and telling you to giddy up."

Ed closed his eyes and started counting backward from a hundred.

"It's all right, he'll stop soon," she reassured Harry. "Although if he gets to sixty, we're in trouble."

"We are?" Harry asked dryly. "Or you are?"

Good point.

Ed reached seventy and stopped, opening his eyes to stare down at her. Whew, that was close.

"And staying at that rundown shack was a long-term solution?"

"No, but I thought it would give me time to save some money for a deposit somewhere else. I admit I underestimated how bad a state it was in."

"The place leaks like a sieve," Harry added bluntly. "It's a wonder she didn't get ill staying there."

"Harry, you're not helping matters."

"He needs to know the truth. And you need to learn to ask for help."

"She's crap at asking for help. Kiesha thinks that everyone should come to her when they need help, but she doesn't feel like she should do the same."

"That's not true. Every time I can't open a jar I go next door and ask Sudsy to open it for me. Sometimes he even does it. You know, if he hasn't been drinking too much."

"Oh, she'll ask for small things," Ed said. "But not the big things, oh no, those things she tries to do all by herself."

"I don't want to be a bother."

Ed sighed and sat back in his seat. "And this is why I eat antacid like it's going out of fashion."

Drat. Now she felt bad. "I'm sorry I'm crap at asking for help. But I just . . . I want to do things for myself. You know how Grandpa was with Mama. He always made her feel so guilty for needing help from him."

Ed sighed. He ran his hand over his face. "I know, Kiki. I remember. But what you don't realize is that we're all here for you. Me and Georgie, Juliet, Brick, and Xavier. Noah and Cleo, Isa and Loki. Heck, most of the town would come to your aid if you needed it, Kiesha. You're loved and you're not alone."

She blinked back the tears that filled her eyes. "I told you no mushy stuff, Ed!"

He smiled at her. "Tough. So next time you need us, tell us. Understand me?"

"I'll try."

"And if she won't tell us I'm relying on you to do it, Harry."

Harry was studying her as though she was a puzzle he was coming to understand. Yeah, she guessed he knew a whole lot more about her now.

Her reluctance to ask for help. To make herself vulnerable. But she was going to have to learn how if she wanted this relationship to work.

She was going to have to tell Harry about Vance. But not now. Not today. Although that was also on her to-do list. Find a way to pay Vance off. What were the odds of winning the lottery?

"So you're staying at the motel with Harry? That's not a good solution. You'll both come stay with us."

She gaped at Ed. "That's not happening."

"Why not?" Ed asked.

She turned to Harry, who looked like he was trying not to smile. "I think I already told you why not."

"Good Lord. Our bedrooms will be far apart. You won't hear . . . anything. Not that you'd hear anything like that anyway."

"Thanks for the offer, man," Harry told Ed. "But I don't think that will work. You guys need your privacy and so do we."

Ed frowned, but nodded.

Oh right, she said it and he ignored her. But when Harry pointed it out, he listened.

Typical.

And rude.

"Juliet has a pool house," Ed said.

"No, not happening." She shook her head.

"We're fine in the motel," Harry said. "And it won't be forever."

"Yeah, I'm thinking of renting that room that Mrs. Yardley has."

Ed scrunched up his nose. "That place smells like cheese."

"Yeah. But I like cheese, so it won't be that bad."

Ed turned to Harry. "You're not going to let her live in a place that smells like rotten cheese, are you?"

"No, of course not. She's staying with me." Harry shot her a look.

Happiness swam through her at that firm look. She didn't want to leave, but she also didn't want to wear out her welcome.

"Now, what I want to know is if you really did hold onto a tailgate behind a truck while on your roller skates?"

Oh, crap.

She'd hoped he'd forgotten about that.

"It was before we were together."

"When was it?"

"Uh, just before you left," she told him.

His eyes turned a steely blue.

"I was running late. I was just trying to get to work quicker. So really, it was Ed's fault for being so inflexible about what time I need to be here. And it was Jonny Jack's fault too. That asshole tattled on me."

Ed sighed, but Harry was frowning.

"What is the deal with this Jonny Jacks? Is he following you around? Do I need to worry about him stalking you?"

Both she and Ed gaped at Harry. Then Ed turned to her. "You want to explain?"

"I, uh, huh . . . he's not stalking me."

"Are you sure?"

"I'm sure. He's just a tattletale, but he, well, he's no danger to me. I promise."

Harry looked like he wanted to ask more, but he didn't. "Then explain about what you were thinking, holding onto that tailgate. Do you realize how dangerous that was?"

"You know what?" Ed said, standing. "I feel like coffee."

"No! We can't kick you out of your office," she said hastily. "That's just rude."

"Since when have you cared about that?" Ed scoffed.

"Since thirty seconds ago when you offered to leave to get coffee," she pointed out.

"Don't worry," Harry said. "I'm just going to walk Kiesha to her desk. Then I'll leave."

Uh oh.

There was some dark promise in those words that she was certain she didn't want anything to do with.

Yep, she had a feeling she was in trouble.

Harry wrapped his large hand around hers and led her over to her desk. "Please sit."

She stared up at him in trepidation then she sat. He moved to her side, crouching down. She'd put her hair up in a ponytail today with a neon pink scrunchie to match her tights.

"Here are the rules for today."

Double uh-oh.

"I'm going to pick you up when you finish work to take you back to the motel room. Where we're going to have a good chat about safety. And what is dangerous. And what things you are forbidden from doing."

She turned to look at him. "We're just going to chat?" Sure, she hated being lectured to. But it was probably better than the alternative.

"Oh no. We're going to do more than chat. You're getting your butt spanked. You're also going to write a hundred lines about obeying Daddy and not putting yourself in danger."

Drat. A hundred lines? Was he kidding?

"Couldn't you just give me more spanks?" she whispered.

"No. Somehow, I think the lines will make more of an impression on you."

Drat him. He wasn't wrong.

Standing, he leaned over and gave her a soft kiss. "Behave yourself. Don't eat too much candy. Wait for me if I'm late for some reason, but I'll text you to let you know."

Behave herself? Don't eat too much candy?

Sheesh. It was like he didn't know her at all.

27

"Pop!" Marisol rushed out of her cabin to throw herself at him. "I'm so glad you're back."

"Hello, sweetheart." He hugged her tight before looking down at her feet. "Where are your shoes? You shouldn't be out here just in socks."

"Drat! They're all wet now. I forgot I wasn't wearing shoes." She ran back up the stairs of the cabin she lived in with Linc. He'd already called Linc to ask if he could borrow Mari for the afternoon. He'd also remembered to ask him about Remy, the guy who watched Isa so closely. Linc had reassured him that Remy was a good guy. But he also said he'd keep an eye on him.

When they got inside, she quickly stripped the socks off and moved toward her room. "Go get comfy."

She walked back out wearing a pair of pink princess slippers that made him smile. He hadn't seen any slippers in Kiesha's stuff. He made a mental note to get her some when they went shopping this weekend.

"Harry? You all right?"

He blinked, looking up to see Mari was standing in front of

him. "Yes, sorry, Banana. I zoned out." He held a hand out to her. "Come sit with me. I have something to talk to you about."

Her eyes widened in horror. "Oh my God! Are you all right? Are you ill? What's happened?"

"Whoa," he said, pulling her in beside him then turning to face her. "Nothing is wrong. I'm not ill. Everything is fine."

"It's only that you were just here and you never visit this often, so I was worried..."

"I'm sorry. I didn't mean to worry you. I promise, I'm fine. There's actually an entirely different reason for me being here."

"What's that?"

"Well, I've met someone."

She stared at him, wide-eyed. "Met someone? Wait, you mean, she lives here? In Wishingbone?"

"Yes. She lives here."

"Oh my God! That's awesome. But how will that work with you living in Houston?"

"I'm going to move here."

"But... wait... how long have you been with her?"

"Not long at all. This is very new."

"And you're moving here? Is that wise? What about your career? Your apartment?"

"Truth is, I haven't been happy at work for a long time. I need a change. And being closer to you can never be a bad thing. I know this is very new, but the feelings I have for this woman are like nothing I've felt before. I know she's mine, Banana."

"Aww, that's so sweet. Who is it? Do I know her?"

"Yes, you do. It's Kiesha."

"Kiesha? Oh, wow, really?"

"You look shocked," he said dryly. He'd known it might take a moment for her to get her head around.

"It's not... it's not... she's just..."

"So much younger than me? Yes, I know. But I really care about her, Marisol." And he didn't much care what anyone else thought. He intended to have Kiesha, to keep her, to claim her. However, he knew it wasn't an accepted thing to go around claiming someone out loud. Or have your ownership tattooed on them.

So, he kept his mouth closed about that part.

But Kiesha was his. And she was going to stay his.

No way he'd ever let her go.

However, most people would probably think him nuts if he said that after only really knowing her a few short weeks.

Best to keep his crazy under wraps for a bit longer.

"No, it's not that. You're not that old, Pop. And you're gorgeous. It's just . . . are you . . . I mean, isn't she . . . urgh, I don't know how to ask this!"

"Just ask."

"I always thought that Kiesha was a Little."

"Oh, yes. She is. Is that a problem?" He didn't see why it would be. Marisol was a Little after all.

"No, of course not!" she said hurriedly. "It's just . . . well, I wasn't sure if you . . ."

Ahh. Now he got it.

"I'm fully prepared to take care of Kiesha. In any way she needs," he reassured Mari. He got why she was feeling so awkward bringing this up.

But he was ready to give Kiesha anything she needed. Including some smacks to her bum when required. He couldn't believe her reckless behavior.

That would have to stop.

He needed to find a house. To give them privacy. But also, to provide the stability that Kiesha desperately needed.

Convincing her to move in with him . . . well, that might be the difficult part.

"Pop? You sure you're all right?"

"Sorry, Banana. Just thinking. To be honest with you, I think I'm the best I've been in years."

"Really? Because of Kiesha?"

"Because of several things. But mainly because of her, yes. She's shown me that there is more to life than work."

"She certainly knows how to have fun. And you could use some more of that in your life."

"So, I have your approval," he teased.

"Of course! Anyone that makes you happy has my approval. And selfishly, I'm glad it's someone who lives around here. Because that means I get to see more of you."

"You really are the sweetest. Now, I have a favor to ask."

"Of course."

"Help me look for somewhere to live?"

"You bet! Oh, this is going to be so much fun." She clapped her hands.

As Mari was getting ready, he got a call and stepped outside to take it.

"Hi, Jeff, thanks for getting back to me. I need you to do some research into someone for me. Full background, the works. His name is Dennis Martin Fryer. Yep, that's his name. I'm going to send you the rest of his details. Thanks."

Dennis didn't know it yet, but his life was soon going to change. Drastically.

∼

Kiesha waited on the police station steps for Harry. He'd texted to let her know he was five minutes away. So, she figured she would wait outside so he didn't have to come looking for her.

Maybe that would get her some brownie points.

And help her poor bottom out.

But when he pulled up to the curb and she reached for the car door, he climbed out with a frown.

"Stop right there."

She stilled.

Oh, right. He liked to open doors. And put on seat belts.

"What are you doing standing out here?" he asked as he came around and opened the door.

"You said you were nearly here so I thought I would come wait out here for you."

He helped her into the seat then placed his hands on her cheeks. "Damn, you're freezing. Don't do that again. You're to wait inside where it's warm and I know you're safe, understand me?"

"Uh, okay."

He fastened her seat belt, then closed her door and moved back to the driver's seat.

Her tummy warmed in happiness at his protectiveness.

"How was your day?" he asked her.

"Uneventful. Yours?"

"I went to see Mari. I told her about us."

"You what?" she asked. "What did she say?"

He shot her a puzzled look. "That she's happy for us."

But was she? Would she approve of Kiesha being with her dad? Well, not her real dad but family didn't have to be blood.

Speaking of Ed, he hadn't wasted time in telling everyone that she'd gotten kicked out of her apartment and had been staying at her grandpa's cabin. She'd had to field a number of grumpy texts from her friends.

Seemed everyone was keen on spanking her ass today.

"She's really happy for us, sweetheart," Harry reassured her as he turned into the motel parking lot. He parked in front of their unit. "I promise. Marisol doesn't lie. And all she wants is for us to be happy. She's pleased I'm planning on moving here as well. And she wants to have lunch with you sometime."

"Okay." Damn, why was her voice so squeaky? It was embarrassing.

"Don't stress. Come on, I have some dinner for us inside. We have a few things to do tonight before bed."

Great. Just what she wanted to hear.

∽

When they got back to the motel unit, Harry led her into the bedroom. She glanced over at the small desk in the room and found it had been set up with a piece of blank paper and a pen.

Awesome.

That seat didn't look all that comfortable either.

"Right, come here." He held out his hand and she moved reluctantly over to him. Instead of drawing her over his lap straight away, he pulled her to stand between his parted legs. Reaching up, he cupped her face so she had to stare down at him.

"Hey," he said quietly. "Are you worried that I'll hurt you? I promise I will stop if you say your safeword."

"I'm not worried about that. I just . . . are you sure I have to write lines? Can't you just add an extra ten on to my spanking?"

"Ahh, I should have known it was the lines worrying you." He shook his head. "No, I can't do that, I'm afraid. I'm really worried about your lack of concern for your safety. And if writing lines stops you from doing something that endangers yourself in the future then it's worth it."

Well, drat.

"What about our neighbors? They might hear you spanking me. And we don't want the police called. Ed won't be on your side then."

"Ed isn't on my side, baby. He just recognizes that we both have a common goal."

"Which is?"

"To take care of you. And anyone who looks out for you is good people in my book."

"Darn it when you say things like that, you just melt all my grumpiness."

"You were feeling grumpy?"

"Well . . . not really. But I thought about it."

"About Ed and I getting along?"

She sighed. "No, not really. But if he starts tattling to you about me then we're going to have words. I don't need another Jonny Jacks in my life."

"Will you tell me the story about him one day?"

"Yes, one day." Old feelings welled inside her, threatening to overwhelm her. "It's complicated and I'm just not ready . . ." She turned her head away, blinking back annoying tears.

"Okay, baby. You don't have to tell me today. Time for your punishment. And you don't need to worry about neighbors. I asked the owner whether there was anyone staying on either side of us and he said not until the weekend."

"Oh Lord! You asked Arnie that? Now he's going to wonder what the hell we're up to in here that we don't want anyone hearing us. And he's a huge gossip. Huge. If he doesn't figure it out he'll probably make something up."

"What?" Harry scowled. "Like hell he will! Don't worry, I'll deal with him."

She stared down at him in shock. Then a slow smile filled her face.

He gave her a surprised look. "What is it?"

"I just like how you always have my back."

"Always, baby. I'll always have your back."

Cupping his face between her hands, she leaned down and kissed him. She put all of her feelings for him into that kiss. All of her needs and desires and wants.

"Thank you, Harry."

"You don't have to ever thank me for taking care of you. That's my privilege."

"It feels good, knowing you're there for me when I need you."

This time, Harry initiated the kiss. And boy, the man knew what he was doing. She felt herself being pulled down to sit on his knee as he kissed her until her lips were tingling and she was breathless.

"You sure do know how to distract a man."

She had to grin. "Yeah? I did a good job? Are you going to forget about that silly spanking and nasty lines and take me to bed instead?"

"Nice try, little girl. But I wouldn't be a very good Daddy if I promised consequences then didn't follow through. That wouldn't give you the sense of stability you need."

Well, damn.

"Nothing will distract me from doing what's best for you." He tapped her nose. "Now, you're going to spend some time in the corner before your spanking."

"What? Why?"

"Because you've said negative things about yourself a few times and that's not allowed, is it?"

Drat.

Standing, he took her hand and led her over to a corner of the room.

"I don't want to spend time in the corner."

"This is what you get for making bad comments about yourself. Now, nose in the corner. I'm just going to adjust your clothing. A naughty girl always has a bare bottom in the corner."

What? That couldn't possibly be a real rule, right?

"Daddy, you can't do this!"

"Am I in charge?"

"Yes," she replied.

"Are you saying your safeword?"

She huffed out a breath as he tucked the bottom of her skirt into the waistband.

"No."

"No, Daddy," he pressed.

"No, Daddy," she repeated. "I'm not saying my safeword."

"Then I can do this," he told her firmly.

She shifted from foot to foot.

"Stay still," he warned. "You're to remain still and quiet while in the corner and think about what happened for you to end up in here."

He drew her tights and panties down under her butt. Then grabbing one cheek in his hand, he squeezed it.

"This is one gorgeous ass, baby. I'm going to have to claim it as well."

He placed kisses all over one cheek then the other. Then he ran his thumb down between them, pressing it on her entrance. She took in a deep breath as trembles of need raced through her.

"My girl likes her bottom being played with, doesn't she?" he murmured. He removed his finger and gave one more kiss to her bottom before standing. "And it's my ass now. Stay still. Think about what you did. And no talking."

Jeez. What sort of hell was this? No talking? Who did he think he was speaking to? Talking was like breathing to her. And staying still was almost equally as hard.

She heard some water running and thought she was safe to shift her weight around.

"Stay still," Harry called out. "Time starts again."

How had he seen her? She blew out a breath.

"Quiet. This is thinking time."

Thinking time? Well, thinking time sucked. And he was timing her? Great, how long did she have to stand here? What did she look like, standing in the corner with her bare butt on display? Sheesh, this was pure torture.

"I don't like torture time," she muttered to herself.

"What was that? Torture time?" he asked.

"Uh-huh, this is torture, Daddy. I can't do it." Turning, she glanced over her shoulder to where he was laying out her pajamas. Yikes. It wasn't bedtime yet. Was it?

"You can do it. And you will. Time starts again."

"Daddyyy!" she cried. "Stop being mean."

"I'm not being mean. You're being punished. And part of your punishment is to stand in the corner and think about what you did and what you could have done differently."

"You mean I shouldn't have opened my fat mouth and said what I was thinking."

"I always want to know what you're thinking, Little Monster," he told her. He walked up to her and placed his hand on the small of her back. "But what I really want is for those thoughts not to be negative about yourself."

"That's kind of an impossible task," she told him. "One corner time isn't going to change the way I think."

"I didn't say it would happen immediately." He kissed her cheek then patted her ass gently. "Now, time has to start over again."

Man, this was really, really hard.

∼

DAMN, it was hard to sit there and not stare at her naked ass. He hadn't been lying before. She had a gorgeous butt. High, pert, and delicious. It was smooth and sweet. The only thing it was missing was a butt plug poking out from between her cheeks.

Next time.

Thankfully, this time she managed to stay still and quiet. He knew this would be hard for her. But he also knew that he needed to start as he meant to go on. Going easy on her wouldn't help her in the long run. But he also didn't need to be harsh.

Striking that balance was difficult.

"Good girl," he praised her. "You can come out of the corner now and get your cuddle."

She spun around so quickly that for a moment he worried she'd fall over. But she managed to balance herself and then reached for her tights and panties.

"No," he said firmly. "Leave those where they are. I'd just have to take them off again."

"Daddy!" she grumbled but she shuffled forward. Reaching out, he drew her onto his lap, cuddling her in close.

"What did you learn from being in the corner?"

"That it's boring."

"Try again," he said firmly.

"Well, it is boring." She shifted to give him a querying look. Whatever she saw must have convinced her that she should think about her answer more carefully. "But also, I suppose I shouldn't make negative comments about myself."

"You suppose?"

"I shouldn't," she said.

He had to grin at the total disgruntlement in her voice.

"Now, time for your spanking." He helped her off his lap then drew her back over so she was lying on her tummy.

He couldn't do anything about the hard-on he was sporting. And he knew she felt it as she wiggled against him.

"Stay still, baby. Is your arm okay?" He'd already checked it, but he wanted to be sure.

"It's fine. Did you like staring at my bare bottom while I was in the corner?" she asked huskily.

"Of course, I did. Your bottom is gorgeous." He rubbed her ass gently. "Do you remember why you're getting spanked?"

"Because Daddy likes touching my ass?" she said cheekily.

He landed two smacks. One on each cheek.

"Ouch! Daddy! I didn't know it was starting!"

"It hasn't started. That was for being cheeky. That wasn't a proper reply and you know it."

"Yes, Daddy. I'm being punished because I didn't listen to you when you told me to stay put. But I really don't like having to stay put."

"I wasn't telling you to stay there for fun. I said it to keep you safe. You didn't keep yourself safe or listen to me give you an order. And that's why you're being spanked."

"Yes, Daddy."

"And you're writing lines because you put yourself in more danger while roller skating behind that truck. That's unacceptable. You could have been badly hurt."

It upset him all over again, thinking about that. He could feel himself trembling at the thought of all the ways that could have ended badly, how she could have been harmed.

"I was fine."

"But you might not have been." She had to see how serious this was. "Baby, you're precious to me and nothing can happen to you, understand me?"

He could hear the fierceness in his voice and so could she if the way she glanced back at him was any indication. "I understand, Daddy. For a long time, I didn't think I had anything to live for after Jonah died. I was lost and I . . . sometimes I still act impulsively."

"I'm going to demand that you keep yourself safe. And if you don't, I will."

"Yes, Daddy. I understand. I think there might be a few more spankings in my future, though," she told him gravely.

He sighed. "Well, it's a hardship but if it has to be done, I'm here for it. Sometimes a Daddy's job is a very tough one."

She snorted out a laugh. "Oh, I'm sure it's so hard for you, Daddy. I think you like spanking my butt."

"Hmm, we'll just have to see, won't we?" He landed two more spanks on her cheeks.

"Ouch! Daddy! No!"

"Oh, my baby. This is only just the beginning." Part of him felt bad for her. But the other part knew she needed this.

Two more smacks. He loved the way she wiggled around on his lap. The movement of her ass as he slapped it.

This time he landed four in quick succession. She moaned.

"No more, Daddy. Please. It hurts."

Worry filled him. Was it too much? But he'd only given her ten.

"You want to safeword, baby?" he asked, cupping one warm ass cheek.

"What? No."

"Are you sure? If this is too much, then you only have to say."

"Daddy, I'm fine. I'm not safewording. Truth is, I kind of like to complain a bit."

"All right. That's okay. As long as you know you can safeword at any time."

"I know, Daddy. Now can we please get on with this? The anticipation is killing me."

"Sorry, baby," he told her. "There's ten more to go. I'm going to make this hard and fast."

He smacked her right cheek twice then her left. Soft gasps escaped her and she whimpered.

"Daddy! No!"

It wasn't her safeword, so he kept going. Two more to each cheek. She was wriggling around, trying to get free but he held her steady.

The last four were given quickly, without hesitation. By the time he landed the last smack, soft sobs were coming from her.

Gently, he turned her over. Tears glistened in her eyes, a few traveling down her cheeks. He wiped them away with his thumbs tenderly. "My poor baby."

Leaning in, he kissed her forehead then chased each new tear, catching it with his lips until he reached her lips, kissing them.

"My beautiful girl. How are you doing?"

"My butt hurts."

"As it should." He brushed wisps of her hair back off her face.

Her lower lip dropped in a pout. "It's not very nice of you, Daddy."

"My poor baby," he commiserated. "You know how to avoid spankings in the future, though."

She sighed, long and loud. "Yes, but it's just so very hard to be good. You know?"

He had to bite his inner cheek so he didn't grin at her words. They were so heartfelt.

"Yes, I know. But the thing is, you're always my good girl. It's just sometimes the things you do or say aren't healthy. And anything you do that puts you at risk is pretty much always going to result in you getting a spanking."

"Yes, I know. I'll try not to put myself in any danger."

"Thank you. It would really help this old man out."

"Yeah, you don't need any more wrinkles or gray hair."

"Hey! Brat." He started tickling her and she shifted around on his lap.

"No, Daddy! Stop! My butt! Ouch!" She giggled in between her protests. "I'm gonna pee!"

He stopped tickling her immediately and then set her on her feet with a light tap to her butt which earned him a huge scowl. "Go pee. Then come back here. I'll get you dressed in your pajamas before you do your lines."

"I think we could forget about that punishment, Daddy. I've suffered enough." She raised the back of her hand to her forehead dramatically.

He shook his head in amusement. But no matter how cute she was, he wasn't letting her get out of her next punishment.

∾

Whoever thought up doing lines while sitting on a hot bottom had a lot to answer for. This was really mean. And her hand was starting to cramp. How many lines had she done? Forty?

This was taking forever.

"How are you doing, Little Monster?"

"Terribly," she moaned. "I need a sucker."

"I think you've had enough suckers today. And it's nearly bedtime."

"I'm never going to get a hundred lines done, Daddy!"

He eyed her for a moment. "All right you can stop at fifty."

Yes! Huh, that was a lot easier than she'd anticipated.

"You can do the other fifty tomorrow night."

Nooo! This sucked.

"I'll do it all tonight, Daddy."

"Sure? I don't want you getting a sore hand."

She sighed. "I'm sure." She settled back into the lines. Harry came over with a glass of water that had a cute bright yellow straw in it. Kiesha loved bright and colorful things.

"Ooh, that's a pretty straw, Daddy."

"I picked up a packet for you today. They change color when the water goes up the straw. I want you to drink all that water by the time you've finished your lines."

"Daddy! I'm already being punished! Isn't that enough?"

He gave her a surprised look. "The water isn't punishment, baby."

She eyed the glass with suspicion. "Are you sure?"

"Yes, I'm sure. How much water do you drink?"

"Well, does hot chocolate count?"

"No, hot chocolate doesn't count."

"I dunno. I drink it when I need to. Are you sure that you don't have any chocolate milk?"

"I don't have any chocolate milk. And from now on, you'll be drinking more water."

"I just don't like the taste."

"I have some ideas for that. You like strawberries, right?"

"Uh-huh."

"What about if we cut them up and put them in a bottle of water for you?"

"Well, okay, Daddy. I'm willing to try it."

"That's my good girl. Now, get writing."

When she was finished writing her lines, she put her hands up in the air. "Done! I am victorious."

Harry checked her lines, even making sure that there were a hundred there.

"Good girl," he murmured to her, pulling her up into his arms and hugging her tight. She wrapped her arms around his neck.

Drawing back, he studied her face. "I want to take you away this weekend."

All right. That was kind of out of left field but she nodded. "Okay, Daddy. Where are we going?"

"That's going to be a surprise. I'll take care of everything including packing your bag. But do you think you could get Friday off work? Is it too late for you to do that?"

"Nah, I can do that. Ed's always on at me to take a day off."

"Good, you take care of that and I'll figure out everything else. Now, I got you something today."

"Daddy, you don't need to buy me anything."

"But I wanted to, and it makes me happy."

"Well, all right. But I'll only accept it because it makes you happy."

"Thank you for your sacrifice."

"You're welcome."

He took her hand and led her back into the living area of the unit. "Why don't you sit down on the couch and I'll get your gift. Then you can play while we wait for dinner to be delivered."

She stared down at the couch with a sigh. It would be better than sitting on that chair in the bedroom while she did lines, at least.

"Should I cover my eyes, Daddy?" she asked.

"Of course."

Oh goody. This was fun.

She put her fingers over her eyes, bouncing up and down on the sofa.

"Here you are, Little Monster."

Something was placed in her lap. Excitement flooded her as she moved her hands away from her eyes.

"Daddy! Oh my gosh! How did you know I loved coloring?"

"Well, I saw the coloring book and thought you might like it."

It was a monster coloring book and totally her. He'd even bought her a full set of crayons.

"I love it! Thank you! Thank you!" She jumped up and wrapped her arms around his neck. "Daddy, you're the best."

"Glad you love it, Little Monster. Now, be a good girl and do some quiet coloring while Daddy gets dinner ordered."

"Daddy, I'm always a good girl."

"Of course you are."

Kneeling on the floor, she colored furiously while he spoke on the phone. Everything else kind of faded into the background while she got in the zone. She was barely even aware of the knock on the door and voices speaking. She was safely hidden behind the sofa.

"Little Monster, dinner is ready."

"Oh, but Daddy, I'm nearly finished. Look!" She held up the page she was coloring proudly. She pointed to a small pink and green monster. "That's me, and this giant, purple, hairy one with the big nose is you. Aren't you handsome?"

"Ahh."

"I think we should frame it, don't you? And write our names on it. So that everyone can see what a sexy monster you make."

"Ummm."

"What's wrong, Daddy? Don't you agree that this super ugly monster is you?" She started giggling, and he grabbed her, tickling her until she screamed for mercy.

"Come on, brat. Dinner. Shower. Bed. And then I'll show you what this hairy monster can do."

"Promises, promises."

28

"Thanks for meeting with me, Mrs. Coster," Harry said, getting up to shake the woman's hand. "If there's anything else you can think to tell me, then you can call me on this number." He handed over his business card to the woman who smiled at him.

It was Thursday afternoon and that was the last interview he'd had lined up. With everything the private investigator found along with all the information he'd gathered, he finally had what he needed.

All of his ducks were nearly in a row.

And soon Dennis was going pay for everything he'd done to Harry's girl.

∾

"So, you going to tell me where we're going yet, Daddy?" Kiesha asked as he buckled her into her seat on Thursday evening after quiz night.

They'd kicked butt. Again. She'd expected they'd be leaving in the morning for their weekend away, but Harry had told her he wanted to leave tonight. After some hasty goodbyes, he'd escorted her out of the bar.

"Still a secret."

Darn it.

"A Daddy shouldn't have secrets from his girl."

"But this is a fun secret."

Right. Unlike her secrets.

The ones she knew she had to divulge to him sometime soon.

He reached over her into the backseat and drew out a blanket and pillow as well as Oogly.

"Oogly, what have you been up to? You been hanging out with Harry all day?"

"He has. He helped me pack your bag and threw himself in the car when I said I was going."

"He's always been the naughtiest of the triplets. A real ratbag."

"I know someone else who's a bit of a ratbag," he told her as he arranged the blanket over her. She wasn't sure why since she wasn't cold.

"Is it you, Daddy? I know it's you."

"No, brat. It's not me. Now, I have a snack for you for the ride." He picked up a small Tupperware container off the floor of the car and handed it to her. She opened it to find one compartment had cheese and crackers while the other had cut up fruit.

"Daddy, I think we need to have a serious conversation about what a snack is. Like, I don't know what you used to eat on road trips as a kid but it's meant to be full of sugar or fat with no nutritional value."

"I didn't go on a lot of road trips as a child."

"That's just sad. I love road trips."

"I know. I remember. I've also filled up your water bottle and there are cut-up strawberries in it. So, I expect it all gone by the time we get to our hotel."

"Okay, but if I have to stop to pee all the time, it's your fault."

"I think I can deal with that. Here's your pillow in case you get tired."

"It's only nine-thirty. I'm fine." Although she did have to stifle a yawn as he closed the door and made his way around to the driver's seat.

Seemed that her body was starting to get used to the early bedtimes he insisted on.

These past few days had been some of the most amazing in her life. Despite the fact that Harry seemed to think she should be drinking more water, eating healthier, and sleeping more.

Oh, and he hadn't fucked her yet.

She'd gotten plenty of good girl orgasms. That's what she'd started calling them. Because he was always praising her. Telling her how beautiful she was. What a good girl she was.

And she lapped it all up like a sunflower turned to the sun.

Of course, if she was naughty, she didn't get any good girl orgasms. Like last night when he'd discovered that she'd been so busy that she hadn't drunk any of her water or touched the lunch he'd sent to work with her.

Yep, he sent her to work with a packed lunch.

Be still her heart.

She'd ended up in the corner for ten minutes thinking about what she could have done differently and then she'd had to write out fifty times that she wouldn't forget to eat her lunch or drink her water.

And worst of all, no good girl orgasms.

Don't get her started on the fact that she hadn't even gotten a glimpse of his cock yet.

Not cool.

Anyway, she had a bit of a plan for next time he wanted to

spank her. A package had arrived at work for her today, which contained a secret weapon in her 'get Harry to fuck her' campaign.

Yes, there was a campaign.

If things got more desperate, she would need to make flyers. Well, just one flyer. For one guy.

Apparently, he was a bit dense. It was up to her to teach him better.

"What music do you want? We can't have a road trip without singing some bad songs." She searched through the stations until she found a good song. "Come on, Daddy. Sing along."

To her surprise, his singing voice was rather good. Better than her own. She was a terrible singer. She messed up all the words then made up her own.

He winced, then quickly hid it as she attempted to reach a high note.

"You know, I always thought I could have a career on the stage. What do you think, Daddy? Should I quit my job to pursue a singing career?"

"Ahh . . . well, that is . . . umm . . ."

She started giggling as he fumbled his way through what to say in reply to that.

He let out a low, rumbling noise. "Brat. Were you teasing me?"

"Yep, I was teasing you. I know I sound like a duck with laryngitis when I sing."

"I wouldn't go that far. But you probably couldn't make a career out of singing."

She giggled. A few minutes later, she frowned as she saw where they were headed. Maybe it wasn't their destination . . .

"Are we going to Bozeman, Daddy?" she asked quietly.

"Yes, we are. Surprise." There was a moment of silence. "Is there something wrong? Do you not like Bozeman?"

"Oh no, it's not that. Not exactly."

This was silly. She couldn't be against a whole city just because some of the worst moments in her life had occurred there.

"What do you mean, not exactly? What's the matter?"

To her shock, he pulled the car off to the side of the road then put it into park before turning to her. Placing one hand on her thigh, he lightly grasped hold of her chin, turning her face toward him.

"What's wrong, Little Monster?"

His voice was soft, and she found herself fighting tears at his caring. What had she done to deserve this man?

Not a lot.

"Bozeman is where Jonah and I lived before he died," she explained.

"Oh, baby," he crooned. "I'm so sorry. I didn't realize that's where Jonah died."

"It's not your fault. And it's silly. It's not the city's fault he died."

He reached for the pocket at the side of the door, pulling out his phone.

"What are you doing?"

"Calling the hotel to cancel our booking. Is there somewhere else that you'd like to go? We could drive to Billings or Big Sky?"

"No, wait. Don't do that." She reached out to grab his wrist.

"Kiesha, I wanted to take you away for a nice holiday. I don't want you to be sad."

She shook her head. "I won't be. I couldn't ever be unhappy when I'm with you."

"I don't think that's true."

"It is," she insisted. "I want to go there with you. Maybe it's time to make good memories to take away the bad."

He eyed her for a long moment. The only light came from the dashboard and the car's headlights, so she wasn't sure how much he could see.

"Are you sure?"

"Please. I want to go there. With you."

"All right, but if it becomes too much I want you to tell me and we'll leave. Promise."

"I promise," she told him.

It wasn't until they were driving again that she thought about Vance and his guys. But it wasn't like they were going to run into them.

29

"Where are we going today, Daddy?"

She was practically dancing around the hotel room. Except it wasn't just a room, it was an entire suite. It was the flashiest place she'd ever stayed. There was a bedroom, living area, and the most enormous bathroom. She walked in there now. She had to pee after drinking a whole glass of water with the breakfast Harry had delivered to their room.

Yes, someone had pushed a trolley into their room and set up breakfast on the small table in front of a window that looked out over the Bozeman skyline.

This place was epic.

"Daddy! What's this other toilet?"

Harry walked in with a smile. "It's a bidet."

"Wow. The thing that cleans your butt?"

"Yep. You want to use it?"

"I only gotta pee." But yeah, she kind of did. Because she doubted she'd ever stay anywhere again with a bidet. Although maybe Harry did this regularly.

"Do you like using it?"

He grinned and leaned against the bathroom cabinet. "No, I've tried it but it's not for me."

Anyway, this was good and all, but she really had to pee. She shifted her weight from side-to-side.

"Daddy, I gotta go."

"I figured that from the little pee dance you're doing. That's cute by the way."

"It's not cute! It's a necessity. Otherwise I might pee my pants. Daddy, go!" She pointed at the door, imperiously.

He narrowed his gaze at her. "Excuse me? Who makes the rules around here?"

"Urgh, this is not the time to go all Dom on me. It's really sexy, but I can't get turned on because I really gots to go."

He just shook his head at her and walked toward the door. Thank goodness.

After peeing for what felt like hours, she washed her hands and moved back into the bedroom. Harry was already dressed for the day and he had an outfit laid out on the bed for her. Turning, he crooked a finger at her. She walked toward him worriedly. He wasn't really upset by her ordering him to leave, was he?

When she was close, he reached out to grasp hold of her chin, holding her face still. "You're adorable, but you also seem to think you're the boss. You're not."

"That's a shame. I think I'd make a good boss. I'd give everyone three-day weekends and candy bonuses."

"I have no doubts you'd make an excellent boss," he told her. "You could rule the world if you wanted to. But when it comes to the two of us, I'm in charge."

"Yes, Daddy. So long as you don't try to watch me pee. Because there are boundaries."

"I don't seem to like boundaries." Grasping her around the waist, he walked her backward until she hit the wall. "I don't like anything between us. I don't like that there is something you won't do in front of me."

She stared up into his intent gaze.

"Some of your crazy is showing," she whispered to him. Not that she cared. She was absolutely here for his crazy.

"Your crazy seems to call to mine." He grabbed her hands in his, pressing them back to the wall by her head. "Is that a problem?"

"Oh no. My crazy really likes your crazy."

"That's good. Because it seems that my crazy is a possessive bastard who doesn't like to let his girl out of his sight. What do you think Ed would say if I set up an office in the police station?"

"I mean, you'd be close-by for people who needed your services."

He leaned in to kiss along her jaw. "And what about you? Would you need my services?"

"Well, that could be nice too."

"Nice?" he growled. "I'll give you nice, brat." Letting go of her hands, he grabbed the bottom of her top and drew it up over her head, exposing her breasts to his gaze.

She gasped and looked over to the window which had the drapes drawn back.

"Nobody will see us," he murmured. "We're too high up. I wouldn't allow anyone to see your naked body but me. Because you're mine." He dropped his hand to her breast, cupping it and squeezing it.

She let out a low whimper.

"I bet you're very naughty at work, aren't you, my baby?" he murmured. "I think that if I was with you all the time, I'd find you breaking all sorts of rules. And you know what I'd have to do, don't you?"

"Nooo," she groaned as he lightly squeezed her nipple. "What?"

"I'd have to call you into my office and lock the door. It would need to be soundproofed. We couldn't have Ed storming in coming to your rescue."

"Ew. Way to ruin the fantasy, Daddy."

"Sorry, I apologize. You're quite right. Let me make that up to you. Keep your hands pressed to the wall above your head. Move them and I'll have to punish you. Do as you're told and you get a reward."

"Your cock in my mouth?" she asked breathlessly.

"That's what you want as a reward? Not an orgasm?" he asked, looking surprised.

Oh damn.

That was a difficult choice.

"I want both," she cried. "But I really, really want to suck your cock. Please. Please."

"My baby does like things in her mouth, doesn't she?" he murmured, running a finger along the seam of her lips. "You'll have to be very, very good."

"I will be. I promise."

"I'll believe it when it happens," he replied. "Where was I? Oh yes, someone needs an apology from Daddy." Bending down, he sucked on her right nipple. She cried out, having to fight against moving her hands away from the wall as he sucked on her hard nub.

God.

So good.

He moved his mouth to her other nipple. "Am I making it all better?"

"Yes. Yes, Daddy."

"Good, because I want to get back to that fantasy of you being naughty while we're working. I'd have to call you into my office."

"Then what?" she asked breathlessly as he knelt in front of her to kiss down her tummy.

"Then I'd have you take off your panties and give them to me. I'll have to keep them for the rest of the day, because you've been naughty. And because they smell delicious. Just like you." He kissed his way along the top of her pajama bottoms. She was wearing her favorite pair.

He started to slowly lower her bottoms.

"Step out of them."

She moved her foot out of one side then the other.

"That's my good girl. It seems you really do want Daddy's cock in your mouth."

She groaned. She wanted that so badly.

"But first, I get to claim another piece of you."

Please let that be her pussy and not her feet or her toes or some other ridiculous part of her.

Because she really needed it to be her pussy.

Then he placed his hands on the inside of her thighs, widening her legs before he licked along the seam of her pussy through her panties.

"After you'd removed your panties and gave them to me, I'd have you bend over my desk so I could properly discipline you. Do you know what I'd do to you?"

"Spank me?" Didn't take a genius to work that one out.

"I'd spank you. But in between spanking you, I'd rub my finger through your slick folds, teasing you, taking you up to the edge, then I'd leave you on the precipice while I spanked you some more."

That sounded like torture.

And yet, she was so here for it.

He drew her panties to one side then flicked his tongue out to tease her clit with light flicks.

"Please! Please!" She couldn't take the teasing. She was already on fire.

"After I spanked you, I'd need to keep you close to me. To

watch over you. A girl that is so naughty can't be on her own after all." He laid a kiss on the top of her slit.

Pulling back, he stared up at her. She gazed down at him, breathing heavily.

"Please. Please."

One lone finger pushed into her wet entrance. Then he thrust it in and out of her.

"I'd have you kneel under the desk while I worked. You'd take my dick into your mouth and suck."

She moaned. Oh hell.

That sounded like freaking heaven.

"Daddy!" she moaned as he moved up to two fingers.

"Yes?"

"I need to come. Please."

Suddenly, he pulled his fingers away.

Nooo. She didn't want him to stop.

"Strip off your panties," he ordered.

Oh, hell yes. Maybe now she'd get to come. And then she'd get him.

Hallelujah.

After her panties were off and flung to who knew where, she stood there, waiting for his next command.

"That's my good girl. Now, I want you to turn around and press your hands to the wall. You're to keep them there."

She turned, wondering why she was in this position.

"That's it. You look so gorgeous. I want you to push your ass back and spread your legs nice and wide. That's my beautiful girl." He grasped hold of her ass cheeks, massaging them firmly.

Then he dipped his mouth down to run his tongue along her lips.

Oh, holy hell. This was a whole new level of insane pleasure.

Whimpers broke out of her mouth with each swipe of his

tongue. Lord, that was so good. Her legs trembled, threatening to give out on her.

Then he spread her ass cheeks and for some reason that only increased her pleasure. His thumb rubbed against her back passage.

When he drew back, she let out a protesting cry. "Please, I need . . . I need . . ."

"What do you need? Tell Daddy what you need, baby girl."

"To come! I need to come!"

He slid two fingers into her passage and drove them in and out of her before moving them up to her back hole. Then he pressed just the tips inside her. It burned and yet it felt so good. The burn only added to her pleasure.

"Remind me that we need to get lube today."

Oh fuck. Yes. She was here for that too.

"Do you still want Daddy's cock?" he asked as he moved his other hand between her legs to stroke her clit.

Fuck. Fuck!

She wasn't going to be able to stay still much longer, to hold back her pleasure. She knew that she needed to. That she had to hold on a bit longer until she had permission to come.

"Yes, yes, please."

He moved away from her and she whimpered but didn't move, didn't give any more protest.

"What a good girl you are," he said. Then she heard him moving. Was he undressing? "You're going to turn around, then walk to me and kneel."

The command filled her with more desire, making it hard for her to breathe as she turned to find him sitting on the bed. He was naked and for the first time she got a full look at him.

There was a light smattering of hair on his chest that led down to his belly button. He was toned. His abs well-defined, his body tan and gorgeous. He had a tattoo on one forearm that looked like a compass.

She loved him in his clothes. He looked so damn sexy. But naked?

Mind. Blown.

"Kiesha? You all right?"

"I just need a moment. I feel like my jaw might be on the floor. Am I drooling? I think I might be drooling."

He let out a low chuckle. "You're definitely good for my ego, baby."

"Believe me, your ego shouldn't have any issues." She stared down at where he was stroking his cock. How was it that big?

Another bark of laughter and a flush of pleasure filled her. "Whoops. Did I say that out loud?"

"You did. But please, feel free to say more."

"Your cock is the most delicious thing I've ever seen," she said as she walked forward, her gaze caught as he moved his hand up and down in long, slow strokes. Her mouth watered.

She really could start drooling at any moment.

Then she knelt in front of him. She heard the hitch of his breath. Saw how he tightened his hold on his dick.

"Please, Daddy, may I suck your cock?" she asked, staring up at him as she licked her lips.

"You little seductress. You know exactly what you do to me, don't you?"

"I'm hoping that I do this to you." She nodded as his erection. "I'm hoping that I do this to you a lot because then I'll get to take care of you. You really have a gorgeous cock. Please, let me taste it."

Reaching down, he placed his hand behind her neck and squeezed. "You do this to me all the time. Now, open your mouth."

She widened her lips as he guided his dick into her mouth.

Oh, yes, please.

More. She wanted more. She wanted all of him. She couldn't wait to make him come. To hear his pants of need. To taste him. Drink him all down. She didn't care that she hadn't gotten to come.

This was something she'd been thinking about for so long she didn't want to wait any longer. Not even for her own pleasure.

Instead of letting her move at her own pace though, he used his hand on the back of her neck to guide her movements. Back and forth, she took him deep, relaxing her throat.

It had been so long. She hummed in happiness and he removed his hand from her neck, wrapping it around her loose hair.

"Fuck yes, baby. That's it."

He rarely swore. But she loved hearing him let go. Knowing that she was giving him this pleasure.

"Good girl. Swallow me down. That's it. You're doing so well. You can take me so deep, can't you? Damn, your mouth is so wet, so hot. Faster now. If it's too much, tap my thigh."

Hell.

He was killing her. She could feel her need rising higher as he moved her mouth up and down his dick.

With his free hand, he played with his balls. And she reached up to hold on to his thighs. She closed her eyes, reveling in the feeling of having no control. Yeah, she liked sucking cock at her own pace. Doing what she wanted. And maybe she'd thought about teasing him the way he did to her.

But what she was finding out was that she might just love this more. There was something about having all control stripped away from her that made her that much hungrier.

That much needier.

"Fuck. Fuck. I can't last much longer. It's been so long. You're going to have me coming so quickly."

Hell. She needed to come with him. She couldn't wait any

longer. She moved one hand down to her pussy. But he drew her off his cock and gave her a stern look.

"Hands back on my thighs. That's your one warning. Break any more rules and this all stops."

Damn, he knew just what to threaten to get her to behave.

She moved her hands back to where they were meant to be and he took his hand away from her hair. She whimpered, staring up at him.

"I'll be a good girl."

"I know you will be. You're always my good girl. Suck my dick now. Make me come, baby girl."

Well. He didn't have to ask her twice.

She moved her mouth up and down his cock, delighting in his groans. She loved doing this for him. There was so much he did for her. And she also adored the fact that in the bedroom he was very different than he was the rest of the time.

It made her feel special seeing a side of him that she bet many people didn't get to know.

Taking him deep, she felt him stiffen before he groaned, coming in her mouth.

After swallowing him down, she licked him clean and kissed the tip of his dick.

Lord, she'd missed this. Missed the intimacy with someone she cared about deeply.

That she might be coming to love.

Closing her eyes, she leaned her forehead against his thigh.

Oh, Lord.

She was falling in love with him. There had been no way of stopping it. Harry was . . . he was everything.

But what if something happened to him?

"Kiesha. Baby, what is it? What's wrong? Did I go too far?"

"No, no," she whispered. She forced herself to lean back and look up at him. Normally, she'd try to hide her emotions behind some outrageous lie or a joke or she'd deflect like crazy.

But Harry had never held back from her. And he deserved to see what she was feeling.

Shock filled his face. Then worry. He cupped her face. "Baby, what is it?"

"I just . . . I'm so scared."

"Of what? Come here." He tried to pull her up into his lap but she shook her head, drawing back.

Worry flooded his eyes and she grasped hold of his hands.

"The deeper I get with you, the scarier it becomes."

"Because you lost Jonah?" he asked, understanding filling his face.

"I nearly lost myself. I thought about . . . my thoughts have never been that dark."

"Baby." He slid onto the floor and drew her into his lap and this time she let him. Because there was nowhere safer than Harry's arms.

She knew that he would always take care of her. She felt it in everything he did. Sometimes it was unnerving having that much attention on her. And she wasn't used to having someone to answer to.

But she knew she needed it. Needed some stability and someone who was reliable.

Damn, that sounded boring but it really wasn't. She'd loved Jonah so much, but they'd had similar personalities.

Harry was different. And she thought that maybe the fact that he was so different from Jonah was why she could love him too.

"You know I can't promise that nothing will happen to me. But I'll do my hardest to make sure that's the case." He ran his hand through his hair, looking stressed. "I'm not sure I should tell you this next part."

"Tell me what?"

He stared down at her pensively. "I don't want you to worry, but I had a health scare about two months ago."

"What? Harry, what happened?"

"I'm fine. I started getting chest pains at work and they called an ambulance."

"You had a heart attack?" She stared at him in horror.

"No, no. I thought that was what was happening, but it turned out to be angina."

"But that's not good either."

"No. But with some lifestyle changes I should be fine."

"What changes?"

"Like getting some balance between work and home. For years, I've worked all the time, I was stressed and burning out. So, I came to Wishingbone for a break. I started eating better. Exercising more. And I met this gorgeous, amazing girl who is showing me there is far more to life than working all the time."

"Is that me?"

"Nah, it was this woman in the checkout aisle at the market—"

"Daddy!"

"Of course, it was you, Little Monster. How can you even ask that? I'm trying to take good care of myself so I can take good care of you."

"Is that why you eat that awful rabbit food? And you're always running or at the gym?"

Urgh, running.

"You're complaining?" he murmured.

"Heck, no. You go to the gym all you like. As long as I don't have to come. Or eat that rabbit food."

"We need to make sure you're healthy as well. Which for you means less candy, more water and more sleep."

"I suppose." She hugged him tight. "I can't lose you, Daddy. You have to take good care of yourself."

"I will." He kissed the top of her head. "I feel the same fear about losing you. I want you with me for a long, long time, baby girl. Forever."

"Forever sounds like a good amount of time. I could do forever." Just the idea of something happening to him sent chills down her spine. But she also knew that he'd already made moves to take care of himself better.

"Thank you, Little Monster. I'm glad you think you could put up with me that long."

She sighed, appreciating his teasing. "Tough job, but someone has to do it."

He tickled her sides and she giggled. Then he turned her so she was straddling his lap, facing him. His gaze moved to her breasts and he ran one finger over a pert nipple. "You know I had something to say and now I can't seem to remember what that was . . . we should really make a pact not to have important talks while naked."

She grinned at his words. She loved the effect she had on him. Feeling bold, she grabbed his hand and cupped it around her breast. "You forgot something else, Daddy."

"Oh yeah, what's that?"

"To make me come."

"Hmm, did I forget that? Or do I just want to drive you mad all day?"

She let out a loud gasp. "Daddy! That would just be cruel."

"Yes, but think of how good it will feel when Daddy finally gives you permission to come."

Hmm, that was something to think about . . .

"I thought about it and I think I'd rather come now, please."

He drew her close, kissing the lobe of her ear. "And I think not. I'm Daddy. So, I win."

Well. Hell.

So not fair.

"You know, I don't think it's fair that you always get to pull the Daddy card. What if I want to be in charge sometimes?"

"Do you?" he asked, lightly tugging at her nipple. "Do you want to make all the decisions? Control me? Tell me what to do? Where to touch you? Withhold my orgasms?"

Worry flooded her stomach at the thought of being in charge.

So that was a no then.

"No," she whispered. "I don't. I like you taking control. I just like to complain sometimes."

He chuckled. "All right, baby. You complain all you like so long as you remember to obey me. Otherwise..." He lightly tapped her ass to finish that sentence and she squirmed on his lap.

"But does that mean I get to come now? Because I was a good girl and told you the truth?"

"This isn't a punishment. Think about it as delayed gratification."

"But I hate delayed gratification. It's awful. Why wait if I can have something right now?"

"Because it will feel so much better later."

"Will it, though? Why can't I have it now and later?"

"Greedy girl. Do you want Daddy's cock inside you?" As he spoke, he ran two fingers through her slick folds then pushed them up inside her.

"Yesss," she hissed. "I want that so bad."

"If you're a good girl and hold off your orgasm, Daddy will give you his cock tonight."

Flipping heck. She thought she might come just from his words alone.

"Can you be a good girl?"

"I think I can."

"I know you can. Because if you're not, then you'll suck Daddy off and get nothing for yourself. That would be sad, wouldn't it?"

"Once I went without candy for an entire day. I thought it was impossible. If I can do that, then I can do this."

"Good girl." With his other hand, he drew her in for a kiss. She parted her lips for him and he teased her, tasted from her while his fingers were still pressed inside her.

She tensed around them, just wanting him to move them slightly. If he just touched her clit . . .

No! Bad girl.

No orgasms for you.

"Ahh, I remember what I wanted to talk to you about now, before you distracted me with these." He drew his fingers free from her pussy and ran them over her nipples, leaving them glistening with her arousal.

"What is it?"

"I really need to get you dressed before I talk." Cupping one breast, he licked her nipple clean then did the same to the other one. Then he cupped her face. "I'm planning on having forever with you, my baby. But I also think we need to have a plan in place in case something happens."

She swallowed heavily, not wanting to think about that. But she nodded. "Like what?"

"You have so many people who care about you. Even if you don't quite seem to realize that. But I think a plan will make both of us feel better. Like, if something were to happen to me, you'd need to immediately call someone. Probably Ed. Straight away. Yeah?"

She nodded.

"No. I need words. What do you do if something happens to me?"

"I call Ed."

"Straight away. Say it," he warned.

"I call Ed straight away."

"And what would you say?"

"I... that I... that you..."

"A codeword. We need a word that you can easily say to explain everything."

"And I tell Ed the word?" she whispered. She hated this conversation, loathed it. But she knew he didn't want her to feel as lost as she had after Jonah's death.

"Yes. And then he comes to you. And he stays with you as long as you need him to. There needs to be a backup person too. Someone reliable. Who has a level head and will look after you?"

She nodded, chewing her lip nervously. "Maybe Georgie. She doesn't panic and she'd come if I needed her to." Any of her friends would. She knew that.

"I agree that Georgie is likely the most level-headed of your friends. But if Ed and Georgie are away that wouldn't work. What about Noah? Or Cleo?"

"Yeah. Cleo would work," she said in a hoarse voice. "I don't like this conversation, Daddy." The last thing she wanted to think about was him dying. It made her feel sick.

"I know, baby." He drew her into his chest and rocked her back and forth. "But do it for me. Okay? For my peace of mind. I need to know you'll always be taken care of. No matter what."

"I'm going to set it all up so you don't have to worry, all right? Everything will be okay, sweetheart. I'll make sure of that."

"I know, Daddy. You take such good care of me." Leaning back, she cupped his face and gave him a fierce look. "But we need to take good care of you. Because I'm not losing you."

Not when she'd only just found him.

"We will. Come on, let's get in the shower. I want to play with that showerhead." He winked at her.

She groaned. She knew that meant more teasing for her. Was it possible to self-combust from not coming?

30

Kiesha stared around the shop in delight. It was new so she'd never been here when she'd lived in Bozeman before. Not that she would have been able to afford anything in it anyway.

But it was magical.

"Wow, Daddy this shop is amazing."

Harry had showered them both, and yes, he'd teased her with the shower nozzle. She'd barely been able to stand and in the end, he'd had her sit on the bench while he'd sprayed the water of the shower head over her pussy.

So mean.

He kept moving it away as she got closer to the edge.

By the time the shower finished, she'd been so turned on it was killing her. She'd actually thought she might come just from him drying her with the towel.

Harry had dressed her in a black dress with yellow and green striped tights and a pair of black Doc Martens. He'd tried to do her hair for her, bless him, but it had ended up in a complete mess. She'd never seen such a disaster.

After spending a good two minutes giggling at the catastrophe, she'd put it up in a simple high ponytail.

"Mari told me about this place," he said to her. "She also said that you have a store on the outskirts of Wishingbone that caters to adult Littles."

"Oh yes, we do. Aunt Marie runs it. I've heard it's really good."

"You haven't been?"

"It's quite a way out of town, too far to get there on my roller skates."

"Would you like to go on our way home?" he asked.

"Can we?" She stared up at him in delight. "That would be so much fun. Although I should warn you, she's a nudist."

"Will she be naked?"

"Depends on what day it is, but likely."

"Right. Well. Okay."

He was so cute when he got all flustered.

"I can't believe this place, though. Have you ever seen such a big toy store?"

"And there's an important area upstairs. Come on." He took her hand and led her upstairs. She couldn't believe everything. There were toys everywhere.

She wanted to stop and explore it all.

"Look!" she cried, tugging at his hand as they moved toward the back of the second floor. "There's a princess photo booth. I can get my photo taken with Cinderella and Snow White and oh, look! There's a giant Legos man." She was squealing as she tugged Harry this way and that.

Well, she tried to tug him. He was very intent on leading her somewhere else. Then she saw it.

The most amazing thing she'd ever seen.

"There's a whole monster area?" she said in a low whisper of awe.

"There is. Come along." He drew her over. She spun around,

shock making her speechless. There were life-sized cut-outs of her favorite monster characters. And the shelves were loaded down with toys. Soft toys, books, games.

She darted from one thing to the next while Harry looked on indulgently. Thankfully, there wasn't anyone else in this area or she might be more self-conscious about her reactions.

"What do you think? Like this place?"

"Like it? Daddy, I love it." She threw her arms around him. "Thank you for bringing me here. It's amazing."

"You're welcome. But you haven't chosen anything yet."

"What?"

"What would you like? This guy is cute." He picked up a yellow alien with tentacles. He looked so weird that he was cute.

"Oh, I don't need anything. Just looking is enough."

Harry's eyebrows rose. "Baby, you can't come to a toy shop and not buy anything."

"But I don't need anything."

"Then buy something you want. What about this?" He picked up a beanie with these two googly eyes on top.

"Ooh, I like that." She chewed her lip. But she couldn't afford it.

Harry placed the hat on her head, then turned her to the mirror. To her surprise, it actually fit. He placed his hands on her shoulders. "Don't stress about what it costs. I'm buying this stuff for you."

"But you already paid for the hotel. And you never let me pay when we eat out. Or for anything back home. I'm beginning to feel like I . . . like I'm freeloading off you."

Instead of dismissing her feelings, he nodded. Then he turned her around to face him. "I get what you're saying, baby. But here's the thing, it's not freeloading when it's something I want. I think you probably have an inkling about how much I enjoy looking after you."

"Just a smidge." She held up her forefinger and thumb. "I mean, you've been awfully subtle about it, but I'm beginning to understand."

"Cheeky brat," he said affectionately.

"That doesn't mean you need to buy me stuff. The things I need aren't material."

"I get that, baby girl." Leaning in, he kissed her forehead. "But it brings me great joy to provide for you. In all ways. I'm not saying that I need you to be completely dependent on me. You have a job you love. And I will support you in that. But perhaps you'd also allow me to spoil you sometimes? Since I enjoy it."

"So, what you're saying is by letting you buy me a toy, that I'll be making you happy."

"Exactly. This is really all for my benefit. Not yours." His eyes danced in amusement as he clearly held back his laughter.

She gave a big sigh. "It's a huge sacrifice, you understand."

"Yes. I get it. A terrible inconvenience to allow me to do this. And to also take you clothes shopping."

She narrowed her gaze at him. "I will allow you to buy me a few things, since you clearly need it so badly."

"Yes, I am forever grateful for your understanding."

"But no getting carried away. I mean it."

"I'll try to contain myself," he replied dryly. "I'm sure you'll tell me if I go too far."

"It's a big flaw of yours, Daddy."

"What is? Spoiling you?"

"Well, I mean, you are only human so I should give you some leeway."

"You're so gracious." He took hold of her hand and kissed the top. "Get the hat. And what about these?" He picked up some alien figurines. She practically vibrated with excitement over them.

"Yes, please! Ooh, can I get this one?" She held up a purple monster.

"Of course, you can."

By the time they headed toward the cash register, she had the monster hat, a couple of monster toys, and a green headband with two googly eyes on the end of its antennae.

They passed a stand filled with squishy toys and she stopped to stare at them all.

"Are these the toys you were telling me about?" Harry asked.

"Yes! We should get you one so you don't have to play with your balls anymore."

Harry shook his head with a chuckle, glancing around before he leaned in. "I don't play with my balls, but if you're offering . . ."

She grinned up at him. "Anytime."

"I don't think I need one, but why don't we get you a couple."

"Really?"

"Really. Which ones would you like?"

"I only need one. But I love this one." She picked up one that had looked like a colorful penguin.

"You sure you just need one? I think he'll be lonely. What about this one? What is it meant to be?"

"It's a catcorn of course."

"Of course, I don't know how I didn't see that. Uh, what's a catcorn?"

"A cat crossed with a unicorn."

"I can see that now."

She rubbed them both against her cheeks. "They're so soft and squishy. Daddy, you're the best! Thank you."

"You're welcome, baby. Let's go get these now."

A younger woman greeted them at the cash register. She had her red hair up in two ponytails and freckles across her nose and cheeks.

"Oh wow! I love monsters."

"You do?" Kiesha asked.

"Uh-huh. Oh, this hat is gorgeous. I need to get it next

paycheck." She sighed. "I hope there's still some left by the time I get paid again."

"Why don't you have this one?" Kiesha said softly, handing over the hat to her. "It would really suit you."

The girl's mouth dropped open and she stared at Kiesha in surprise.

Then Kiesha winced, realizing that she'd given away something Harry had actually paid for. "If that's okay with you?" She gave Harry a guilty look.

But he just stared down at her warmly. "Of course, it is. It's your hat. You can do what you like with it."

She felt bad now, though. He worked hard for his money. Maybe he wouldn't appreciate her giving something away.

"Wow, thank you," the girl said. "That's really kind of you. But I can't accept. I'd get in trouble with my supervisor. She's a real stickler for the rules. But I don't think anyone has done anything this nice for me in forever."

"I wish you could take it," Kiesha told her. "It's really a cool hat."

"Oh, do you know what? Have you seen the store, it's about two blocks over but it has the coolest clothes and footwear. I got these light-up shoes there." The girl walked around to show off her sparkly, pretty shoes which had the base lighting up as she moved.

"Those are so cool."

"I know," she replied. "And they have these monster onesies and the cutest clothes. You need to go. I'll write down the name for you."

"Thank you," Kiesha told her, taking the piece of paper.

"No, thank you. That was a really kind thing you wanted to do."

Harry took the bag as the girl packaged it up. Then she waved to Kiesha before they walked through the toy shop. Harry was silent as he held her hand and she worried that she'd done the wrong thing. An odd feeling came over her. Almost like she was being watched. She turned her head, but the only person she could see had their back to her.

Strange.

When they got outside, she stopped and looked up at him. "I'm so sorry."

He stared down at her. "Sorry? For what, sweetheart?"

"For trying to give away the hat," she said hurriedly. "I know how it must appear and it's not that I wasn't grateful for it. I love it. I really do. I could just see how much she liked it and the offer came out of me before I knew—"

She stopped as he placed his hand over her mouth. "Hush, sweetheart. I'm not mad."

"You're not?"

"No. How could I be mad when you were being so kind? I thought that was an amazing gesture and it's just more proof of what a wonderful person you are." He bent and kissed her and she stared up at him with a huge smile.

"Thank you so much, Daddy. I love everything you got me, even though you didn't have to. I sometimes have trouble accepting gifts."

"Glad you love them, baby girl."

That feeling came over her again and she spun, trying to look around. There were a number of people on the street and a few people were looking their way.

"What's wrong?" he asked.

"I dunno. I just had this weird feeling of being watched. Silly, huh?"

He wrapped an arm around her, then glanced around. "It's not silly. Did you see anyone?"

"No. Really. I think it's my overactive imagination." She tried to laugh it off. But Harry was still frowning.

"Let's go get some lunch," he told her. "Then we'll go to that shop the girl told us about."

⁓

Turned out the shop was an amazing little hidden gem. It had all sorts of things, from onesies, to the cutest tights with all sorts of designs, to an adult area in the back with sex toys.

Yep, he'd had some fun purchasing a few things to use on her. Including handcuffs, a babydoll nightie, a blindfold, and some butt plugs. Oh, and lube. Yeah, he'd bought plenty of lube.

But the best find was a pair of monster horns. They were pale pink and blue twisted together. One end went in her bottom and the other in her pussy.

After paying for everything, he glanced around for Kiesha. Seemed she'd wandered off. He frowned. He hadn't made it clear enough that he expected her to stay with him.

When he returned to the other part of the shop, with a discreetly named bag in hand, he found her looking at a drink bottle with aliens all over it. It had a straw attached. Reaching over, he picked it up. "This would be perfect for your water."

"Really?" Her eyes lit up. "I love aliens. I was on an alien hunting team once and we encountered a real alien." She rubbed her nose then sighed, closing her eyes.

It had been a while since her last story. He wasn't sure why she'd stopped.

Suddenly, she leaned into him, burying her face in his chest. "Sorry, Daddy," she whispered. "I don't even know why I said that. I've been trying really hard not to make stuff up. I don't even know why I do it half the time. Sometimes it's to make myself feel better when I'm worried or upset, but other times it just comes out."

"Shh," he told her, concerned by the way she trembled. "I'm not upset."

"Are you sure?" She stared up at him worriedly.

"I'm sure." He brushed her hair back off her face. "Stop stressing, all right? I wonder if we'll be able to find a similar sippy cup at the store outside Wishingbone."

She gave him an excited grin. "And a pacifier?" Then she bit her lip. "I mean, maybe?"

"If that's what my baby wants, that's what my baby gets."

"Yes, well, what your baby wants right now is to get these slippers and this onesie then go pee."

"I think there's a toilet at the end of the shop, come on I'll pay for this stuff and then I'll take you."

"I really gots to go. I can find it myself."

"I don't like you leaving my side. Like when you wandered off while I was at the cash register before."

"Oh, um, I didn't think I needed to be there while you bought butt plugs and lube," she told him in a low voice.

She was starting to dance around.

"I'll walk you over, then get the stuff." He grabbed everything then guided her over to the restroom. "You wait here for me to come back and get you, understand?"

"I understand."

"Good girl. I wonder if they sell those baby restraint systems at that Little shop in Wishingbone? I think we might need one."

He grinned, whistling to himself as he left her outside the restroom door, gaping at him.

~

Sheesh, he wouldn't really get a harness for her, would he?

She couldn't imagine that. She was a free range Little. She liked to go where she wanted to go. Nothing would tie her down.

Although, if Harry wanted to tie her to the bed then she wouldn't object.

But her Little side liked to roam free. How could she get

around on her roller skates if she was on a baby leash? All right, that's not what they called them, but it was what it felt like.

Nah, he'd just been teasing her.

After peeing, she walked out the door. And had that weird feeling again. Okay, was there something wrong with her? Was she having a hot flush? Because this wasn't normal. It felt like there were eyes on her, watching her movements.

Discreetly, she glanced around but didn't see anything.

"There she is." Harry wrapped an arm around her.

"Right where I'm meant to be. See, Daddy? No need for a leash."

"A leash? I hadn't quite thought of it like that. It's more of a way of keeping you close, where I can keep an eye on you."

"I need to roam. You can't keep me on lockdown."

"No, I know I can't. And I wouldn't ever want you to feel uncomfortable. Come on, there's one more shop I want to go to. Then it's home for a nap and some playtime."

She sure hoped that playtime included sexy time. Because her body was still buzzing from his teasing earlier today.

Wait. Nap.

Noooo.

31

"Come on, Oogly," she coaxed her toy from his hiding place. "It's okay. Your new friends won't hurt you."

"Kiesha?" Harry walked into the room. "What's going on?"

Harry had just taken a phone call in the bedroom. She guessed that it was something work-related.

Even though he'd given his notice, he said he still had things he had to work through.

They'd stopped off on their way back to the hotel to buy Harry some sexy pajamas. She couldn't wait to see him in them later. Then strip him out of them.

Unfortunately for her, he'd been serious about the nap. She didn't know why, since she hadn't been the slightest bit tired. What she had to learn to do, though, was hide her pouting.

Because she'd complained and dragged her feet for so long that he'd ended up tipping her over his knee and giving her ten heavy smacks.

Yep, she'd gone to sleep with a warm bottom and slept like a baby.

Darn it.

When she'd gotten up, he'd dressed her in her new onesie and set her up with a snack and her new water bottle.

She was such a lucky girl.

"Oogly is scared of the new toys," she said with exasperation. "He's being so silly. I've tried to explain to him that he's bigger than all of them, but he's worried they'll gang up and attack him."

"He's just a big baby, huh?"

"Daddy!" She put her hands over Oogly's ears. "Don't say that to Oogly, you'll give him a complex. But yes, he is a bit of a gentle giant. I think he's feeling lost without his brothers."

"Poor Oogly, do you think he'd like to stay in tonight and get room service rather than going out?"

"I think that's a good idea, Daddy. Oogly does like to be around things that are familiar to him."

She and Oogly had that in common.

"Who was the call from, Daddy?"

"Just work. Nothing for you to worry about." He ran his hand over her head and she frowned at his words. They didn't sit right with her.

But you aren't telling him everything either, are you?

She'd made a decision about that, though. She was going to tell him by the end of this weekend. And hope like hell he didn't think that she was coming clean because she wanted his money to pay the debt. And that she didn't cause him too much stress.

She knew her worries stemmed from living with her grandpa. He'd treated her mother horribly. He'd made her do everything, while reminding her of how much she owed him. But Harry wasn't her grandpa. They might have only known each other a few weeks, but she knew that for sure.

He settled on the sofa and drew out his phone. There was a tension in his face that she didn't like. She moved over to where he sat then straddled his lap. He looked up from his phone with a frown. "Everything okay? I thought you were playing?"

"Uh, yeah. I am. I guess." She fidgeted. It was a stupid idea to say anything. "Sorry for interrupting."

She tried to get off his lap but he grabbed her hips with a groan, settling her further into his lap. "No, I'm sorry. I didn't mean to sound dismissive."

"I know you've got things to do but I just . . . I mean . . ." She blew out a breath. This wasn't like her, to be so hesitant. And she didn't like it. "Just because I'm a Little doesn't mean you can't confide in me or lean on me. If something shitty is going on, I want you to tell me, Harry. I don't want this to be all one-sided. I get that you're the Dom, the BBDIC."

"BBDIC?"

"Big Bad Daddy In Charge."

"Ahh, I don't know how I didn't figure that one out."

"You're distracted." She patted his cheek lightly. "It's all right. It's not your fault if you can only concentrate on one thing at a time. It's a man thing."

"Indeed, and you're quite right, sweetheart. I shouldn't have been so dismissive. It's just, this isn't really anything you can help with."

"I can still listen. I mean, if you can talk about it. What's going on?"

"That was work. They want me to go back. They don't seem to understand that I really meant it when I said I was quitting."

"That sucks. Maybe you should just lose their number."

"I'd love to. Unfortunately, there are still some things I need to wind up. They'll get the idea, they're just being persistent at the moment. But you know what? There's no reason I have to answer them while I'm on holiday with my baby."

She squirmed in delight. "You want to send them flyers telling them to shove off? I'm really good at flyers. And glitter. I am excellent with glitter."

"I'll keep that in mind. Maybe we could send them one of those singing groups."

"Ooh, good idea, Daddy. Or one of those airplanes that writes things in the sky?"

"Now, you're thinking big."

"Or . . . or . . . a woman who jumps out of the cake and says surprise! Harry is quitting, now get with the program!"

He chuckled and those lines of tension left his face, his shoulders relaxed down from around his ears. "Thank you, sweetheart. I feel a lot better now."

She smiled. She loved being able to do things for him.

"You know, I think I need a nickname for you." She tapped her finger against her chin. "I know, what about Merry Harry? No, that doesn't rhyme that well. Hmm, I know, Hairy Harry! That's perfect. It rhymes and it's alliteration."

"Very clever, but not happening. You already have a name for me. Daddy."

"Daddy Waddy? Ew, no that was terrible. I can do better. Baddy Daddy. It's not terrible."

"How about just Daddy?"

"Just Daddy? But it doesn't have rhyme or alliteration. I mean, that's kind of sad."

"Brat." He tickled her until she cried for mercy. "Now, why don't we help Oogly come out of his hiding place. I'm sure we can convince him that his new friends aren't scary."

She sighed. "We can try, Daddy. But I'm not holding my breath. And I can hold my breath a long time."

"You can?"

"Yep, when Mom and Grandpa would fight, I used to hold my breath and count in my head. It used to make Mom mad when she saw me doing it, though."

"I'd rather you didn't hold your breath, all right? Not unless it's really necessary."

"Like when there's a bad smell or you go over a bridge or see a ghost."

"See a ghost?"

"Yeah, don't you know you hold your breath when you see a ghost?"

"No, I didn't. I actually haven't seen a ghost."

"Poor Daddy, you really have been leading a boring life, haven't you?"

"Yes, I have. But I think from now on, it's going to be anything but. But why would you hold your breath?"

"You know, because the ghosts are jealous."

"Ahh, like when you go past a cemetery."

"Yeah, that's it. We could go visit a cemetery tonight and find you a ghost so you can have your first ghost sighting."

"I think I'll have to pass."

"Scared?"

"No."

She patted his hand. "It's all right, Daddy. It's okay to be scared. Even when you're Hairy Harry. Are you sure you don't like that one? It rolls off the tongue really easily."

"It's a firm pass." They both sat on the floor and Harry glanced over at Oogly. "What's that behind him?"

"Ahh."

Drat.

Why hadn't she removed that? Tipped it down the kitchen sink when he wasn't watching?

Silly Kiesha.

"Nothing, Daddy."

"Really? Nothing? Because it looks like it's the still-full drink bottle and the yogurt that I got for you. And look, here are the carrot sticks."

"Oh, I wondered where those had gone. Naughty Oogly, he must have stolen them."

"Do you think so?" He took the food to the kitchen and threw it out.

Now she felt bad. After all, Harry had taken the time to make her something to eat and she'd hidden it from him.

Albeit, she hadn't exactly hidden it very well.

"Yep."

"Well, that is naughty. I suppose he'll have to be punished."

She gasped, grabbing hold of Oogly and holding him tight against her. "Daddy, no! You can't punish Oogly."

"If he's naughty that's what happens. Oogly has to follow the rules."

Poor Oogly.

Could she let him take her punishment? Wellll . . .

She looked from Oogly to Harry who held his hand out for the toy.

"Noo! I can't do it. It was me! It was all me!"

"Was it just?" He crouched down in front of her, his face serious and stern.

Uh-oh.

Surely it wouldn't be too bad of a punishment, right?

"While I'm glad you came clean in the end, you hid the evidence of not eating your snack and drinking your water, and then you put the blame on poor, innocent Oogly."

Feeling terrible, she dropped her head. "I'm sorry, Daddy."

"That's good to hear, but you're going to have to be punished. You know that, don't you?"

"Yes, Daddy."

"Now, if you'd come clean straight away I would have settled for some corner time and five smacks to your bottom. But lying, well, that's a much harsher punishment."

"What are you going to do, Daddy?"

"I think I'm going to have to increase your spanking to ten and you're going to be plugged for the rest of the evening."

She gasped. Plugged? That was terrible.

"You wouldn't really stick something up my butt, would you, Daddy?"

"You mean you don't like the idea of having something in your bottom, Little Monster?"

No, that wasn't what she meant at all. She rather liked the idea. But only during sexy times. Not for punishment.

"Just so you know, if you hadn't come clean, then you wouldn't have been allowed to come tonight."

"Daddy, that would have been just mean!"

"Perhaps next time, you won't try to hide things from Daddy, hmm?"

"I'm sorry, Daddy!" She reached out and wrapped her arms around his neck, almost sending him toppling to the floor. "It won't happen again. I promise."

"Good girl." He hugged her tight. "I'm going to go get things ready. I want you to drink a third of that water."

She sighed. "All right, but I like when you put the strawberries in it."

"Oh, I'm sorry, sweetheart," he told her, looking chagrined. "I completely forgot about the strawberries."

"It's okay, Daddy," she said hastily, hating to seem like she was complaining.

But plain water? Gah.

"You were busy."

"But I'm never too busy for my baby. She always comes first."

Jeez, he was just the sweetest.

He returned with a fresh bottle of water with cut-up strawberries in it. "Thanks, Daddy."

"Welcome." He leaned down and kissed her forehead. "Now,

I'm going to go get the plug ready. I want you to bring that bottle with you so I can see that you've drunk some."

Darn it. And then he had to go and ruin it all. How could he be so sweet and yet so mean?

32

Harry set the butt plug and lube on the nightstand. He couldn't believe he'd let himself get pulled away by work. That was exactly what he was trying not to do.

That was why he'd given his notice. Because he wanted time for other things in his life. Namely the gorgeous girl in the other room. And let's face it, she needed close watching.

Not that he could spend all his time just looking after her. If he tried, he had no doubt that she'd smother him in his sleep. No, he'd need to find something else to do because he couldn't fill his days with gym workouts, runs, and taking care of Kiesha.

But whatever he chose to do, he'd do it at a far slower pace. He wanted plenty of time to take long weekends away with his girl, or take her out on a picnic or shopping or whatever she wanted to do.

What he couldn't do was allow himself to get dragged back into a lifestyle of work, work, work.

Barbara was just going to have to learn that he'd meant it when he said he was leaving.

Or he would have to stop answering her calls. He wouldn't be answering any more this weekend.

Right. Focus.

"Kiesha? Come in here please."

She walked in slowly, her drink bottle dangling from her fingers. It was half gone, he noticed, which was impressive for her. She wore the cute monster onesie they'd picked up today. It was blue and white and there were monster horns on the hood, which was currently over her head. She looked adorable.

He'd made sure to buy one with a dropseat.

He crooked a finger at her as she lingered in the middle of the room, looking very sorry for herself.

"Come here, sweetheart."

"Look, Daddy! I drank half of my water."

"Good girl. Do you need to pee before your punishment?"

She shook her head.

"Sure?" he pressed. "Because if you need to go after you have your plug in, then I'll have to take it out for you and reinsert it. And trying to pee with a butt plug in . . . well, you can see how that could end up, right?"

He grinned as she quickly moved into the bathroom. "I'll pee! I'll pee!"

Yeah, he thought that might be the case. When she returned, she looked a bit sheepish and worried.

"Uh, Daddy?" she asked as she moved slowly closer.

"Yes?"

"Just how long are you intending to leave the plug in my bottom?"

"I was thinking an hour to begin with. But it depends how you do. If it's too uncomfortable, we'll work up to you taking it longer."

"I think it's going to be way too uncomfortable, Daddy."

"Let's see. Come here." He grasped hold of her as she came closer, pulling her between his legs. "Why are you being punished?"

"For not eating my snack and drinking my water."

"And?"

"And hiding the evidence."

"And?"

She sighed. "And pretending that Oogly was at fault."

"That's right. For not drinking your water or eating your snack, you're getting ten minutes in the corner. For hiding the fact, you're getting ten spanks. And for pretending it was Oogly, you have to wear a plug. Understand?"

"Yes, Daddy."

"Then come here." He positioned her on his lap so her legs were over one side and her body dangled over the other side.

"Hands on the floor and keep them there."

He reached for the back of her drop seat, opening it and drawing the flap down to reveal her yellow panties. He paused, staring in disbelief at what sat above her ass cheeks on her lower back.

"What's this?"

"Oh that? It's my new tattoo. You like it?" She turned her head to look up at him.

"Like it? When did you get this?" He knew it wasn't a real tattoo. Just as well, because if it was . . . they'd be having a very serious discussion. While he applied his belt to her butt.

Because written above her bottom in bright green, were the words: *No Spanking Allowed*.

"Uh, well, a little while ago."

"When I spanked you earlier, it wasn't there."

"I put it on in the bathroom. It's a fake tattoo, Daddy. It will come off in a few days."

"A few days?" he asked.

"Don't you like it, Daddy?"

"No, I don't. And unfortunately for you, it's not going to stop you from getting a spanking that you've earned."

She sighed. "That's too bad. If it had worked, I might have

gotten a real one."

"If you'd gotten a real one, you wouldn't have been able to sit for a week, naughty girl."

"Daddy, I didn't know you were against tattoos."

"I'm not against tattoos. What I do object to is brats who write naughty things on their bodies. Now, it's ten with my hand unless you want to double it?"

"Nope, Daddy. I'm good with ten."

Sheesh what kind of a question was that? Who in their right mind would turn around and ask for double the number of spanks?

Then again, if it wasn't a punishment spanking maybe she would.

There was a vast difference between a fun spanking and one for punishment and usually it had to do with the way she felt.

Like right now, she was feeling really guilty for not eating the food that Harry had taken the time to get ready for her. He really was a good man and Daddy.

So, when he lowered her panties and started smacking her bottom, she was surprised to find herself almost immediately in tears. The relief the spanking brought her made her feel a bit emotional.

After a few spanks, he stopped and rubbed her lower back. "Baby, you okay? I've only given you four and you're already upset. Were they too hard? Especially after your earlier spanking."

She'd gotten ten then as well and hadn't cried at all so she could understand why he was worried.

Sniffling, she turned back to look at him. "I'm okay, Daddy. I just feel kind of bad for not eating the snack and hiding it."

"Ahh, I see. Well, remember, after your punishment everything is forgiven and forgotten, you can just let it go. All right?"

"Yes, Daddy."

"That's my good girl. Six more and then I'm going to insert the plug into your bottom."

He didn't waste any time in finishing off the spanking, which she was grateful for. Sobs wracked her body and her bottom was definitely hot and throbbing.

"That's it. Good girl. Let all the tears out. I have you. Are you ready for the next part?"

"Yes, Daddy. I'm ready." Maybe. It had been a long time since she'd had anything in her bottom. She didn't count when Harry pushed the tip of his finger in there.

"Right, I'm just going to put some lube on the plug. I want you to try and relax."

"Daddy, you can't tell a person to relax when you're about to stick a piece of plastic in their ass," she informed him.

"I can't? Huh, I'll take that under advisement for next time."

"Daddy!" she cried. "There won't be a next time."

"I think there will. We have to get you ready. Unless you don't want Daddy's cock in your bottom?"

Oh, no. She wanted that. Almost desperately.

"Well?" he asked.

Darn it. Why couldn't he just let some things slide?

"Yes, Daddy. I want that."

"I thought so. Deep breath in. Just relax. That's it. Good girl. How does that feel?"

"Like someone is sticking a piece of plastic in my ass," she grumbled.

"Don't you like it, baby? Maybe next time you think about hiding things from Daddy you'll remember how this feels."

Yeah. She wouldn't bet on it.

The plug was pushed right in, then he twisted it. She groaned as burning pleasure engulfed her.

She had to try and breathe her way through the waves of need and hunger engulfing her.

Holy. Heck.

"That's it. Good girl. This plug looks so pretty peeking out of your cheeks. Now, you're going into the corner. I want you to push that naughty bottom right out so I can see the plug."

He helped her stand, holding onto her hips to keep her steady as the blood rushed from her head.

"That's it." He stood and led her to the corner. Bending, he cupped her chin. "You feeling okay?"

"I have a sore bottom. Inside and out."

"That's what you're meant to have. Any other pain or anything uncomfortable?"

"No," she grumbled.

He ran his thumb over her cheek and she found herself melting. "My good girl. Turn around now. You know the rules of being in the corner."

Yeah. The boring rules.

No talking. No moving. Bottom out. Nose in.

With a long, loud sigh, she got herself into position. Who ever thought of this for a punishment? It was horrid. She hated staying still. And not talking. Hmm, what could she think about? She needed to design some new T-shirts. She should find some cheap T-shirts while she was here and—

"Are you thinking about what you did wrong, Little Monster?"

Ahh, drat.

She shifted her weight around, feeling the plug move in her bottom. She couldn't have this in her bottom for a whole hour. That was just ridiculous.

Plus, she was already so turned on. She wondered if Harry—

"Focus. Concentrate."

Right. Concentrate. She'd been naughty. That's why she'd been spanked and was standing here with her bottom on display. Because she'd tried to hide stuff and lie.

Bad Kiesha.

"That's better. Come here now."

Whoop! Corner time was over. She spun around and moved over to Harry as quickly as she could with her bottom. She threw herself at him.

"Careful!" he admonished. "You'll hurt yourself."

Not likely.

They landed on the bed, him on his back with her lying on top of him. She pulled herself up so she could look down at him. "Hi, Daddy."

"Hi, sweetheart. Did you think about your behavior?"

She nodded, chewing on her lip. He reached up and released it for her. "And?"

"I'm sorry, Daddy. I didn't mean to be so naughty. I shouldn't have hid my snack and water and I definitely shouldn't have blamed Oogly."

"No, you shouldn't have. You also owe Oogly an apology."

"You're right, Daddy. I should do something nice for him. Do you forgive me?"

"Of course, I do. Although, I hope you remember your sore bottom next time you think about doing something like that."

"Daddy! There will never be a next time."

"Uh-huh." He sat up and settled her on his lap. She could feel her bottom hanging out of the onesie she was wearing and squirmed around.

"Now, why don't we go play with your new toys and then we'll have dinner and I'll remove the plug?"

"Okay, Daddy."

He settled her on her feet then righted her clothing. As they moved into the living area of the suite, she looked up at him. "Daddy, do you think we could go shopping somewhere with cheap clothes?"

"I suppose. Why is that? What do you need?"

"Some cheap, plain T-shirts."

"You need T-shirts?"

"I like to do designs on them."

"You do?" he asked as they settled onto the floor.

She knelt, no way she could sit on her bottom. She picked up Oogly, giving him a hug and a kiss in apology.

"Are all your T-shirts your designs?"

"Not all of them. I don't have any equipment that prints on them or anything. I just use T-shirt paint. It's fun."

"Sure, we can do that, Little Monster and get you some more supplies if you need."

"One day it would be awesome to have all the proper equipment."

Harry's phone rang a few times while they were playing monsters versus aliens. But he didn't answer, even though she told him he could.

She had to admit it made her feel pretty special that he was ignoring everyone else to spend time with her. However, by the time he ordered dinner, she was ready to be able to sit comfortably again.

"Daddy, I need to pee. And take out this plug."

"All right. Go into the bathroom, put your hands on the counter, and stick your bottom out."

Sheesh. Really?

"Can't I take it out?"

"Nope. You ever try to take a plug out yourself and I'll strap your bottom. Unless you're in pain and I'm not around. But I'd never leave you while you were plugged."

"All right, Daddy. But can't I go over your knee again?"

"No. Now go do what you were told without arguing." He gave her a firm look.

"Yes, Daddy." She gave him a very pitiful look, though, to let him know exactly how she felt about this.

33

She walked into the bathroom and moved to the counter, grabbing hold while she studied herself in the mirror.

She loved this onesie, she looked so adorable in it. And there was an extra sparkle in her eyes right now. She felt so happy. Carefree. Sure, there were a whole lot of worries, but she pushed them to one side.

Harry walked in and stood behind her. He reached around to wash his hands. Embarrassment flooded her as she realized he was really going to make her stand here while he removed the plug.

Yikes.

Down went the drop seat and her panties and he stared into the mirror at her.

Closing her eyes, she dropped her head. That was way too intense.

"Uh-uh," he told her in a low voice. "Look at me."

Crap. She should have known that was coming.

"I can't."

"You can," he told her in a firm voice. "I know it's hard but I want you to look at me while I remove the plug."

"Daddy."

"Look at me, sweetheart."

Raising her head, she opened her eyes and stared at him as he twisted the plug. A low moan escaped her.

"Do you like that?" he asked. "Do you like the feel of me moving the plug inside you? Are you thinking what it would feel like if it was my cock inside you? Taking your ass?"

"Yes," she groaned. "I want your cock so badly."

"Is your pussy wet at the thought?"

"Darn it, Harry," she told him. "Do you have to talk like this?"

He drew the plug out slightly before pushing it back in. "You're complaining? You want me to stop?"

Stop? Hell no.

"No, no, I don't want you to stop. It's just so . . . urgh, I'm so turned on and you won't let me come."

"You have to wait, don't you? Poor baby girl. Having to hold off on her pleasure. But just think about how good it will feel when you finally get to come. I'm going to eat you out first, for a good long while. Then I'm going to fuck you. I don't know how I want to take you. On the bed on your back. Or with you bent over the edge of the bed. Or on your hands and knees on the floor."

"All of them," she replied breathlessly as he started slowly drawing the plug out. "All of them would be good."

"Yes, wouldn't it? Unfortunately, I'm not as young as I once was and you might have to take pity on an old guy and give him a rest in between."

She let out a deep breath as the plug left her bottom. He stepped back and moved to the sink.

He started cleaning the plug and she glanced over at the toilet. Once the plug was clean, he washed his hands. A knock came from the door of the suite. "That's dinner. You come out when you're ready."

A few minutes later, she walked out to find dinner set out on the small table in front of the large windows.

Instead of the chairs being opposite one another, he had hers pulled around beside his.

He settled her on the seat and she bit her lip as she realized he'd put a cushion down.

"Thanks for the cushion, Daddy," she told him.

He winked at her, then removed the covers over their plates. On his plate was a steak with a large salad. On hers were crumbed chicken pieces, broccoli, and mashed potato.

"Yummo!" she said, grabbing her fork.

"Wait," he told her, reaching for a cloth napkin. "Let's put this napkin around you since we don't have a bib."

"Daddy! I don't need a bib. I'm a big girl."

"Well, big girl, let's just see how you do. You don't want to get your new onesie all dirty, then have to wait to wash it before you can wear it again, do you?"

"No, I guess not. All right, Daddy. I'll wear the bib." She let him tie the napkin around her.

He cut up all of her food, then blew on it before feeding her. He was always careful to make sure her food wasn't too hot.

"Well, Little Monster," he said once she was finished. "I'd say the bib was a good idea, wouldn't you?"

She stared down at herself in shock. There were food stains all over the napkin.

"Uh, maybe, Daddy."

"Just maybe? Bibs are going on my shopping list."

"What shopping list?"

"For when we go to that store in Wishingbone." He undid the napkin and carefully pulled it off her. "Just wait here and I'll get a washcloth to clean you up."

She tidied up their dishes as she waited for him.

"I would have done that, Little Monster," he chided gently as he returned. Crouching, he wiped each of her hands, getting between her fingers. Then he cleaned her face.

"I like helping, Daddy."

"You're a good helper," he praised. "But little girls need to be careful that they don't hurt themselves. It's always best to ask Daddy first if you want to help, okay? Only because I want to keep you safe, not because I'm upset."

She nodded, giving him a smile.

"That's my girl." Leaning in, he kissed her lightly. "I'm going to set this out in the hall. Why don't we get you under a blanket in the bedroom, watching some TV while I take care of it?"

"Okay, Daddy."

When he came into the bedroom ten minutes later, she was engrossed in a movie about vampires. She jumped as he appeared in the doorway, letting out a small scream.

Frowning, he walked in and looked at the screen. "This isn't very age appropriate. It'll give you nightmares."

"I've seen it before, Daddy." And yeah, she might have had a nightmare afterward.

Clicking his tongue, he switched the television off, turning to her with a stern look. "I could swear that I left you watching a safe cartoon."

She shrank into her cocoon of blankets and pillows. "It was boring, Daddy. I won't have any nightmares."

"You need reining in, don't you, my baby?"

"No, Daddy. I'm telling you, I'm a free-range Little. I can roam around, do what I want, eat what I want, it's how I thrive."

"I don't think so. I think you thrive from a watchful eye, some firm rules and discipline when you're naughty. Since you've been with me, those bags under your eyes have disappeared, your color is better and you're eating better."

"I think our definitions of eating better differ greatly. I've only had one sucker today. One!" She was practically going through withdrawal.

"My poor baby, you're doing things tough, aren't you?" he crooned.

"I am!"

"Do you need Daddy to make everything better?"

There was a husky note to his voice which immediately made her skin tingle and her insides clench. She licked her lips and his gaze zeroed in on her mouth.

"Yes, please."

He climbed onto the bed then knelt over her, placing his hands on the headboard as he bent in to kiss her softly.

He nuzzled at her cheek then along her jaw and down her neck. "What part of you haven't I claimed yet?"

"My back," she whispered. "My shoulders. My arms. My hands. My feet and legs."

"Goodness. I need to start with your . . . feet."

Her feet?

That didn't seem very sexy. He moved away then grabbed the blanket and drew it back.

To reveal what she was wearing underneath. She watched as heat filled his face.

"Now, this is a surprise. Here I thought you were still wearing your onesie."

She was wearing the babydoll nightie he'd bought her earlier and she loved it. Deep red and lacy, it was tight under her breasts then went out in a flare.

"Delicious. Like unwrapping a present and finding all of your dreams have come true."

Wow. Just wow. How did he know exactly what to say to turn her on? He tugged on her ankles until she lay flat on her back on the bed. Then climbing off the bed, he grabbed the bag that had held the nightie.

And drew out the handcuffs and rope from earlier. Her heart raced at the sight.

"I'm going to tie you up for this next part, sweetheart," he told her. "Hold out your hands."

He put the handcuffs over her wrists. They weren't so tight that they hurt, but they definitely felt weighty.

"If at any time you feel uncomfortable or frightened, you're to say your safeword, understand?"

"Yes, Daddy."

"Good girl."

He used the rope to secure the cuffs to the headboard, so her arms rested above her head. Immediately, she tugged at the restraints, moaning with delight and pleasure as she found herself well secured.

"You like that, don't you? Like being tied down by Daddy?"

"Yes, Daddy," she told him.

"Good. Because I like it too."

Which just pushed up her own pleasure. She watched, her breath growing faster, as he drew out a blindfold.

"You okay, my baby?" he asked, watching her carefully.

"Yes."

"Sure? You trust me to blindfold you? It's all right if you're not up for that."

"No, I . . . I am. I want that. I just won't get to see you." She pouted up at him.

He grinned and shook his head. "I promise, you'll get to see me. I won't keep you blindfolded the entire time." He fixed the blindfold over her eyes and it added a whole other level of tension and pleasure to the experience.

She sucked in a breath and he kissed the tip of her nose then her lips. "I like that you enjoy looking at me. That you want to see more of me. But most of all? I like you."

Yeah, well, she had him beat on that since she loved him.

But she wasn't ready to say it. She didn't know why. Maybe because this felt too new. Or perhaps she was waiting for the other shoe to drop.

He moved his lips down her neck and along the edge of the nightie. Then his mouth found her nipple through the lace and he sucked until it was a hard nub. She groaned, pulling at her restraints.

"Easy, my baby. You're going to get to come. I promise. In fact, this time you can come as often as you like without waiting for permission. Isn't Daddy good to you?"

"Yes."

"What do you say?" he murmured before brushing his tongue over the lace covering her hard nub.

"Thank you, Daddy, for being so nice to your girl."

"She deserves it. I know it wasn't easy waiting for tonight to get to come. But it will be worth it."

She sure hoped so.

He turned his attention to her other nipple, pushing the lace to the side before lightly scraping his teeth over the nub.

She cried out, her clit throbbing in delight.

More. She needed more.

She sure hoped he wasn't going to tease her for too long. But he spent his time playing with her nipples until they were so sensitive that she didn't think she could take much more. He plucked at them, licked and sucked until she was squirming on the bed.

"Please, Daddy. Please!"

"What do you need?"

"Your mouth on my pussy. On my clit. I need to come!"

"But I haven't claimed the other parts of you yet." He moved his mouth over her shoulders. "Another part of you that is now mine."

He obviously didn't realize that all of her was his already. But she wasn't going to tell him.

Not when it meant she got his mouth all over her body. He was now working his way down her right arm and hand, then he kissed the tips of her fingers. "Is your pussy wet? Is it ready for me?"

Oh, Lord.

Surely he knew that? He'd just been playing with her nipples for a good ten minutes, he couldn't honestly think that she wouldn't be wet after that, right?

"Answer me."

That firm voice sent waves of arousal through her.

"Yes, I'm wet."

"Good girl." He kissed both wrists just above where the handcuffs sat, then worked his way down her left arm. "I can't wait to taste your pussy again. It's addictive. I'm going to eat you out and you're going to come on my tongue, aren't you?"

She'd do whatever he wanted her to do as long as she got to come.

"Yes, Daddy."

"That's my girl." He slid down her tummy and grabbed her feet, pushing her legs back so they were bent and her feet were flat on the mattress.

When he parted the lips of her pussy, she tensed up. She knew what was coming and she was so here for it. Then he blew his breath out over her clit and wet lips and she whimpered in frustration.

That wasn't what she wanted or needed.

She needed more.

"Shh, baby. You're okay," he soothed. He flicked his tongue out over her clit. He drove her nuts with his soft, slow licks. Then he moved lower, pushing her thighs further apart so he could lick over her entrance before pushing his tongue in deep.

A moan escaped her.

With his thumb, he played with her clit, driving her closer and closer to the edge. Then he slid his fingers into her passage as he tongued her clit.

"Oh, pumpkin pie and whipped cream, please let me come already!"

A chuckle escaped him, the breath of air making her even more sensitive.

He was torturing her. She couldn't take it.

"Whipped cream, huh? Things must be bad."

They were. They really were.

And then he quit playing around. Or maybe she was just so close she couldn't take it anymore. He moved his tongue back and forth across her clit with firm, fast flicks that sent her spiraling. She screamed, her entire body buckling under wave after wave of intense pleasure.

It was almost too much. The day of build-up had put her so on edge. But eventually, she drifted back to earth. Her lungs were working overtime as she tried to get air into them, her body trembling.

"Daddy, Daddy," she called out.

"You're all right. Shh. I have you." He wrapped her up in his embrace. "That was intense, huh?"

"Yes."

"You look so beautiful when you come and the way you taste . . . so delicious." He took her mouth with his, and she could taste herself on his tongue. She hummed with pleasure.

"Now, for round two."

Oh holy heck. He was trying to kill her.

By the time he'd finished feasting on her, she'd come three times. He slid off her blindfold then undid the cuffs and rubbed her arms. Then he moved her onto her knees, her face buried in the pillow as he ate her out from behind, sending her into another orgasm.

"Baby, you've killed me." He lay back on the bed, breathing heavily.

She was lying on her front. She couldn't move. Couldn't breathe. She was done. Stick-a-fork-in-her done.

At some stage while she was blindfolded, Harry had stripped off so he was just wearing a pair of black boxers. And damn he looked hot lying there with his chest on display.

Hmm. Maybe she had a bit of energy left. Moving toward him, she snuggled up under his arm.

"Hello there, my baby," he murmured.

"Hello, Daddy." She ran her hand up and down his chest, over his nipple. He had a few tattoos on his lower arms. They were hidden when he wore his shirts so most people might not even know they were there.

One was a compass. She ran her finger over it.

"To provide protection and guidance," he told her. "And help guide me home. Not that I even knew where home was. Not until I met a certain dark-haired, gorgeous, crazy, beautiful woman."

"Daddy, can I explore?"

He studied her for a long moment. "You don't want to go to sleep?"

"Oh no, I don't need too much rest between rounds. I'm not ancient like you."

"Why, you little brat," he growled. Rolling her onto her tummy, he straddled her lower legs and lifted her nightie. Then he landed several stinging smacks onto her ass. She cried out and moaned in pleasure simultaneously.

"Just for that, you're going to suck my dick in apology."

Oh hell. That was the sort of apology she liked. If that was how she had to apologize all the time, well, she might just have to do more things to say sorry for.

"If I have to, Daddy. I mean, it's a huge problem for me, but I was naughty when I called you old and I should apologize."

"A huge problem, is it?" He moved off the bed and stripped off his boxers as she rolled onto her back.

She studied his cock. "Oh yeah, it's enormous."

He shook his head with a grin. "On your back, put a pillow behind your head."

Lying back, she watched, her heart racing in anticipation, as he grabbed his dick in his hand, stroking it with long, firm strokes.

Her mouth watered. That was her cock. And she wanted it in her mouth. What was he playing at?

"Daddy, please," she asked, giving him a pitiful look. "I want to touch you."

"Hmm, I'm not sure that a naughty girl gets to touch Daddy."

"Then how am I meant to take your cock into my mouth?"

He moved over her, straddling her upper chest and pinning her arms to her body. "Open your mouth."

Oh. Holy. Heck.

Was he serious? She'd never done this, but she opened her mouth, wanting to taste him. Needing to. He slowly fed her his dick, inch by glorious inch.

She murmured in pleasure, sucking on him as he slid into her mouth.

"Yes, baby. That's it. Good girl. Look at you." He grabbed hold of the headboard. And drew back out of her mouth before slowly sliding in again.

"If it gets too much, slap my leg."

Yeah, she doubted she would have to do that. But she murmured a yes around his dick. Damn, he was thick. And gorgeous. He kept his movements slow for a start and she found herself wanting him to speed up.

"Have mercy. I can't last much longer," he moaned.

Good. Because she wanted him to come. Now.

But instead of driving deep and coming down her throat, he drew back and moved so he was kneeling next to her instead.

"No, Daddy. Come back."

He shook his head. "I'm not coming in your mouth this time. I want to be inside you. I want you to get up, then turn and face the headboard on your knees."

She moved, turning around to face the headboard. She'd never been dominated like this in the bedroom.

And she was so here for it.

"Good girl." He ran a hand down her back to her ass. Then he followed his hand with his mouth, kissing his way down her spine to kiss each butt cheek. Then he shocked her by parting her ass cheeks and placing a quick kiss on her back hole. No one had ever done that before.

"Now lean forward and grab hold of the headboard. Wait, condom."

He moved away to the nightstand and grabbed a condom. She watched as he rolled it over his firm, thick dick. That was going to be inside her soon.

And she could not wait.

Then he was behind her again, his fingers ran through the lips of her slick pussy, pushing inside her.

Her breathing grew faster.

"Who does this pussy belong to, baby girl?"

Lord help her. Those words. They were everything. Her thighs trembled and she took a better hold of the headboard to keep herself up.

"You, Daddy."

"That's right. It's my pussy. To do with what I like. And what I want right now is to feel this pussy around my dick."

He removed his fingers and ran them along her ass cheeks. "This is the best ass I've ever seen. And it's all mine, isn't it, baby?"

"Yes, Daddy. All yours."

"Mine to discipline, mine to squeeze, mine to fuck."

Was he going to do that tonight? No, she knew that he wouldn't. Harry was nothing if not extra cautious of her safety and health. He'd make sure she was ready to take him there.

Then he positioned his dick at the entrance of her passage, pushing inside her.

And oh God, it was better than she ever expected. He was stretching her, but in a good way. In a way that made her breathing grow faster, deeper.

"Please. Please. More."

"You'll get more when I give it to you. I don't want to hurt you."

That was so mean. Couldn't he see that he was killing her here? And hurt her? He had to feel how wet she was. How ready for him. But he kept up that slow pace until he was fully inside her.

They were both breathing heavily by now. He was surrounding her; his chest was pressed to her back and his heat engulfed her.

"You have no idea how good you feel. You're killing me here, baby."

She was killing him? What did he think he was doing to her?

Then he started moving. Slow at first but he built the pace up faster and faster. She loved the feel of him inside her. The sharp, short thrusts followed by long, slow glides of his dick.

Reaching around, he toyed with her clit, flicking it firmly.

"I want you to come on my cock."

"I can't," she groaned. "I can't come anymore."

"You can. You will. I want to feel you come around me. You can do it. Come for me, baby. Come for me."

She didn't think it was possible. She was still shaking her head as he managed to get her over that edge again. A cry shook its way through her as she clenched down on his dick.

That was so intense. She was shaking by the time she came back to earth.

"Thank you, my baby." He drew slowly out of her pussy.

"No! What are you doing?" she cried out.

"Shh. I want to see your face as I'm fucking you."

He moved her onto her back, then he was inside her again. And she swore that her eyes rolled back in her head.

So good.

The man had some stamina. He held her hands above her head as he fucked her until she didn't know where she was. Didn't know if she could speak or heck, even what her name was.

All she knew was that she belonged to this man.

Her everything.

And then he threw his head back as he came, his shout of satisfaction filling the room and making her smile as she clenched around him.

Carefully, he moved to the side of her then drew her in against him.

"Thank you, sweetheart."

"For what? I think I should be thanking you," she slurred. "That was amazing."

"It was. I don't think I can move for a year."

"Poor Daddy Waddy."

He was groaning even as he started laughing.

34

It was their last night in Bozeman.

She was going to miss being here with Harry. Having time together. She was also nervous, because after dinner tonight, she intended to come clean about the money she owed Vance. She didn't know if that was why she'd had a dream last night about losing Harry. Or if it was to do with something else.

The waiter in the restaurant held out her chair and she sat, glancing around.

"Everything all right?" Harry asked.

She nodded. "Yep. All good."

"What do you feel like?" he asked, picking up the menu.

"I don't suppose they have chicken tenders and fries here."

His lips twitched. "No, but they've got pasta."

"I do like pasta."

An hour later, she scraped her plate clean. Damn, that was good. Also, her tummy was really full now.

"I think I ate too much."

Harry leaned over and wiped her chin with his napkin.

"That chin obsession is back." She groaned, rubbing her tummy.

"Poor baby. No dessert then?"

"What? No! There's a separate tummy for dessert." Everyone knew that, right?

"Are you sure? I don't want you to be in pain."

"I'm sure. Totally sure. I just need to go to the restroom. If the waiter comes back, can you order me the Bombe Alaska?" She'd always wanted to try that.

"You want to share it?" Harry asked.

"What? No. Why would I want to share?"

"Uh, because it's a dessert for two."

"Pfft. So they say. Really, that's just a guideline. I can fit it in." She patted her tummy, and he shook his head. Knowing him, he'd probably order sorbet and diced fruit or something.

She made her way into the really posh restroom. This place was gorgeous. As she was washing up, the door opened. She didn't pay much attention until she realized the person hadn't moved toward a stall.

Turning, she froze as she saw the man standing there. He was dressed in a dark shirt and dress pants. But the nice clothes couldn't hide the evil lurking underneath.

At least not to her.

"Jerome? What are you doing here?"

"Eating dinner, of course."

"This doesn't really seem like your type of place." When she'd known him, he'd been into pizza, ribs, and beer. And that was pretty much it.

"Well, you don't know what I'm into anymore, do you, Kiesha? I could have changed."

She doubted it. You could dress a pig up and it would still be a pig. Not that she was comparing Jerome to a pig. She liked pigs.

"What do you want? Why have you barged into the women's

restroom?" Why hadn't she brought her handbag in here with her? Then she'd have her Taser and phone. Not that her Taser was charged. She really had to get onto that.

"Maybe I just wanted to come say hi."

"We're not friends, Jerome. And I don't want to say hi. Now, go away."

"That's not very nice of you, Kiesha. I came in to offer you a deal."

"What sort of deal?" She really needed to get back to Harry before he came looking for her.

"If you're waiting for someone to come rescue you, I wouldn't hold my breath. I put an out-of-order sign in front of the door."

That wouldn't hold Harry back for long.

"What do you want?"

"Who's the old man? He your sugar daddy?"

Yeah, like she was going to tell him any personal information about herself.

"Because I've been watching the two of you, staying in that fancy hotel, him buying you shit all weekend."

"Oh, my God. You've been following us?"

That's what she'd sensed? She felt ill at the thought. Jerome had always been an asshole, but a dumb one. She didn't think he was capable of following her without her seeing him.

Seems she was wrong.

"What do you think Vance will think about you parading around his town with that old man?"

"Vance can kiss my ass."

Jerome's eyes narrowed in anger. It probably wasn't her brightest idea to mouth off about Vance to one of his men. But she was mad, and she didn't give a shit right then.

"I could take you to him right now," he threatened. "Vance should never have let you just walk off. That was a pussy move. He should have tied you to his bed and kept you there until you stopped being so fucking mouthy."

Holy shit. Was he criticizing Vance? Was he high?

His face grew softer. "I'm just trying to help you."

Yeah, right. Jerome cared about no one but himself.

"So I won't tell him that you were here or about your sugar daddy so long as you do something for me."

Fear bubbled in her stomach. "And what's that?"

"I want ten grand and your mouth on my dick. Right now."

She threw back her head and laughed. She laughed until her stomach ached and tears ran down her face. Jerome's face darkened in anger. He stepped toward her, grabbing her arm. Hard. He shoved her against the wall. "Don't fucking laugh. Why are you laughing, bitch?"

"Because that was hilarious. You're a funny guy. Now let me go."

"I don't think so. You're going to get down on your knees and suck my dick, or I'm going to tell Vance about your friend. And how loaded he is. You planning on milking him for money? On using him to pay your debt?"

"No, of course not!" She'd never do that.

Jerome leaned in and she could smell his breath. It wasn't pretty.

"Dude, what have you been eating? Garbage? Your breath is bad enough to fell an elephant."

"Shut up, bitch!" he snarled. He shook her, making her head smash back against the wall.

Shit. He definitely had to be on something. She had to get away from him before Harry came searching for her. The last thing she wanted was for him to get hurt.

Without allowing herself to think about it too hard, she drew her foot back and then smashed her knee up into his balls. He let out a choked groan, his hand slipping from her arm.

"Stay away from me. And from Harry."

Shit.

She should have told Harry about all of this earlier.

Stupid, so stupid.

When was she going to learn? She needed to learn how to ask people for help.

"Watch your back, bitch," Jerome spat out. "I won't let this lie. I will make you pay."

"I'm so scared."

That was the problem, though.

She was scared.

Scared that the best thing she'd ever had in her life was going to walk out on her once he realized just how messy her life was.

And that he could well be in the middle of it.

~

Harry didn't know what was wrong with Kiesha. But he'd had about enough of her staring off into the distance, and not noticing anything else around her.

When she stepped out onto the road without looking, he grabbed her arm and quickly drew her back. She let out a cry of pain as a car sped past, tooting at them.

"Kiesha? What is it? Did I hurt you?" he asked, turning her to face him. Was it the arm that she'd hurt at the Wishing Well? But no, that had healed, and he'd grabbed her other arm, so it couldn't be that. Her sleeve was too tight for him to push it up and check, but they were only a few minutes from the hotel.

"What? Oh, I'm fine. Guess I was a bit distracted."

"A bit distracted? You've been like this since you came back from the ladies' room. Out of it. I don't think you've heard a word I said, and you didn't eat your dessert."

To be honest, that worried him more than anything. It wasn't like her to not eat something sweet put in front of her.

"Are you not well? Is that it? Do I need to call a doctor?" He put his hand over her forehead. "You're not hot. I need to get a thermometer."

"I'm fine. I'm not sick."

He frowned. "Then what is it? What's wrong with your arm? Did something happen?"

"I . . . I . . . yeah, something happened," she whispered. "Can we go back to the hotel room before I tell you, though?"

"I think that's a good idea. But you're going to hold my hand so you don't wander off. Got me?"

"Yes, Daddy." She stared at him sadly. What on earth had happened?

When they got inside the hotel room, he turned to her. "Show me your arm."

"What?" She gave him a surprised look, her other hand moving to her arm protectively. "Why?"

"Because when I grabbed you, you made a noise that sounded like you were in pain. I want to see your arm and make sure it's all right."

"It's fine, Daddy."

"No. No, I want to see it. Now." He made his voice firm, giving her a strict look. To his surprise, tears filled her eyes.

"What is it? What's wrong?" he asked.

Okay, now he was even more worried. Gently taking her hand, he led her to the sofa and settled on the couch with her on his lap.

"Oh, Harry. I'm so sorry."

"What is it? Baby, just tell me."

"I've messed up. I always mess up. It seems to be my one talent in life."

"Hey." He grasped hold of her chin, tilting her face back. Reaching over, he grabbed a few tissues to clean her up. "I don't want to hear you saying things like that. You know you're not to talk badly about yourself."

"How can it be talking badly about myself when it's the truth? I'm a complete mess. My life is a mess. I tried to fix it. But everything just seems to get worse. And now I've gone and gotten you involved. I don't know what he'll do. He might not care or he might decide to somehow use you—"

"All right, slow down. I want you to take a deep breath. Everything is going to be all right, I promise."

She shook her head. "Don't promise that. You can't promise that. You don't know what he's capable of. I thought he was trying to help me, but I don't think he's capable of any sort of empathy or sympathy. All he feels is a need to own anyone he thinks will be useful to him."

"Kiesha, listen to me. Whoever this person is, whatever he's done to you, he's not infallible. He's a person, not a monster, and we can defeat him. Together."

"Well, I know he's not a monster. I like monsters. I don't like Vance."

"Vance who?"

"Vance LaRue. He's this crime boss here in Bozeman, and now he's going to know about you because Jerome will tell him. That's just the sort of thing that evil little weasel will do because he doesn't get his own way and I didn't suck his dick—"

"Whoa. Okay, I'm going to need you to stop. Take another deep breath."

He waited until she'd settled a bit more, then he turned her so she was straddling his lap. He held her hands gently in his, frowning when he found them freezing. Reaching over, he snagged a blanket that she'd been snuggling under this morning when they'd first gotten up. They'd sat together and watched morning cartoons while he'd drunk coffee and she'd had chocolate milk. He wrapped it around her, tucking the front in under her thighs.

"Tell me. Start from the beginning. And tell me all of it."

He didn't like that she'd been holding something big back from him. But he had to remind himself that things between them were still new. They'd only known each other a month. He couldn't expect to know it all.

"From the beginning?" She rubbed her hand over her face. "I don't know where to start... I mean, I guess I have to start with Jonah. He... I told you that he got really sick, right? With cancer. Well, we didn't have any health insurance, and the bills kept piling up. I just told myself that he'd get better and we'd figure it all out later. That's always what I do. I just hope that things will get better. I can't go through life just hoping for the best. Because life always seems to kick me in the butt."

"You were left with a lot of medical bills?"

"Yes," she whispered. "And I had no way of paying them. You know things were bad for me after Jonah died. I was in a dark place and nothing seemed to matter. Vance figured out how bad things were and he moved me into his place. I didn't put up much of a fight. And by the time I realized what was going on, well, Vance had found all the bills and paid them."

"What? Why would he do that?"

"So he could own me."

"That mother-fucking bastard."

"Vance likes to get his own way. No one really tells him no. By this time, Ed had realized I had moved and was on the warpath. I told him I'd gone on a road trip to get my head together."

"Why not tell him the truth?"

"Because Vance is really dangerous, and I didn't want to put him or my friends in danger. And because it was my problem to solve. I hate feeling like a burden. My Grandpa made my mom feel like a burden every day she lived with him. He never stopped reminding her of what she owed him. It was awful. I swore I would never owe anyone anything like that. And now I suddenly owed Vance all this money."

"What did Vance want?"

"A wife."

His eyes widened. That wasn't what he'd expected her to say. "What the fuck? Are you saying that he wanted to buy you?"

"Yeah. Sounds crazy, right? Vance is a good-looking guy. He's rich. There are probably dozens of women who would fall all over themselves to marry him. I mean, he'd probably make a pretty crappy husband. He's gone all hours of the night. Not sure he could be faithful because I'm pretty sure he's not capable of loving anyone. Well, anyone except April."

"And who is she?"

"His daughter. She's the one redeeming feature about that asshole and the reason that I'd never try to go against him. Well, that and the fact he'd probably squash me like a bug. He has this gorgeous little girl, and she thinks the world of her Daddy and he feels the same about her."

He tried to figure this all out. "Where is her mother?"

"I don't know. No one ever mentions her."

"So Vance wanted you to marry him, to be his wife and a mother to his daughter in return for paying Jonah's medical bills."

"Yeah, he'd wipe the debt if I married him. I suppose he couldn't marry just anyone because he couldn't trust them. I think I'm one of the few people in this world that he thought he could trust because of my bond with April." She rubbed at her chest. "We were at a BBQ at his house once, on one of the rare occasions when April was around. And she started choking. No one else seemed to realize what was going on. But I grabbed her and gave her the Heimlich. She was so tiny, I was scared I was going to hurt her. And when she spat out what she'd been choking on, and I came back to awareness, I found myself surrounded by ten scary assholes with guns aimed at me."

"They thought you were hurting her."

"Jonah threw himself in front of me. And then this deep voice yelled at everyone to get back. There he was. Vance. He's kind of terrifying. He's huge. He spends hours every morning in the gym. And he raced over and picked up this little girl, holding her so tenderly. It was the sweetest thing I'd ever seen. And then he ordered me and Jonah into his office. Pretty sure I wet myself. I can't quite remember because I also went numb."

"What did he do?"

"He . . . he just stared at me as April sat on his lap and I thought this was it. I thought I was dead. Then April climbed off his lap and walked over to me. She doesn't talk. I'm not sure why. That's something else no one speaks about. What happened to her mother and why April doesn't talk. But that doesn't mean she can't communicate. She grabbed my hand and pulled me down into the chair and then she climbed up into my lap. Apparently that was strange behavior for her. She doesn't like strangers or anyone except for Vance and his closest bodyguards. Anyway, Vance was shocked. But then one of his bodyguards, who he seems really close to, came in and whispered something in his ear. He must have seen what happened. When Vance learned what I had done, things really eased up. I mean, he didn't suddenly become this awesome, friendly guy or anything. We went home straight away, but I seemed to be on Vance's radar."

"What does that mean?"

"He would invite us around for dinner and stuff. It made Jonah a bit uncomfortable, but Vance isn't a man you just say no to. He's used to getting his own way. So we'd go when he would invite us and April would usually be there. She and I got close. She's such a sweet kid and so not what you thought she'd be like with her father. Not that Vance wasn't a good father. He was, surprisingly."

"Did he try anything with you?"

"No. I don't think he was ever interested in me like that. Jonah was still worried, though. But then he got ill and everything was a mess. I was a mess. I was trying to be strong for him, but the truth is that I'm not strong at all. I'm weak and I didn't know what to do, and I was so scared. So I did what I always do. I buried my head and hoped for the best. But the best didn't happen."

"You're not weak."

"I am. I know you don't like me saying bad things about myself, but this is true. I'm so freaking scared. All the time. I bluff my way out of things, make shit up. I pretend that I'm having the time of my life, but underneath it all I have no idea what the fuck I'm doing."

"Believe it or not, most people are."

"You aren't."

"Baby, I am far from perfect. I have my moments where I don't know what I'm doing. Where I'm scared."

"Really?"

"Really," he replied firmly.

"When I finally clawed my way out of the darkness and grew aware of what was going on, I told him I couldn't do that and that I wanted to leave. I loved April, but I couldn't stay there. If I did . . . I was going to lose myself. I'd likely give Vance whatever he wanted. He wasn't cruel or nasty. He was more indifferent, I guess. Anyway, he wasn't happy at that."

"He didn't want you to leave."

"No, and I was dumb. Really dumb. I should have rejected him in private. Instead, I did it where some of his men could hear. Vance told me if I left that I would have to pay back every cent of what I'd borrowed. With interest." She ran her hand over her face.

"He had to follow through to save face."

"Right," she said in a whisper. "He told me I had three months to get my shit sorted, then he'd be sending a guy to me each month. They'd expect installments and if I didn't pay them, he'd bring me back to him."

"So you've been paying him all this time?"

"Yeah."

"How can you afford that?"

"I got a second job," she admitted. "You remember that time you came to my apartment and Dennis the dick said I was out?"

"You were at your other job? Where?"

"A few towns over at Chubby's Bar. Horrible place, but it paid well."

"Paid?"

"I got fired a while back. I had an altercation with a handsy customer."

"What? And they fired you? They can't do that!"

"Well, they did. So I missed the last payment when Bodhi came to get it."

"Bodhi? One of his men?"

"Yeah, one of his personal bodyguards. Bodhi is . . . he's actually a decent guy. When he came to get the money, I'd already been evicted, and I forgot. I didn't have the cash, anyway."

"But you weren't taken back to Vance."

"No, because Bodhi gave him money. From his own pocket."

Harry's eyes narrowed. "And what happened tonight?"

"One of Vance's men must have seen us while we were out shopping or something. He decided to confront me in the restroom."

"What the hell? He cornered you? Wait, why is your arm sore? Was that him?"

She nodded hesitantly, knowing he wasn't going to be happy.

Harry's face turned to granite. "I want to see your arm. Right now."

He lifted her off him and stood up. Then he helped her pull down the top of the long-sleeved dress she wore. She stared down at her upper arm, wincing as she saw that the skin was starting to discolor already.

"That fucking bastard!" Harry snapped, making her jump. "You should have told me as soon as you got back to the table. He could have done anything to you! Damn it. This is fucking unacceptable! What the hell was I thinking, letting you go to the ladies' room on your own?" He paced back and forth.

"Harry, calm down." She chewed at her lip worriedly.

"I can't calm down. You were in danger."

"But you have to calm down. I don't want you to get sick!"

He stilled, then turned to her. Understanding filled his gaze. "Baby, I'm not going to get sick."

"Too much stress isn't good for you and this is stressful. Maybe I shouldn't have told you."

"You definitely should have told me. I want to know everything that happens in your life, understand me?" He drew her up into his arms, holding her tight. "I promise that I am going to take good care of me and of you."

She hugged him just as tightly. "I couldn't bear to lose you."

He kissed the top of her head. "And I couldn't stand to lose you. From now on, you're not going anywhere alone anymore."

Her mouth dropped open. "Uh, Harry, you realize I have a job and stuff, right? I have to go some places on my own."

His gaze narrowed as he stared at her. "From now on, I take you to and from work. Once you're in the building, you'll be under Ed's supervision. No leaving until I return to pick you up. Anywhere else you need to go, I will go with you. And you need to keep your Taser charged and with you at all times."

"That's a bit over-the-top, don't you think?"

"Some guy cornered you in the restroom of a public restaurant and fucking assaulted you while I was out in the dining room, looking at the fucking dessert menu. Not acceptable."

"He didn't hurt me."

"Do not lie to me," he said in a low voice. "I can see the evidence of where he hurt you."

"Yeah, but he just grabbed me, pushed me against the wall. It's not a big deal."

"No. No, Kiesha. You don't get to try and pretend what happened doesn't matter or that you've got it handled. You can't tell me that someone who works for some criminal kingpin trapped you, grabbed you, and I'm guessing, threatened you, and that it's okay. It. Is. Not. Okay."

She took a deep breath and let it out slowly. What was she doing?

He was right. Not. Okay.

Sitting on the sofa, she could feel her body trembling as she leaned her elbows on her thighs and pressed her face into her hands. "You're right. I'm sorry, you're right. What he did . . . he did hurt me and he scared me. I should have told you straight away. I should have screamed for help. What's wrong with me?"

She stared down at her shaking hands.

"Hey, there's nothing wrong with you."

To her surprise, her freaking out seemed to calm him down. He walked over and sat on the coffee table in front of her. Reaching out, he took her hands lightly in his.

"I was going to tell you about Vance tonight. I swear I was. I just wanted to wait until the end of the weekend before I ruined it."

"Hey," he said, cupping her face in his hands. "You didn't ruin anything."

"It's a lot, Harry."

"A problem shared is a problem halved. I'm going to help you with this, and you're going to let me."

"I don't want you to get hurt. It's my problem."

"Nope, baby girl. It's our problem. Say it."

"It's our problem," she whispered with another shiver.

"You're freezing." He grabbed the blanket at the end of the sofa and wrapped it around her. She realized that her dress was pooled at her waist, leaving her just in her bra.

"There is something wrong with me," she told him. "I try to ignore everything that makes me uncomfortable or scares me. Just sweep it into the too-hard basket and hope that it will get better. But it's not getting better. I was working two jobs. I was keeping stuff from you. I can't keep living in this fantasy world."

"There's nothing wrong with hoping for the best. But you have to ask for help when you need it. Because there are so many people who care about you, Kiesha. You just have to reach out and tell us what's going on."

Tears drifted down her cheeks as she nodded. "You're right. I just . . . I didn't want to endanger anyone."

"Are you sure he's not interested in you sexually? I don't see why he wouldn't be."

"Aww, as sweet as that is on my ego, I'm certain he's not. He never tried anything with me."

"You were in mourning."

"I don't think Vance's the sort of guy that cares about a mourning period. And truthfully, if he did want me, I think he'd just take me. I wouldn't be playing this game with him. I don't think he even wants me anymore. It's all about saving face."

Harry didn't look convinced. "Do you ever see his daughter?"

"I video call her. I mean, I do all the talking and she just nods or shakes her head. I wish I could see her in person, but I don't think it's a good idea for me to go near her."

"Because you think he won't let you leave?"

"Maybe," she whispered.

"What did this Jerome guy say? Was he after the money?"

"No, I still have a few weeks. Him seeing us was just a coincidence, it sounds like. He said . . ." Shit, Harry was going to lose it.

"He said what?" he asked in a low voice.

"He said that he was going to tell Vance that I was here and about you, that I had a sugar daddy. I guess he saw you buying me things and made assumptions. He said I should be milking you for the money I owed. Then he said if I got down on my knees and gave him a blow job, plus ten thousand dollars, he wouldn't say a word to Vance. I laughed in his face and that's when he got really angry and pushed me into the wall."

"What happened next? How did you get away?"

"I kneed him in the balls," she said. "He fell to the floor and made some more threats about how I was going to pay while I ran out of there."

Sitting on the sofa next to her, he drew her onto his lap. "Baby, I hate that that happened to you. Especially when I was so near. Vance was Jonah's friend. He should have taken care of you, not tried to manipulate and hurt you."

"I know. Jonah would be horrified. I guess Vance might have justified his actions by telling himself he was watching over me."

"Have any of his men threatened and hurt you before tonight?"

She swallowed heavily. "He mostly sends Bodhi and he wouldn't harm me. But the time before last, Jerome came to collect. And he . . . you remember those bruises on my wrist?"

"Yes," he growled. "I'll fucking kill him."

She buried her face in his chest. "I don't want you to get hurt. I don't want anyone to get hurt because of me."

Harry tilted her chin up, so he was staring down at her. "None of this is your fault. If anyone gets hurt, it's because of Vance. Understand?"

"Yes. I know."

"I had no idea you were in danger. This asshole Jerome could have taken you and I wouldn't have known. We're also getting you one of those GPS trackers. We'll grab that tomorrow on our way home."

"I don't think that's—"

He gave her a stern look that dared her to finish that sentence.

"Do you think they have neon pink ones?" she said.

"We'll see." He stared at the wall, clearly thinking. But she couldn't help but wonder what he was thinking about. Was he wondering why he'd ever gotten involved with her?

A shiver of worry raced through her.

His gaze turned back to her, warming. "You're cold. Let's get you in the bath, then into bed. I want to get some stuff for that bruise as well."

"The bruise is okay. I've had worse."

"Doesn't make a difference if you've had worse. You're in my care now. Which means you'll be getting something for that bruise. Let me get you in the bath, then I'll call down to the desk."

"Okay, that sounds good."

"Don't worry, baby. We'll get this straightened out."

She hoped so. Somehow, she didn't think it would be that simple.

35

Kiesha fiddled with her new bracelet as they drove back to Wishingbone the next day. It had a gold chain and a pendant with a GPS chip so that she could be tracked. She wasn't sure how she felt about that.

"Do you not like it, sweetheart?" Harry asked.

She startled. He'd been so quiet since she'd told him everything last night. She was too scared to ask what he was thinking in case he told her that he had decided she wasn't worth the bother.

She wasn't sure her heart could take it, if that's what he was thinking. Better to wait until he was ready to tell her.

"Oh no, I do." It wasn't her usual style, and the sales assistant had given her a weird look when she'd asked if they had a monster pendant. In Wishingbone, she wouldn't get that look.

"You sure aliens can't track me through it?" She waited for him to dismiss her worry as stupid.

"I admit that was a concern of mine as well, but I'm pretty sure aliens don't have our technology or they would have taken over our world already."

She thought about that. It seemed plausible.

The bruising on her arm looked a lot nastier today, even though Harry had iced it last night, then put some arnica cream on it this morning, which he'd sent someone out to get.

They were on the outskirts of Wishingbone when he spoke again. "Can you direct me to the shop with the Little stuff? Mari said it's not actually in the township."

She gave him a surprised look. "We're still going there?"

"Why wouldn't we be going there?" he asked.

"I don't know. I thought, maybe . . . you take this street up here on the right," she directed.

He turned, but instead of driving down the street, he pulled off on the side of the road. Turning the car off, Harry undid his belt and spun around to face her. She kept her gaze on her fingers, which were twisting into one another.

"Kiesha, look at me, please."

She let out a deep sigh, then glanced up at him. His gaze was kind but firm.

"Why wouldn't I take you to the Little shop?"

"I . . . I . . . you've been quiet. Since I told you about Vance."

He frowned and nodded. "I have."

"And I guess I was thinking . . . have you changed your mind, Harry? About me?"

He cupped her face between his hands. "Never. I'll never change my mind about you. That's something you need to work on believing. But you will. Maybe weeks from now, months, years. Doesn't matter. Because I'll be here. Always. And you will grow confident in my feelings for you."

"Your feelings for me?" she asked, clearly fishing. But she was feeling damn vulnerable and needy, and she hated that.

Today's T-shirt said: *I'm All Good. It's All Good. Everything Is All Good.* And there was a picture of a frazzled sloth on it. It wasn't one of her designs, but she thought it suited her mood.

She was all about mood T-shirts.

"This wasn't the way I was planning on telling you," he murmured. "But, my baby, I think you're the most amazing person I've ever met. You approach life like you do most things, with energy and enthusiasm. Life is never boring with you around. I love your loyalty and your care, and I know that I want to spend the rest of my life with you. I don't care if anyone says it's not long enough for us to know. I'm sick of analyzing everything in my life, of being cautious. I know you're mine. And that I'm yours. And frankly, I'm too old to fuck around on this."

She giggled.

"I love you, Kiesha. With all of me."

She leaned in, pressing her forehead to his, then kissing the tip of his nose. "And I love you, Harrison Taylor. I love that you ground me. You accept my crazy side—"

"I adore your crazy side," he corrected.

"You support me and never try to change me. You also don't let me go too far. You're stern when I need you to be, understanding the rest of the time. I'm not sure I could spend another day without you in it. And even though I'm scared it will all end and I'll be alone again, I know it's worth that worry just to be with you for the time we have."

"If I have my way, we'll have forever." He clasped hold of her face and kissed her. Hard. Deep. Full of love.

When he drew back, her head was spinning slightly. Unfortunately, real life worries pierced that haze of happiness.

"Why were you so quiet, then?" she asked.

"Just thinking about what to do about Vance and his goons."

"Oh."

"The easiest way to get rid of him would be to pay what you owe," he murmured.

"No, I don't want you to do that. You shouldn't spend your money on me."

"I would spend every last penny I have to keep you safe. Don't you know that? I can earn more money. What I can't ever find is another you."

"Darn it, Harry." She sniffled. "You're killing me with sweetness."

He smiled, then put his belt back on and started the car. "I think the first thing we do is go to the Little shop and get you the things we need. Then we call Ed. It's time to tell him, baby."

"Oh man, he's going to want to smack my ass."

"I won't let him do that."

She gave him a huge smile. "My hero."

"Because that's my privilege and right."

"Are you going to spank me for not telling you straight away about Vance?" she whispered.

"I get why you didn't tell me. You wanted to protect me. Plus, things between us are new. At the same time, you put yourself in danger. I would never have taken you to Bozeman had I known. I can't protect you if I don't know everything."

She directed him to the Little shop. It was in a big red barn. The woman that owned it lived in a cute house next door.

Harry parked, then turned to her. "But I think you've been through enough, so I'm not going to punish you. However, keep anything like that from me in the future and my belt will come off."

She should be relieved. Instead, she felt this hard ball of guilt inside her.

"Is there anything else you're keeping from me? Have you had any issues with anyone else?"

"Ahh, just Dennis the dick, which you know about. And you know about my arch nemesis. I . . . there's stuff to tell you, but he isn't a threat to me. Oh, then there's the guy whose balls I broke."

"What?"

"Well, I don't know if they're broken. Can balls break? I might have to research that. But I did knee him in the balls. I've got to tell

Georgie how well her self-defense classes are paying off. Of course, I've always thought I had secret ninja skills. Maybe I was one in another life."

"Kiesha, focus, baby. What guy?"

"Oh, at Chubby's Bar. Remember, I said that one of the customers got handsy and I was fired? Well, I might have broken his nose and kneed him in the balls. And then I lost my job. So did the other waitress. She wasn't very happy with me."

"But you came to her rescue."

"I know, but she really needed that job. Our boss was a real bitch who didn't care about her employees, but she paid well. I needed it too."

"Not anymore," Harry said darkly as he undid her belt. Aunt Marie walked out of her house, coming toward them. "And it sounds like you're well rid of it."

When he got out, he greeted Aunt Marie, who was completely naked. Kiesha watched as Harry went red. He was so cute. She waited impatiently for him to come get her out. She knew better than to do it herself.

Harry loved her.

Harry wasn't going anywhere.

And she was the luckiest girl in the world.

36

"This place is so awesome!" Kiesha said. She took a few running steps and then jumped onto the back of the shopping cart, which was designed for an adult to be able to sit in the seat facing whoever was pushing it.

Kiesha had refused to sit in it, claiming she was a big girl. But Harry was starting to see that he should have insisted on it. Reaching out, he wrapped an arm around her waist and grabbed the shopping cart before it went smashing into a display of protein powders.

"No," he said firmly.

"But Daddy, I was just having fun."

Aunt Marie, the owner, had been kind enough to let them have free rein of the shop, telling them to call for her when they were finished. He was grateful, considering how awkward it had been talking to her while she didn't have clothes on. He'd thought Kiesha was teasing him when she'd told him the older woman was a nudist. But she'd probably regret leaving them if they toppled over her carefully stacked display.

"It's dangerous."

Something caught his gaze and he reached over to pick up a harness with a leash attached.

Kiesha's mouth dropped open as he held it up.

"Either you wear this or you sit in the shopping cart."

"I'll be a good girl, I promise. I'll even hold onto the cart. See?" She grabbed hold of the handle with her hand.

"I'm sorry, Little Monster, but those weren't your choices."

"Daddy!" She stomped her foot. Then her eyes widened and she stared down at the limb. "Whoa. Where did that come from?"

"I'd say it came from Kiesha," he said dryly.

"Daddy. I didn't tell my foot to do that. Are you sure the aliens aren't controlling me through this bracelet?"

"If they are, it's going to be rough on you since you'll be the one getting spanked for being naughty."

"Daddy! That's not fair. You can't blame me for the things the aliens make me do."

"Life's tough," he agreed. "But yes, I can. Now, harness or seat?"

"Not much of a choice," she grumbled. "Seat, I guess."

"All right. But I think I'll get this just in case." He put the harness in the cart.

"No! Daddy!"

"Already done."

"You can't buy that."

"Excuse me? Pretty sure I can."

She was adorable when she was cross. But as cute as she was, she was also being a bit too sassy.

Taking hold of her hand, he led her to an area of the store that had a chair facing the corner. *Time-Out Chair* was painted along the back of the chair.

"Daddy, noooo."

"You're being a bit too sassy. And you need to remember that stomping your foot and arguing isn't good behavior."

She gave him a look filled with regret and chagrin. "I'm sorry,

Daddy. You're right. I'm not sure . . ." She put her hand over her tummy. "Now, I feel terrible."

"Which is why you're spending five minutes in the corner. Sit on the chair and I'll come back for you soon."

She sniffled and he nearly relented. But he couldn't give in every time she got a bit tearful.

"Okay, Daddy." She sat in the corner, her shoulders slumped, sounding like she was struggling to hold in her tears.

He reached for her, then took a deep breath.

Be strong. This is what she needs. To know that you'll pull her back if she goes too far.

He moved back to the shopping cart, but he never took his eyes off her. Letting her out of his sight was going to be difficult. He didn't know how he was going to cope with her going to work tomorrow.

The GPS bracelet helped a bit. But it wasn't enough.

He wondered if Ed would agree to him putting cameras in the police station? Or if he could get access to the cameras they likely already had there. Now there was a thought. Checking the time, he moved back to her.

"All right, Little Monster. It's been five minutes. All done." To his shock, she launched herself out of the chair, straight at him.

She was trembling as he gathered her close, holding her tight. "Hey, hey, hey. You're all right. You're all right."

Damn it. Had that been the wrong move?

"I'm so sorry, Daddy. I'm sorry I was naughty."

"You weren't that naughty. And everything is forgiven now."

She shook her head. "I don't think so. I think we should leave. I don't deserve any of these nice things."

That seemed like an overreaction. He tilted back her face with his hand under her chin. "Hey now, what's this all about? Of course you deserve these things."

"I don't! I really don't! I don't deserve anything nice. I kept i-important things from y-you. I should h-have told you about V-Vance and now who k-knows what he's going to do? What if you're in d-danger?"

"Hush. Hush, sweetheart." He cupped the back of her head, thinking furiously. He hadn't thought she'd feel this terrible about everything. How could he make this better?

"Daddy?" she asked.

"Yes?"

"Could you maybe spank me?"

"What?" Shock filled him. That wasn't what he'd been expecting her to say.

"I think I'd feel better if I was punished."

His initial thought was to say no. But if she was feeling awful and a punishment would make her feel better . . . hell, maybe it was what he needed too. In order to get this tight knot in his gut to disappear. He knew she would have told him and that she'd been scared of losing him.

But the fact is, she should have told him when she realized they were headed to Bozeman. She had to learn to trust in his feelings for her. Because if anything had happened to her . . .

And that was the main cause of the knot in his stomach. The idea that she could have been harmed made him feel ill. And knowing that asshole had his hands on her, was threatening her while he had no clue?

Yeah. It pissed him off.

"All right. Aunt Marie said there is a private room here for discipline."

"What? We're doing it now?" she squeaked.

"Better to get it over and done with. Otherwise, you'll worry about it. We do it now, then you can feel better."

And so could he.

. . .

Kiesha couldn't believe that Harry was going to spank her now. She hadn't meant for him to drag her into some room and smack her bottom.

"What if Aunt Marie comes in?" she asked worriedly. "What if she hears us?"

"She said the room was soundproof. And that she wouldn't return unless we called for her."

"Well, you two had quite the conversation, didn't you?" she grumbled as he reached a discreet door in the back. When they walked in, she saw it was set up as a playroom and nursery. There was a toy kitchen along one wall. And some storage drawers that she guessed held more toys. Along the other wall, there was a cot and a rocking chair.

Did people come in here and play and sleep? Another door was off to the side, and Harry walked in there, still leading her. How did he seem to know where to go? This room had a padded bench with stirrups. There were restraints attached to the stirrups and under the bench on either side.

Good Lord.

He wasn't going to put her on that thing to spank her, was he?

But there was also a long couch and a hard-backed chair. He led her over to the couch and she let out a sigh of relief.

"Stay here."

She watched as he moved to the free-standing closet. She gasped as she glanced at all the implements hanging inside it or resting on shelves. Dildos and butt plugs still in their packaging. She guessed you used them, then paid for them after.

There was also an enema kit, blindfolds, gags, and more restraints. Then hanging from pegs attached to the back of the closet were paddles of all sorts and shapes. Wooden, leather, round, long, square.

Yikes.

He picked up a black leather paddle. It was rectangular in shape and it looked absolutely horrible.

"Can't you just use your hand, Daddy?" she asked, putting her hands back to protect her bottom.

She needed a cushion to stick down her pants. Or a coating of iron.

She needed to be Iron-Girl!

Crap.

"No, I think this needs something more than my hand. I'm going to give you ten with the paddle."

"Daddy, nooo."

He raised his eyebrows calmly. "I can make it twenty."

What kind of an offer was that? It was a shitty sort of an offer, that's what.

She shifted her weight from foot to foot nervously. She'd never been paddled before. Thoughts of how much pain she was going to be in flitted through her head.

"Little Monster, look at me."

She stared up into his eyes.

"I'll put it away if it's too much. Okay? We'll do twenty-five with my hand instead."

Twenty-five with his hand? Sheesh, his offers just got worse and worse.

"No. No, Daddy. I can handle it."

He gave her a skeptical look.

"I can. I just . . . maybe try two first and then check with me?"

"Of course, my baby." He kissed her lightly. "This is meant to impress on you that keeping things from Daddy like this isn't acceptable. But mostly it's to erase that guilt you feel. Okay?"

"Yes, Daddy."

"All right, let's get this over with."

Less than five minutes later, she found herself lying over his lap, her bottom bare, her tights and panties down her ankles and her hands scrunched together into fists.

"Do it, Daddy."

Smack! Smack!

She wasn't going to lie. It hurt. But it wasn't the blinding pain she'd feared it might be. It stung, but she knew she could handle it.

And she'd feel better afterward.

"Sweetheart?" he asked gently, rubbing in the pain. "Are you all right?"

"I'm good, Daddy. You can keep going."

"Are you sure?"

"Please, Daddy. I just want it done and I can handle it."

"All right, say your safeword if you need to."

The next two slaps were worse. After six smacks she was considering saying her safeword. Her feet were drumming on the sofa and the room was filled with her sobs.

The last four landed and she just collapsed on his lap, crying her heart out. He gently turned her over, wrapping her up tightly in his arms. Her poor bottom was resting off to the side of his lap.

Harry pressed kisses to the top of her head and held her, rocking her slightly until she calmed down. Then grabbing some tissues, he cleaned her up, making her blow her nose and everything.

Gross.

"I'm not sure the paddle is going to be something we use that often," he confessed. "I prefer my hand."

"I prefer your hand too, Daddy." She leaned back then kissed him gently. "But thank you. I needed that. I feel so much better now. Lighter. Like a weight has lifted off my shoulders."

He nodded. "Good, my baby. I'm here to give you what you need."

"Daddy, I really don't think we need all this stuff."

It hadn't been much fun sitting in the shopping cart after being paddled. But she still refused to use the harness. That was not happening.

Nope.

Harry gave her a stern look as he put a baby's bottle with cute aliens on it into the cart. There was already a sippy bottle, a plate that had different compartments so food didn't touch, an alien onesie and bib as well as mittens. As well as a monster pacifier that had made her squeal in excitement. And a time-out chair which did not.

Now he'd picked up some monster slippers and pajamas.

"Remember I said that this is as much for me as it is for you."

"The pacifier is for you? How am I only just hearing about this side of you?"

"Brat. These things will help me take care of you. Now, how do you feel about enemas?"

"I think that I am never, ever having one, that's what I think."

"No enemas. For the moment. That reminds me. I need a medical kit." He pushed the overstocked cart down another aisle.

For the moment? Yikes.

"Ah, here is what I was looking for." He pulled up in front of a display of necklaces and picked one that had a brightly-colored donut on the end. The donut looked like it was made of rubber and was quite large.

"Cute necklace."

"Isn't it? The best thing is that it's chewable."

"What? Really?"

"Yes, all of this jewelry is. Instead of having so many suckers, we could get you a few necklaces to chew on."

"Oh my gosh! That sounds amazing."

She picked out a necklace with a round pink disc pendant and one with a purple disc. They were so cute. She couldn't wait to try them.

Kiesha shifted around on the seat of the shopping cart.

"Do you need to use the toilet, baby?" he asked as he picked up a kit, which claimed to have an extra-large anal thermometer. Yikes! Why would they need to make that extra large?

Not. Cool.

"No!"

"Are you sure?" He gave her a firm look. "It seems like you do."

She thought about it. Did she? Drat. It seemed she did.

"Yes, Daddy. I gotta go. Really badly." How had she not realized? Shoot. Where was the restroom?

Without saying anything about how silly it was that a grown woman hadn't realized she had to pee, he wheeled her over to the restroom. The door had a picture of a unicorn on it which was cute.

Undoing the belt holding her into the seat, he lifted her down before taking her hand.

"Daddy, I can pee on my own."

"Yes, but you didn't even realize that you needed to go. I think you're feeling younger than usual right now, aren't you?"

Was she?

Sheesh. Maybe. How did he know that, though? Her Little was usually around four or five. Which is why she'd wrinkled up her nose at the idea of a baby's bottle. Although a pacifier appealed. So perhaps she could go younger.

He led her into the toilet, stopping in front of it. Oh cute! There were frogs on the toilet lid. Crouching, he reached under her skirt for her tights and panties, pulling them down and helping her sit on the toilet.

"Daddy, I've got a shy bladder."

"I'll run the water and turn around," he promised. "But I'm not leaving."

Sheesh.

To her surprise, she started peeing even before he got the water on.

After she tidied herself and stood up, he turned and helped her wash her hands.

"Thanks, Daddy."

"You're welcome, Little Monster. Now, let's get this stuff paid for and head back to the motel."

37

They were driving toward the motel when Harry got a call. He pulled the car over to the side of the road. Kiesha was chewing happily on her donut necklace. It was amazing.

"Yes? What? Good. Yeah, we'll be there. Thanks."

As he ended the call, she drew out the donut and glanced over at him. "What's going on? Who was that?"

"That was Ed. You want to go watch Dennis the dick being evicted?"

"Evicted? How can you be evicted when your uncle is the landlord?"

"Because you're a dick?" He grinned over at her. "Well?"

"Oh yeah. I want to see. This ought to be good." She rubbed her hands together with a grin.

They pulled up outside of her old apartment building and it was better than she'd expected. Dennis the dick was standing outside while some guys in a moving van packed all his stuff away. He was red-faced and stomping his foot as he yelled at them.

And he was dressed only in his boxers. Gross.

"I'm not sure I should let you see this," Harry stated, placing his hand over her eyes.

"Ew, hate to say it but I've seen it all before."

"Which just makes me want to go punch the little prick."

"He's not worth it. Besides, it seems like he's getting what he's owed."

He moved his hand away. All of the residents of the building were out watching him. Many of them were taking photos or videos. Harry helped her out of the car. They stood for a moment, just watching. Ed, who'd been talking to his deputy, Jace, walked over and kissed her on the forehead, then settled in to watch as well.

"Couldn't have happened to a nicer person," Ed commented.

"Do you know what's happening?" she asked.

"Someone discovered that there were a number of current building violations. Things that Dennis had been given money to fix. Instead, he'd pocketed the cash and didn't fix them. That same person contacted his uncle to let him know about the violations. They also managed to get a number of residents to write complaints about Dennis and these were passed on to his uncle. Who is furious, by the way. I would not want to be Dennis right now."

"Did someone?" she murmured, looking over at Harry. "Would that someone be you?"

Harry shrugged. "I did a bit of digging, looked into Dennis' uncle and then brought his attention to these violations." He stared down at her. "Nobody upsets my baby."

She hugged him tight then leaned up on her tiptoes to speak to him quietly. "I didn't think it was possible to love you more. Thank you."

"You never have to thank me for looking after you."

"I forgot how good you are," Ed said. "After what happened with Dave Rhine I shouldn't have forgotten."

"Who?" Kiesha asked.

"Senator Rhine," Ed told her. "The one who was disgraced and lost everything a while back after all his corruption came to light. That was Harry."

Darkness filled Harry's gaze. "When Mari was younger, he terrorized her. I was just giving him what he deserved."

Dennis screeched and she turned with a wince. Ouch. That hurt her eardrums. She saw a well-dressed man exit the building. Immediately, Dennis stopped his tantrum, walking over to the man, his hands out at his sides as he said something. The older man shook his head, giving Dennis a look of disgust.

Was that his uncle? The other man took out his phone, moving away. Dennis turned around, spotting her. He came storming across the road toward them.

Immediately, Harry and Ed stepped in front of her. She sighed. She couldn't see a thing now!

"You! I know this is your fault, Kiesha!" Dennis yelled.

"Guys, let me see him." She peered around Harry's shoulder.

"Stay there, Kiesha," Harry said firmly, putting his arm back to keep her there.

"You did this! You did this!" Dennis screamed.

Whoa. He was losing it.

"Actually, I did this," Harry told him in a deep voice. "Not Kiesha."

"What? Why the fuck would you ruin my life?" Dennis spat at him.

"Because you dared to upset my girl. You evicted her without cause, leaving her homeless. You wanted revenge on her because she wouldn't touch your pathetic little dick."

"You asshole!" He lunged for Harry, but Ed stepped between them.

"Dennis, calm down."

"Nooo!" Dennis kicked Ed in the shin, then attempted to

punch him. Ed easily subdued him, forcing him to the ground and cuffing his hands behind his back as she looked on in shock. His boxers started falling down his ass and that was not a sight anyone should have to see. She hadn't realized that an ass could be that hairy.

Ed started to read him his rights through his protests.

"What are you doing? You can't arrest me! Uncle! Uncle, stop them!"

She glanced over as Dennis' uncle approached. He nodded to Harry. "Thank you for bringing all of this to my attention, Mr. Taylor."

"Oh, it was my pleasure," Harry replied.

"Dennis, shut up!" his uncle told him. "You attacked the sheriff. Of course he can arrest you."

"Jace!" Ed called out to his deputy who was headed their way. "Take him back to the station."

"Sure."

Dennis continued to spew profanities as Jace got him into the back seat of his police car. Ed and Dennis' uncle started talking quietly.

"Whoa," she said in shock. "I can't believe this is happening."

"Excuse me."

She glanced over to find Dennis' uncle staring at her.

"I've heard about the way my nephew has treated you, ma'am," he said without preamble. "My deepest apologies. I've decided not to collect rent from any of the residents for the next three months as an apology. But for you, I have something else." He handed her an envelope. He nodded at Harry. "Hope this meets with your approval."

"It does," Harry said. "So long as all those violations are fixed."

"They will be. And I promise that Dennis will no longer be an issue."

He turned and walked away. She gaped after him in surprise. Had that just happened?

When the crowd had died away, Ed turned to face them both.

"Are you sure you don't want to move back in here?" Ed asked her. "Free rent for three months is a good deal. And it would be better than the motel."

"We're not going to stay at the motel forever," Harry replied. "And like I've said before, Kiesha stays with me."

She turned to Ed. "I get you're looking out for me and I love you. But I'm an adult and I know what I want. And that's Harry. He gets me. He doesn't look at me and think: how can I change her to make her more like everyone else? He likes me as I am."

"More than like," Harry told her.

She grinned over at him. "More than like. Harry's my person, Ed."

To her surprise, Ed reached out and pulled her close, hugging her tight. "Good. I'm glad. That's all I've ever wanted for you. You deserve someone who allows you to be yourself while still keeping you safe."

Harry dragged her out of Ed's arms and into his, kissing her in a show of possession that made her roll her eyes.

"What's in the envelope?" Ed asked.

She opened the thick envelope, gaping in shock at the wad of cash inside.

"Holy crap! How much money is this?"

"Thousands," Harry stated.

"I think I better pretend I never saw this," Ed said dryly.

"I can use this to help pay off my debt!" she said excitedly. She'd never seen this much money in her life.

"What debt?" Ed asked.

Oh. Crap.

"Uh, well . . ."

"That's something we need to talk to you about," Harry said.

Ed looked from her to Harry. "I'll head to the station now to help Jace with Dennis, but I can meet you at my office in a couple of hours."

"Actually, we could use Georgie's perspective on this," Harry told him.

Kiesha sighed. "I should probably tell everyone together. They're all going to be mad at me so I might as well get it over with at once."

"I don't like the sounds of this," Ed said slowly. "But I'll get everyone at my place in an hour's time. That work?"

"That works," Harry replied.

∼

HARRY WALKED UP to Ed's front door with Kiesha. There were no other cars in the driveway so it didn't look like anyone else was here yet. Instead of knocking, Kiesha just opened the door and walked in.

"Kiesha!"

Harry stepped inside to find Georgina had Kiesha in a big hug. "I heard what happened with Dennis! About time someone dealt with him."

"I know. I need to stress eat." Kiesha walked past Georgina into the kitchen. To Harry's surprise, she started pulling things out of the pantry.

"She makes herself at home." Georgina winked up at him. "Can I get you something? Tea? Coffee?"

"Coffee would be great. Black."

"I tried to tell him that only psychopaths and creeps drink black coffee," Kiesha told Georgina.

"I drink black coffee," Ed said, coming into the room.

Kiesha sent Harry a look. He grinned.

"I rest my case," she muttered. "Jeez, this candy was all the way in the back behind the sauerkraut. By the way, who the heck eats sauerkraut? What were you guys trying to do? Hide the candy from me?" She came out with three suckers in her mouth.

"Lord forbid we do that," Ed said. "You're going to rot your teeth." He reached for one of the sticks and she bared her teeth at him.

"Fine. Fine. Get holes." He held up his hands, stepping back.

"Kiesha," Harry said in a low voice.

She turned to him. He hated how tense she was. How worried. He knew she was concerned that her friends would be angry with her for keeping this from them.

But he also knew she'd feel better after she told them.

"Just one at a time."

She drew the suckers from her mouth. "But I've already opened them. It would be a terrible waste to throw them away."

"I'm sure it won't matter." He held out his hand.

With a huge sigh, she put two on his hand. The sticky parts went onto his palm. Yuck.

After throwing them out, he washed his hands. By then, everyone had started to arrive. Loki came in first with Isa, his big voice boomed out greetings to everyone while Isa went around and gave everyone hugs, including Harry.

Then came Noah and Cleo. Cleo frowned and grumbled about the interruption to her Sunday afternoon until Noah whispered something in her ear that had her blushing. Georgina got everyone coffee and cookies. Kiesha moved up to him as they waited for Juliet and her men. They were the last to arrive. Brick held Juliet's hand, while Xavier, who was yawning, had his arm slung over her shoulders.

"What's happening?" Loki asked. "Why're we all here? Not that I don't appreciate the cookies. I do."

Kiesha sighed and moved forward, glancing around at all her friends. She rubbed at her temples. Harry wrapped an arm around her before leaning in to kiss the top of her head. "It will be okay. Everyone will understand."

"Understand what?" Isa asked, looking concerned. "Are you all right?"

"What's going on?" Cleo asked, leaning forward. "Is this to do with Dennis the dick? Because I heard he got kicked out by his uncle and completely humiliated himself."

"About time someone took care of him," Loki boomed. "Thought I was going to have to go teach him a lesson. Can't be letting anyone treat our Kiesha like that."

Harry watched as the tension eased in her shoulders. "No, it's not about Dennis. But yeah, he did get kicked out with a bit of help from Harry."

"He was an idiot," Cleo muttered. "Glad he's gone. You going to move back into your apartment, Kiesha?"

"No," Harry replied. "She's not."

"I'm staying with Harry," Kiesha said firmly.

He could tell she was nervous, and he didn't like pressing her to do this. But the more people that knew about Vance, the better chance he had of protecting her.

"Is that why we're here?" Brick asked. "To discuss Dennis?"

"No," Kiesha replied, glancing around at all of them. "There's something I need to tell you all. Something I should have told you when I first returned to Wishingbone."

∼

KIESHA TOOK a deep breath and told them all of it. About her depression after Jonah's death. The medical bills Vance had paid. How he'd moved her into his house, how he wanted her to marry him because of April. And how she'd rejected him. Finally, she confessed that she'd taken another job in order to pay off the debt.

After she was finished, she closed her eyes for a long moment.

When she was feeling braver, she opened her eyes to study her friends.

They were all staring at her with a mix of concern and confusion.

Finally, her gaze went to the most important person in the room after Harry.

Ed was pacing.

Back and forth. Back and forth.

Her heart raced as she waited for him to say something. She licked her lips. "Ed?"

"Fuck. Fuck! Why didn't you tell me about the medical bills? You said they were covered."

"Well, it wasn't exactly a lie."

"I would have paid the damn debt, Kiesha."

"Watch the way you speak to her," Harry growled, getting to his feet and pulling her to him. "I get that you're upset, but you can't take that out on her."

"I could have protected her from all of this!" Ed said.

She knew that was why he was so upset. Because, at his heart, Ed was a protector. All the men in this room were.

"We all would have helped," Isa said quietly.

"And we'd never have asked for anything in return," Cleo added.

Juliet whispered something into Xavier's ear. "Juliet says that she has plenty of money. Why wouldn't you have let her help?"

"Because I don't want to be the charity case," Kiesha blurted out. She closed her eyes, regretting it as soon as she said it.

The room erupted, everyone yelling something until Ed whistled. They all quieted as Harry sat in the chair with her on his lap, holding her tight.

"We can leave if this is too much," he told her.

She shook her head. No, this was well overdue. She'd been an idiot, keeping this all to herself.

"This is because of your grandpa," Ed said, staring at her solemnly. "The way he treated your mom."

She nodded, knowing that of everyone, he'd get it.

"What do you mean?" Georgie asked. "What about her grandpa?"

"When my dad took off, my mom was left with a lot of debt. We would have been homeless if my grandpa hadn't agreed to take us in and pay the debt. My mom worked three jobs to pay him back, and every day he humiliated and belittled her. He made her do everything for him." She stared around at them all. "I know you guys wouldn't do that to me. But I don't ever want to be a bad friend. I know I'm a lot to take—"

"You stop right there, Kiesha," Isa said fiercely. "You are not a lot to take."

"Yeah, what bullshit is that?" Cleo snapped.

"Total bullshit. Why would you think that?" Loki asked.

"I had it pointed out to me recently that I'm a terrible friend. That I stick my nose where it's not wanted and make things worse. That I'm ridiculous and I don't know when to stop."

Everyone stared at her.

"Juliet wants to know who said that to you," Xavier told her in a tight voice. "So she can destroy them."

She gave Juliet a teary smile. "Thanks, babe. But it's true."

"It is not true!" Georgie protested. "You're the best friend anyone could ever have."

"You always take care of us," Isa said.

"You're the first person to volunteer to help if we need it," Cleo added.

"The whole town would be lost without you," Loki boomed.

"You need your ass spanked for believing any of that bullshit," Noah added.

Juliet got up, then came over and hugged her tight. Kiesha wrapped her arms around her, holding on.

"Thanks, guys," she told them in a croaky voice as Juliet returned to sit between Brick and Xavier. "I really am sorry I didn't tell any of you. I thought I could handle it myself. But then I lost my job at Chubby's Bar because of some asshole customer who got handsy with one of the other waitresses and I interfered. I couldn't make the last payment. And finally," she let out a deep breath, "one of Vance's goons saw me in Bozeman last night."

"What happened?" Ed asked.

She told them about Jerome cornering her and his threats.

"That fucking bastard!" Ed snarled.

"What's Vance's last name?" Georgie asked, tapping on her phone.

"Vance LaRue," she told Georgie. "I don't think Vance will harm me. He's had plenty of opportunity and he never has."

"I don't like the threats this Jerome made against you," Ed said. "We need to look into him. It sounds like he could come after you."

"That's my worry as well," Harry said. "We'll need to watch out for him. We need to get a meeting with Vance."

"What? Why? No, you don't," she said hastily. "You shouldn't go near Vance. He's dangerous."

Everyone sent her incredulous looks.

She groaned. "Shit."

"I also want to know more about what happened at Chubby's Bar," Ed said. "And who said those things to you."

She sighed and rubbed her hand over her face. "We have more important things to worry about."

They all stared at her. She threw up her hands into the air. "Fine. This meathead grabbed my fri—urgh, the other waitress and wouldn't let her go. He pulled her over his lap and started spanking her. So I hit him in the face with my drink tray. Think I broke his nose. When he came after me, I kneed him in the balls.

Then the bouncer dragged Margo and I into Geri's office. She's the owner."

"And what did she do?" Georgie asked.

"Fired us."

"That bitch," Cleo snarled.

"How could she fire you?" Noah asked. "You were attacked."

"Because she's a terrible person. She also knew she could easily get other waitresses to fill our spots. Margo, she . . . she was really unhappy with me for interfering. She's the one who said those things to me about being a lot to handle."

"Sounds like we need to pay her a visit," Isa said, looking to Loki, who nodded.

"Please don't," Kiesha said. "She was only upset because she was worried about supporting her daughter."

"I know you, Kiesha." Isa frowned. "There's no way you would have just left her to struggle. You'd have offered to help. She rejected you, right?"

"Yeah."

"And after you came to her rescue," Loki rumbled. "Not. Cool."

"I know, but please leave her alone."

"All right, we'll leave her be," Ed said. "But this Geri can't be allowed to do things like this."

"She won't be," Harry said coldly.

"Let us know if you need any help with that," Brick told him.

"All right, so how do we set up a meeting with Vance?" Ed asked.

"I will meet with him," Harry said firmly. "You can't get involved."

Ed scowled at the other man.

"He's right," Brick said. "You're the sheriff. I can go, though. You'll need some back-up."

Harry studied the other man, then nodded.

"You guys are nuts," Kiesha told them. "You can't come with

me. You don't know how he would react. What if he . . . what if he hurts you?"

"He won't hurt me," Harry said.

Urgh. He was frustrating! "But he might!"

"We need to deal with him, Kiesha," Ed said. "You can't have this threat over your head. It's this or the authorities."

"I have some contacts at the FBI that I can use," Georgina offered.

"No. No! I don't . . . I can't do that." Not because of Vance. But because of April and Bodhi and a couple of other guys she remembered treating her kindly. "No, I want the meeting. But on my own."

Harry squeezed her lightly. "Not happening."

Shit.

"Have you got a way to get in contact with him?" Brick asked.

"Um, well, I have a contact number for Bodhi. I can text and ask to meet him."

"Do that," Ed said.

"Right now?" she asked.

They all nodded. She got off Harry's lap and walked over to where she'd dumped her handbag. She searched through it and drew out her phone.

"Um, okay. What shall I say?"

"Tell him you want to fully pay off the debt you owe, but that you need a meeting with Vance first. And that you'll bring someone with you," Harry said. "Brick can drive us."

She typed that out, even though she still didn't want Harry to go with her. That's if Vance would agree to a meeting. "But he'll be mad when we don't pay off the debt in full."

Harry just shot her a look.

She shook her head. "Harry! I can't let you do that."

"You're not going to let me. I'm insisting. You can't continue to live with this debt. I'm not going to sleep until the threat is gone, Kiesha."

She bit her lip. It was so hard to accept help. Especially this much help.

But he had a point.

"Let me help you, Little Monster."

Everyone else faded into the background as she sat back on his lap and hugged him tight.

"Okay. Thank you."

"While we're waiting for the meeting to get set up, I'll do some research into this guy," Brick said.

"I'll put in some discreet inquiries to my contacts," Georgie offered.

"Juliet says she'll talk to Reuben," Xavier said.

They all stiffened.

"Maybe not the best idea, Twink," Xavier told her gently.

Juliet frowned, then nodded.

"What if he won't meet with you guys?" Georgie asked.

"We'll figure that out if it happens," Harry said. "But until then, Kiesha needs to be watched at all times. The only time I will allow her out of my sight is if she's in the police station under your watch," he said to Ed.

"Allow?" Kiesha asked.

Isa whistled.

"Jeez, nice knowing you, Harry," Cleo told him.

"Yes," Harry said sternly. "Allow. Because nothing will happen to you. You were hurt once under my watch, that won't happen again. You're my heart, Little Monster."

Damn it. There he went being all sweet.

"And I'm in charge."

And then he ruined it.

"So you will do as I say."

"Why isn't she kicking him in the nuts?" Loki asked, sounding confused.

"Because she likes him," Isa said. "It's so sweet."

"Juliet thinks she's still going to get him in the nuts. She's just lulling him into a false sense of security," Xavier stated.

"That would be something Kiesha would do," Brick grumbled.

Sheesh. Had he still not gotten over the time he'd nearly run her over?

"You should move in here," Ed said.

Georgie nodded.

Kiesha shook her head. "We've talked about this. No." She and Ed would kill each other.

"Or the pool house," Xavier offered. Brick frowned and Juliet smiled.

"Actually, I have another idea," Harry said slowly. "But I need to talk to you first, Brick."

Brick looked surprised. "Sure."

"We'll stay at the motel for now," Harry stated. "Kiesha, I'll continue to take you to and from work. When you're there, you stay there. No going anywhere else on your own."

Great. Goodbye privacy. She had a feeling this next week was really going to suck.

38

She was right. This week did suck.

And it was only Tuesday.

"Why don't you just lock me up in a jail cell," she moaned. "I'd have more freedom.

She moved her scrambled eggs around on her plate. Harry had cooked them breakfast this morning in the small kitchen.

"I know it's hard. But it's for your own safety," he told her, not even looking up from his phone.

Harry had barely been sleeping. He hadn't even unpacked the things they'd bought. She hadn't used her monster pacifier or her slippers or even the baby bottle.

But she wouldn't complain, because she knew he was busy. He was often on the phone to Brick. And yeah, maybe she was feeling a bit forgotten, but it was only temporary.

Standing, she put her plate up on the kitchen counter.

"What are you doing?" he asked.

"I was going to brush my teeth."

"You haven't eaten."

"You mean you noticed?" She winced as she said that as his head shot up to look at her. "I'm sorry, I didn't mean it like that."

He studied her, then set down his phone and took off his reading glasses. Those reading glasses were sexy as hell. "I think you did. And I think you're right to say it like that."

"What?"

He opened his arms. "Come here, my baby."

She walked over slowly, letting him draw her onto his lap and hold her tight.

"I'm sorry, sweetheart."

"What? Why? I should apologize. I just sounded so ungrateful and all you're trying to do is help me."

"No," he said firmly. He grasped hold of her chin, turning her face so he could kiss her gently. "You're not ungrateful. I'm sorry that I haven't been paying much attention to you. I know I tend to throw myself into a task and ignore everything else around me. I don't want to do that with you."

"But you're doing it to protect me. I get that it's only temporary."

"It is, but it's still no excuse for ignoring my girl. I'll try to do better. What do you say if tonight we have a movie night?"

"Really?" she asked excitedly.

"Really." He kissed her again, wrapping his hand around the back of her neck. "I have to go get in the shower. Eat some more breakfast, please. Then I'll take you to work."

"Okay, Daddy." She ate several more bites. A knock on the door had her frowning.

She walked over. "Who is it?"

There was a beat of silence. She moved to the window and kneeling on the chair, peered out, coming face-to-face with an older woman dressed in a dark blue skirt and matching jacket, along with a white shirt.

Kiesha let out a startled scream, falling off the chair onto her butt.

"Ow, ow, ow."

"Kiesha!" Harry called out. "Kiesha!" He raced into the room, water dripping down his chest, a towel wrapped around his lower half. "What is it? What's wrong?"

"I broke my butt."

"What happened?" He came over to help her up.

Kiesha rubbed her bottom. "There's a woman outside. She was knocking at the door. I got a fright when I saw her trying to peer in."

"What?" Moving to the door, he opened it.

The woman on the other side had her fist raised to knock again. She let out a startled gasp. "Harrison!"

"Barbara? What are you doing here?"

"You know her?" Kiesha walked over to stare at the woman. She looked about Harry's age.

The woman glanced away from Harry's bare chest to look at Kiesha. Her eyes widened further. Kiesha wasn't sure why she was staring.

"Do I have something on my face?" she whispered to Harry.

He turned to look at her. "What? No. Why?"

"She's staring. Is she okay? She's not having a stroke or something, is she?"

"What? No," Barbara said stiffly.

Harry sighed. "Kiesha, this is Barbara, a work colleague. Barbara, my girlfriend, Kiesha."

"Hi." Kiesha waved at her. "Do you want to come in?"

"I'll get dressed," Harry muttered, placing a kiss on Kiesha's forehead. "Good girl for not answering the door. That will get you a reward later."

"A reward?" Barbara said as Harry walked into the bedroom.

Kiesha bounced on the balls of her feet. "Lucky me, huh? So, you worked with Harry?"

"Ah, yes, I work with Harry."

"He quit, though. So how come you're here?"

"Oh, I know he said he was quitting, but I don't believe it. Harry is a work-a-holic and I'm certain he'll miss it. I don't know what he could find to do here that would in any way keep him interested and engaged. No, he'll soon get bored and return back to us."

Worry filled her. Would living in Wishingbone be enough for Harry? What would he do with himself? He was smart and driven and dedicated. Would he get bored?

He'd said he was buying a house here, but had he even gone looking for one? Or was he staying in the motel because he knew, subconsciously, that he didn't want to live here long-term?

Harry walked out, looking as pressed and tidy as ever. He glanced between them both, then he turned to her. "Sweetheart, what's wrong?"

And it was like all her doubts disappeared. Maybe Barbara was right. Perhaps Wishingbone wasn't enough for Harry. Or he'd need more.

But if that happened, they'd talk about it. And she knew that they would decide what to do. Together.

However, no matter what happened she wasn't leaving him and he wasn't leaving her.

"Barbs here just said that you're going to get bored of living here. This place isn't enough for you and that you'll move back to Houston eventually."

Barbara gasped.

"Did she just?" Harry murmured, turning to Barbara. "Then why bother coming here if you expect me to return anyway?"

"Because we're losing clients! We need you, Harrison! I need you."

"You can't have him," Kiesha told her. "He's mine."

"What? No! Not like that." Barbara shook her head. "I need his mind."

"She doesn't want me, sweetheart. She wants the money I bring in."

"That sounds terrible when you put it that way," the other woman said. "But you have to admit, Harry, that this place isn't for you."

"Actually, this place and the people who live here are exactly what I need. And I'm sure I can set up my own firm here if I want."

"That's a great idea!" Kiesha told him with a broad smile.

"Sometimes, I have them," he said dryly. "Barbara, we need to leave. I have to get Kiesha to work."

Barbara eyed Kiesha. "I'm sure she can get herself to work."

"No, she can't. Now, we have to go."

"But . . . but I've come all this way to . . . to see you," she stuttered over her words as Harry ushered her out the door. "What am I supposed to do?"

"Go home, Barbara."

"Bye!" Kiesha said to her as Harry grabbed her hand and walked her to his rental car. "Poor Barbs, she looks a little out of her element."

Harry handed her into the car then did up her seatbelt before he cupped the side of her face. "You didn't believe what she said, did you?"

Kiesha shook her head. "No. Not really. I mean, if you did get bored and wanted to go back, I'd go with you. You're stuck with me. I'm like bubblegum on your shoe."

"Well, that's kind of gross. But you're right. It's you and me. Forever."

She leaned her forehead against his.

"However, I have no plans to leave. In fact, I want to show you something after work today."

"A surprise?"

"Yep."

"A good one?"

"I think so."

"Yay! I hope it's a lifetime supply of suckers."

"You might have to adjust your expectations," he warned.

"Bummer."

∼

"Hey, Little Monster. Ready to go home?"

She glanced up with a smile as Harry approached her desk. "Yep, I'm all ready."

"She's been ready all day," Ed said as he poked his head out of his office. "Not sure if she did any work."

"I did! I'm just excited about my surprise." And their movie night.

"Well, make sure you get some sleep tonight. I don't want to see you here tomorrow with bags under your eyes." Ed pointed to her sternly.

"See what I have to put up with?" she said to Harry. "No other boss would talk to me like this."

"No," Harry agreed. "Aren't you lucky?"

She sighed. "Yeah, I really am. Bye, boss man!"

"Behave." Ed disappeared into his office.

She slid her hand into Harry's. "How was your day?"

"Busy. I spent most of it with Brick going over stuff. He has some information on Geri and Chubby's Bar, but not enough. You didn't hear from Bodhi?"

"No, I told you I would call you straight away if I did." Bodhi had texted back the same day she'd sent a message asking for a meeting, saying that he would set one up. But she hadn't heard from him since. It made her nervous as hell.

Harry led her to a dark blue truck she'd never seen before. "What's this?"

"Our new vehicle. I was sick of the rental car and I need something for when the snow hits. Like it?"

"I do! I love it! Although neon green or pink would have been better."

"They were all out of those colors."

"Rude." He opened the door, lifting her up then fastening her seatbelt.

Ooh, leather seats.

And that new car smell. Delicious.

Once he was in the driver's seat, she turned to him. "So you didn't see Barbara?"

"No, I'm sure she's gone home. Now, there's some water for you in the cup holder. I want half of it gone by the time we reach our destination."

She held in her groan, but picked up the water as he drove her across town. They finally pulled up outside the house she'd told him she loved when they were walking Oscar.

"What are we doing here?" she asked as they drove up the driveway. It was actually looking a lot better. Someone had been cutting back trees and the outside had been painted. "Has someone bought this place?"

"Yes. We have."

She turned, gaping at him. "What? How? When?"

"I bought it a week ago. I looked at other houses with an agent, but I kept coming back to this one. Truth is, I fell in love with it as much as you did. But it wasn't really habitable. I've had people working non-stop to fix it up. It's still not quite ready. I've been talking to Brick about putting in a security system and they're still painting the interior. But I wanted to show you our new house, so you know that I'm being very serious when I say I want to live here."

"Oh, Harry. I can't believe this. Thank you! Thank you!" Tears dripped down her face. "This place is amazing. Can we go inside?"

"Perks of being the owners." He winked at her.

They spent the next hour until it grew dark exploring the house. As he drove them back to the motel, she couldn't stop talking excitedly about the house and her plans for it.

"Can we get a dog? Please?" she asked as he parked.

He chuckled. "All right, baby. We'll get a dog."

"Yes! And a cat! And a rabbit. Maybe two. They might get lonely."

"We'll talk about that later." He lifted her out of the truck. As she settled her feet on the ground she saw someone approach Harry from behind.

Harry stiffened as the man grew close.

Oh, hell.

"Kiesha, Vance wants to meet. You can come quietly or I can get out my gun, shoot this guy, and take you with me."

"No need for a gun, Pete. We want the meeting." She glanced up at Harry and he gave her a reassuring smile.

"Good. This is what is going to happen. My associate is in the dark car behind me. You're going to leave your phones and handbag in the truck, then get in the back seat without a word. Got me?"

Pete moved back and Harry turned, walking toward the car. She followed along behind him, her legs trembling with fear. She caught movement out of the corner of her eye and saw Barbara standing there, looking pale. The other woman disappeared from sight. Probably for the best. She wouldn't put it past Pete to take out any witnesses.

She just hoped like hell that Barbara told someone what she saw or they were in deep, deep trouble.

Getting into the backseat, Harry drew her in against him. This wasn't what she'd been expecting.

"It's going to be all right, my baby," he whispered.

God. She hoped so.

"I couldn't grab my Taser," she said quietly as Pete turned and frowned at her.

"It's all right. They wouldn't let you keep it."

"Shut up, you two," Pete barked.

They waited a few minutes until he relaxed in the front passenger seat, then Harry leaned into her again.

"When we get there, stay behind me. Let me do the talking."

Yeah. That wasn't happening.

39

Harry walked into the large office. It was richly-appointed, with two leather chairs in front of an open fire to his right. Bookshelves flanked the fireplace and ahead of them was a huge wooden desk.

But it was the man sitting behind the desk that held his attention. They hadn't been able to dig up much information about him, which made Harry think that he hadn't been born as Vance LaRue. That everything they'd found on him was smoke and mirrors. He looked to be in his late-thirties, with deeply tanned skin, dark hair and eyes. Dressed in a well-tailored suit, he looked every inch the mafia boss.

As Harry studied him, he expected to see satisfaction or happiness or even annoyance. What he got was nothing. Absolutely nothing. The man was a cold abyss, letting nothing slip through that mask.

Or else he actually did feel nothing. Could that be the case? Maybe. In which case, that made him even more dangerous. Because he wouldn't even hesitate to order their deaths.

Harry hoped someone realized they were missing sooner

rather than later. Ed had the ability to track Kiesha's bracelet. But to do that, he'd have to realize that they were gone.

And by the time he did, they might have already disappeared for good.

No matter what happened, he had to protect Kiesha. Even if that meant giving this guy whatever he wanted. He cleared his throat, ready to offer him anything to let Kiesha go. But before he could speak, Kiesha stepped forward and slumped down in the seat across from Vance.

"Was the pat-down really necessary?" she snapped, reaching over to grab something from a bowl on his desk.

"Couldn't risk you bringing in a phone or mace or an AK-47."

Did Vance just make a joke?

"Pfft, that's just silly. What help would mace be? You're immune."

Vance nodded solemnly. Was there a softening in his face? It was hard to tell.

How could he be immune to mace?

Also, he was going to tenderize Kiesha's butt once they were safe. In the car ride over, he'd told her to stay behind him and let him do the talking.

She'd done the exact opposite.

Then Vance turned his gaze to Harry. And any hint of softness was gone. He was icy cold.

"Let's cut the bullshit. Why'd you send Pete to get me? He threatened to shoot Harry."

Vance's gaze moved to Harry. He shrugged. "So? I don't care about him."

"I do."

They were staring at each other, and Harry moved forward, standing behind Kiesha. He put his hand on her shoulder, hoping to break the tension.

"You care about him?" Vance finally asked.

"I love him."

There was no reaction from Vance. Maybe Kiesha had been right, Vance didn't have feelings for her. At least not romantic ones. But he thought there was something else going on here.

"Why have Pete force us back here? That wasn't cool."

"You said you wanted a meeting."

"A meeting is where two parties make a time and agree to meet in a place that suits them both. It's not being forced into a car and dragged back here."

"You should have stipulated that."

Kiesha sighed. Harry squeezed her shoulder, not wanting her to antagonize him.

She unwrapped the piece of candy she'd taken from the bowl on his desk and popped it in her mouth. "Urgh!" She spat it into her hand. "This is mint flavored."

"Yes. And?"

"I hate mint. You know I hate mint."

"Do I?"

"Yuck, yuck, yuck. Get it off my hand!"

Harry reached forward and took the sticky candy from her palm.

"Only psychopaths and creepers like mint-flavored candy."

"I like mint-flavored candy," Vance deadpanned.

Harry slid his free hand over Kiesha's mouth so she wouldn't say it.

Please, don't say it.

He also didn't point out that he liked mint-flavored candy.

Vance's eyes narrowed as he looked from his hand, then up to Harry. "Take your hand off her."

This was it. Do or die. He was likely going to die. But he had a feeling that if he didn't take a stand, this asshole might try to take his girl.

Never going to happen.

"She's mine."

There was a beat of silence. Harry reached for her, drawing her up and behind him. "Stay behind me."

"Harry, what are you doing?"

"I want to speak to Vance. Now, stay behind me."

To his shock, she didn't argue.

Vance rubbed his chin. "I've never seen you obey someone, Kiesha. This guy threatening you?"

Kiesha sighed and rested her forehead against Harry's back. "No, he's not threatening me. Harry loves me, Vance."

"Then why is he bossing you around?"

"Seriously? You're objecting to him trying to protect me?"

Vance gave Harry a thoughtful look. "Are you protecting her?"

"I will not allow you to harm her. Or to take her from me. I love her and she's mine."

Kiesha wrapped her hand up in the back of his shirt, but to his suprise, she didn't speak.

"I know you want the money Kiesha owes you." Did he, though? Harry doubted it. He got the feeling Vance didn't care one bit about the debt. Vance peered around him, trying to see Kiesha. But she stayed behind him.

Maybe he'd half the spanking she was owed. Maybe.

"It's a vast amount." Vance wrote something on a piece of paper and slid it toward him.

As he reached for it, he realized he still held the sticky mint candy. Grabbing a handkerchief from his pocket, he wiped it off and picked up the piece of paper.

He was careful not to let any emotion show on his face. Vance was looking for a reaction. There was no way she owed that amount.

"Fine. How would you like the payment? Cash?"

The two men stared at each other.

"Yes. Cash."

"And then all ties to Kiesha are severed. No more of your men coming around and harassing her."

"Harassing?" Vance asked. "Kiesha? Who harassed you?" There was a silky note of darkness in his voice.

Kiesha stepped around beside Harry. "Jerome."

Vance's eyes narrowed. "Tell me."

She explained about how Jerome hurt her when he'd collected the money she owed, as well as what happened last weekend.

When she was finished, Vance hit something on his desk. "Bodhi, come in."

Harry didn't look back as Bodhi walked in behind them. As much as he hated to have his back to a threat, he knew who the biggest threat in the room was.

Vance sent him a look like he knew what he was thinking.

"Yeah?"

"Find Jerome. Bring him to me."

"Sure."

Vance sat back after the door closed.

"Jerome didn't tell you about seeing me?" she asked.

"No, he did not." He turned to Harry. "I will speak to Kiesha alone now."

"Not happening."

Kiesha slipped her hand into his. "Harry, it's all right."

"No. Whatever he has to say can be said in front of me. We're paying the debt. You're free from him."

The door opened again before Vance could speak. But this time, Vance stood, looking concerned. "April? What's wrong?"

A blonde-haired little girl flew past them and into Vance's arms. Harry caught sight of tears streaming down her face. She was tiny. Like a doll.

"April," Kiesha whispered as Vance held the little girl on his lap.

Shock filled Harry as he took in the changes in the other man. The softness on his face, the way he cradled the girl so gently.

This small girl was why he wanted to keep Kiesha.

Kiesha tried to move closer, but he grabbed her hand. "April? What's wrong?"

The little girl turned, and delight filled her face. Getting off Vance's lap, she threw herself at Kiesha, wrapping her thin arms around her neck.

Vance raised his head and met Harry's gaze. And in it was everything he wouldn't say. That this girl was his world. And he'd do anything for her.

But he couldn't force Kiesha into something she didn't want. And there was no way that Harry would give her up.

To his surprise, Vance seemed to get it as he gave him a nod. There was a commotion at the door and a woman walked in.

"April! What have I said about interrupting your father! Come here, you naughty girl."

Fuck. Wrong thing to say.

Vance drew himself up, glaring at the woman. Harry turned to study her, noting how pale she went.

"I'm sorry, sir. I didn't know she was going to come in here."

Did she really think that was the reason Vance was so angry?

The woman made to move forward and grab April, but Kiesha stood, stepping back. April wrapped her legs around her waist.

The woman, who was about Kiesha's age and dressed in a tight dress that showed too much cleavage, frowned. "Give April to me."

"Back off, Mother Gothel," Kiesha spat back. "You're not having her."

"What? My name is Rebecca."

"Don't you know who Mother Gothel is?" Vance asked her.

"I . . . what?" Rebecca gave him a confused look.

"She's the evil crone in *Tangled*. Which is April's favorite movie. I'd think you would know that since you are her nanny."

"What? Of course I do. Yes, the evil crone. Wait . . . you're calling me an evil crone!" She glared at Kiesha.

Kiesha snorted. "Really? Not very smart, is she?"

"No, she's not," Vance said coldly. "You're fired. Cooper!"

"Yo!" A huge, muscular guy walked in. "Kiesha, babe, you're back."

"Not for good," Kiesha said, eyeing Vance. Then she carried April back to the chair she'd been sitting in before, sitting with the girl on her lap. Harry took a seat next to them.

"Escort her out." He waved at the nanny. "She's fired. Make sure she's properly debriefed."

"Sure thing."

"What? No! You can't do this!" the woman yelled.

Vance sat with a sigh once she was gone. He leaned his forearms on the desk and stared at April and Kiesha. "You should be here."

"No," Kiesha said firmly. "And you know that I can't come back."

Vance scowled.

"Were you making her pay that debt in the hope she'd come back here?" Harry asked.

Vance turned that scowl on him.

"Except you made a mistake in thinking that she couldn't survive on her own. That she couldn't pay the debt. And that she would come crawling back."

"She's more resilient than I thought," Vance muttered.

"I'm not coming back, Vance." April made a noise and Kiesha drew her back. "But not because I don't love you, sweetie. I do. With all my heart. And we can still call each other."

"Nobody loves her like you do," Vance said.

"Well, we'll just have to find someone who does, won't we?" Kiesha said, running her fingers through April's hair. "Because anyone would be lucky to look after my girl. We'll find someone."

"You'll help?" Vance asked.

She looked at Harry. And he knew he couldn't deny her. But he had stipulations.

"Yes, you can help. But I want the interviews to take place somewhere neutral. And if for some reason you need to come, I'll come with you."

Vance sucked in a breath and Kiesha appeared worried. But then April leaned away from Kiesha to look at him. She studied him for a long moment. Then she reached over and patted his cheek.

From the way Kiesha sucked in a breath, he got the feeling this might be unusual behavior. Then she smiled.

Kiesha glanced over at Vance.

"Fine," he grumbled. "You find someone suitable to help. And I'll pay you."

"You don't have to pay me."

"I'll pay you," Vance countered. "Here is my offer."

Harry reached for the piece of paper Vance held out to him. And saw it was the exact amount that he'd written down before as Kiesha's debt.

"Accepted," Harry replied.

The door opened suddenly, and another guy walked in.

"Vance, we've got a fucking problem. There's a whole fucking lot of people standing at the front gate, demanding entrance. The boys don't know what to do. One of them says he's the sheriff of Wishingbone. Hey, Kiesha."

"Axel," she said back. "Ed isn't going to leave until he sees that we're safe. He's annoyingly persistent and stubborn."

Vance eyed her. "Much like someone else I know."

∽

HARRY HELPED her out of the back of the car, then slid his arm around her waist. Probably just as well, since she was feeling kind of shaky.

They'd made it out of the lion's den alive.

Not that she'd been worried about herself. No, all her fear had been for Harry. But somehow, April smiling at Harry had helped push Vance into doing the right thing. And she didn't care if she had to help find someone to take care of April. She'd find her the best person possible.

Her debt was wiped clean.

She couldn't believe it. Before they'd left, Harry had asked for reassurance that Jerome wouldn't be a problem. Vance had given him a chilly look and told him not to question him and to get out.

But she figured that was a yes.

As they stepped through the gates, her mouth dropped open in shock as she took in everyone standing there.

Yeah, she'd expected her friends to be there. But there were far more people standing there than she'd thought. In fact, it looked like half of Wishingbone had come.

"There they are!" someone cried. They all cheered, the noise was almost overwhelming.

Ed stepped forward and she rushed at him, throwing herself into his arms.

"Pop!" someone cried and she glanced over to find Mari hugging Harry, Linc at her side. She spotted several people from Sanctuary Ranch, including Clint and Kent Jensen. There was Red and Irish Mick and even Remy. He was staring at Isa, but he was here.

"What is everyone doing here?" she asked, pulling back.

Harry reached for her, wrapping his arm around her.

"We all came to help you," Georgie told her.

"How did you know we were here?" Harry asked.

"I told them that I saw the two of you being hustled into a dark vehicle." Barbara stepped forward. "I went straight to the sheriff. I didn't think it looked right."

"Thank you, Barbara," Harry told her.

"Yeah, Barbs, we owe you," Kiesha added.

Barbara nodded regally. But Kiesha thought she saw a hint of a smile. Maybe.

"And then the whole town rallied around to come rescue you both. I . . . I've never seen anything like it." Barbara moved closer to Harry. "They're all nuts. But I get why you want to live here."

"The town is amazing. But the main reason I won't be leaving is right here." He turned Kiesha to him and kissed her deeply. "It's because of you. My heart, my world. My life wouldn't be the same without you in it." Then he leaned in to whisper in her ear. "But I'm still blistering your butt later for disobeying me."

She broke into a laugh. Because she wouldn't have her life any other way.

40

Kiesha sat up with a sob, staring around the room frantically.

"Daddy! Daddy!"

Harry rushed into the bedroom of their motel.

"Baby." He sat next to her, and she threw herself into his arms. She'd had another bad dream about Harry being taken from her.

"You're all right, my baby. Everything is fine."

It was Friday, two days after most of Wishingbone had turned up to rescue her and Harry.

They'd been disappointed that no rescue attempt was necessary. So instead, they'd all gone back to Sanctuary Ranch and had a party. It was surprising what you could conjure up last minute. There had been food, dancing, laughter, and stories.

Mari had pulled her aside to have a conversation with her about Harry. She'd thought that the other woman might have been going to warn her off. Instead, Mari had pulled her into her arms and thanked her for making Harry so happy. They'd ended up talking for ages until Harry and Linc came and found them.

Mari had even warned her not to let Harry do her hair,

because he was terrible at it. Yeah, she'd already figured that out. But then yesterday, she'd found him watching a video on how to take care of textured hair.

And her heart had melted. So the next time he offered to help do her hair or wash it, she was going to let him. And if he did a shit job, she'd just re-do it herself.

Ed had given her as much time off as she needed. She knew there was a reason she loved that big teddy bear. Because she wasn't ready to let Harry out of her sight.

"I'm here. You're all right." He rubbed his hand up and down her back until she calmed. "Same nightmare?"

She nodded. "Yes."

"Nothing is going to happen to me. I'm right here with you."

"I know, Daddy. Sorry for being silly."

"Hey, you're not being silly." He leaned back, then cupped her chin in his hand. "I don't want to hear you say that, understand?"

"I understand."

"That's my good girl." He ran his fingers through her hair. "Think you could go back to sleep? It's still early."

She shook her head. No way that was happening.

"All right. I want you to go pee, and we'll get you settled on the couch with your pacifier and some cartoons. I want you to rest some more."

He helped her out of bed, and she moved into the bathroom. When she walked into the living area of the motel, she found he'd put her pacifier on the coffee table, next to her bottle which was filled with milk. Oogly, Doogly, and Moogly were on the sofa along with a warm blanket and pillow.

Harry took hold of her hand and led her to the couch. Sitting, he drew her onto his lap and pulled the blanket over her. Grabbing the baby bottle, he pressed it to her lips.

She opened her mouth, and he pushed the nipple inside. She sighed in pleasure. They'd discovered that she found being given a bottle like this soothing. It made her feel secure and loved.

Harry flicked through the channels with his free hand until he found a funny cartoon movie about a bear.

Eventually, she finished the bottle and gave a sleepy yawn. She glanced at the time with a wince. Five-thirty. Yuck.

Harry settled her on the sofa and stood. "All right, my baby?"

"Yeah, Daddy. I'm good."

He tucked the blanket around her and pressed the pacifier between her lips. She lay on the sofa while he did some things on his laptop.

Jerome had somehow disappeared. She knew that Harry had his private investigator trying to find him, but she figured if Vance couldn't find that asshole, then no one could.

"Little Monster?"

She turned her head to look over at Harry, pulling her pacifier from her mouth. "Yeah, Daddy?"

"What would you like for breakfast? I'm going to get something delivered."

"Sucker."

"No suckers for breakfast," he said firmly.

"But it's what I want, Daddy. You asked me what I wanted."

"So I did. I should have said, what would you like for breakfast that isn't candy. Suckers aren't good for you."

"You have some real strange ideas, Daddy. It must be from living in the city."

"Yes, that's where I get my strange ideas from," he said dryly. "Now, any requests?"

"French toast with extra syrup and chocolate milk."

"French toast with a side of cut-up fruit and orange juice coming right up."

She sighed. "Daddy, we have to do something about your hearing. It's getting worse."

"I'll get onto that."

After breakfast, where he'd made her eat a bite of fruit for every piece of syrupy toast she ate, he had her lie back on the bed so he could dress her in a pair of striped yellow and green tights, a black skirt and one of her T-shirts on which she'd written: *I Like Sugar And Maybe Four People.*

"Would you like to do some crafting? Coloring? Or maybe you want to play with your stuffies?"

"I want to do some crafting, Daddy!" she said excitedly.

"All right. Let's brush your teeth and we can get you set up."

Twenty minutes later, she was sitting in front of the coffee table with some of the plain T-shirts they'd bought in Bozeman. She chewed on her donut necklace as she decorated them.

Harry took a few calls, but she didn't pay much attention. She had her stuffies lined up along one side of the coffee table, watching her work.

"Daddy!" she called out.

"What is it, baby?" he asked, walking over.

"What do you think of this one?" She held up a big white T-shirt. On it in blue writing she'd put: *Lucky Enough To Be A Daddy To The Cutest, Sweetest Girl In The World.*

He grinned at her. "I think it's perfect."

"Oh no, it's not perfect yet. I've got more to add. Go back to what you were doing. Shoo, Daddy! Shoo."

He gave her a firm look, but walked back over to the small dining table. "After you've finished that, I want to go check on progress at the house. Then we'll have lunch and you can have a nap."

"No nap."

"Yes, nap."

"No nap, Daddy. I don't need it."

"Unfortunately for you, Daddy is in charge. And Daddy says you need a nap."

"Daddy needs to read this T-shirt." She held up the same T-shirt, and he gave it a curious look until she turned it around. Then he crossed his arms over his chest as he read what she'd written.

Daddy's girl is always right and should be given everything she wants.

She grinned at him. "See? The T-shirt doesn't lie, Daddy. You have to do what it says. It's the law or something."

"Really? And here I am, a lawyer with no idea that was the law."

"That's a bit sad, Daddy. Your education is very lacking."

"You're having a nap, brat. Any more arguments and you'll find yourself over my knee first."

Well, she wasn't putting that on a T-shirt.

"Come on, let's go to the house."

"Can I skate there?" she asked excitedly.

"All right. As long as you listen to Daddy and don't get too far out in front of me."

"Of course, Daddy. I'm a good girl. I always listen to my Daddy."

"Now, I'd like to see that on a T-shirt."

∼

"Kiesha, wait up!" Harry called out with a frown. She knew better than to get so far ahead of him. "Don't cross the road without me."

"I know, Daddy!"

They were nearly at the house he'd bought, and he was regretting letting her skate. She kept getting ahead of him and he didn't like it. He was still feeling the effects of their meeting with Vance. Of not knowing whether he could protect her.

When he got close to her, he gave her a sharp smack on the ass. There was no one else around, but she still gasped.

"Daddy! You can't do that here."

"You were warned to stay close, Little Monster. I think someone needs some corner time and a red bottom."

"Yes, Daddy. You do."

He took her hand in his as they moved toward the house. "Not me, brat. You're going to spend ten minutes in the corner once we get home and then you're getting ten smacks on your ass. And if I have to tell you again not to move too far ahead of me, it will be another ten."

She gave him a sad look. "Daddy, it's really hard to go slow on roller skates. You just don't understand."

"I understand that you're going to end up napping with a very sore bottom, if you don't mind me."

"All right, Daddy." They moved quietly up to the house and just stood there for a moment, looking up at it.

"Can you believe we get to live here?" she asked.

"No," he replied. "I can't."

"It's so beautiful." She leaned her cheek on his arm. "But the best part of it is that I get to live here with you."

"That's the best part for me too, baby girl. Come on, I need to talk to Saul before he leaves for the day."

∽

Kiesha stared at the stairs.

She knew she shouldn't.

She would definitely get her bottom smacked if she did it.

But, oh, it could be so worth it.

She'd found the perfect piece of cardboard outside. It had just been lying there, waiting for her to use.

If she wasn't supposed to do this, then the cardboard wouldn't have been there, right?

Harry was outside talking to the contractor. He was hoping

they could move in next weekend. She settled the piece of cardboard down close to the top stair. She'd taken off her roller skates at the bottom of the stairs. She wasn't crazy. No way would she attempt to go up all these stairs wearing them.

No one else was here. They'd all gone home. This was perfect timing. She took hold of the sides of the cardboard.

"What do you think you're doing, Little Monster?"

Drat.

She'd felt sure he would be talking to Saul for a while.

"Um, well, I thought I'd test out this cardboard. It's really solid cardboard, Saul. And the stairs look fantastic." She smiled at the burly contractor who stood behind Harry. He just shook his head at her, giving her a stern look.

She'd known Saul for years. He was used to her antics by now.

The staircase was amazing. It was curved and perfect for gliding down on a cardboard sled.

Harry folded his arms over his chest. "Really? And then what were you going to do?"

"I don't know what you're insinuating."

"I'm going to head off," Saul told Harry. "You're okay locking up?"

"Yeah, thanks, Saul."

"Bye!" Kiesha said to Saul, waving to him.

"I know exactly what you were about to do. Are you allowed to slide down the stairs?"

"No, Daddy. But I didn't do it."

"But you would have if I hadn't come along and stopped you. I want you to carefully get up, pick up your sled, and then come down here. Walk slowly."

Grabbing the sled, Kiesha moved down the stairs toward him, giving him a wide-eyed look. "Surely, you can't punish me for nearly doing something, Daddy?"

He grasped her chin, tilting her face back. "Sliding down the stairs is dangerous. You could hurt yourself and that's unacceptable. Understand?"

"Yes, Daddy." Her shoulders slumped.

Taking hold of the sled in one hand, he placed it by the front door.

Bye-bye, Mr. Sled.

"Are we going back to the motel, Daddy?"

"Nope." He led her into the room he'd chosen as his office. There was nothing in here except a sawhorse and some mess that had been swept into the corner.

When he moved to the sawhorse, she had some idea of what was going to happen.

"I want you to lean your forearms on the sawhorse, then stick your bottom out.

"Daddy! No."

He cupped her face between his hands, then leaned down and kissed her. "Yes. You need this. It will help settle you. And you deserve it for nearly sliding down the stairs like that. It was very dangerous. While I don't want to ruin your fun, I'm never going to allow you to put your safety at risk."

She knew Harry was always conscious of riding that line between keeping her safe and letting her be herself. And she loved him for it.

But she should probably try to make it a bit easier on the poor guy.

"I'm sorry, Daddy. You're right. It was a silly thing to do."

"It's okay, my baby. All is forgiven."

"So no spanking?"

"Oh no, you're still getting your butt spanked." He gestured at the sawhorse and she turned with a sigh, putting her lower arms along the sawhorse, then pushed her ass out.

He raised the bottom of her bright pink, long-sleeved, oversized sweater dress over her ass. Then he drew her tights and panties over her bottom.

"Spread your legs as far as you can," he commanded.

Drat.

She pushed her legs apart, and he didn't give her any warning before the first smack landed.

"Daddy, ouch! No!"

"Daddy loves you, my baby."

Smack! Smack! Smack!

"And he's not ever going to let you do something that might harm you."

Smack! Smack! Smack!

"That was naughty to sneak off like that! Especially when the house is still under construction."

Smack! Smack!

"Walking around in socks isn't acceptable either!"

Smack! Smack!

By the time he finished, she was crying and her bottom was throbbing painfully.

But then he helped her stand and turned her, holding her in his arms as he swayed back and forth.

"Shh, shh, shh," he murmured to her. "You're all right, my baby. Daddy has you. Daddy will always have you."

~

KIESHA WOKE up to a ringing phone and the sound of Harry cursing quietly. Which wasn't normal for him.

"Sorry, baby girl. I thought my phone was on silent."

"It's okay," she murmured. Her mouth was so dry. "Need a sucker."

"No sucker. Try to go back to sleep."

"No more sleep."

Something was pressed to her lips, and she opened them, sucking on the nipple of the bottle. Cool water soothed her throat, chasing away some of the yuckiness in her mouth.

When she'd had enough, she pushed at the bottle.

"Good girl. Here's your pacifier. Sure you don't want to nap some more?"

Urgh, that's right. Harry had put her down for a nap after lunch. She hated napping.

She hated even more that she'd needed a nap.

He slid her pacifier into her mouth, and she sucked on it happily. It wasn't a sucker, but it was okay.

When she finally opened her eyes, she found him sitting on the bed with his laptop. For someone who'd quit his job, he still had plenty to do.

Harry's phone rang again, and he frowned down at it. "It's Barbara. I'll take it out in the other room."

Barbs had left the day after their meeting with Vance. She'd seemed to have a good time at the party, though, and Kiesha wondered if she would come back to visit.

She made a noise of protest, reaching out to grab hold of his leg. He was wearing jeans and a dark shirt today. And he looked so sexy. She was pretty sure he only wore jeans because she'd told him she loved the sight of his ass in jeans.

He patted her shoulder. "Okay, I'll stay here." He answered the call. "Hello, Barbara. All right. Tell me. Is that so? Interesting. Yes, we'll be there. Good work. Thanks, Barbara."

She tuned out the rest of what he was saying as she decided she wanted something other than her pacifier in her mouth. Reaching over, she started to undo the button at the top of his jeans, then glanced up at him.

He simply raised an eyebrow at her.

She took that as all the permission she needed. If he didn't want his dick sucked, he could just tell her.

Might make Barbs blush, though.

After opening the button, she drew down his zipper. Harry raised his hips slightly so she could push his jeans down. Leaving him in just a pair of snug black boxers. His cock was hard, pressing against the material.

Yum.

She pushed the material down over the tip, then drew her pacifier out so she could suck the head into her mouth.

Ahh, much better.

He sucked in a sharp breath. "What? No, I'm fine. No. No pain. I've been good. Thanks. Yep. She is. Yep, she's right here with me."

Kiesha pushed his boxers further down so she could wrap her hand around the base of his dick. She continued to suck on the head of his cock, like it was her favorite treat.

The sound of Harry talking was a soothing background noise. The feel of his cock in her mouth kept her happy, grounded. He ran his fingers through her hair as he spoke. Then he ended the call to Barbs and made another short call.

She didn't pay much attention, though. She just liked being here, in the moment.

"Baby girl? You still with me?"

Sighing, she slid his dick from her mouth and glanced up at him. "Yeah, Daddy?"

"You all right? Want to stay like this for a while longer?"

Did she? Or did she want something else? Her body stirred, telling her exactly what she wanted. Sitting, she straddled his lap.

"I want you, Daddy. Inside me. I want you to take me."

"Do you just?" He took off his reading glasses, putting them on the nightstand beside him. "You best strip off then, hadn't you?"

She moved back, quickly taking off her clothes as he drew his jeans and boxers further down his thighs. But he didn't strip off fully.

She loved when he was still partially dressed while she was naked.

"Come here and kiss me," he commanded.

Straddling his lap again, she kissed him like it was their last. As though she'd never taste him again.

Eventually, he wrapped his hand in her hair and drew her back. "Are you wet? Did it get you all hot sucking on my dick while I was talking on the phone?"

"Yes, Daddy. Yes."

He twisted her nipple between his finger and thumb, making her gasp as pleasure-pain flooded her.

"Show me," he ordered.

Reaching down with two fingers, she swiped them through her slick pussy lips and held them up to him. He slid his tongue over her fingers, gathering up the moisture.

"Not enough. Push them into your pussy. Hard and fast until I tell you to stop."

Holy. Crap.

Kiesha pushed her fingers into her passage, her breathing growing faster as she moved them in and out.

"That's it. That's my girl. Right, show me your fingers. I want to taste my pussy on your fingers."

Lordy. He was killing her.

But she held up her fingers, and he took them deep into his mouth with a groan.

"You taste like heaven. Come here." He put his hands around her hips, his grip firm but not punishing. Then he slid her carefully onto his dick. They'd both decided to dispense with condoms.

She moaned, her head tilting back in pleasure as he kissed up her neck.

"I'm going to take you hard and fast, my baby. You ready for this?"

"Yes. Yes, please, Daddy."

He drew her up, then slammed her down. Over and over until she was a mess of need. Until all she knew was the feel of him inside her, claiming her. Making her his.

Then he drew her fully off him. "Get on your knees, arms stretched out in front of you, legs pushed apart."

She moved into position, glancing back to find him stripping.

"Uh-uh, naughty girl. Head down." He slapped her still tender ass, making her groan.

Then he moved in behind her, his dick piercing her with one smooth movement. Holding her still with his hands on her hips again, he fucked her with hard, deep thrusts. She was so close . . . so close . . .

"Daddy, please! Can I come?"

"Not yet."

"Daddy! Please!" She sobbed, uncertain she couldn't hold out much longer. She didn't care whether there was anyone in the motel room next door who could hear them. All she cared about was coming.

Then his hand reached around her, flicking her clit with firm brushes of his finger.

"Come, my baby."

She didn't need any more encouragement. She came with a scream that he quickly muffled with his hand. As she quieted, he ramped up his movements until his own shout of satisfaction filled the room.

Sated, exhausted, they tumbled back onto the bed with her lying half on top of him.

"You're going to kill this old man," he told her, brushing his fingers through her hair.

She tightened her hold on him. "Don't say that, Daddy. Never say that!"

"Shh, I'm not going anywhere. I promise."

She leaned up to look down at him fiercely. "You better not. Because I'd follow you and then I'd kick your ass."

"The only one getting a sore butt around here is you." He lightly patted her backside as he kissed her.

Kiesha snuggled in against him.

"So, how would you like to go out for a drink?"

"To the Wishing Well?" she asked.

"Actually, I had somewhere else in mind."

∽

Kiesha stared out at the building. "Why are we here?"

"Well, you know I started looking into Geri and this place once you told me what happened."

"Yes. But I told you that you didn't have to."

A dark look crossed his face. "Yes, I did. No one treats my baby badly."

Aww. He was so sweet. And sexy.

"Barbara offered to help me after someone told her what happened to you here. And Barbara, well, she's a shark. Once she senses blood, she goes after the kill and she moves surprisingly fast." His phone buzzed and he checked it. "Brick moves fast too. Baby, is this the guy that assaulted you here? The one whose nose you had to break?"

He turned his phone to show her a photo.

"Yes, that's him. How did you find him?"

"Barbara had someone ask a few questions and someone knew who he was. Hmm, seems he got arrested for assault last weekend. And because he was on probation, he's gone back to jail. Too bad. Oh, well. At least we can still take care of your old boss. Shall we go in?"

Her brain was spinning. "But I don't know if they'll let me in."

"They will," he told her in a dark voice.

He came around and opened her door. Reaching over her, he undid her seatbelt. He was still insisting that she wear the suffocating thing. After helping her down, he wrapped an arm around her.

Reggie stood at the door, scowling down at her. "No, nope. You gotta leave. Geri banned you."

"She didn't ban me. She just told me to get out," Kiesha countered.

"Same thing. Fuck off and take the old dude with you."

"Reggie Smith, right?" Harry said calmly, squeezing her.

"Yeah? What of it?"

"Funny, I thought your last name might have been Sinclair."

Reggie blanched. "W-what? How did you know that?"

"I make it my business to know everything about anyone who does my girl wrong. Now, unless you want me to let your family know where you are, you're going to let us pass. Understood?"

Reggie nodded, looking at Harry with wide eyes. He stepped aside, then stumbled down the steps and ran off.

"What was that all about?" she asked, staring up at Harry.

"Reggie's hiding from his family. Seems he tried to poison his older brother so he could take over as head of the family. They're a big deal in the New Mexico crime scene. I don't think we'll see Reggie again."

No great loss.

Harry led her inside. "This place is unpleasant, isn't it?"

It was early on, but there were a number of patrons here. Waitresses in barely there uniforms moved between the tables, their faces blank.

"This is the place where dreams come to die."

He wrapped his arm around her, squeezing her tight. "After this, you'll never come here again."

That made her feel better. They sat in the middle of the room, where everyone could see them.

"Welcome to Chubby's, where the customer is always right," a deadened voice said from behind her.

Frowning, she turned to see Margo standing there. The other woman's eyes widened. "Kiesha? What are you doing here?"

"What are you doing? I thought Geri fired you as well?"

"I came back and begged for my job." Margo looked at her, then Harry curiously. "You need to leave. Geri is going to be so mad."

"I don't care whether she is or not."

"Kiesha, I'm sorry about what I said to you that night. I was totally out of line. I don't expect you to forgive me, but I was mad."

"I get it," Kiesha said quietly. She understood, even though she wasn't certain she could forgive her.

"What would you like to drink?" Margo asked.

"Nothing from here," Harry said coldly.

Margo nodded and walked away. Kiesha chewed her lip. She hated confrontation or upsetting people.

"I should have been nicer."

"No, you shouldn't react in any way that makes you uncomfortable. If you can't forgive her, then that's what she deserves for how she treated you. Or you can give it time."

Yeah, maybe time was what she needed.

"What are you doing here?"

Kiesha sighed as she saw Geri walked toward them. She wore a short, sparkly blue dress and ridiculously high heels.

"Are you sure coming here was a good idea?" she asked Harry.

"Patience, sweetheart."

"Well? How did you get in here? Where is Reggie? If you came begging for your job, you're going to have to start at the bottom. The very bottom."

Kiesha wasn't sure exactly what the bottom was, since she hadn't really been at the top before.

Harry stood, drawing Geri's attention. Kiesha noticed the way she took him in, taking note of his expensive clothes and confident demeanor.

Immediately, she changed, becoming more coy, pressing out her chest. "Hello, who are you?"

"I'm the man who is going to make you pay for allowing my girl to be mistreated while she worked for you, then firing her without justification. Hope you enjoyed your nice life. It's now over."

Geri drew back. "W-what?"

Someone stepped through the door and her attention was drawn to the woman that walked in. She wore a boring gray suit and her hair was drawn back into a bun. She looked no-nonsense and slightly scary.

Geri turned to sneer at her. "I think you're in the wrong place."

"No, I believe I'm in the right place. My name is Enid James. I'm a health officer for Madison County. I've received several concerning complaints about this establishment and I'm here to do an inspection."

"But . . . what . . . no, there's a mistake. I always deal with Mike."

"Mike has been fired. It appears he was taking bribes, both monetary and sexual." Enid looked Geri up and down. "You won't have that problem with me. I'll start in the kitchen."

"What? No, you can't do this." Geri started after Enid, complaining fiercely.

Kiesha looked at Harry. "You and Barbara did this?"

"Yes," he said with satisfaction.

They settled back, watching in amusement as Enid ran circles around Geri, who was screaming at someone on her phone.

Kiesha's eyes nearly fell out of her head as Geri turned her ire on Enid.

"You can't shut me down! This is preposterous."

"She's shutting her down?" Kiesha said. "Holy shit." Her attention turned to the door once more as the local sheriff and two of his deputies stepped into the room.

Geri glanced over, then around, appearing as though she was going to flee. The sheriff seemed to sense that too as he moved forward toward her.

"Geraldine Lewis, I have a warrant for your arrest."

"What? No! Why?"

The sheriff continued to read her rights to her, while cuffing her hands behind her back. Geri was screeching like a banshee.

Harry stood and reached down, holding out his hand to her. He smiled as the sheriff half-carried Geri past them.

"You!" Geri screamed as she saw him. "This was you!"

Kiesha looked up at him. "Was it?"

"Turns out Geri hasn't been declaring all of her income or all of her employees. She's in some serious trouble for tax evasion."

She grinned. "Remind me not to get on your bad side. Or Barbs'."

Harry led her toward the door.

"So that's it? Geri is gone, and this place is being closed down?"

Kiesha glanced over at Margo and blanched at how devastated she appeared.

"Actually, I've had word that a new bar is opening close by soon," Harry told her. "If anyone here wants a job, they're hiring shortly."

"Really?" Margo asked.

"Yes. Here's some cards with the owner's details. You can pass them around." Harry drew out his wallet and pulled some cards out, passing them to Margo. "The pay will be fair."

"T-thank you." Margo turned and fled.

"How did you know about that?" she asked.

He shrugged. "I knew if I went after Geri, this place would likely close and so I did a bit of research. It wasn't hard."

No, maybe not. But not everyone would have done it. She hugged his arm as they walked to his truck.

"You're a good man, Harry."

He stopped and turned her to him, kissing her lightly. "And so are you, my baby."

"That's everyone taken care of."

He frowned. "Not quite. Jerome is still in hiding."

"Vance's guys will find him. For the first time in a long time, I feel so light, so free."

"I'm glad, my baby. That's all I want. For you to be safe, healthy, and happy.

"I'm always happy when I'm with you."

41

Kiesha snuck along the hall in her sock-clad feet.

Quiet, quiet, like a mouse.

She was chewing on one of her chewable necklaces. She loved them. And she could wear them wherever she wanted. Unlike her pacifier, which she mainly used when she was sleeping or feeling out of sorts.

She snuck up to the door that she knew she wasn't supposed to open. Harry had told her it was going to be a surprise, but she couldn't wait any longer.

They'd moved into their house last weekend. It still had a number of things that needed fixing, but neither of them had wanted to stay at the motel any longer.

It had been a week and a half since their meeting with Vance. Jerome still hadn't been located, much to everyone's frustration. Harry was still being extra protective, but she had managed to get back to work. And while she'd been working, Harry had been working on a secret project behind this door.

Now, it was Friday evening and she had to know what was going on behind door number one.

"And now... behind door number one is..."

"A naughty girl about to get her butt spanked," a deep voice said from behind her.

She squealed and jumped into the air. Then she turned, leaning back against the door with a hand over her chest. "Daddy! You nearly gave me a heart attack. Don't sneak up on me like that!"

"If you weren't trying to sneak around you might have heard me."

"I wasn't sneaking around!"

"Then what are you doing here?" Harry asked, crossing his arms over his chest and giving her a stern look. "In the place where you know you're not allowed to be."

She looked around with faux-surprise. "Oh my gosh! Look where I am."

He held out his hand to her, drawing her over to him. "You know exactly where you are and that you're not supposed to be here. Ten minutes in the time-out chair."

"Daddy, no!"

"Oh, yes." He turned her away from the door and gave her several hard pops on the ass. "Off you go. Any more arguments and I'll add ten swats to your bottom."

She quickly made her way to the cozy second living area at the back of the house, slowing down when he warned her not to run. This living area was just for the two of them. It was small with a chaise sofa and a large television set over the gas fireplace. In one corner sat the time-out chair that Harry had bought at Aunt Marie's shop.

Sitting with a huff, she folded her arms over her chest and stared at the wall, feeling sorry for herself.

One small peek wouldn't have hurt, right?

But Harry had been working hard on whatever was behind that door while she'd been at work this week.

And he'd been so excited about showing her.

She'd nearly ruined that. Dropping her arms, she leaned her head forward into the corner with a sniffle. She was so naughty. A sob escaped her.

"Hey, Little Monster, what's the matter?" he asked.

"I'm sooo n-naughty!"

"Come here, my baby."

She turned to find him sitting on the sofa with his arms open. "Noo! I don't deserve cuddles."

"You always deserve cuddles. There is nothing that you could ever do that would make me not want to cuddle you. Now, come here."

Jumping up, she raced over and threw herself at him. He let out a loud "oomph" as she landed against him. "Watch the crown jewels there, baby."

"Sorry," she said, rearranging her legs so she was straddling him. "That would be a tragedy of epic proportions."

"It certainly would." He gathered her close, hugging her to him. "Now, you weren't that naughty."

"I was going to peek, though! And after all your hard work. I would've ruined it."

"You wouldn't have ruined it. But I would have been a bit sad if you'd seen it without me."

Tears dripped down her face and she leaned into him, burying her face in his neck. He rubbed his hand up and down her back.

"I really am sorry, Daddy."

"I know you are, my baby."

"Are you gonna spank me?"

"Do you think you deserve it?"

She hated when he made her decide. "Yes."

"Then yes, I'll spank you. But there is something else we need to address. I wanted to give you some time to process everything that happened first, but it's come time to address it."

She sat back, feeling puzzled. "Address what?"

"What did I say to you in the car on the way to Vance's compound? About what I wanted you to do once we got there?"

She bit her lip. "To let you take the lead, to stay quiet and behind you. But Daddy, I did! I hid behind you and didn't talk."

"Not in the beginning, you didn't." He gave her a firm look. "You could have provoked him into harming you. Or taking you from me. Neither of which were acceptable. You disobeyed me when it came to your safety."

"You're going to spank me for that too?"

"Yes. I am. First, I'll give you five with my hand for tonight. Then it's ten with the paddle."

She sniffled, tears racing down her cheeks.

"Then you're going to wear a butt plug until bedtime."

"Okay, Daddy."

"Right now I want you to stand and strip off completely since you'll be getting straight into your pajamas after your punishment."

"Yes, Daddy."

He helped her off his lap, watching as she took off her clothes.

"Does it make you sad or worry you that I can't ever give you children?" he suddenly blurted out.

She paused as she reached around to undo her bra.

"What? Why would you ask that?" Kind of odd timing.

He glanced away. "I know you said you didn't know if you wanted children, but after seeing you with April, it was clear how much you both adored each other."

She was silent for a moment. "I don't want children at the moment. April is special to me. But just because I love her doesn't mean I want a child. However, I can't guarantee that in a few years' time I won't change my mind."

He sucked in a breath.

"But there are other ways to have kids, right? I mean, there're lots of children who need fostering. But if that's not something you want to consider, then I'm fine with it." She came and knelt between his legs. "Because all I need in life is you, Harry."

He cupped her face between his hands. "And all I need is you. But if you ever did decide you wanted to foster or adopt then I think you would make an amazing mother. Although I'd have to watch how much candy you fed them."

"Candy is good for the soul, Daddy. I'm a bit worried about your negative opinions about sugar. We might need to find you someone you can talk to about that. It's not normal."

He just grinned. "Right, rest of your clothes off. Enough stalling."

She stood and finished stripping.

"Go get the paddle, butt plug, and lube."

They had a special drawer in the built-in cabinets where he kept that stuff. He'd told her they would find somewhere better to keep it eventually.

With a sniffle, she dragged her feet as she walked back with the implements. He took them from her one by one, setting them down on the sofa next to him. Then he patted his lap.

"Come on, my baby. The sooner we get this over with, the sooner I get to cuddle you."

She climbed over his lap, facing the paddle which sat on the sofa in front of her. Harry positioned her where he wanted her, then rubbed her ass.

"The first five is for your behavior tonight, Little Monster."

"Yes, Daddy. I'm sorry."

The first two smacks were light, but the next two were heavier, the final one landing with a loud slap on the middle of her buttocks. Her butt felt warm, but it wasn't enough to have her wriggling around or sobbing.

Yet.

He picked up the paddle and she let out a low moan as he rubbed it over her stinging cheeks.

"What's your safeword?" he asked calmly.

"Red, Daddy."

"Good girl. Say it if you need to. Ten smacks of the paddle. And I want you to remember this spanking next time you think about disobeying an order given for your safety."

She didn't even have time to reply before the paddle landed. Four smacks in quick succession, setting her butt cheeks aflame. She gasped for air, her feet kicking against the sofa as she tried to hold in her sobs.

Slap! Slap!

Her ass was burning. She was never going to sit again.

Slap! Slap!

Would this ever end? She was going to get rid of that damn paddle once this was over.

Slap! Slap!

Sobs escaped. Tears coursed down her cheeks.

"Shh. Good girl. It's all over. Well done. You're doing so well. Shh. All is forgiven now."

He rolled her over, holding her on his lap with her bottom off to the side of his thighs. Rubbing his hand up and down her back, he whispered to her quietly. Reaching over, he grabbed a tissue to clean her up.

Grasping hold of her chin, he tilted her face back. "You doing okay, Little Monster?"

"Yes, Daddy. I really am sorry."

"I know. And all is forgiven now, understand?"

Maybe. But there was something more she wanted to do for him. If he'd let her.

Sliding off his lap, she kneeled on the floor between his legs once more. "Daddy?" She glanced up at him, saw the growing heat in his gaze.

"Yes?"

"Can I also apologize in another way? Please?"

He raised an eyebrow. "You want to suck my cock as an apology?"

"Uh-huh."

"You know that you won't be getting any pleasure since you were just punished."

"I know. I just... I really want to do this. I need to. May I?"

"Since you asked so politely, you may." He helped her take off his jeans and boxers, which left him in just a tight black T-shirt. Yep, he'd been dressing down lately while he worked on the house. And it was just as sexy as his shirts and pants. Maybe more so.

Leaning in, she put her hand around the base of his cock, then licked her way up to the head.

"Fuck, baby." He rested his arms along the back of the sofa and let her do whatever she wanted.

She loved when she could play a bit with him. Moving her hand from his shaft, she cupped his balls. His breathing grew faster, a low moan filling the room.

"Yes. Good girl," he groaned as she took his shaft deep into her mouth.

The taste of him made her hum in approval. Satisfaction flooded her as she felt him tense. His dick was rock hard. She ran her tongue over the head then brought her hand back around the base of him, running it up and down as she swallowed him down.

"Fuck. Fuck, baby."

She had to grin. When he was close to coming, he often seemed to forget himself and started swearing. She loved that too.

Taking him into her mouth quickly, she took her time moving back up his shaft.

Up. Down. Up. Down.

His harsh pants filled the room. His thighs were tense. She took him as deep as she could and swallowed.

His moan was one of pure need. Pure pleasure.

"I'm close, my baby."

And she was ready. She moved faster, taking him deep each time until he groaned, coming in her mouth. She swallowed all of him, licking her way back up his shaft once he was finished and placing a small kiss on the tip.

He drew her up into his arms and kissed her, not seeming to care that he could taste himself. Pulling back, he stared down at her.

"I love you so much, my heart."

"I love you too," she whispered back.

"You're it, Kiesha. You're the person I've been waiting for all these years. The piece of me I was always missing. The road I traveled led me to you. And there is nowhere I would rather be."

"Oh, Daddy. You say the sweetest things." She wrapped her arms around him.

"All of it was true. Now, I want you to lie on your back on the sofa."

What? Why?

He helped her lie back, then he kneeled on the floor next to the sofa.

"Daddy? What are you doing?"

"Time for your plug."

"But . . . aren't you going to have me lie over your lap?" She didn't like this position.

"Nope. I want you to bring your legs back against your chest and hold them there."

"Daddy, do we have to do it in this position?"

"Yes. We do. Now, if you keep complaining, I can also rewarm your butt in this position."

"It doesn't need rewarming! It's hot enough to fry eggs!"

"Is it? Doesn't seem that way considering you're still not doing as you were told."

She quickly drew her legs back, exposing her ass and pussy. The sternness in his voice sent a shiver of pleasure through her.

"Oh, someone likes the idea of Daddy smacking her bottom. Or was it giving her Daddy a blow job that she enjoyed?" he asked.

"The blow job, Daddy. I love doing that."

"What a good girl you are." He ran a finger through her slick lips. "It's too bad you don't get to come tonight."

She closed her eyes as he parted her bottom cheeks again, putting a dab of lube on her back hole. Then he pushed his finger inside her, moving it in and out. Her breathing quickened. She really needed to come.

When he drew his finger free, she whimpered in disappointment.

"Poor baby, she does like having her bottom hole played with, doesn't she?"

She figured that was a rhetorical question since the evidence was clear.

But then he slapped her bottom. "Open your eyes and answer me."

Drat.

She opened her eyes hastily, watching as he coated the plug with lube. "Yes, Daddy."

"Good girl. Now, keep those eyes open. I want you to look at me while I'm plugging you."

With a groan, she stared up at him as the plug was slowly pushed into her bottom. It stretched and burned. It was the biggest one she'd taken yet and she wasn't sure she could do it.

But then he dropped one finger to her clit, flicking it softly. A wave of pleasure rushed through her as he pushed the plug deep, seating it inside her.

To her frustration and disbelief, he removed his finger from her clit then helped her up.

"There we go, baby girl. All plugged up and spanked. Now, I've got to wash my hands and then we'll get you into your pajamas, yeah? Would you like to watch a movie?"

No, she didn't want to watch a movie. She wanted to come.

"I have some ice cream too," he added.

"Real ice cream or that stuff that's sugar-free and dairy-free?" She eyed him skeptically.

"It can be a surprise."

Uh-huh. Sure. She knew exactly what that meant.

∼

SHE WOKE in a glaze of pleasure. Something ran over her clit, making her groan. Opening her eyes, she stared around the barely lit room. She reached for Harry in her half-awake state, then groaned as two fingers worked their way deep into her pussy.

"Harry?"

He pushed the covers off. He was lying between her open legs, his mouth teasing her pussy.

"Is this why I wasn't allowed to wear anything to bed last night?" she asked sleepily. If so, she was totally down with it. She'd go naked to bed every night if she got to wake up to him eating her out.

He continued to play with her, taking her up to the edge then pulling back.

Torture. Pure torture.

"Please," she begged. "Please, let me come."

"Not yet, sweetheart. Reach over and grab the lube for me."

With her breath catching in her throat, she half-rolled to grab the lube from the top drawer. She handed him the lube.

"Thank you. Now, bend your knees, feet flat on the mattress and raise your hips."

He slid a pillow under her lower back before squirting some

lube on his fingers. Then his mouth returned to her pussy as he slowly slid his wet fingers into her ass.

Oh God.

It felt amazing. She squirmed, needing more. Needing to come so badly that she could practically taste it.

"Please, let me come. Please!"

He rose and shook his head. "Not yet. I want you to get your vibrator."

She bit her lip but grabbed her vibrator from the top drawer. When she turned back, he directed her to kneel and hold onto the headboard with her free hand.

"Push your ass out now. That's a good girl." He ran his hand over her bottom, squeezing it. She hissed. "Still sore?"

"Yes, Daddy."

"I'm going to fuck this ass, my baby. I can't wait any longer to feel you clenching down around my cock. I want you to turn the vibrator on low and hold it to your clit but don't come."

She did as directed, holding on tight to the vibrator in one hand and the headboard with her other hand.

A low moan escaped her mouth as he pressed his dick against her back hole.

"That's it, nice and easy. Take a deep breath in. Let it out slowly. Good girl. Doesn't that feel so good? You're so hot. So tight. Fuck, baby girl. I could come before I fully get inside your ass."

"Me too."

"No coming until I give permission," he warned.

"Nooo," she moaned as he pushed deeper inside her.

It was too much. Too much pleasure. Too much burn. She couldn't take it. She couldn't hold back. Her clit was so sensitive.

"Please, please, please."

Finally, he seated himself deep. His hands held her hips still and she could hear him trying to calm his breathing.

"I love you, my baby."

"I love you too, Harry. But for the love of all things holy. Will you fuck me?"

He chuckled, but then he started to move. And it was like nothing she'd felt before. The vibrator buzzed against her clit. He stretched her ass, brushing up against her sensitive nerve endings.

"Put the other end of the vibrator in your pussy," he directed. "You can come whenever you like once you've done that."

As he drew free of her ass, she pushed the vibrator deep inside her. The other end still buzzed on her clit.

He drove forward. Then out. Then in.

And she felt herself growing closer and closer to the edge.

"Come for me, my baby. I want to hear you cry my name. I want to feel you milk my cock."

It was all she needed to send her over. To make her scream out his name as she clenched down around his dick. And it must have given him that final nudge over the edge too. Because he drove even deeper inside her, coming in her ass with a shout.

She quickly switched off the vibrator, pulling it out of her as he slid himself free. She collapsed onto her tummy on the bed. She expected him to fall down next to her. Instead, he surprised her by kissing her toes, then along the arch of her foot, up over her calf. The back of her knees and thighs. Along one ass cheek and up her back. Her shoulders and neck. Then he rolled her, and kissed his way down her body, including her arms, wrists and fingers. When he finished at her toes, he straddled her hips and grinned down at her. "You're all mine. I've claimed all of you."

"Daddy, I always have been. Just like you're all mine."

∽

"Let's put this blindfold on."

"I don't need a blindfold, Daddy! I can just put my hands over my eyes."

"You'll try to peek."

"I will not!"

"Uh-huh, so I didn't catch you trying to peek in the room last night?"

She pouted. "You weren't very nice about that, Daddy! You smacked my butt!"

"You needed it."

Well. She could argue that, but she decided not to. See? Sometimes she made good decisions. "You also made me sit in the corner."

"Yes, I'm a mean, mean man."

"As long as you know it, Daddy."

"Do you want your surprise?" he asked.

"Yes! Yes!" She jumped up and down, clapping her hands. "Is it a lifetime supply of suckers?"

"Yes," he deadpanned.

"What?" Seriously?

"But mint ones only."

"Daddy! That's not very nice to tease!" She smacked him on the chest with her hand.

"Who said I'm teasing?"

"You are! You wouldn't get me a lifetime supply of suckers, you're always trying to stop me from having them. It's not nice, Daddy. Not nice."

"I'm sorry, my baby. But I worry about the state of your teeth and your health. Is that a bad thing?"

"It is when it means no suckers. I don't even know how to function without fifty percent sugar running through my veins."

"Only fifty?" he said dryly. "I would have said more."

Yeah. That was probably a fair call.

It was Saturday morning and she was spending the entire weekend in Little headspace.

He'd dressed her in a pair of bright yellow and green socks

that went high up her thighs. A black, pleated skirt and a T-shirt that said: *Underestimate me. That will be fun.*

She also had alien slippers on her feet.

She looked freaking adorable.

He fitted the blindfold over her eyes.

She bounced up and down in excitement.

"Careful," he warned. "I don't want you falling. Hold Daddy's hand."

Anticipation flooded her as he walked her along the corridor. They came to a stop and then he opened a door and led her through.

"Stand still. I'll take off your blindfold."

He removed her blindfold and for a long moment, she just stood there, gaping in shock at the awesomeness that was this room.

"Daddy! It's a monster room!" she squealed.

"Yep, a playroom fit for a Little Monster," he agreed.

She could barely take it all in. There was a bunk bed against the wall ahead of her. It had stairs leading up to it at the side then an actual slide that came down the front. Underneath the single bunk, he'd created a cave-like area with cushions on the floor and fairy lights hanging from the base of the bunk bed.

A monster mural had been painted along one wall, with lots of brightly-colored monsters and little alien ships flying in the sky. Another part of the room was made for toy storage. There were a lot of colorful baskets set into open shelves.

"Daddy! This is amazing! I can't believe you did this." She threw herself at him.

"You need a private space where you can play and nap. Oh, and this corner is for time-outs." He pointed at a free corner. "I'm going to move your chair in here."

"Yeah, you don't have to do that, Daddy."

"You'd rather leave it out in the living room?"

Urgh, no. Maybe not. "Okay, Daddy."

"There's something else I have to show you. Are you ready?"

She nodded excitedly, even though she couldn't possibly understand what else he could have done. It wouldn't top this, anyway. He led her out of that room and to the room next door.

Opening the door, he drew her inside.

For a moment, she was confused. Why would he take her into his office? Then she realized this wasn't his office. It was for her. She gasped in shock. "You got me a printer? And a computer? And a press? Daddy!"

"I had to do some research on what you needed for your T-shirt designs. I hope I got everything you need. The computer has a graphics program on it, but if you don't like it we can change it."

She threw herself into his arms. She could feel herself trembling. "Daddy, it's amazing. It's perfect. But I don't know if I deserve it."

"Hey, enough of that," he said in a low, growly voice. "You deserve this and more. You deserve the world. In fact . . ." He drew something from his pocket then got down on one knee.

She gasped in shock, staring down at him with watery eyes. "Daddy?"

"Kiesha, my baby, my Little Monster, I love you so much. I can't imagine my life without you in it. Please, will you marry me?"

"Oh, Harry! Yes!" She cried as he opened the ring box. The ring was gorgeous, it was a yellow diamond, surrounded by clear diamonds. And just perfect. He slid it onto her finger.

After he stood, she threw herself into his arms.

"I want to give you the world, Little Monster."

"I love you. You're the best Daddy a girl could ever dream of."

"Just remember that next time I have to spank your butt."

She giggled.

EPILOGUE

"I'm just headed out to do some errands, boss man!" Kiesha called out.

"Wait. Where are you going?"

She paused, sighing. She'd nearly gotten to the door. Slowly, she turned. "You losing your hearing? I've heard that happens as you get older. Especially with men. I think it has something to do with the extra hair in your ears. Blocks the sound. Do you have issues with extra hair in your ear, boss man?"

Ed glared at her. "Where are you going?"

"Got to go to the post office and send this to April." She held up a brightly-wrapped gift. They'd managed to find the perfect nanny for April. Kiesha had known it as soon as she'd met her.

She'd been dressed in a denim pinafore with green and blue striped tights, and black Docs. Oh, and she was the girl from the toy shop. The one that had loved the hat Kiesha bought. As soon as she'd walked in, Kiesha had pointed to her and told Bodhi that she was it.

Bodhi had wanted to interview her, though. He was such a stickler for the rules. But he'd been impressed too. Plus, she'd managed to answer all of Kiesha's questions about *Tangled* correctly. None of the other applicants had done that. Her introduction to April had gone really well too.

Not so much her meeting with Vance, but what did he matter? Penny wasn't going to be his nanny.

"You'll go straight there and straight back?"

"Yes, boss man."

"Make sure you do."

Sheesh. Everyone was a whole lot more overprotective since Vance had her and Harry brought in for a meeting. She didn't get why. All the bad guys were caught. Two days ago, Bodhi had told her that they'd found Jerome. She was shocked it had taken them that long, frankly.

She carefully made her way down the steps of the police station and glided along the pavement, waving to everyone who called out to her. She was still shocked by the sheer number of people who'd gone to Vance's to rescue her. It showed her how much they all cared.

After sending off April's present, she realized she'd forgotten her phone. Ahh, well, she'd be back in the office soon. But maybe she'd grab an iced chocolate from the diner. She deserved some sugar, after all.

And what Harry didn't know, wouldn't hurt him.

As she stepped off the road, she paused to admire the sun glittering off her ring. She really was so lucky.

Grinning, she started across the road just as she heard the roar of an engine.

Glancing up, she stared in horror as a car pulled out of a park and raced right toward her. It was going to hit her!

Move Kiesha!

People started screaming as a red truck zoomed past her. She closed her eyes, bracing for impact. A loud smash made her scream.

She was going to die! She just knew it! And just when everything in her life was finally going well.

"Kiesha! Kiesha! Are you all right?"

Hands grabbed her arms, someone shook her but she couldn't seem to breathe. Panic grasped hold of her lungs.

"Kiesha, snap out of it!"

Smack! Pain flared on her cheek and she opened her eyes. Gasping for air, she glared down at Leslie.

"Ow."

"You were panicking."

"Oh, and you felt so bad about slapping me, right?"

"Not even a bit."

"Kiesha!" A loud roar from further down the street had Leslie ducking away. And that's when she saw it. The mess in the road from two vehicles colliding. The car that had been headed right toward her was one she didn't recognize. She frowned as she saw someone lying on the ground while Red gave them CPR.

Was that? But how could it be?

"Jerome?" she whispered.

"Kiesha! Are you all right?" Ed suddenly appeared in front of her. Just as the sight of the other vehicle registered. The one that had likely saved her by smashing into the other car.

"Jonny Jacks!"

∽

Harry rushed into the hospital.

He couldn't believe that Kiesha had nearly been run over. He spotted Cleo standing by the entrance.

"Harry, she's in here. We all are." She beckoned to him and he followed her into a private examination room. He'd just been leaving Sanctuary Ranch when he'd gotten the call.

Isa and Loki were sitting on two chairs to the side of the room.

Brick was on his phone, leaning against the wall. Noah pulled Cleo into his arms as soon as she entered the room. Harry's gaze went to Kiesha who was sitting on the bed, tears racing down her cheeks. Juliet was on one side, Georgina on the other, trying to soothe her.

"Little Monster," he breathed out, coming forward quickly. She practically threw herself into his arms.

He felt like he'd lost years off his life when Ed had called him. And he wasn't sure he'd taken a proper breath as he'd raced here.

"Are you all right? Where are you hurt? Where is Xavier? Why isn't he checking you over?"

"I'm f-fine. I didn't e-even get a scratch."

Unable to believe her until he checked for himself, he drew back to examine her. She looked frazzled and frightened but there were no visible injuries. He cupped her cheeks between his hands. "What happened?"

"I went to the p-post office to send April's gift. I was crossing the road to go to the diner when this car came out of n-nowhere. It was heading t-toward me and it was getting faster. He was trying to run me o-over."

"Who?" he asked in a dark voice.

"Jerome," she whispered. "It was Jerome."

"I'll fucking kill him," Harry roared, making her jump and cry harder.

Shit!

"Sorry, baby, sorry. Don't cry. I'm sorry." He gathered her close and rocked her as she sobbed.

"What happened next?" he asked.

"Another vehicle hit Jerome's car," Georgina said. "It stopped Kiesha from getting hit."

"What? Who?" Harry asked.

"Jonny Jacks," Cleo whispered.

Really?

"Is he all right? What about Jerome?"

"Jerome is dead," Noah told him in a tight voice. "We're not sure about Jonny. Xavier is with him and Ed is interviewing witnesses."

"L-leslie slapped me," Kiesha said, pulling away from his chest.

"What? Why?" He took the tissues Juliet gave him to clean her up.

"Kiesha was panicking," Isa told him.

"Yeah, but she enjoyed slapping me. Bitch." There was no heat in her voice and her face crumpled again. "Oh, Harry, what if Jonny is seriously injured? It will be my fault."

"How is it your fault?" he demanded. "It's Jerome's fault. Jonny saved you." And he'd have Harry's undying gratitude for that.

"He's always saving me. Even when he's tattling on me, he's just looking out for me. And all these years, I've t-treated him like public enemy n-number one. What if he d-dies and I can never t-tell him how grateful I am?"

He sat on the bed next to her, gathering her into his arms.

"We'll give you both some privacy," Georgina said. "We'll be out in the waiting room." He nodded as they all filed out.

He grabbed another tissue and held it to her nose. "Blow."

She cleared her nose. "Thanks, Daddy."

"I was so scared, my baby. So very scared. Please don't ever scare me like that again."

"I don't think I'll be in any h-hurry to cross a road again," she told him solemnly.

"I don't think I'll let you out of my sight again." He spotted her skates across the room by the door.

"I'm going to have nightmares for months. I'm also going to kill Vance. Why the hell didn't he tell us that Jerome escaped?" he asked.

"I don't know. Maybe he doesn't know. Shit, I need to text Bodhi but I think I left my phone in the office."

Harry drew out his phone. He'd left his phone in Mari's cabin while he'd gone outside to find Linc for her. And when he'd gotten back, it had been ringing with the call from Ed so he hadn't checked it. But now he saw he'd four missed calls and five text messages.

He quickly called back Bodhi.

"Harry, you have to get Kiesha somewhere safe. Jerome's free."

"We know," Harry replied. "He tried to fucking run her over. How the hell did he get free?"

"Fuck. Is she all right?"

"Shaken up, but she's all right. A friend intercepted Jerome's car."

"He dead?" Bodhi asked.

"Yes. Died on scene."

"Fucking asshole. He died too quickly then."

"What the hell happened?"

Bodhi sighed. "Angel, the guy guarding him let him go. Jerome somehow convinced him that Kiesha was lying. That he didn't deserve to get locked up because of her. It sounds like Jerome blamed her for his life falling apart, for Vance coming after him. Guess he decided to get revenge on her."

"I take it you're taking care of this guy better than you did Jerome?" Harry snapped.

"Careful," Bodhi warned.

"Kiesha nearly died because you guys couldn't keep Jerome locked down."

"Vance feels deep regret over that. If Kiesha needs anything, I'm a call away."

Harry wasn't sure about that. Vance seemed to have trouble feeling much of anything.

The call ended and Harry swore quietly.

"What did he say?" she asked exhaustedly.

Harry repeated everything back.

"Bodhi says if you need anything to let him know."

"Awesome," she muttered. "None of that helps Jonny. I can't believe he saved me."

"I'm so very glad he did. I want to take you home."

"I can't. I need to wait and see if he's going to be okay. They took him into surgery. Please."

"Of course, my baby. Hush, it's all right. We'll wait. But you need to lie down with me, all right? You've had a fright and we need to take care of you too."

He lay back and tucked her in against him with her head resting on his chest. There wasn't a lot of room on the bed, but he didn't care. He just needed to feel her against him.

"Do you remember me telling you how my mom would send gifts and pretend they were from my dad?" she asked. "And how she made him sound like a good person?"

"I remember."

"Well, one day when I was nineteen I got this call from a lawyer who said my dad had died. He'd been given instructions from my dad to call me with details of the funeral. That's all he told me. I was devastated. I'd just finished school and I'd had these plans to go find him. I had this romantic view of him thanks to Mama and I thought he was a good guy."

"What happened?"

"I got to the funeral and there are these people there. This woman got up to speak who says how much she'll miss her husband. These twin boys, they're around sixteen, they get up and speak about their dad who was wonderful. And this younger boy stood between them but didn't say anything. And I knew they were my dad's kids because they looked just like the photos my mom had of him. They had his eyes. I didn't look a thing like him, I take after my mom."

"Oh, baby."

"I still had hope. I thought I'd go introduce myself and maybe get to know them since I missed out on getting to know my dad. They didn't even know who I was. They didn't believe me. They thought I was lying to get some of my dad's money. Because he never said a word to them about me. He didn't care enough to tell them he had another kid. I was devastated. I caught the bus back home, because I hadn't told Mama where I was going. When I got home, I told her everything and she got mad at me for going to the funeral. That's when she told me the truth about what an asshole. How he'd racked up all this debt in her name and then took off. How he found another family and forgot about us. All the lies she'd made up to shield me."

He tightened his arms around her. "I'm so sorry, baby."

"I just . . . I lost it. I took off. I grabbed some clothes and money and started walking down the road. I had my thumb out when Jonny Jacks pulled up in his red truck. Told me to get in. He drove me to a diner the next town over, sat me down with pie and made me tell him all of it. He told me not to blame my mama. That she was just trying to do her best. I knew he was right. But I just needed to get away for a while."

She took in a deep breath. "I got up and told him I was leaving and when I turned around, standing there were Ed and my mom. I know it's stupid, all right? I know how foolish it is to hold a grudge. But it was the worst day of my life and my dad was dead and I just . . . I was angry that he'd called them. It seemed like one more betrayal. But I didn't hate him."

She shook her head, twisting her fingers in his shirt. "All these years I've never hated him. Sometimes . . . sometimes it's my . . . my rivalry with him that has been the only thing getting me up in the morning. That's kept me going. Knowing that I could do something outrageous and he'd be there to catch me, it became a game I guess. But what if he thinks I hate him?"

"I'm sure he knows you don't, baby." He kissed the top of her head. "And you'll be able to tell him all of this soon."

"I hope so."

"Did you ever find out why the lawyer called you?"

"Oh yeah, it turns out he did leave me some money in his will. I didn't want it, though. I gave it to my mom."

She was sleeping an hour later when Xavier came into the room. He just gave Harry a thumbs up then disappeared. Harry breathed a sigh of relief at the sign.

Jonny would be okay. Thank God, because his girl really needed to catch a break.

~

THE NEXT MORNING, she tiptoed into the dark room. Kiesha hated hospitals. Sure, not many people liked them. Maybe doctors and nurses did.

But not her.

Still, she wasn't leaving until she got this off her chest. She moved up to the older man lying still in the bed. He was hooked to an IV and a heart monitor.

He'd broken some ribs and had lots of bruises. They'd had to operate to repair his fractured shoulder, but Xavier said he'd make a full recovery.

Thank goodness.

"Kiesha?" he asked in his gravelly voice. She stared down at his face, into those dark brown eyes and smiled. "Am I dying then? Since you're visiting me? Or am I dreaming?"

"No, you're not dying or dreaming. I'm here."

"You come to smother me in my sleep then?"

"Tempting, but no. I've come to tell you something worse. You're coming home with me to live. I'm going to nurse you better."

His eyes widened in horror. "What? No! That's not necessary."

"It is necessary. I'll be a great nurse. I'm not wiping your butt for you, though. I draw the line at that."

"No one is wiping my ass and I'll hire a nurse."

"It's already being set up. Harry's figuring it all out."

"You sure I'm not dreaming?" he groaned.

"No. Why'd you do it, Jonny? Why save me?"

"Because I love you, darlin'."

"Even though I've been awful to you all these years?" she asked in a small voice.

"Darlin', you've never once been awful. Hell, those years you didn't live here were the most boring years of my life. Chasing around after your ass since you moved back is what's keeping me alive."

"You're not that old, you bastard."

"No, I've got a few years left in me."

She brushed a hand over his short afro which was steadily growing gray. It made him look distinguished. Then she leaned down to kiss his forehead. "I love you too, you douchebagette."

He laughed and then groaned. "You're gonna be a terrible nurse."

"I know! We'll have so much fun though."

∽

SHE WALKED out of the room once Jonny fell asleep and moved straight into Harry's open arms. "Everything okay?"

"Yep. Everything is perfect."

He led her out to his truck.

"Oh, but on the way home can we get a nurses uniform and an extra-large anal thermometer?"

"Do I want to know?" he asked as he climbed in the driver's side.

"Nah, you want plausible deniability. Just a bit of a prank to keep Jonny going. I'm the only reason he can get up in the morning, you know. He depends on me."

He grinned, then reached out and grabbed her around the back of her neck, drawing her close. "Life is never going to be boring with you, Little Monster."

"I sure as heck hope not, Daddy."

Thanks for reading Daddy's Sassy Sweetheart. Hope you loved Harry and Kiesha as much as I do! And don't worry there are plenty more stories to come!

Printed in Great Britain
by Amazon